THE
BUTTERFLY
ASSASSIN

PRAISE FOR THE BUTTERFLY ASSASSIN

THE
BUTTERFLY
ASSASSIN

FINN LONGMAN

SIMON & SCHUSTER

First published in Great Britain in 2022 by Simon & Schuster UK Ltd

Copyright © 2022 Finn Longman

This book is copyright under the Berne Convention.
No reproduction without permission.
All rights reserved.

The right of Finn Longman to be identified as the author of this work has been asserted by them in accordance with sections 77 and 78 of the Copyright, Designs and Patent Act, 1988.

1 3 5 7 9 10 8 6 4 2

Simon & Schuster UK Ltd
1st Floor, 222 Gray's Inn Road
London WC1X 8HB

www.simonandschuster.co.uk
www.simonandschuster.com.au
www.simonandschuster.co.in

Simon & Schuster Australia, Sydney
Simon & Schuster India, New Delhi

A CIP catalogue record for this book
is available from the British Library.

PB ISBN 978-1-3985-0734-0
eBook ISBN 978-1-3985-0735-7
eAudio ISBN 978-1-3985-0736-4

This book is a work of fiction. Names, characters, places and incidents are either the product of the author's imagination or are used fictitiously. Any resemblance to actual people living or dead, events or locales is entirely coincidental.

Typeset in Times by M Rules
Printed and bound by CPI Group (UK) Ltd, Croydon, CR0 4YY

FSC www.fsc.org MIX Paper from responsible sources FSC® C171272

Content Warning:
This book contains: on-page depictions of murder, death, and associated violence; flashbacks to and discussion of past child abuse; hospital scenes and references to past medical abuse; and descriptions of illness, including vomiting.

For Caspian and Eleanor,
who have known Isabel almost as long as I have.

'For there lives in this house
a certain form of anger,
a dread devising everrecurring everremembering anger
that longs to exact vengeance for a child.'

Agamemnon by Aeschylus
(translated by Anne Carson)

MAP OF ESPERA

NW CHECKPOINT

N

GANTON

SHERBURN

HESLERTON

FOXHOLES

16

6

5

NEWTON

10

1

WEAVERTHORPE

LUTTON

3

2

4

13

GRINDALYTHE

COWLAM

SLEDMERE

LANGTOFT

SW CHECKPOINT

DISTANCES

NW CHECKPOINT TO SW CHECKPOINT
——— 7.5 MILES

NW CHECKPOINT TO EASTERN TRADE ENTRANCE
——— 15 MILES

COMMA

NEUTRAL ZONE

BOROUGH BOUNDARIES

HUMMINGBIRD

INDUSTRIAL: MANUFACTURING

MAJOR ROADS

CIVILIAN

INDUSTRIAL: FARMING

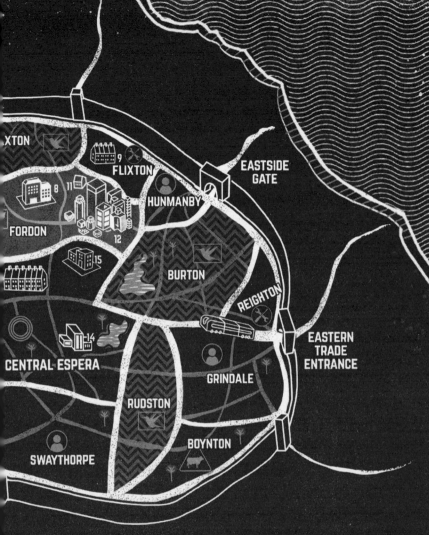

KEY

1 – FRASER SECONDARY SCHOOL
2 – ISABEL'S FLAT
3 – MORTIMER'S HOUSE
4 – EMMA'S HOUSE
5 – THE SUNSHINE PROJECT
6 – CHADWICK GREEN HOSPITAL
7 – GAUNTLET DRIVE
8 – LINNAEUS SECONDARY

9 – KATIPO
10 – GRACE'S HOUSE
11 – RYANS' HOUSE
12 – COCOON COMPLEX
13 – CEMETERY ENTRANCE
14 – UNIVERSITY OF CENTRAL ESPERA
15 – UCE MEDICAL SCHOOL
16 – DANCEJO

1

ERARO (MISTAKE)

That first night in her tiny flat, she cuts off her hair and her name. The brown strands are easily binned, but *Isabel Ryans* is harder to get rid of. When she looks in the mirror, that's who she sees, despite the asymmetrical crop of hair that half obscures her face. Not *Bella Nicholls* – the name on her new papers, her school records, the bank account with barely enough stolen money to cover next month's rent. Isabel can't hide from herself.

Which means she can't hide from *them*, either.

She keeps trying anyway. Every night she triple-checks her locks and wedges a chair underneath the door handle, because if it won't stop them, at least it'll give her prior warning if – when – they come for her. Each undisturbed night is both relief and agony, and she spends her days waiting for it all to fall apart. They know she's here. They must know she's here. Nobody can hide from the guilds; they're too good at what they do.

The fact she's still alive just means they're biding their time.

After two sleepless nights, Isabel starts keeping a knife under her pillow. After three, she abandons her bed for the battered settee where she has an unobstructed view of the door. She wakes every morning with a crick in her neck that nothing can entirely ease, unable to shake off her fear.

I got out, she tells herself. But is that even true, when she can't bring herself to sleep in her own bed? This is nothing but a temporary reprieve, a moment's breath before things get a hundred times worse. She shouldn't have left. She's going to spend the rest of her life looking over her shoulder.

Every morning she removes the chair, unbolts the locks, and reminds herself that she's free. Then she clips back her hair, already regretting the fringe, and sets off at a jog, hitting the streets as the world transitions from night to day. In those hours, the city is empty of life but for a handful of early commuters and a trudging paperboy starting his morning round.

It's on one of these early morning ventures that Isabel finds herself a job – a paper round that won't pay her rent but at least keeps her from starving. The *Echo*'s circulation is small enough to complete before school and large enough to be worth Ashvin's time to hire someone to replace a kid who moved out of the borough. Ashvin is the newsagent, and Isabel's tether to

2

the real world. His shop feels real in a way that school doesn't, those early mornings and newsprint smudges on her hands doing more to convince her that she got out than any pile of homework. Sometimes she almost forgets that she heard about the vacancy because she was curled up in the alleyway behind his shop, shaking in the grip of a flashback.

And so it goes, for two and a half weeks. Two and a half weeks of normality, two and a half weeks of paranoia, until the night she's proven right. The sound of her shitty locks giving way wakes her, and the sigh of the chair sliding across the floor as the intruder eases the door open has her reaching for her knife.

There's somebody in her flat.

Isabel sits up slowly, willing the sofa springs not to squeak. The intruder's attempt at stealth is ruined when they trip over her school bag, packed for the morning and left beside the door. No professional would make that mistake, unless they were trying to lure her into a false sense of security.

She reaches out and takes a second knife from the coffee table, keeping her movements slow. Here on the settee she's invisible, shrouded in shadow, but as the intruder steps further into the flat, she can see his outline against the harsh, fluorescent lighting of the hallway.

He ducks to search her school bag for valuables, and Isabel throws the first of her knives. It embeds itself in the wall, inches from his head, and he shrieks, dropping the tablet he's taken from her rucksack. The screen shatters on impact. By the time he spots Isabel, she's already aiming the second knife.

'Close the door,' she orders him, because she has a good relationship with her neighbours. 'Keep your hands where I can see them.'

He's young, she realises as he shuts the door with a trembling hand and takes a single step towards her. Barely in his twenties, if she's any judge. 'I'm—'

'Quiet.' Weighing her knife from hand to hand, she listens. All she hears is the lacklustre hum of the elderly heating system. There's no sound of anyone waiting in the hallway outside and no indication that he's woken the rest of the building. She gestures with the blade towards the table. 'Sit.'

After a moment's hesitation, he obeys, hands on the table so she can see he's unarmed.

Isabel closes the distance between them too quickly for him to flinch. With one hand, she slams her knife down, through his hand and into the table. With the other, she snatches up a tea towel and stuffs it into his mouth to muffle his scream. She waits until he subsides into ragged breaths before yanking the cloth away and taking a seat.

'Mi havas du demandojn,' she tells him, almost conversationally. 'Kiu sendis vin tien ĉi, kaj kiel vi trovis min?' *I have two questions. Who sent you here, and how did you find me?*

He shakes his head, skin shiny with sweat. 'I don't understand. Please . . .'

Isabel leans forward and applies pressure to the handle of the knife, watching his face as the blade twists. She's met some good actors, but there's no hiding pain – or fear. The stench of urine mingles with the scent of blood in the air, and she realises exactly how terrified he is.

Amateur, she thinks, but a deeper instinct still asks, 'La gildoj. Kiun?' *The guilds. Which one?*

'Please,' he begs. 'I don't . . . I'm not . . .'

He's not acting. There's a civilian's desperation in his contorted face, and pain has stripped away any artifice.

Isabel leans back in her seat, folding her arms. 'You don't speak Esperanto,' she says. 'Which means you're not guild. Why are you here?'

'I . . .' He's pale. Shaking. 'I was planning to rob you.'

'You picked the wrong flat.'

'I can see that now,' he manages, voice tight with pain. He glances at his hand as though considering pulling the knife out, but turns a sickly shade of white at the sight of the blood and hastily looks away. 'Please don't kill me. I'm sorry. I-I'll apologise to whichever guild you're from, or whatever you want.'

'Say a word to the guilds and I'll cut out your tongue.'

'Fine,' he agrees at once. 'I won't say anything. Please. I didn't take any—'

'Tell me,' she interrupts. 'Why this flat? Why me, of everyone in this building?'

He swallows. 'I knew you lived here alone. That you were young, that you haven't changed the locks yet. I didn't think . . . I mean, it's Lutton, the guilds don't—'

'You were counting on me being a civilian,' she says.

Of course he was. Even the most daring of thieves wouldn't

5

chance an encounter with Comma or Hummingbird, the two murderous guilds who dominate the city of Espera. Arms dealers and intelligence agents, poisoners and contract killers: their members have a diverse and bloody skill set.

And it never occurred to him that Isabel might be just as dangerous.

'Yes. I'm sorry. I ...' He glances at his hand again and retches. When he looks back at Isabel, his eyes are wide and petrified. 'Are you going to kill me?'

'I haven't decided. What's your name?'

'Ian.'

Oh. 'That's not a good answer.'

'I'm not lying. My name's Ian Crampton. I can ... I can prove it.'

A civilian and an idiot, giving his full name to somebody he thinks is guild. Either he doesn't think he'll make it out of here, or it hasn't occurred to him that he's given Isabel all the information she needs to call a hit on him.

'I didn't say it wasn't true,' she says, and reaches over to grasp the knife, pulling it from his hand as easily as she put it there. Blood gushes from the wound and she tosses him the tea towel. 'Put pressure on it. More,' she adds. 'Unless you *want* to bleed to death in my kitchen.'

She thinks he might be sobbing, but it's hard to tell if the dampness on his cheeks is sweat or tears.

'You've put me in a difficult position,' Isabel confides. 'It would be different if you were called, I don't know, *David*. But *Ian*? It's not a name that puts me in a good mood.'

'Then – then I can be David,' he stutters. 'Whatever you want. Please.'

'Too late.' She dumps the bloodied knife in the sink and adds, 'You know it's a school night? I was trying to sleep.'

'I don't get it,' he says. 'You're only a kid. You can't be . . .'

Isabel turns, leaning against the edge of the counter. 'Can't be what?'

'A contract killer.' Ian stumbles over the words. 'An assassin. The guilds don't . . . they don't train children.'

Funny the way everyone still believes that. 'And I thought Lutton had a low crime rate,' she says. 'But it seems tonight is a learning experience for us both.'

'I didn't know,' he insists. 'I didn't know you were guild.'

Killing him would cause problems, especially here in her flat. She'd have to deal with the body. It was a lot easier with Comma behind her. With her parents behind her.

Isabel disguises her shudder as a sharp movement towards the kitchen tap, rinsing the blood from her hands. When she's composed her expression, she looks back at Ian. 'Let's get one thing clear. I'm not guild.'

'But you—'

'Get up.'

He staggers to his feet. 'You can call the police. Turn me in. Whatever you want.'

'Walk towards the door. Stay in front of me.'

He's unsteady, but does as he's told. Isabel yanks her other knife out of the wall as they pass and keeps it in her hand as she directs him down the stairs and out of the fire exit. To the right, the glittering solar panels of the main road send their coloured lights into the night. She tells Ian to turn left, towards the encroaching shadows of the narrow alleyway that runs beside her block of flats.

'Do you know who I am?' she asks him.

His face is ghostly-white in the gloom as he turns to look at her, washed out by blood loss. He manages to shake his head. 'I don't know anything.'

'Let's keep it that way.'

'You're letting me go?'

'Looks like it. Now piss off before I change my mind.'

The thief looks at Isabel. He's got half a foot on her, at least, but he cowers before her. 'You're fucking scary, you know that?' he says, his fear tinged with grudging respect. Then he half runs, half stumbles down the alley away from her.

Ian. It's not a name she associates with good things.

He's maybe ten feet away when she throws the knife.

It hits him in the back and he crumples before she has time to register the absence of the hilt in her hand. She doesn't remember deciding to kill him, choosing to take aim, but when she approaches him and bends to retrieve the weapon, his breath bubbles uncertainly through bloody lips, pain electric in his eyes.

It won't take him long to die, but it'll be long enough to hurt.

Isabel slits his throat, half mercy and half reflex, and the pain shatters into lifelessness: burglar to body, civilian to corpse, a vicious magic trick of a transformation that somehow feels like it should take longer.

It's beginning to drizzle, the dampness clinging to her pyjamas and her hair. Fine droplets catch the inadequate glow of light from the open fire escape. When she checks her battered watch, it tells her it's three in the morning.

She looks down at the body.

Fuck.

This is the last thing she needs.

'Morning, Bella. Rough night?'

Isabel glances up at the boy waiting by the tram stop, his blond hair an unruly mass of curls as usual. Nick Larrington. He attached himself to her on the first day of school because they were both new transfers with no other friends. He doesn't seem to have caught on that they have nothing else in common, and she can't figure out what it is that he wants from her. She'd half hoped that missing her usual tram this morning would mean she could make the journey unremarked. Apparently not.

She narrows her eyes at his question. 'Why?'

'You look shattered. Plus your jumper's inside out.'

By the time Isabel had dealt with the body, there was no point going back to bed before her paper round. Now she's exhausted but wired, a hair's breadth from snapping. Her paranoia whispers that Nick knows something, but logic points out that if he knew how she'd spent the night, he wouldn't still be talking to her.

He's smart enough that she's yet to catch him actively badmouthing the guilds – even in a civilian borough like Lutton, that's a sure-fire way to end up on a watchlist for suspected abolitionist activity. But on their third tram ride together, he admitted that he sometimes cries reading the death notices in the *Echo*, the week's kills neatly broken down by borough and guild, and if he's not desensitised to murder after seventeen years in Espera, he never will be. She hadn't realised that was possible.

'Didn't sleep well,' she says, scanning the crowd. It looks like the usual mix of students and commuters, but she hasn't lived here long enough to notice anyone out of place.

She screwed up. She screwed up so badly. At least she dumped the body far enough away not to scream *ISABEL RYANS IS HERE* to anyone who cares to look, but there's no way an unclaimed kill in a civilian borough will go unnoticed for long. Maybe they'll send someone she knows, or maybe she'll never see them coming and she'll be nothing but another name on the list for Nick to cry over.

She should have called the police. Before throwing a knife at him, before giving away that she is – was – guild, when there was no risk in letting him walk away. That's how it's done in civilian boroughs, isn't it? The Espera Met stays out of guild business, but a thief they could have handled.

Instead, she killed him.

Fuck.

'Tram's coming,' says Nick. Soon she's swept up in the crowd boarding the packed vehicle. That's okay. She can hide in a crowd. They can't do anything here, on a tram, in public . . .

Isabel wedges herself in a corner next to the emergency exit, too far away from Nick to chat. He looks disappointed, but it's a relief to drop the façade of normality. Two and a half weeks. Eighteen bloody days. That's all she managed.

She reaches out to grab the metal pole for support and catches sight of her nails. *Shit.* All that time spent scrubbing her hands in the sink last night and there's still blood under her fingernails. There's nothing she can do about it here without drawing attention to herself, so she shoves her hand in her pocket and tries to forget about it.

By now she's had plenty of practice ignoring the blood on her hands.

2

TROMPO (DECEPTION)

Located in the middle of the civilian borough of Lutton, Fraser Secondary School is a mess of mismatched architecture, the grass-roofed extension with its glass and solar panels nestled against the brutalist concrete pile of its original building. It's also the closest thing Isabel's going to get to a new start. From now on, she's an ordinary seventeen-year-old girl who is going to go to school, get some qualifications, and not kill anybody.

Else. Not kill anybody else.

Isabel's an experienced liar, but establishing herself at the Fraser required more than a confident tone and an innocent expression. Being abruptly pulled out of school eighteen months ago by her parents means her real academic record is patchy, and smoothing over the gaps is a delicate operation. She forged herself a set of Level Two qualifications since, without them, she'd be limited to industrial jobs and apprenticeships. It doesn't feel too dishonest: if she'd been given the chance to finish fifth year, she'd have taken them at sixteen like everybody else. But she can't forge memories she doesn't have, and it's easier to drop down a year and start Level Threes from the beginning than try to muddle through with a year's worth of missing knowledge.

The extra year also buys her time, putting off the moment she has to figure out what's next. The University of Central Espera is theoretically neutral, but it's a pie the guilds have their fingers in, and it's not like she could afford the civilian fees. And if there's a job out there that would let her stay hidden, she hasn't found it yet. School is the safest place for her – the longer she can stay here, the better.

Her teachers have been told that Bella Nicholls was homeschooled due to poor health, which isn't *entirely* a lie. This non-specific tragic backstory does double duty as an easy explanation for why she sometimes has to duck into an empty classroom when the chaos and noise of the crowded school corridors become overwhelming, and why she's not up-to-date on all the pop culture references that pepper her classmates' conversations. But blending in is about more than what's on paper, and every day Isabel is confronted by the differences between herself and her classmates.

At Linnaeus Secondary, the highly selective Comma-funded school she used to attend, her path was clear. Top grades in the sciences would have earned her a place in the specialist track for pupils the guild was interested in sponsoring for training. Her academic classes would have been supplemented by specialised vocational courses designed to pave the way for future study: classes in poisons, weapons development, codebreaking ... But those options are limited to spons – guild-sponsored schools – which means she won't find them at the Fraser, even if she wanted (or needed) them. Here, the required vocational electives are geared towards civilian jobs. Woodwork. Textiles. Food Science. Training for a life Isabel was never expected to lead.

Her late transfer left her with limited options, of which Woodwork was the least objectionable. Mortimer Sark, the teacher, is known to staff and students alike by his first name and rewards exceptional homework with biscuits from a bright orange tin he keeps on his desk. She'd hoped that meant he was a soft touch, but so far he's anything but.

'Everyone else in this class,' he told 'Bella' in their first lesson, 'took Level Two Woodwork with me. That means they've sat through my lectures and demonstrations on workshop safety. They're bored to tears of the topic, but at least I know they won't saw off their own fingers. You, on the other hand ...'

'I'm not going to saw off my fingers.'

'So you say, but I have no proof that it's true.' He placed a thick lever-arch file on the workbench in front of her. 'I understand that your old school didn't offer Woodwork, which is fine. Well, no, it's tragic, but it's not an insurmountable issue. However, since we don't have time to cover everything you've missed, I'm going to need you to work through this by yourself. When you're done, I'll test you. If you pass, you get to use sharp things.' He gave her a wry smile. 'Yippee.'

Isabel eyed the folder. 'Is this really necessary?'

'You'd be amazed at the variety and quantity of accidents students managed to have before I rewrote the safety documentation. So, yes, it's necessary. And,' he added, 'you're staying on this bench where I can see you.'

It's like he knew Isabel had been planning to find the darkest corner of the room to crawl into. 'Anything else?'

He gave her a placid, disarming smile. 'Not yet. I'm sure I'll think of something.'

Two and a half weeks of diligently working through the folder later, she's still barely a third of the way through and, as such, Mortimer has yet to let her touch anything more lethal than sandpaper in his classroom. Sometimes she's sure he's deliberately testing her patience, though it's difficult to hate him when it's clear he's motivated by genuine concern for his students.

Today, slowed by exhaustion, Isabel's the last to leave, and he catches her. 'Bella, if you need any help with the safety documentation, I'm happy to go over it with you in a free period. I know it's a lot to work through alone.'

'I'll bear that in mind,' she responds non-committally.

She expects him to try harder to convince her, but all he says is, 'I'm not holding you back to be difficult, you know.'

'I know that.'

They're alone in the classroom, and Mortimer is between

15

Isabel and the door. She tries not to notice things like that, but old instincts die hard.

'I was sorry to hear about your poor health,' he says, apparently sincerely. 'But your Level Two scores were excellent. I'm sure you'll catch up quickly.'

Her Level Two scores are a lie. 'Thanks,' she says awkwardly. 'I'll do my best.'

'I do wonder, though,' he says, 'why you would move from Fordon to Lutton to attend an underfunded civ without the resources to support you properly.'

And there it is. It's possible Mortimer's remarks are innocent – anyone might question why she'd leave a guild borough and its opportunities behind for a civilian school like the Fraser. But the fact that he's paying attention at all is dangerous. It means he's looking at the joins where *Isabel Ryans* becomes *Bella Nicholls*, the places where truth and lie intersect. And she has no good answers for him. Her Level Two grades may be fake, but they're not implausible: the teachers at Linnaeus honed her younger self to academic sharpness and, if she'd stayed, she could have continued along that trajectory. Few people would move to a civilian borough if they had the choice, since guild jobs have better pay and better benefits; fewer still would make the change before they'd even finished school. Mortimer probably assumes that either she's an abolitionist, or she got expelled.

'I'm not trying to pry,' he says, clearly reading into her silence. 'But I'm concerned that the Fraser can't give you all the support you need, especially with your background.'

'My background?' She scrubbed her record of anything

suspicious, anything too close to the guilds. And unless he knows about last night . . .

He doesn't know about last night. Nobody knows about last night.

'Your health issues,' Mortimer clarifies.

'I'm fine,' says Isabel. 'I was ill for a while, and now I'm not.' The damage has been done. All that's left are the scars, and her medical exemption from PE means nobody here will ever see those.

'Okay,' says Mortimer, sounding unconvinced.

She swings her rucksack onto her shoulder. 'I'm late for Chemistry,' she informs him, and leaves before he can ask any more questions.

She's good at Chemistry. It's one of the few subjects where she has to pretend to know less than she does, although little of what she learned in her father's lab is on the syllabus. And Dr Garner is the kind of teacher Isabel can deal with: impersonal, straightforward, efficient. She's strict enough that some of the other students dislike her, but Isabel appreciates it. At least she always knows where she stands.

Today, though, it's hard to focus. She killed someone. A burglar, a civilian, an innocent. She dumped the body, but they'll find it eventually, and they'll trace it back to her. Maybe they already know. If they're watching her – they *must* be watching her – they'll have seen everything.

Eighteen days of freedom. She thought she was afraid before, but now it's like she can feel the blade hanging over her head, waiting to fall.

Lack of sleep isn't helping, and her notes grow messier as the textbook blurs. The words are a jumble of elements and properties, swimming on the paper. Isabel closes her eyes, and the voices of her fellow students fade. She feels only the cold resin of the table under her fingertips, her feet resting on the bar of her stool. It could be any lab.

No. Not *any* lab.

The fear is as instant as it is irrational, her left hand curling instinctively into a fist that couldn't protect her then and won't protect her now. She can't feel her nails digging into her scarred palm, but she can feel her knuckles burning as she tries to remember how to loosen her grip.

'Are you sleeping in my class, Bella?' asks Dr Garner.

Isabel's eyes snap open. Her panic-frozen muscles relax as the colourful classroom displays come into focus. She's at school. She escaped, and she's at school, and – and Dr Garner looks distinctly pissed off.

It takes every ounce of her willpower not to flinch. 'Sorry,' she mutters, staring down at the desk. 'I was ... thinking.'

Silence. She waits for punishment, but when she dares look up at her teacher, Dr Garner only frowns a little and says, 'About covalent bonding, I hope.'

Is that what they're studying? Isabel hasn't taken in a word. 'Yeah,' she says vaguely. 'Sorry.'

Dr Garner leaves it at that, but it's a long time before Isabel can unclench her fist. She fights to stay present for the rest of the lesson, pressing the tip of her pen into her palm every time she feels herself drifting back into a flashback. By the

18

time the bell rings, there's a constellation of dots adorning the damaged skin.

Nick, inevitably, catches her at the tram stop after school. 'Bad day?'

Is it that obvious? She doesn't know how Nick reads her so easily – what signals she's giving out, or how to stop them. 'Feels like this week has lasted a month already,' she admits.

'It's Tuesday.'

'Well, then, kill me now and put me out of my misery.' Isabel dredges up a smile and pretends she's joking. Talking to Nick is at least better than staying stuck inside her own head, running through the potential consequences she might face for what happened last night. 'Never get a paper round,' she tells him. 'Getting up at five isn't worth it.'

Like *that*'s her biggest problem right now.

'Wasn't planning on it, but thanks for the tip. Is that why you always look so tired?'

Isabel scowls at him. 'Wow, flattering.'

He pulls a face. 'Sorry. That came out wrong. Obviously, I meant that the city of Espera is grateful for your noble sacrifice.'

She laughs despite herself, adopting a heroic expression. 'Come rain or shine, brave newsies of the city are there, delivering the *Echo* to your door. Now for the low, low price of three shillings a week, you too could have the latest headlines with your breakfast.'

Nick snorts. 'And by "latest headlines", you mean death, death, and . . . oh! More death.'

Isabel drops the pose. 'That's a little unfair to the *Echo*,' she says. 'Last week they had a *fascinating* exposé on Lutton Borough Council's mismanagement of local recycling services.'

'Scintillating journalism,' he agrees. 'I apologise for maligning your employer.'

'And it could be worse,' she points out. 'It could be the *Times*. They put their kill column on the second page, as though you might somehow miss it. At least the *Echo* keeps the obits at the back, and misses out the lurid details.'

'There's always the *Bulletin*,' says Nick, and Isabel's smile fades. He catches sight of her expression and gives an awkward shrug, hunched and nowhere near as casual as he wants it to be. 'What? I didn't say I read it. I'm just saying it's out there.'

The *Weekly Bulletin of the Free Press* – known widely as the *Bulletin* – is the illegal newssheet of the abolitionists, the people who want the guilds disbanded. Nobody's ever identified the leaders of the Free Press, if it's even a single organisation and not a convenient smokescreen for a dozen radical factions, but the guilds have certainly tried. Isabel knew Nick was soft-hearted, but there's a difference between squeamishness and revolutionary politics. 'Didn't peg you for a radical,' she says.

'I'm not,' he says, immediately defensive. 'But, you know, not every paper has to follow the guilds' agenda.'

Which is as good as saying he sympathises.

'Somehow,' she says, carefully pasting humour over her discomfort, 'I don't think the Free Press is recruiting kids for paper rounds.' It makes Nick laugh, and they change the subject.

But the whole way home, all Isabel can think about is what Nick would do if he knew she was one of them. If she told him the things she's done. That would be one way to make him leave her alone, to ensure her journey to school is undisturbed by any attempt at friendship. He'd be afraid of her.

Maybe he should be.

Maybe they all should be.

3

MEMOROJ (MEMORIES)

Her hands are barely large enough to grip the gun. She strains to reach the trigger, feeling the pull in her fingers. This gun wasn't designed with children in mind.

That's because it isn't her gun. She wasn't meant to need one. This isn't how today was supposed to go.

When she looks up, he's still got his back to her, radio in hand. If he calls for help, it's already too late. Her mother's voice urges her to fire, to get it over with.

And she always obeys her mother.

The discordant screech of her alarm wakes Isabel with a start. Five a.m. The fact she slept through the night is more surprising than the nightmare, though she'd thought she was past the night terrors. She'd also believed she wasn't going to kill the first person to threaten her precious freedom, so she doesn't know herself as well as she thought.

Isabel sighs and sits up, steadying her breathing. *I'm alive. I got out, and I'm alive.* At some point in the night, she threw her blanket halfway across the room, but better the blanket than the knife under her pillow. She tilts her head, listening to her neck crack after another night on the settee, and tries to ground herself. In the weird pre-dawn light, the flat hardly seems real.

Maybe it isn't. There's something dreamlike about the silence as she hunts for coffee. Where are the sirens, the click of guns being cocked, the steady breathing of a Comma agent waiting to take her out? The tap water thunders into the kettle, deafening in the absence of other sounds.

Who will notice the body first – the guild or her parents?

Ashvin's on the phone when she gets to his shop, but her bag of papers is waiting for her. She grabs it and sets off, shoving the *Echo* through letterboxes without looking at what she's doing. Twitchy with nervous energy and walking faster than usual, she's covered half her route by the time she slows down enough to read the headline screaming from the front page.

UNCLAIMED KILL IN LUTTON

Isabel stops dead, midway up somebody's garden path. Her world narrows to the thick, black letters on the page, proclaiming her mistake to everyone in the city. They found the body. They found the body, and with a headline like this, the guilds will know too. She's surprised they haven't sent somebody for her already. She wonders how much longer she's got.

Muscles rigid with the effort of keeping calm, she folds the paper and pushes it through the house's narrow letterbox. A dog barks inside as the *Echo* hits the doormat, and Isabel walks steadily down the path, through the gate and around the corner. There, out of sight, she sinks to the floor, back against a lamppost, and tries to breathe.

Unclaimed kill.

She could read the report. Find out what they know, guess how long it'll be before they join the dots. But it's not worth it. It's safest to assume they're already a step ahead, and that all the newspaper can offer is sensationalist speculation.

Get up, she tells herself. *Somebody will notice. Get up.* She knows how to follow orders, even from herself. Some defensive instinct forces her to her feet and back to her task, mechanical and efficient. When the final paper has been pushed through its letterbox, Isabel tucks the empty bag close to her body and begins to run: first a steady jog, then faster. The air is crisp and autumnal, but the pavement beneath her feet is dry.

It should feel like freedom. But the thunder of her pulse in her ears can't drown out the memories following her like spectres: her mother in the training hall, giving orders; her father and his lab, full of cruelties; a woman with moss-green eyes and a much-broken nose, signing the order that almost killed her. They chase her through the safe civilian streets of Lutton, inescapable as dread.

The headline is a reminder that there are some things she can't outrun.

She gets back to her flat with enough time for a shower and a rest before school, but her blood's static with anxiety and she can't sit still. She ends up leaving early, catching a tram before the morning rush. In a just world, this would mean a morning without Nick, but the city of Espera is anything but just: there he is at the tram stop, bleary-eyed and clutching a thermos of tea.

'You're early today,' he says.

'Ashvin's trialling a new stimulant on his minions,' she tells him, her tongue sharpened by exhaustion and resisting efforts at sincerity. 'We're all seeing double, but, on the plus side, we're moving twice as fast.' The joke is a friendlier lie than anything else she might have offered, but Nick's eyeing her warily, so she adds, 'I'm kidding. Though I wouldn't say no to some caffeine right now. What's dragged you here so early?'

'Homework.' He shrugs. 'The library seemed like the most reliable way to escape my brothers long enough to finish it.'

Isabel has yet to set foot in the library. The rows of shelves and the hushed atmosphere intimidate her, like the books know she doesn't belong. 'How many brothers do you have?' she asks. It's possibly the first time she's shown an interest in Nick's life.

'Four, and a sister. So it's pretty hard to hear myself think sometimes, as you can imagine.'

She can't, but she nods vaguely anyway, and the rest of the journey passes in silence. Tiredness makes Nick quiet – and clumsy too, stumbling as they disembark outside the Fraser. His bag falls open, vomiting books and pens across the pavement. He swears, crouching to gather them up, and Isabel darts forward to save a pen from disappearing down a drain.

She holds it out to him. 'Here. Rescued from the sewer.'

'Thanks,' says Nick, reaching out to take it. And then he notices her hand.

It's not the worst of her scars, only the most visible, but Nick's expression is horrified as he takes in the ugly, damaged skin of her left hand and the crooked fingers that no longer fully straighten, warped by scar tissue. Revulsion flickers across his face before he can hide it, and she flinches, curling her fingers around the injury and stuffing her hand in her pocket.

'Accident,' she says, forestalling his questions. 'I don't want to talk about it.'

This is the part she hates – the moment horror turns to pity. 'What happened?' he asks in a hushed voice. 'Some kind of burn?'

'What part of "I don't want to talk about it" didn't you understand?' Isabel snatches up the last couple of pens and hands them to him. 'Maybe zip up your bag next time.'

Without waiting for an answer, she sets off towards the school.

'Wait—' Nick's wheezing slightly as he jogs to catch up with her. She remembers him mentioning his asthma, during one of those early conversations where he talked incessantly in her direction and she answered in monosyllables. 'I'm sorry. Really. I didn't mean to make you uncomfortable.'

She wonders how he'd react to the rest of her scars. 'Don't let me keep you from the library,' she says, without looking at him.

'Come with me,' he suggests.

Now she glances at him, at his expectant expression, but it answers nothing. 'Why?' she asks. 'Because you feel guilty for staring at my hand?'

'Because I could use the company.'

She wants to refuse, but she doesn't have a better plan for how to kill the forty minutes until the bell goes; hanging around on the cold playing field is less than appealing.

'Fine,' she concedes, without softening her tone. 'Lead the way.'

The library is on the top floor. Nick marches confidently in and dumps his stuff on a desk, but Isabel freezes at the sight of the packed shelves, books jostling for space. The last time she was in a library ...

'You look bewildered,' says a voice, and she turns to see a short-haired woman in an ugly grey jumper. 'I'm Grace Whittock. The librarian. Anything I can help you with?'

Do you have any books on getting away with murder when they've already found the body? 'I ...' *What do you know about flashbacks and nightmares and how do I make them stop?* 'I haven't been up here before. I'm new to the school.'

'Well, this might help a little.' Grace Whittock hands her a bookmark printed with the library classification system and layout. Isabel takes it despite having no intention of checking out any of the books. 'I'd give you the grand tour, but I have a staff meeting in five minutes. Do you have a name?'

It takes Isabel a moment to remember the correct answer to that question. 'Bella. Bella Nicholls.'

'Nice to meet you, Bella,' says the librarian. 'Come back at break sometime and I'll get Emma to show you around. It's less confusing than it looks.'

'Right.' She has no intention of doing that either. 'Uh, thanks.'

The woman smiles. 'Great! In the meantime, I think your friend is waiting for you.'

Isabel follows her gaze and sees Nick beckoning to her from his table. 'He's not my friend,' she says automatically.

'Does he know that?' asks the librarian, and leaves before Isabel has time to answer.

She wants to turn around and walk straight out of this book-filled room, but Nick looks so expectant that it feels cruel, so she pulls out the chair across from him and sits down. He already has his homework spread across the table.

'So,' he says, 'is it true you were homeschooled?'

'For a while,' says Isabel, with no intention of elaborating on that answer. 'I thought libraries were supposed to be silent.'

'Ms Whittock isn't here.'

If she'd realised that following him to the library meant she'd agreed to reciprocate his attempts at friendship, she wouldn't have come. 'We're not doing this,' Isabel tells him, pulling out her History book. 'I'm here because there's half an hour until the bell rings and I don't have a better way to fill the time, not because I want to talk about myself.'

Nick shrugs. 'Fine. You can help me with my Latin homework.'

She snorts. 'You're better off without my help there.' Latin's for civilians – for people who don't need a modern language because they'll never leave Espera and who haven't been raised with the guild tongue of Esperanto everywhere around them. 'How about you help me with my History essay?'

He grimaces. 'Go on, then. Hit me.'

'Espera and Europe in the 1940s,' reads Isabel, with considerable distaste. 'Question one. Explore the implications of Esperan neutrality on the movement of refugees. You may choose to focus on specific aspects of the 1942 Sanctuary Act.'

'Ugh,' says Nick. '*That* module.'

Isabel feels the same way. The Fraser requires at least one humanities subject at Level Three, and History seemed like the easiest option. But she's painfully aware that, at best, the syllabus offers an incomplete picture of Espera's past; at worst, it's propaganda designed to flatter the guilds and their power. The Fraser may have a more balanced curriculum than Linnaeus, but it still tends towards the sycophantic. Isabel knows her teachers are expecting an essay about Espera, the City of Hope, which took in refugees from bombed-out cities across Europe and gave them security and a new life behind its high walls – not Espera, the City of Fear, which murdered its way to independence and built those walls in the first place.

But for a brief moment, she allows herself to wonder what would happen if she answered truthfully.

'Sure you can't do it for me?' she asks Nick.

He grimaces. 'I'll stick to Latin, thanks.'

Probably a good choice. 'Quod nocet saepe docet.'

'What's that?'

'The only Latin I know. *What harms often teaches*. It's what—' She breaks off, realises Nick's looking at her, and gives him a lopsided smile. 'It's what my father used to say.'

His look is a little too understanding, though whatever conclusion he's come to is only a fraction of the truth. 'He sounds ... lovely.'

Isabel hides her expression by rummaging through her school bag for a pen. 'Yeah, homeschooling was a right bundle of fun,' she says finally. She can't even bring herself to make it sound like a joke, because none of this is funny.

UNCLAIMED KILL IN LUTTON scream the papers lying on doormats across the borough, her own death warrant hand-delivered. She swallows, uncaps her pen, and pretends she can't see her hands shaking.

And she'll say this much for Nick: he does her the small kindness of pretending he can't either.

4

SEKVOJ (CONSEQUENCES)

The rest of the day passes in a haze, Isabel's fear tearing at her stomach like claws. She's never noticed students reading the newspaper before, but by lunchtime she's seen half a dozen of them huddled around a single copy of the *Echo*.

'They're saying it's a freelancer,' says one boy.

'Bullshit,' says his friend. 'In Lutton? My money's on a crime of passion. There's probably some big drama behind it.'

'On the radio, they said it was too good to be a one-off,' says a third. 'They think the killer must have been trained.'

'Doesn't mean it wasn't personal,' says the second student. 'It could be a guild killer settling scores, and they didn't claim it because it wasn't a commission.'

'I don't think it works like that,' says the first boy, but

he sounds uncertain. Which is understandable, given that knowledge of how the guilds' contract killers conduct business isn't easy to come by. 'And why would a guild killer be in Lutton, except on a hit?'

Isabel leaves them to their speculation without contributing, but she hears it echoed again and again before the end of the day. It feels like nobody's talking about anything else, and by the time the final bell rings, she's tense enough to snap.

She tries not to look over her shoulder on the way home, but she can't shake the feeling of being followed. When she finally reaches her flat, she locks the door and wedges a chair under the handle before she's even put her bag down.

Somebody clears their throat.

She thought they might be following her. She never imagined they'd have beaten her home. But there at her table is a man in his thirties, wearing black suit trousers and a grey shirt with the top button undone. The colour matches his eyes, which aren't friendly. Leaning against the leg of the table is a slim, officious-looking briefcase.

'Isabel Ryans,' he says. It's not a question.

She swallows. Knowing this was inevitable doesn't make it any easier to face now that it's happening. 'Is this ... What's this about?'

'Ni bezonas paroli,' he says. *We need to talk.* His language choice punctures any hope she had that he isn't guild. 'Why don't you take a seat?'

It doesn't look like he's armed, which only means he's too important to carry his own weapons. Isabel puts down her school bag and forces herself to cross the room, pull out a chair and sit down, as though he doesn't scare her at all.

His slight smile suggests he's not fooled. 'I'll be frank with you,' he says. 'I'm here on behalf of Comma.'

'How did you find me?' she asks. Her mind is screaming: *run, run, run*.

'We never lost you. We had no reason to seek you out before now.'

Until she killed Ian. She should have let him live. If Comma already knew she was here, it wouldn't have mattered if he'd talked. But his death is a problem. His death makes *her* a problem.

'Be honest with me, Miss Ryans,' he says. 'What do you know about the whereabouts of your parents?'

It takes a moment for his question to register. 'Wait, *what*? You're not here about—'

'That young man you killed? We'll come to that, but no, it's not my primary concern. Your father is missing.'

Missing. A word so passive has no business being applied to her father. If he can't be found, it's because he doesn't want to be. 'I don't know anything.'

'Are you sure?' His voice is calm, but she can see the tension in his posture.

Missing. What does that even mean? 'You think he's been abducted or something? That he's in danger?'

The man pauses. 'Maybe.'

So that's a no, then. 'You think he's defected.'

For a second, he considers lying to her; she sees it in his

momentary hesitation. Then he says, 'We're considering the possibility.'

Defected. She thought she was the only one trying to leave. 'That sounds like a *you* problem,' she points out.

'It is,' he responds tightly. 'Your father's absence, whatever the explanation, is economically problematic for the guild. It's important that we retrieve him as soon as possible.'

'And my mother?' she asks, noting the wording of his questions.

'Also missing,' he admits. 'But Judith is close to retirement and only takes a few contracts these days. We're far more concerned about Ian.'

She tries not to flinch at the name, of the reminder that she let her emotions get the better of her two nights ago. 'You have other poisoners,' she points out.

'Not like him.'

No, her father's brand of monstrosity always was unique. The poisons he develops secure Comma's dominance in the industry, not only against Hummingbird, their rival within Espera, but worldwide: governments have killed for the chance to obtain a nerve agent from Ian Ryans' lab. No wonder they're freaking out about losing him.

'I don't know or care where my father is,' she says. 'I haven't spoken to my parents in weeks. If that's all you came for, then we're done.'

'You haven't heard from them since you ran away.'

It isn't exactly a question, but Isabel nods. 'If anyone knows where they are, it'll be Michael.'

The man looks up sharply at the mention of her parents' protégé. 'Do you know where he is?'

'Michael? No, last time I—' She breaks off as the implication of his question sinks in. 'He's missing too?'

'We spoke to him shortly after you left, but since then we've lost contact. We don't know if he's with your parents.'

'Probably,' she says dismissively. 'Michael's a coward. He'll do whatever they tell him.'

'And yet I understand that he helped you, the night you ran away.'

Helped is a strong word. 'He didn't stop me,' she clarifies. 'That's not the same thing.'

'Your parents don't seem to have seen it that way.'

'They punished him?'

His nod is small and sharp – uncertain, Isabel realises. He's unwilling to commit to acknowledging her parents' capacity for cruelty. She has no difficulty believing it, but it's hard to know what to feel about Michael suffering for her. Vindication, that he finally experienced what he always denied? Regret, that the boy who once saved her life should bear that punishment? Neither feels like enough, but it doesn't matter. Michael made his choice. He, unlike her, actually had one.

'Maybe he's with them, maybe he's not,' she concedes finally. 'But if anyone knows anything, it'll be him. Are we done here?'

'Not quite.' He appraises her. 'I'll admit, you've pulled an impressive fugitive act. But you're a valuable asset, Isabel. We'd be shooting ourselves in the foot to let you walk away like this.'

'I'm not an asset,' she says. 'I'm a person. And I don't want to be a Comma agent.'

'But you killed that young man.'

Of course it comes back to this. 'It was a stupid mistake, and it won't happen again.' A stupid mistake that's ruined everything. She knows he wants more from her than an apology. 'What are you going to do to me?'

He drums his fingers lightly against the table. 'When you left, I was in favour of leaving you alone. You're young, and a few years of education will do you good. But now that this little *mistake* of yours has made the news, Hummingbird will have noticed. You might as well have publicly announced that there's a trained killer in Lutton who isn't affiliated with a guild – someone to be either neutralised or assimilated.'

'I don't understand.'

'They want you, or they want you dead.'

Oh, shit. She's been so focused on Comma and the target already on her back that she almost forgot about the brand new one she's painted. 'I . . . didn't think of that.'

'Of course you didn't.' He leans forward suddenly, and she recoils. 'Say Hummingbird find you. What next? They'll see you're a child and put two and two together to equal Cocoon. Maybe they'll try to recruit you, maybe they'll kill you – either way, it's not in any of our interests. You're too useful a weapon to lose.'

Isabel's mouth is dry. She knew she'd screwed herself over, but she hadn't even thought about the impact on Comma if news of Cocoon leaked to Hummingbird or the public.

Cocoon: the guild's final secret, kept hidden from all but a select few, with the power to undermine every shred of credibility in their promises.

The guilds don't train children. Except Comma did.

'I'm not a weapon,' she manages, voice hoarse.

'But you've proved you have no problem with killing.'

'So what?'

'So why did you leave?'

The question catches her off-guard. 'Why the fuck do you think?' she spits. But despite the vicious bite of her words, her voice cracks as though she's about to cry. She hates herself for letting him see that, but not as much as she hates him for watching.

There's a moment's pause, and then he says, 'I see,' in a tone that suggests he doesn't. From his briefcase, he takes a couple of sheets of paper and places them on the table. 'Let's discuss how we're going to resolve your current predicament, Isabel.'

The pages are densely typed, with enough brackets and numbers for Isabel to guess it's a legal document before she's read a word.

'What's this?'

'Comma are prepared to offer you a deal.'

It's what she expected. It still takes all her restraint not to push back her chair and walk away, and what stops her is less interest in what he has to say and more the knowledge that she has nowhere to go.

'There's nothing you could offer me that would make me come back.'

'We'll claim the kill.'

Which means no police investigation, no Hummingbird target on her back; the body will be dealt with, and she can move on as though she didn't screw up her one chance at freedom. It may be in Comma's interests to keep Isabel out of their rival's hands, but they won't give her this for free.

'What do you want from me?'

'Shockingly little, under the circumstances. Simply that when you finish school, you join us.'

It's not a bad deal. But it feels like a death sentence, like cold metal around her wrists. 'No.'

'You told Michael you wanted to go back to school.' Did she? She doesn't remember letting herself be that vulnerable around him. 'This way, we both get what we want.'

'I wanted out of Comma, not to be dragged back to my parents the moment I pass my exams.'

He regards her steadily. The silence is so tangible she can taste it, bitter and sharp as bile. At last he says, 'So it's about your parents, then.'

'Why do you ask so many questions when you already know the answers?'

'What makes you think I know the answers?'

'Because ...' *Because they told me that you did. That Comma knew and approved, so nobody was going to listen to my stories.* 'Because the guild knows everything, doesn't it?'

'If only.' His mouth twists in what might be a smile. 'There's more to Comma than your parents, Isabel.'

'I don't care. I'm not making the deal.'

He pushes back his chair and stands. 'You know,' he says easily, 'some of my colleagues are placing bets on whether the police or Hummingbird will find you first.'

'Which did you bet on?'

'Neither. I'm more intrigued to see how long you survive on your own.' He returns the contract to his briefcase and snaps the clasps shut. 'My name's Ronan, by the way. Ronan Atwood. I highly doubt this will be the last time we cross paths.'

Isabel says nothing. At the door, Ronan turns back as if to speak, but only shakes his head and leaves the flat.

She crumples, pulling her feet up onto the chair and hugging her knees to her chest. Her whole body feels sticky, unclean; the scars under her clothes burn as though they're days old instead of years.

They weren't meant to come here. This flat is hers, and only hers.

But they knew all along, and they sent Ronan Atwood to deal with her.

She knows the name, even if this is the first time she's had a face to put with it. It's impossible not to have heard of him when he controls half of Comma; everybody knows he's aiming to be Director one day, and he's most of the way there. If he came to see her in person, she's in even more trouble than she realised.

As for her parents, she doesn't believe for one second that they're really gone. They won't have left the city. That Comma can't find them is ... significant, she supposes, but it doesn't mean she's safe. If anything, it's the opposite.

Isabel can't be sure how long she stays curled against the wall, one arm wrapped around her knees, but her legs are half numb by the time she stumbles into the kitchen. She opens the cupboards and stares at the contents, but she has no appetite, so she locks her shitty locks, stacks her textbooks on top of the chair underneath her door handle, and puts a clean set of bedding on the settee.

But she already knows she won't be sleeping tonight.

5

MENSOGOJ (LIES)

The borough of Lutton is afraid. Isabel sees it in the faces of the civilians waiting for the tram, senses it in the Espera Met officers patrolling the streets and in the taut atmosphere of the school. The excitement of rumour has given way to fear now that the victim has been identified:

> Ian Crampton, 21, worked as a shop assistant and was the primary carer for his sister, who suffers from a rare autoimmune condition ...

Everyone wants to know who's next. Everyone wants to know why Ian is dead.

Isabel wants to know that too – and why, having already

fucked up her life beyond repair, she didn't take Ronan's deal. This morning, watching the police walk their pointless beat, last night's decision feels rash. Childish. *Not safe, not safe, not safe.* She should have taken it. What does she have to lose?

Only the rest of her life. Only the belief that she can be anything more than a weapon.

Isabel's afraid too, in her own way. She's afraid of the memories that assail her throughout the school day: a mess of disconnected images, flashbacks full of ragged holes. The lab. A notebook. The spiders, always the spiders. She'd say they're the worst of it, but she doesn't know what other horrors lurk in her mind, nor why her memories are full of dropped stitches and moth holes, patchy and incomplete. Maybe that was deliberate, her father's vicious cleverness taking her memories from her.

But some things remain vivid and sharp as a knife, and for a moment she's not in her overwarm, dusty History classroom, trying to stay focused on today's half-truths and blatant propaganda. She's watching her younger self, as if from a distance: seeing again and again her shaking hands, the shattered flask of acid, her father furious as he takes her by the wrist and presses her hand down into the pool of liquid.

You've got to learn, he says, as she sobs in the corner of the lab, no strength left for screaming. *You think this is cruelty, but it's not. I'm teaching you. You won't forget what you've learned today.*

What she learned was that he would do anything.

And she remembers that like it was yesterday – the agony of

the burn and the awful clarity of realising that no matter how hard she tried to please her father, it would never be enough to keep her safe. But that only makes the blank patches in her memories more concerning. Why does she remember this and not the rest? What did her father do?

Where did her father *go*?

She told Ronan she didn't care, but she cares. She cares because as long as he's out there, her father is a threat she can't fight.

Closing her fingers around the scarred mess of her left palm, Isabel forces her mind back to the lesson. She doubts Mr Branagh believes half of what he's telling them, but it's hardly his fault – out here, in the civilian world, the real history of the guilds is often obscured. Not erased, as such, but a point's been made of ensuring it's more trouble than it's worth to seek out, and certainly too risky to teach. After all, the guilds have no interest in emphasising their origins. It's better to encourage the impression that they've always been there, a power without beginning or end. The emphasis, of course, on *without end*.

Within the guilds themselves, it's a different story. Once you get close enough, there's no need for lies and grandstanding: the reality of their power is everywhere, and far more intimidating than any illusion they've created. Espera may know the guilds first and foremost as assassins, but the contract killings within the city are the least of their bloodstained activities. The rest of the world knows them as the most powerful arms dealers on Earth, answerable to no one but the highest bidder, and their influence goes further and deeper than any Esperan civilian could possibly know.

But Bella Nicholls has no place pointing this out, so Isabel sits silently and takes notes on the version of the story she's supposed to believe.

'So,' Mr Branagh continues, 'can anyone tell me the terms of the agreement that Comma and Hummingbird signed?'

'Not to undercut each other,' says a student in the second row. 'Or poach each other's employees.'

A voice from the third row says, 'Not to train minors.'

Isabel freezes midway through tapping her pen against the textbook. She dimly hears the teacher's correction, the fact that they never wrote that into law, but his voice sounds like it's coming from miles away. Of course they didn't formally codify that. No one thought either guild would stoop so low – the verbal agreement should have been enough.

Except the promises of murderers aren't worth the blood that paid for them. The most surprising thing about Cocoon is that it didn't exist sooner.

Another student is speaking, but all Isabel hears is her own heartbeat pounding in her ears and the slight hitch of her breath. Her chair screeches against the floor as she stands.

'Where are you going, Bella?' asks Mr Branagh.

'I think I'm going to be sick.' She grabs her bag, already stumbling towards the door. 'I . . . sorry – I've got to go.'

The classroom door swings shut behind her. She takes a deep breath, then trips her way down the stairs as fast as she can and into the nearest toilets, shutting herself in a cubicle.

The guilds don't train children, said Ian Crampton, 21, who had a *sister*, a sister who would have waited for him to come home, who needed him . . .

The guilds don't train children, he said, as if the fact that she was young would protect him, when it was never enough to protect *her*, so why the fuck should he get what she didn't? Why should any of them get to feel safe, when she's never felt safe in her life, when she can't sleep in her own bed and she's got nowhere left to run?

The Fraser was meant to be safe, whatever that even means. It was meant to be a new start – a place that Comma couldn't follow her and a route to another life, a civilian life, like the one the rest of these kids were given without having to fight for it. She could have been Bella Nicholls for real and left it all behind, if only she hadn't fucked it up.

Isabel wants to laugh, and she wants to cry.

She does neither. She fumbles the lid of the toilet open and throws up until it feels like there's nothing left in her stomach. Shit. Is she sick? She hasn't eaten yet today and acid burns her throat, but her hands are shaking too much to unzip her bag and retrieve her water bottle. She can't catch her breath. She can't catch her breath. She can't breathe.

Is this how she dies? After everything she's been through, she'll suffocate in a school toilet that reeks of vomit?

'Hey,' says a voice. 'Are you okay in there?'

She didn't hear them come in. She left herself vulnerable, didn't watch her back, because she's an *idiot*. Every decision she's made in the past week proves that. Isabel tries to stifle her gasping breaths, waiting for whoever it is to leave, but instead of retreating footsteps, she hears the soft rustle of a bag being placed on the floor.

'Are you having a panic attack?' they ask.

Just leave, she thinks, but she doesn't have the lung capacity to say it aloud. Her breath hitches, her heart slamming desperately against her ribcage like it's trying to escape.

'Okay,' says the voice. 'You don't have to talk. I want you to breathe with me. Can you do that?' Their voice is gentle and steady. 'Let's hold our breath for five seconds. I'll count them. One, two . . .' Isabel fights for control of her breathing. 'Now breathe out. Let it all go. You're doing brilliantly. One, two . . .'

Isabel feels dizzy, and she's fairly sure she's going to throw up again, but she lets the voice guide her breathing. The tight band around her chest loosens a little, five counts at a time.

'Can you tell me five things you can see right now?' asks the voice.

'What?'

'Anything you see around you. It doesn't matter what.'

'Toilet,' she says. 'Bin. Toilet roll. Crisp packet. Graffiti.'

'That's great. You're doing great. What about five things you can hear?'

That's harder. 'The cistern filling. One of the taps is dripping. The class next door.' Isabel struggles to fill the remaining gaps. 'Cars on the road outside. Your voice.'

'Good. That's really good. You okay?'

Isabel no longer feels like she's suffocating, but she's shaking and exhausted. 'I don't know.'

'Why don't you come out of the cubicle and wash your face? It might help.'

She doesn't want to be seen like this, but she can't stay here for ever, and clearly the stranger isn't planning to leave. It takes three attempts before Isabel's shaking legs will support her weight, and she has to lean on the cistern to flush the toilet, wiping her face with a piece of tissue. Then, hesitantly, she unlocks the cubicle.

The voice belongs to a brown-haired girl wearing glasses and a concerned expression. 'Hello,' she says.

'Hi.' Isabel's voice is hoarse.

'I'm Emma.'

She manages, after a moment's thought, to give the correct name. 'Bella.'

'Was that the first time you had a panic attack?' asks Emma.

'Yes.' No. The fear isn't new, the crushing terror an old ghost that's haunted her all her life. But nobody's ever stayed with her, talking her through it. Nobody's ever helped her come back to herself. 'I don't want to talk about it.'

'I wasn't going to ask.' Emma holds out a water bottle. 'Here.'

Isabel's words have abandoned her, and it seems incomprehensibly difficult to explain that she already has a water bottle, so she takes it and manages to drink a few sips. Emma watches her like she expects her to collapse at any moment.

'Thanks,' she says finally, screwing the lid back on the bottle and wiping her mouth. 'I should get back to class.'

'Maybe you should go to the nurse,' says Emma. 'Or at least sit on the bench outside for a minute until you feel better.'

47

Until you stop shaking, she means, and Isabel momentarily hates Emma for seeing her like this. 'I'll manage,' she says, though she doubts she can walk back up the stairs to her History lesson without her jelly-legs giving way.

'At least let me walk with you.'

Isabel shakes her head. 'I can manage,' she insists. Emma's concern is misplaced: this panic's entirely rational given the shit she's in, and Isabel deserves worse. She can't explain that, though, and if she lets Emma be kind to her any longer, she's going to shatter before she can rebuild the walls holding her together. So instead she says, 'You don't even know me.'

Emma shrugs. 'No, but I know panic attacks. Nobody should have to be alone through that.'

Being alone means not being in anyone's debt. Means not letting anyone see her at her weakest. 'I should go.'

Emma still looks worried, but she doesn't try to stop Isabel as she heads for the door. 'I'll be in the library at lunch if you need company,' she says. 'You know ... if you wanted to talk about it.'

The last thing she wants is to talk about the complete clusterfuck she's made of her life. 'Thanks,' she says, 'but I'm okay.'

Isabel doesn't go back to History; the thought of explaining to Mr Branagh why she left is too much to contemplate. She walks until she finds herself outside the nurse's office instead, and the door opens before she has a chance to overcome her hesitation and knock. There's no opportunity to extricate herself before she's ushered inside to be fussed over, having her temperature taken and answering a dozen rapid-fire questions.

Eventually, she convinces the nurse that she doesn't need to call Isabel's parents to authorise sending her home early, and then she takes the midday tram back home.

Her flat feels no safer by day, but she curls up in bed anyway, a miserable heap of blankets hidden from the world. She stays there until it's dark outside, and then she drags herself to the kitchen table and Mortimer's safety documentation, letting rules and regulations smooth away the fear. Finally she falls asleep with her head resting on the paper, and wakes an hour later from a nightmare with her father's face.

The night is long and fearful, but Isabel's only sick twice more. She counts it as a victory that when her alarm screeches it's able to wake her, because that means she slept, but in her momentary panic at the sound, she reaches blindly for her knife and grabs the blade instead of the hilt.

Only the blood tells her she's injured at all. She stares down at her hand for too long before reaching for a bandage, waiting for the pain. It should have hurt.

But it was her left hand, and the scarring across her palm has warped it ugly and tough enough not to feel.

6

INFORMO (INFORMATION)

Isabel has a free period, the result of her medical exemption from PE, and she's spending it in the library, resenting her endless History homework and her ongoing nausea in equal measure. As she stares down at the textbook and tries to make sense of its lies, she finds herself remembering the insomniac nights of her childhood and how she would creep from her bedroom along the darkened corridors like a shadow. She became good at finding new places to hide. One of them was a library, if you could call it that – a small, dusty room with a few scuffed shelves of outdated textbooks. For a while it was a safe place, and she used to perch on a step stool and work her way through the tattered volumes.

You'd never find those histories in the Fraser's library.

From them, Isabel learned about the city's origins, more than a century ago, as a research base dedicated to weapons development and intelligence operations to support the Allied war effort. Scientists and spies: those were Espera's first inhabitants, Europe's best and brightest, and they had a dozen languages between them, a barrier that somehow nobody had anticipated. It was a young French radio operator who suggested Esperanto as a way to bridge their differences. After all, it was a project about hope – hope of cooperation, hope of victory. *Hope that the weapons they developed would kill the enemy's children instead of their own*, thinks Isabel bitterly. She wonders how the early Esperantists would feel about their language of unity becoming a tool of violence for the guilds.

But the project was successful, for a given definition of success. The trouble began when the war ended and the funding was cut. Those scientists and spies found they had a taste for death-dealing and wouldn't willingly give it up. It wasn't long before they realised how lucrative the business of selling their wares across the world could be. When the ministers in charge of the project objected, they killed them. When the British government tried to beg exclusivity in exchange for the English land ceded to the growing town, they raised their prices. In the space of a few short years, it went from a clandestine wartime operation to a major commercial operator in the world of weapons and intelligence, and it had no plans to go back.

What really fascinated Isabel in those books were the pictures: aerial photographs of that early complex of wartime

51

buildings and the settlement that grew up around them, hardly recognisable as the seed of the city of Espera. It's almost unbelievable that within a century those huts, research laboratories, and factories, separated from their Yorkshire neighbours by a barbed wire fence, could grow into a closed city that's all but self-sustaining. But the photographs clearly mapped its rapid development, the fence posts repeatedly pushed back as the town consumed the farmland around it, until the day they became concrete walls instead. And when the walls were done, another war looming on the horizon, Espera closed its gates and issued its ultimatum of independence.

It's hard, after all, to do anything much against a city with weapons to rival those of the bloodiest nations in the world.

In those days there was only one guild, known as Flight, but the unity didn't last. Isabel had almost reached the chapter that explained the schism that formed the two guilds, her torch batteries running low, when the green-eyed woman flicked on the light and said, 'Reading by torchlight will ruin your eyesight, little Moth.'

Toni, her name was. Toni Rolleston. The sound of her voice almost sent Isabel toppling off her step stool – a dangerous mistake, to have let herself get so engrossed she'd lowered her guard. After that, the library never felt safe again, so her history remains incomplete. She never learned what Espera told the world in those early years that meant that, for the rest of the century, refugees saw it as a place of asylum, bolstering its population and technological advancement. Or when and why the guilds turned their murderous attention inwards, accepting commissioned hits on their own citizens, though she suspects that's a simple story – a deadly combination of boredom, money, and bloodlust.

Incomplete or not, it's more than this textbook will teach her.

Isabel sighs and slams the book shut, resisting the urge to throw it across the room.

'I take it History isn't your favourite subject,' says a voice.

She looks up. The library – nothing like Cocoon's little book room, nothing to be afraid of – resolves into focus, and the librarian with it.

'Sorry,' Isabel says warily, eyeing her. 'Was I being too loud?'

'You're fine,' Grace Whittock assures her, pulling out the chair opposite and sitting down. 'I wondered if you needed any help.'

'I need a nap,' says Isabel, with the most naked honesty she's displayed in days. She spent the night pacing her father's lab, deciding to leave, pulling open the door, only to find another lab behind it, and another, and another, until finally she reached her bedroom and realised there were no more doors. She hammered on the blank walls with a hand made of fire, and woke up just as the plaster cracked. Knowing it was only a nightmare should help, but the fear lingers, vying with her stomach ache for the privilege of ruining her day.

'All I can offer is books and friendly advice, I'm afraid.'

'Thanks, but I'm good.' Isabel leans back in her chair. 'You heard about the murder, right?'

'Of course,' says Grace uncertainly. 'Why?'

It's a risk, asking Grace what she thinks, but Isabel gets the impression the librarian might have a more rational and considered opinion than the rumour mill. 'I wondered what you thought about the whole freelancer theory.'

If Hummingbird really thinks someone in Lutton is setting themselves up as an unaffiliated contract killer, they're not going to stop looking until they find them. The last time there was a freelancer in a civilian borough was ten years ago and, unfortunately for them, the guilds found them before the police did. It wasn't pretty.

'I think it's unlikely,' says Grace. 'If someone was going to take that kind of risk, they wouldn't do it in Lutton.'

'Because people in Lutton can't afford to hire them?' Isabel guesses.

'Because people in Lutton wouldn't want to.' The librarian looks around, as though checking for eavesdroppers. 'For a start, it has the highest *Bulletin* circulation outside the industrial boroughs, and rising. A freelancer would be better off picking a wealthier civilian borough like Grindale or – even safer – taking a guild job.'

It's true that Lutton's deprivation breeds dissatisfaction, but Isabel hadn't realised it was *quite* such a hotspot for abolitionist activity. She wonders if the guilds know. As far as she's aware, none of the raids in search of the Free Press have brought them this far west.

'How would you know that?' Isabel asks. 'About the *Bulletin*, I mean?'

'I'm a librarian,' says Grace. 'It's my job to know things.'

Isabel narrows her eyes, but Grace's expression is unreadable. 'So if they're not a freelancer,' she says, 'what's your theory?'

'I think ...' The librarian weighs her words carefully, regarding Isabel as she speaks as though looking for clues. Isabel flushes and tries not to look away. 'I think it was personal. Instinctual. The killer knew what they were doing, that's obvious, but I think they killed him because they wanted him dead. Nothing more.'

And isn't that the truth, really?

I didn't want him dead, Isabel thinks. *I wanted to be safe.* But for a moment, that had seemed like the same thing, and now she has to live with the aftermath.

She's trying to think how to redirect the conversation when they're interrupted. 'Grace, I was wondering where these—' begins a girl holding a stack of books, a 'LIBRARY PREFECT' badge pinned to her hoodie. *Emma*, Isabel remembers: the girl who talked her down from her panic attack, now smiling at the sight of Isabel. 'Hey, Bella! You're looking better.'

Isabel looks like death, her fear and sleepless nights carving hollows into her cheeks and pressing bruises into the soft skin under her eyes. But she concedes that she probably looked worse yesterday after throwing up in the school toilets. 'Thanks,' she says.

'How's my favourite delinquent today?' asks Grace. Isabel does a double-take to confirm she's really talking to Emma, prefect badge and all.

Emma grins back. 'Oh, you know, same old. Haven't set fire to anything so far, but it's only two p.m.' She looks at Isabel. 'What did *you* do that's illegal enough to get Grace's attention?'

'She wasn't doing *anything* illegal,' chides the librarian. 'I came over to see if Bella wanted help with her History homework.'

'And?'

'And we got sidetracked into talking about the murder.'

Emma rolls her eyes. 'Feels like that's all anyone is talking about.'

'Is that so surprising?' says Grace mildly. She gives Emma's pile of books a once-over and adds, 'Those are for the English department, if that's what you were going to ask me. Mrs Dunmore put in a request.'

The girl pulls a face. 'Great. More stairs.' But her smile's back in seconds as she adds, 'Glad you're feeling better, Bella!' and then she's gone.

'So,' says Grace, 'you've met Emma.'

Isabel finds her voice at last. 'Why did you call her a delinquent?'

'An old joke.' The librarian smiles wryly. 'Ask her how she became my shelving assistant while on probation for spray-painting the bike shed; she tells it better than me. I made her a prefect eventually, thought it might keep her out of trouble.'

'Did it work?'

'Well, she's learned to avoid getting caught.' Grace's expression is mischievous, and she hardly seems like an authority figure at all. Maybe that's why Isabel smiles back, a shy twist of her lips that feels like giving something away.

Her smile fades as her nausea intensifies, accompanied by a vicious, stabbing cramp severe enough to make her gasp.

'Bella?' asks Grace. 'What's wrong?'

It's like something's ripping her guts apart from the inside. 'Stomach ache,' she manages through gritted teeth, biting her lip until she draws blood. Slowly the pain recedes, and she forces her breathing back to normal. 'I'll – I'll go to the nurse.'

Grace looks worried as she helps Isabel gather her books and shove them into her bag. 'You're sure you can get there by yourself?'

She nods, although she doesn't actually know. The last thing she wants is company.

Outside the library, she finds a gap between two sets of lockers and curls up on the floor. She could go to the nurse's office, but she was there only yesterday, and they'll notice something's up. Maybe if she sits here for a moment, it'll pass.

I've survived worse, she tells herself, but the reminder doesn't help.

She puts her head between her knees and focuses on dragging oxygen into her lungs. In, out. Easy. In, out, her breath deafening in the silent corridor. She's supposed to use her free period to catch up on homework, but curling up on the floor and waiting for death seems like an acceptable substitute.

The pain resolves into a dull knot in her stomach, the threat of acid sharp in the back of her mouth. Tentatively, she raises her head. The world spins and settles, colours coalescing into shapes and images. One more lesson before the day's over: fifty minutes of Biology with soporific Ms Murray. She can manage that.

When she finally gets home, she checks her post out of habit. There's a folded sheet of paper at the bottom, which she opens while climbing the stairs, expecting another advert for the takeaway down the street.

Instead she sees the gruesome, stylised bird of Hummingbird's logo.

Isabel stops in her tracks. They know. Somehow, they *know*. They might not know who she is – there's no note, no name, and her mailbox says *Bella Nicholls* – but they know someone in this building made that kill. This is a warning.

They're coming.

I wanted to be safe.

But safe was this flat. Safe was this life. Safe was Bella Nicholls and school and no guild, no parents, no target on her back, and she fucked it up, completely and irrevocably.

At this rate, it'll be her own damn fault if she gets herself killed.

7

DOLORO (PAIN)

It's the middle of the night, and she's been stabbed in the gut.

Isabel gasps, curling up and pressing her hands against her stomach to stem the bleeding, but when she lifts one shaking hand, it comes away dry and clean. She rolls off the settee and stumbles halfway to the light switch before she understands: there is no wound, no knife, and there are no weapons that can protect her from an enemy that's inside her.

Poison. It's the obvious answer. She should have twigged the first time she threw up, but she'd put that down to fear, because she thought at least they'd look her in the eyes when they killed her.

But Isabel Ryans knows poisons. If she can identify this

one, she can mix an antidote – and Comma know that. So either this isn't their work, or they aren't trying to kill her.

Or it's something you can't fix, she thinks. And if that's true, then it's hopeless, because she has nowhere to turn for help. Comma know *that*, too. Maybe Ronan Atwood ordered this the moment she turned him down, to force her to beg them to save her.

Nausea overwhelms her and she staggers to the bathroom to throw up. When she straightens and wipes her mouth, her eyes are dark pits in the mirror. The pain makes her mind brittle, all blood and broken glass, destroying any hope of sleep.

She's shivering. The flat's cold, but not cold enough to warrant the cost of heating; her breath mists the bathroom mirror as she braces herself against the sink, trying to stay upright. She wraps her towel around her shoulders for warmth and walks shakily back into the main room.

This is bad.

She could call a doctor. Tell them her name, her *real* name, and let them turn her in, so that she doesn't have to grovel at Ronan's feet. But a doctor is unlikely to see her on the basis that Comma *might* cover her bills. And meanwhile she's vulnerable, the sickness giving leverage to anyone who might want to use her. Her only hope is that her parents are too deep in hiding for the news to reach them.

Isabel groans, slumping at the kitchen table and wishing for unconsciousness. The stabbing sensation is interspersed with periods of dull agony, as though her internal organs are trying to turn themselves inside out. It's a long time before exhaustion overwhelms the pain, but finally she sinks into oblivion and stays there until nightmares chase her back to bitter wakefulness.

On Monday morning, after a restless and pain-ridden weekend, Isabel swallows as many painkillers as she dares and trudges through her paper round in a haze, thoughts as grey as the ink smears on her hands. Then she heads straight for school and, after a moment's hesitation, the library.

Grace Whittock is sitting at her desk, sorting through her in-tray, but she glances up and smiles. 'Something you need, Bella?'

This seemed like a good idea until she was actually here. Now she wants to turn and run. She forces herself to stay put. 'I need to find a doctor and I don't know where to look. I thought maybe you could help.'

The librarian immediately looks concerned, compounding Isabel's sense that this was a mistake. All she's done is draw attention to herself. She'd have been better off looking it up on the school computers – it's unlikely the guilds are monitoring those. Anything's safer than walking up to a virtual stranger and declaring that she's sick.

'Is this about the stomach ache you had on Friday?' asks Grace.

Isabel turns away, wrapping her arms around her torso as though she can hold herself together. 'This was a bad idea. Forget I asked.'

'The school nurse might—'

'It's fine. Don't worry about it.'

'Wait,' says a voice. Not Grace's. She looks back to see Emma emerging from behind a bookshelf, her hair a little wild. 'I can help. I'm sorry, I wasn't trying to listen, but . . . I know a clinic that might be able to help. They don't have, like, a lot of resources, but it's free, and they're good people.' The words tumble out in a rush.

Isabel looks at her, at the earnest expression on her face and the way she's trying to tuck her hair behind her ear as though that'll tame it, and remembers Emma talking her through her panic attack. She loosens her grip on her shirt and says, 'Really?'

Emma nods and comes over. 'It's called the Sunshine Project. It's in Central Espera, and it's a non-profit clinic for low-income civilians, which . . . well, I don't want to make assumptions, but, that's you, isn't it? No offence.'

Civilian. It's not a word Isabel ever imagined being applied to herself. It takes her a moment to realise it's the 'low-income' part that Emma thought might offend her.

'They're pretty busy, but they can usually make time for emergencies. I can give you the number. It can't hurt to try, right?'

Emma waits expectantly for an answer. Isabel has never been good with words – English words, especially, tend to abandon her at the slightest provocation – and it takes her a moment too long to figure out how to reply. Emma's face falls.

'Or not,' she says. 'I'm sorry. I shouldn't have said anything. I always do this. My mum must've said a thousand times that I—'

'No,' interrupts Isabel, stammering out the syllable at last. 'No, it's okay, I'm ... thank you.' The words take considerable effort, but she gets them out. 'I would like the number, please.'

Emma relaxes, the crease in her brow disappearing. 'Okay. Good. Grace, do you have a pen?'

The librarian purses her lips. 'I'm not sure if I should ...'

'Sunny's is legit, you know that,' says Emma.

'That's not what I'm worried about.' Grace glances at Isabel. 'Do your parents know that you're ill?'

Isabel should never have brought her into this. 'I don't live with my parents,' she says tightly.

'That's not what I asked.' But Grace must see from Isabel's face that she'll get no further answers, because she slides out from behind her desk, passing Emma a pen and a block of sticky notes as she does. 'Okay. But I didn't witness this, understand? Because if I did, I'd have to tell the nurse, and she'd want to make sure your head of year knew ...'

It's not a threat, but it feels a little like one. 'Understood.'

'I have to go down to IT for a second. Don't break anything while I'm gone.'

Whether that's true, or just an excuse, it still leaves Isabel and Emma alone in the library together. Isabel stares at the floor, the display of new books, a hangnail that won't pull free – anywhere but at the other girl. Emma doesn't seem to notice. She scrawls the number on the top sticky note and hands it to Isabel.

'Here. Just ask for the next appointment they've got.' She

sees Isabel's hesitation and adds, 'You can borrow my phone if you don't—'

'I've got a phone,' Isabel says, accepting the note. 'But thanks.'

The corridor outside the library is deserted, so she doesn't have to go far for privacy. She types the number, but it takes several seconds before she can bring herself to press *call*. The phone rings once, twice, and Isabel's transported back to stolen minutes and a stolen phone, desperately trying to lay the groundwork for her new life.

She was so hopeful, and so afraid, and this was meant to be her chance.

The phone rings again and she hears the small click of the line connecting, but she's already got her thumb on the end call button. Her breath comes ragged as she presses it, sinking to the floor and letting the phone clatter to the ground beside her.

Make the damn call, Isabel, she tells herself, but today that's an order she can't follow. She worked so hard, fought for so long to get here, and now what? She's sick, and too afraid to make a phone call?

The library door opens. 'Hey,' says Emma, crouching down beside her and picking up the abandoned phone. 'You're okay. It's okay. Do you want me to call them for you?'

What she wants is to be capable of making the fucking phone call herself, because she's not a child and she doesn't need a stranger to do this for her. If she can't call them, maybe she doesn't deserve their help anyway.

She doesn't say this. She doesn't say anything. But Emma

shuffles back so that she's sitting next to Isabel and says, 'You know, at one point I was having panic attacks every single night. Like, *every* night. My sister used to sit with me, but it was months before I felt safe enough for them to stop.'

Isabel's voice feels scratchy as she says, 'I'm not having a panic attack.' She's not sure if she's lying.

'But you can't call them right now,' Emma guesses. She says this like it makes perfect sense. 'So, how's this? Today's Monday, which means my brother will be at the clinic. He volunteers with their admin department. I could call him and see if he knows how things are looking for appointments. It might be better than calling the front desk anyway.'

She waits.

It's clear that what she's really saying is, *Here's something you couldn't have done by yourself, so you don't have to feel ashamed about letting me do it for you.* Isabel can tell she's being manipulated, but Emma's doing it with more tact and kindness than anyone else ever has, so she swallows and pushes the phone towards the other girl.

Emma smiles and picks it up, dialling a number from memory. 'Hey, Leo?' she says, after a moment. 'It's Emma. How busy are things over there?' Whatever he says in response makes her roll her eyes. 'No, I'm *genuinely* asking for a friend here, so don't call Mum.' She listens, frowns, and puts her hand over the phone. 'It's an emergency, isn't it?' she asks Isabel.

Isabel nods, a lump in her throat.

'Yes, it's urgent,' says Emma to Leo. 'Well, can you check the— Ugh, okay, well, can you call her if there's a cancellation?

Yes, I mean it, top of the— I don't care about Mr Conroy's appendix, Leo. Put her at the top of the damn list.' She covers the phone again. 'Bella, what's your surname?'

Every time she lies it's a little easier. 'Nicholls.'

'Bella Nicholls. This is her number I'm calling from. Yeah, see you tomorrow. Don't forget you're bringing the picnic. Bye.' She hangs up. 'No appointments right now,' she says. 'But don't panic. Leo's putting you top of the list for cancellations, and there's a good chance he can make that work.'

It's easy for Emma to be optimistic when she's not the one who's dying. Isabel hugs her knees close to her chest, trying not to let despair overwhelm her, and searches for the words to explain that she doesn't need Emma to wait with her. It's hard when that feels like a lie.

She's spared by the shrill, tinny ring of her phone. Cautiously, she answers it. 'Hello?'

'Good news, Miss Nicholls,' says – well, presumably Leo. 'As soon as Emma hung up, a cancellation came through for tomorrow. Quarter past four. How's that for you?'

A lifeline. She swallows the sudden lump in her throat and confirms she'll be there, barely taking in his instructions to arrive early to fill out some paperwork. He rattles off a script about the clinic's policies and finishes by assuring her that Dr Vernant is very good at his job and will do whatever he can to help her.

Isabel takes a deep breath, as though compensating for the lack of pauses in Leo's speech. 'Thanks,' she says. 'I appreciate it.'

'I'm just glad we can help,' says Leo. He sounds like he means it. 'I'll send you a text with the details.'

'Thanks, Leo.' She hangs up and gives Emma a tiny, fragile smile. 'Tomorrow, after school.'

Emma's look of relief surprises her. 'That's great. Do you know who you're seeing?'

'It began with V, I think.' Her phone bleeps with the confirmation text and she checks. 'Dr D. Vernant.'

'Oh, Daragh! He's everyone's favourite. You're lucky – his waiting list is *huge*. He's only there two days a week. I think he's at some fancy private hospital the rest of the time.'

'Leo didn't boot someone else out to fit me in, did he?'

'Probably not,' says Emma cheerfully. 'But if he did, I expect they deserved it.' She grabs Isabel's hand and squeezes it before she can react to the unexpected contact. 'Well, whatever's wrong, Daragh will fix it.'

Emma's hand is warm, and Isabel feels a curious reluctance as she extricates hers. It's reassuring that the other girl has such faith in this doctor, since she has no idea what she'll do if Daragh Vernant *can't* fix whatever's wrong with her.

'Thank you,' she says. 'For helping.'

'Any time.' Emma pushes herself to her feet and holds out a hand to help Isabel up. 'Maybe I'll see you later? And, Bella,' she adds, 'it'll be okay, whatever it is. You'll get through this.'

'You don't know that,' says Isabel.

'Sure I do,' says Emma. 'I'll personally fight the universe on your behalf if you don't. And that's a threat.'

You hardly know me, Isabel wants to say, but the words

67

catch on the lump in her throat and before she can speak, Grace comes up the stairs with a box of printer paper, saying, 'Are you threatening people in my library, Emma? We've talked about this.'

'Technically, we're outside the library,' says Emma, her smile offered as readily as her friendship. 'And technically, the abstract concept of reality and fate is not a person, so I can threaten it as much as I like.'

Grace quirks an eyebrow. 'All right, I won't ask. But the bell's about to go. You should get to class.'

'We're going!' says Emma, and she's already halfway down the stairs, Isabel trailing in her wake.

8

KOLOROJ (COLOURS)

The pain wakes Isabel several times in the night. At three a.m., she gives up on trying to sleep and tackles Mortimer's safety file instead, hoping that it'll numb her into unconsciousness. She finishes it ten minutes before she has to leave for her paper round and, later, has just enough energy to appreciate the surprise on Mortimer's face when she drops the heavy folder on his desk at the start of sixth period.

'Already?' he says.

'No point hanging around,' she says. 'What happens now?'

He flicks through the pages, pausing at each end-of-section quiz dutifully completed in Isabel's variable handwriting. Then he takes a cardboard wallet from his desk drawer. 'Now,' he says, rummaging through it, 'you get the incalculable joy of taking this safety exam.'

The question paper he hands her is shorter than she expected. 'Is this it?'

'And then you'll watch me demonstrate proper usage of all the tools, and you'll sign a disclaimer saying it's your own fault if you get hurt, but, yeah, that's it.'

She's fairly sure Mortimer's faffing her about, but she doesn't feel like arguing in front of her classmates. She takes the exam back to her desk and starts filling in the cover page.

Bella Nicholls.

Ronan Atwood is the only person to have called her 'Isabel' in weeks. She didn't realise she'd missed it. She hated the sound of her name in his mouth, but she's tired of wearing lies.

Isabel stares down at the exam paper and sees that her hands are trembling. The bandage on her left hand hides her scarred palm, but she still balls it into a fist rather than look at it.

Comma have known where she is all along.

She killed a man, and Hummingbird and the police both know about it.

Her parents are missing and could be anywhere.

And she's sick.

The dots aren't hard to join, even if some of the picture is still missing. She killed Ian Crampton, and now somebody's decided she needs to be taken out before she makes herself even more of a threat. It hardly matters who's behind it – she can't outrun any of them.

The sound of metal against wood momentarily distracts her.

Mortimer's placed the biscuit tin in front of her, and his voice is gentle as he says, 'Take one.'

She looks up. He nods encouragingly and she takes a biscuit, but her mouth's too dry to bite into it. The noise of her classmates getting on with their work will mask anything she says to Mortimer, but she still feels exposed. Watched.

The biscuit snaps and crumbles between her fingers, and she stares down at it. 'I'm sorry,' she says helplessly. 'I'm sorry, I didn't mean ...'

'Okay,' says Mortimer. 'It's okay.'

It's not okay. Wordlessly, she looks at him, at the exam paper, at the mess she's made – another mess, another way to draw attention to herself – and he must see the despair in her face, because he takes the test from her and helps her brush the biscuit crumbs into the bin.

Then he says, 'I wouldn't be able to concentrate with the noise in here either. Do you want to sit in my office to take the exam?'

She doesn't care about his stupid test, but when she looks at Mortimer, it's clear he knows that. He's offering her an escape from the eyes of the class. She nods mutely, taking her bag and following him into the little office that opens off the classroom, feeling like she's about to unravel.

The room's dominated by a large colour printer and a shelf crammed with folders, but it's immaculately tidy. She's not sure why that's surprising.

Mortimer places the test on his desk, which is as neat as the rest of the room. He puts the biscuit tin next to it. 'If you want to take the exam,' he says carefully, 'it's here. Or you can sit here and do nothing for half an hour. I don't mind.'

Isabel's seen Mortimer speak to enough of her classmates after something has gone wrong to know that this is how he talks to people he thinks are about to start crying. He's usually right, and the fact that he's using this voice on her makes her hyperaware of her prickling eyes and the lump in her throat.

'I've got to get back to the others,' he says. 'Bella ... look, it's not my business to ask what's wrong, but if you want to talk, I'm here. If I can help, I will.'

For half a second, she considers telling him – that she's not Bella, she's Isabel, and she thinks she might be dying. Maybe he can figure out which rules and regulations she has to follow to stay alive. But she might as well hand him a knife and expect him not to stab her with it: the fact that he's so quick to notice when she's not coping means he's watching her, and that makes him a threat.

He takes her silence as an answer. 'Feel free to help yourself to biscuits,' he says, and heads for the door.

Isabel clears her throat. 'Thanks,' she manages. It's pathetic and inadequate, but it's all she's got.

When he's gone, she stares down at the exam paper. She can't face answering it. The office is better than the classroom, but she'd rather not be here at all. But where else could she go? It's not as if her flat's safe. It's not as if there's anywhere in the city where the long arm of the guilds doesn't reach, where they couldn't hurt her if they wanted to.

That's assuming they haven't already. That her sickness isn't their work.

Isabel presses the metal tip of her mechanical pencil against her bandaged hand until she can almost feel it, and resists the temptation to crawl under Mortimer's desk and hide.

When the bell finally rings, she waits for the rest of the class to leave, then hands Mortimer her nearly blank exam paper. 'Sorry. I'll do it next time.'

'Okay.' He asks no questions as he places the paper with its single falsehood – *Bella Nicholls* – inside the wallet on his desk.

Isabel doesn't have words to express how grateful she is not to be asked for any more lies.

The tram Isabel takes to her appointment is nearly empty. She sits at the back, next to the emergency exit, and watches as a final passenger dashes up and slips through the gap in the closing doors. They brush their hair out of their face and she sees that it's Emma, panting slightly from the run.

Her face brightens when she spots Isabel. 'Hey, Bella,' she says, swinging down into the seat next to her. 'Feeling any better?'

'Not massively.'

'That's shit. Nervous about your appointment?' She's the one who seems nervous, twisting her hands around the straps of her rucksack and weaving the hanging ends together and apart, together and apart.

'Only about finding the place,' says Isabel; half a lie.

'I can show you the way,' says Emma. 'It's easy enough. You follow the art.' She smiles like it's nothing. Show her how she can help, give her the knowledge to do it, and there it is: joy. The Sunshine Project. A ridiculous name – but when Emma smiles, Isabel begins to understand what it means. *Hope.*

'Art?' she echoes, confused.

'You'll know when you see it. I'll take you. It's on my way, anyway.' Emma smiles again, letting go of her tormented rucksack straps, and adds, 'You'll be fine. Like I said, everyone loves Daragh.'

Isabel nods and glances out of the window. A sign marks the boundary of the borough of Weaverthorpe, one of the larger Comma boroughs and a nice enough place to live and work, if the idea of taking guild money doesn't make your skin crawl.

She looks back at Emma. 'What about you?' she asks. 'Where are you going?'

'Oh,' says Emma, as though the question is unexpected. 'I . . .' Her smile turns small and sad. 'It's my sister's birthday,' she says finally. 'I'm meeting Leo at her grave.'

It's Isabel's turn to make a small, round noise of surprise. 'I'm sorry,' she says. The words feel sticky with the blood on her hands.

Emma shrugs uncomfortably. 'She had cancer. That age-old impartial bitch.'

It shouldn't be a comfort to Isabel to know it wasn't guild, but somehow it is. 'That sucks.'

Emma stares into the middle distance for a moment, then tugs again on the straps of her rucksack as though grounding herself. 'Yeah, well,' she says. 'It's shit, but it is what it is. I'll drop you off on my way. It's not far.'

'You don't have to do that.'

'No, I don't. But nobody should have to be alone when they're sick.' She gives Isabel a lopsided smile. 'I'd offer to come in with you, but—'

'I'm fine.'

'Yeah, I thought you'd say that. I'll take you to the door, at least. Some of the city's best murals are around there and I'll take any excuse to see the art.'

Isabel hunts for other reasons to make the journey alone and finds none. 'Thanks,' she says at last.

They lapse into silence, each lost in their own thoughts. Only towards the end of the journey does something occur to Isabel. 'On the phone yesterday, you told Leo to bring a picnic.'

Emma shrugs. 'Yeah.'

'Were you kidding?'

'Absolutely not. I'm starving.'

'You're going to have a picnic at your sister's grave?' Isabel knows she doesn't have the most conventional relationship with death, but that seems odd, even to her.

Emma screws up her face, searching for the words to explain. Finally, she says, 'Jean would have wanted us to. We go and tell her stories about what she's missed. We did it when she was sick, and then we never stopped.'

'And that helps?'

'Sometimes. Sometimes it's just a reminder of how proper shit it is that she's gone. But we do it together, and that's the whole point – that it was never just the one of us dealing with any of it.' Her voice wavers. 'It gets both easier and harder every year.' She stands. 'Come on, this is us.'

Isabel follows her off the tram and through the narrow streets of Central Espera. The whole borough is a chaotic neutral zone, the only place where guild employees and civilians might live side by side without knowing it. Wide commercial streets vie for space with rabbit warrens of crowded residential tenements. The main roads are paved with the usual solar panels, the pedestrian crossings dancing green under their feet, but as the streets grow narrower, the solar panels give way to cracked paving slabs, and weeds sprout in the shadows of the buildings that loom overhead.

All of Espera's houses are colourful; in many cases, the paint serves to hide their shoddy construction and the dismal grey of old concrete. But each borough has its own style: the neat block colours of Fordon are as different from the peeling paintwork of Lutton as they are from the patterned brickwork of Grindale. And Central Espera is a riot of murals and graffiti, street art crawling over every flat surface in a dozen styles. One house has been carefully painted with a trellis of roses, so detailed that from a distance they look real; the next house shimmers with gold and silver as twisting leaves and knotwork surround the windows and door. Faces stare out at them – some human, some animal, some otherworldly and unsettling. Isabel has only ever seen the city centre's art in passing, and the effect of so much of it at once is dazzling.

She's beginning to understand why Emma told her to follow

the art. It lines their path, drawing them onwards to see what new explosion of colour will be next. She sees the delight with which Emma points out little details she'd otherwise have overlooked, highlighting the small animals poking their heads around drain covers or the vines creeping down from gutters, and a nugget of information comes back to her.

'Grace said you once painted the bike sheds,' she says.

Emma grins, a feral smile that chases away the melancholy shadowing her face ever since she mentioned her sister. 'Yep. See that?' She points to a luminous, rainbow paisley design that spreads across a broad expanse of wall at the end of the street. 'That's mine.'

'You painted that?' Isabel wants to stop and examine it more closely, to follow each swirl of colour to see it twist and melt into the others, to run her hands along the gold outlines to discover if they feel like metal or sunlight. But if she stops, she'll be late for her appointment. 'It's beautiful,' she says honestly. It's a kind of beauty she never realised Espera could have.

'I almost got in trouble for that too,' Emma confides. 'I mean, the art's part of this district. Technically, it's a free-for-all, but it's usually considered polite to ask before you paint somebody *else*'s house. I might have forgotten to do that. Still,' she adds cheerfully, 'if they hated it, they'd have painted over it.'

She leads Isabel down a particularly narrow alleyway and out into a small courtyard dominated by a low, colourful building, every inch of its walls decorated with fine, faded art.

Above the door, in curling ultramarine script, somebody has painted THE SUNSHINE PROJECT. A bright yellow sun peeks out from the middle of the O.

'This is it,' says Emma. 'You sure you're all right from here? Leo will understand if I'm a bit late.'

'No, I'm fine,' says Isabel. 'Go and find him. I hope . . .' She hunts for the right words. 'I hope today is easier, not harder.'

Emma's smile outshines her mural. 'And I hope Daragh can fix whatever's wrong,' she says, and leaves Isabel to mount the wooden steps to the front door alone.

9

VENENO (POISON)

The inside of the clinic is cool and dark. Isabel gives her name to the receptionist and fills in half a dozen forms, then takes a seat on one of the wobbly chairs and settles down to wait. The smell of antiseptic is acrid in her throat, so she picks up one of the newspapers from the table and tries to distract herself from the memory of other hospitals and other doctors.

It doesn't help. The *Gazette* has a report on the Lutton murder, and she lacks the self-control not to read it. It's a useless self-flagellation that leaves her feeling even more nauseous: Espera Met are still chasing geese, but the effort that's going into the Ian Crampton case means it's only a matter of time before they represent a legitimate danger to her. And then what?

She returns the newspaper to the table and shoves her hands in her pockets to stop them from shaking. Hummingbird are closing in, and now the police too. She's been distracted by her illness, but the other blade above her head is as sharp as ever and waiting to fall.

'Bella Nicholls?'

Isabel looks up. 'That's me.'

'I'm Daragh Vernant. Come on through.'

The doctor is in his thirties, dark-haired and kind-looking. She expected a white coat or scrubs, but his badge is pinned to a green cable-knit jumper. Isabel follows him into a small room and hears the door click behind her with a mixture of relief and fear.

'Take a seat and tell me what seems to be the problem,' says Dr Vernant.

Everyone loves Daragh, Emma told her. *He'll fix it.* Isabel forces herself to unclench her fists and say, 'My stomach. It hurts so much it's been waking me up.'

'I'm sorry to hear that. When did it start?'

'Last week. Friday. It ... came out of nowhere. I was fine, and then I wasn't.'

'Can you tell me any more about your symptoms?'

Stumbling a little over the words, she describes her stomach pains and disturbed nights, the nausea and the agony. Daragh makes careful notes, and when she's finished, he takes a moment to review them, expression thoughtful.

'When did you last have your period?' he asks.

Isabel hesitates. She should have known he'd ask this. She

could lie, but what if it matters? He can't help her if she's not honest about her medical history. 'Eighteen months ago,' she says reluctantly.

The doctor looks up. 'Oh?'

'I'd prefer not to talk about it.' That seems to be her catchphrase these days. 'It's not a menstrual problem, I know that much.'

'If there's any chance it's related, I need to know your medical background.'

'It's not. Related, I mean.' She hopes. If it is, this has been going on longer than she thought.

Daragh looks hard at her, but doesn't press the point. 'Any dizziness? Headaches?'

Isabel nods. 'Bad ones. Making it impossible to think.'

'Hmm.' He makes a note. 'Your intake forms didn't mention any underlying conditions. Is there anything I should know about?' She shakes her head. He reads through his notes again, tapping his pen against the page. 'No diarrhoea?'

'No.'

'Not norovirus, then. Do you think there's a chance you've been poisoned?' His tone is casual, but he's watching her reaction closely.

Isabel freezes. 'I . . .' she begins, and gets no further.

'Most people wouldn't have hesitated on that question.' The doctor leans back in his chair. 'So you do think there's a chance.'

'I don't know,' she confesses. 'It doesn't make sense.'

'It's unusual,' he agrees. 'You're very young to be a target.

That doesn't mean it's impossible. Is there any reason someone might be targeting you?'

I killed Ian Crampton. 'No.' She looks up at him – his kind face, his too-clever words – and says, 'Do *you* think I've been poisoned?'

Daragh purses his lips. 'I think it's a possibility we should consider,' he says. 'I wouldn't normally leap to that conclusion, but it would explain the severity and abruptness of your symptoms. If it's a guild hit, though, it's surprising that the effects have been non-lethal. Which is good,' he adds, 'obviously. Perhaps whoever did it was incompetent, or you're highly resistant to poisons. Or maybe they don't want you dead.'

'I'm . . .' Isabel begins, her mouth dry – 'I'm fairly resistant, I think. I've been . . . exposed to a number of poisons and survived.'

The doctor puts down his pen. 'You've been exposed to a number of poisons?' he repeats, as though he's not sure he heard her correctly. 'On purpose?'

She shouldn't have said that. There's no way to explain without making it worse. 'Kind of?' It occurs to her that he might misinterpret this, so she adds, 'I wasn't trying to hurt myself.'

'I was more worried that somebody was trying to hurt *you*,' says Daragh. 'But thank you for the clarification. I take it your parents aren't adjacents?'

Adjacents – shorthand for everyone the guilds employ outside of their central body, from admin and janitorial staff to teachers and manufacturing workers. Technically, Comma calls them *Hedylidae*, ever since some smart-arse renamed all their departments after butterfly taxonomy, but in practice everyone calls them adjacents. The term encompasses the majority of people living in guild boroughs, and anyone who knows that Isabel used to live in Fordon, like the teachers at the Fraser, will have assumed her family falls into this category.

Unless she gives them a reason to think otherwise, like stupidly admitting some of the fucked-up details about her life.

'I—'

'Bella,' Daragh says sternly, 'I can only help if you tell me the truth. You're from a guild family, probably fairly senior, with all the dangers that go with that. Am I right?'

She says the only thing she can. 'I left. I'm not part of it any more.' He has to know that she's not Comma, that they won't help her, that she's alone in this.

The doctor regards her for a long moment. 'All right,' he says, and slides a sheet of paper and a pen across the table towards her. 'Write down any poisons you know you've been exposed to in the last year. If you're taking any other medication, make a note of that too, no matter how insignificant it seems.'

Isabel picks up the pen, but doesn't begin to write. 'What happens if I've forgotten something?'

'I'll be slightly more confused when I detect it in the blood samples I'm about to take,' says Daragh. 'This is to help me interpret the results and predict any complications that might arise during treatment. If something's missing, it's not the end of the world. Just tell me what you can.'

She writes the list while Daragh readies his equipment. It looks a lot worse, written down. No wonder she's sick, after everything her body's been through.

He raises an eyebrow when he reads it, but doesn't ask any questions. 'You'll need treatment,' he says. 'The antidote first, but there might be internal damage.'

And treatment isn't free. 'I'll deal with it.'

'If Comma—'

'I said I'll deal with it.'

Silently, he draws a few vials of Isabel's blood. Then he hands her a urine sample bottle and says, 'There's a bathroom off the waiting area. Leave the sample at reception, and I'll get back to you with the results as soon as I can. We'll work out a treatment plan from there.' He looks like he wants to say more – some useless reassurance, perhaps – but Isabel pulls her jumper on and stands before he has a chance.

At the door, she pauses and looks back. 'How long do you think I've got?'

'I don't know. It depends on the poison, and on what the poisoner is trying to achieve.'

He doesn't lie to her. She respects that. 'Better hope they're not in a hurry to see me dead, then,' she says, and leaves the room.

Back at her flat, Isabel rummages through the duffel bag she brought from her parents' house until she finds the book she's looking for. It's no page-turner, but it might have answers. *Poison*. Something she's not resistant to, something that could be used to hurt her but not – so far – kill her.

What do they want, whoever they are? Is it even *her* they want? If she believes Ronan Atwood, then her parents are missing. Maybe somebody thinks that poisoning their only daughter will lure Ian and Judith Ryans out of hiding. But it won't. If this kills her, her father will be more disappointed by her failure to make the antidote than saddened by her death.

It's more likely he's the one who poisoned her.

She pauses midway through turning the page. Now that she's allowed herself to think it, the idea sinks its teeth in, sending venom like ice into her blood. Her father. He had dozens of chances to poison her before he pulled his vanishing act, and she'd never have suspected. But he of all people knows the dose required to kill her, so if this is his work, he doesn't want her dead.

Just weak. Desperate. Willing to do whatever he wants.

She looks back at the book. If Ian Ryans created this poison, it can't help her. His poisons are unique concoctions designed to turn your own body against you, to convince your immune system to shut down and your nerves to shred themselves. Once upon a time, Isabel knew how they worked, but now when she tries to recall what she learned in her father's lab, she finds only meaningless scraps of recollection, devoid of context and content and anything that might save her.

She slams the book shut and shoves it away just as somebody knocks sharply on her door. Isabel can count on one hand the number of people who have her address, so she's only mildly surprised to find Ronan Atwood leaning against the wall in the grotty hallway.

Wordlessly, she stands aside to let him in, and he takes a seat at the table. He's in monochrome again, though today his grey shirt is lighter and he's wearing a thin, black tie. There's no sign of a weapon, but he's still a threat.

He indicates the book. 'Poison? I thought you weren't interested in our world.'

'I'm not,' says Isabel. 'But I'm sick, so I guess I've got to care about it one way or another.'

His eyes widen slightly, enough to tell her this sickness isn't his idea of an appropriate punishment for killing Ian Crampton. 'Who would poison you?' he asks.

'Your guess is as good as mine.'

Isabel needs a cup of tea, and she refuses to stand on ceremony for Ronan Atwood. It's easier if she pretends he's not basically in charge of Comma, if she fills the kettle as normal and ignores the fact that she has her back turned to one of the most dangerous men she's ever likely to encounter. She's proud of how steady her hands are as she reaches for the mug at the back of the cupboard.

He doesn't try to guess. Maybe he already knows.

She makes her tea, keeping her movements steady and unbothered. As she returns the milk to the fridge, she notices that he's playing with a coin – a new shilling, shiny and polished as the day it was minted. It flashes between his fingers and disappears momentarily before reappearing in his palm. She wonders what point he's trying to make.

'I'm here about your parents,' he says finally.

'I can't help you.'

'I disagree.' He takes a thick cardboard wallet from his briefcase and places it on the table. 'We recovered these documents from your father's files, and I think you can help us read them. You know how his codes work, don't you?'

She knows enough to know that they're a nightmare. Her father always refused to follow Comma's internal comms policy, preferring to use his own esoteric ciphers. Cracking them is less about algorithms and logic, and more about knowing how Ian Ryans' mind works.

She's beginning to see why Ronan's here.

'Even if I did,' she says, 'what makes you think I would help you?'

'We'll claim the kill. You won't be under our protection, and the delay will make Hummingbird suspicious, but it'll get the police off your back. We'll provide medical care if that's something you need, and it sounds like it is. All you have to do is tell us what you know.'

When he puts it like that, it sounds almost reasonable, which means that's only half the story. 'And then you'll never bother me again, I suppose,' says Isabel wryly.

'It's not a bad deal, Isabel,' he tells her. And that would be true, if she trusted him as far as she could throw him. But this is Ronan Atwood, and anything he offers comes at a price.

She reaches over and opens the wallet, glancing at the first few printouts. It's enough. Pushing it back towards Ronan, she says, 'I can't help you.'

'I don't believe you.'

'You have an entire department of codebreakers. They'll get

through this in half the time I would. I know a lot less about my father's work than you seem to think.'

'But you used to help him in the lab.'

Is it fury or fear that burns through her now? '*Help* him?' she says. 'Is that what you call it?'

'His notes suggest you were crucial to some of his biggest breakthroughs. If there's anything you can tell us . . .'

She laughs. She can't help herself. '"Crucial",' she repeats. '"Help him". He *experimented* on me, Ronan. I was his lab rat.'

Ronan is silent for a moment. When he speaks, it's only to swear under his breath, so quiet it's barely more than an exhalation. 'I didn't know.'

It's not what she expected him to say, and she has no idea how to respond. All these years of thinking the guild knew everything, and yet they were blind to what was happening right under their noses. Unless, of course, Ronan's lying.

After a long pause, he says, 'So that's why you left. Why you wouldn't consider my first offer.'

'It's a factor.' Isabel sips her too-hot tea rather than meet his eyes. 'I'm not coming back, Ronan. No matter how many times you ask me.'

'Why didn't you tell anyone what your father was doing to you?'

Isabel stares at the gathering ripples on the surface of her tea for several seconds until she has the presence of mind to put the mug down before the liquid spills. She hides her shaking hands under the table as though she can keep Ronan from noticing her fear.

'Who would I have told?' she asks. 'They said you already knew. That you approved.'

'Approved of what?' says Ronan. 'Testing on you?'

Why does he keep asking her these questions? He should know this shit already; she shouldn't have to say it. Her throat's closing up, and she's not sure she could speak, even if she wanted to.

'Isabel,' he says. His voice is firm, but the harsh tone has gone. 'I need you to tell me what happened.'

Tell him and he'll leave you alone. She wants him gone, but— *He'll say it was on Comma orders*, whispers another voice. *That it happens to everyone in training. He'll say you're delusional, that you did it to yourself, because you've always been a nasty little liar, haven't you, Issy dear?*

The voice is her mother's. She tugs herself free of her doubts and back into reality. 'I won't help you find my father,' she tells Ronan instead. 'The guild's better off without him.'

'Isabel—'

'I'm *sick*, Ronan. I don't know about you, but it feels like there's probably a correlation between that and the disappearance of one of your master poisoners. And that strongly suggests he doesn't give a shit about me. So why would I know anything you don't?'

He can't argue with that, but he tries anyway: 'This isn't only about you.' There's an edge to his words, and the coin slips between his fingers and hits the table, rolling until it falls to the floor and comes to rest by Isabel's feet.

She picks it up, the cool metal barely warmed by Ronan's hand.

She thought it might be something special, but it's an ordinary shilling, embossed with a maelstrom of wings representing both guilds. Last year's issue, still new enough to shine.

'It feels like it's about me,' she says, putting the coin on the table. 'But, by all means, tell me why I should care how this affects the guild.'

They're both looking at the shilling when Ronan speaks. 'Espera's situation is . . . precarious. Comma's more so. If the outside world stops trading with us, that's it, we're done for. That won't happen as long as they need what we sell, and as long as we follow through. But if we fail . . .'

'Is that likely?'

'Your father was working on a commission. He never made the trade. He took his notes and samples and he disappeared – and that's trouble for Comma, financially and politically. Our stability and prosperity depend on having something to offer, and your father's poisons are one of our greatest assets. He absconded too late for us to limit the damage, and now we have a pissed-off buyer and a strike against our reputation. We'll be lucky if they ever buy from us again.'

Her father's always been good at leaving a mess behind. 'So Comma lose money. Hummingbird gain a client. Why do I care, again?'

'And if the client doesn't go to Hummingbird – if they stop buying from Espera completely? This city is only independent because it has enough leverage to ensure it stays that way. All it takes is for one powerful client to walk away and it could trigger a mass exodus – one that threatens the whole system.'

Isabel tosses the coin back. Ronan catches it neatly. 'If one deal can bring it all down, your foundations are pretty shaky in the first place,' she points out.

'Espera exists on a knife-edge. That's always been true. Do you understand now why this matters?'

She understands why Ronan's bothered. She doesn't know how finding her father will help. Unless they can track down his notes and samples, they've already lost this commission, and it's not as though they'll ever trust him again.

'I can't help you,' she says, folding her arms. 'I don't know what he was working on, I don't know why he left, and I don't know where he is. I don't—' *I don't remember*, she almost says, but admitting to the gaps in her memory feels like giving Ronan too much power over her. 'I don't know any more than you.'

He taps the pile of documents. 'And these?'

She doesn't know her father half as well as Ronan thinks she does. That doesn't mean she can't decode those files, but it does mean she doesn't *want* to, because she has no idea what she might find.

And because collaborating with Ronan Atwood is less than half a step away from re-joining Comma after all.

'I can't help you,' she says again. 'Figure it out yourself.'

Frustration flickers across his face but disappears quickly behind his usual mask. He indicates the book on poisons. 'You must have a great deal of confidence in your ability to stay alive without us,' he says smoothly, 'to turn down an offer that could save you.'

Isabel hates him. She hates the careful way he picks his words, how he fakes outrage and concern over what was done to her. He *knew*. He must have known. He's too important not to have known.

'I've been surviving without your help for seventeen years,' she says. 'I can manage a few more.'

Ronan takes a pen and scrawls a phone number on the inside cover of the book, then stands. 'Let me know when you change your mind,' he says, and leaves Isabel alone with her traitorous, poisoned body in a flat that's no longer (has never been) safe.

10

KONFESO (CONFESSION)

LUTTON MURDER CLAIMED BY COMMA

Isabel does a double-take when she sees the headline plastered across the front page of the *Echo*. She has to flip to the next paper in the pile, and the next, to be sure she's not imagining it.

They all tell her the same thing: Ronan claimed the kill. The police are abandoning their investigation – they stay out of guild business – and now that Hummingbird knows a claim has been staked and the killer isn't theirs to target, Isabel's safe . . . from this mess, at least.

'Everything all right, Bella?' asks Ashvin, and she realises she's standing stock still in the middle of the newsagent's, staring at the papers like she's never seen one before.

'Yeah, sorry, I . . . Big news about the murder, right?'

'Big news,' Ashvin agrees, watching her load the papers into her bag. 'Circulation's up. Make sure you check the list.'

A clear sign to get on with her job. Isabel takes the hint.

Why would Ronan do this? Because she's a 'valuable asset', too valuable to fall into Hummingbird's hands? Or because he thinks she'll change her mind about helping Comma? She won't. He left her the folder of her father's documents, but Isabel shoved them in the bottom of her wardrobe as soon as he was gone and has no plans to retrieve them.

Or maybe, just maybe, Ronan Atwood is trying to help her.

But she knows his type. More than that, she knows his reputation. He's ruthless, ambitious, calculating – not benevolent. He'll want something in return for this apparent act of mercy, and she doubts she'll get much choice when he comes to collect her debt.

Isabel tries to put it out of her mind, but if she doesn't think about Ronan, she has to think about what the doctor said, and that's worse. She's simultaneously impatient for answers and dreading the moment Daragh tells her what she already suspects: that he can't cure her.

Her updated route takes her most of the way to school. It's still early when she stuffs the empty delivery bag in her locker and heads towards the library to kill time until the bell rings. She can hear voices – Grace must already be in.

As she approaches, the noise resolves into words. 'You must have noticed her hand, Grace.'

Mortimer. Isabel ducks out of sight and listens.

'So she's got a nasty scar,' comes Grace's voice. 'It could've been an accident – a hot stove, a spilled kettle . . .'

'She's got a nasty scar, she's obviously traumatised, and her school record says she used to be at Fordon Borough School, which I know for a fact is a lie. I have a friend in their admin office, and he says they never had a Bella Nicholls.'

Shit. They're talking about her. She presses herself more closely against the wall, as though that'll help.

'What are you implying, Mortimer?'

'You don't think that's suspicious? That she'd lie about her school?'

'Not as much as you do, apparently.' Grace sounds exasperated. 'What, you think she's a double agent?'

'I don't know what to think. You've heard the rumours about the spons—'

'And half of them are bullshit. The guilds might fund the schools, but they leave the kids alone until sixth year at least.'

'Then why would she lie?' Grace is silent, and Mortimer pushes the point: 'That scar on her hand looks like an acid burn. How would a teenager get a scar like that, unless they're caught up in something they shouldn't be?'

Isabel's heart is pounding so hard against her ribs that it almost hurts. She clenches her fist, knuckles against her teeth, trying not to make a sound.

'I think that's a stretch,' says Grace. 'Maybe she has an abusive family.'

'Is that what she told you?'

'I know she doesn't live with them. Beyond that, we haven't

talked about it. We talked about the murder, we talked about her History homework – conversations I've had with five other students this week.'

'You talked about the murder?' echoes Mortimer.

'She wanted to know what I thought.' Grace pauses. 'Mortimer, you've got that look on your face. Don't tell me you think—'

Isabel can hardly breathe, an unyielding band of fear tightening around her chest. *No, no, no.* Comma claimed the kill. She wasn't supposed to have to worry about this any more.

'I'm not saying she did it,' says Mortimer. 'But she was visibly upset in my class, and the more I learn about her, the less things add up.'

'Comma claimed that kill.'

'It took them a week. Something's going on, and I think Bella's involved.'

Grace scoffs. 'She's a teenage girl.'

'Yes, she's seventeen. They take people from sixteen, don't they?'

'Only in exceptional circumstances. If you're scared of Bella Nicholls, you're in the wrong profession.'

'I'm not scared of her. I'm scared *for* her.' Isabel wasn't expecting that, or the way Mortimer's voice softens. 'Grace, if she's got Comma's attention to the point she's had to move halfway across the city and lie on her school record to get away from them, she might be in danger. Maybe they killed that man to scare her into compliance.'

There's a heavy thump, as though Grace has dropped a pile

of books on the desk. 'I know you've convinced yourself you have a moral duty to protect every student who enters your classroom, Mortimer, but if Comma want Bella Nicholls, it's not your job to get in their way.'

Grace is right. If Mortimer's interpretation of events was in any way correct, interfering would get them both killed. And it's not like Isabel expected them to help her. But it still stings to hear the librarian say she wouldn't protect her, if it came to it.

'And if you think she's a risk to your other students,' Grace continues, 'then deal with it, but don't bring your wild speculation to me.'

Isabel can't stay here. Any second now, Mortimer will storm out of the library and find her cowering in the corridor, and he'll know she's heard. She can't have that conversation now, without lies ready to shield herself. So she steals away, taking the stairs as fast as she can, and almost crashes into Nick at the bottom.

'Bella!' He seems pleased to see her. 'You weren't on the tram this morning. You all right?'

I've been poisoned, my Woodwork teacher suspects me of working with the guild, and I've got a Comma agent in my flat every other minute. 'I'm fine,' she says. 'Bit tired.'

'Aren't we all?' His laugh is a little forced. 'Good thing I bumped into you, actually. I wanted to ask you – there's this club in Weaverthorpe some of my friends go to, and apparently they have an underage night every couple of weeks. I wondered if you wanted to come with me sometime?' She stares at him blankly, and he hastily clarifies, 'With *us*. Not like a date. I thought it could be fun.'

Maybe it's the brain fog that comes from being in constant pain, but it takes Isabel far too long to realise he's inviting her to go clubbing, as if she's his friend. She should say no: clubbing feels like an unnecessary risk, and clubbing in a Comma borough is just asking for trouble.

But instead she hears herself say, 'Yeah, maybe. Sounds fun.'

Nick's face breaks into a grin. 'Really?' he says, apparently as surprised as she is by this answer. 'Great! I'll text you the details.' He looks expectantly at her until she twigs he wants her number.

Well, what harm is there in giving it to him? It's the normal thing to do, and Bella Nicholls is normal. She types her number into his phone and they exchange a few more snippets of small talk, and by the time she gets back to her locker, the tight band around her chest has loosened a little.

But the fear is far from gone.

The following evening sees Isabel back at the Sunshine Project. She suspects Daragh's rearranged his hours specifically to see her – it's late, and the clinic's almost empty, except for a tired-looking receptionist who waves her straight through.

'So.' Isabel sits down. 'How bad is it?'

The doctor purses his lips. 'Bad,' he says. 'The test results were … complicated, but it's hard to tell how much that's the result of your prior exposure to poison. I suspect that while that's not the primary cause of your current illness, it isn't helping.'

No, being repeatedly poisoned isn't great for one's health. 'So what is the primary cause?'

'I don't know,' he confesses. He's looking back and forth between a dozen heavily annotated printouts as though the numbers might suddenly make sense. 'The toxicology screen's inconclusive: this is no poison we've ever seen before. You have vitamin deficiencies worse than I've seen in a malnutrition patient starving to death; your white blood cells are through the roof; your adrenal gland has gone haywire. In other words, your immune system is eating itself and your whole body is in crisis. No ordinary poison could do this.'

The meaning of his words is slow to seep through the sludge of Isabel's dying brain. When the sense of his diagnosis finally settles, she says, 'No ordinary poison could. But that kind of thing was – is – my father's speciality.'

There's a pause, and then Daragh says, 'Parnassiinae.' She looks up sharply, but his expression's inscrutable. 'Am I right?'

Parnassiinae. The code name of her father's lab – one of three forming Comma's biological and chemical weapons development division, and by far the most notorious for the vicious nerve agents and poisons it produces.

Not that Daragh should know that.

She's on her feet before she's thought through what she's going to do next. 'Did you – how did you—'

'It's okay,' he says, in a placatory tone; he doesn't seem in the least bit surprised by her alarm. 'You don't have to be afraid of me. After I saw these results, I did some research, tried to work out who could be responsible. That's all. I didn't realise you had a family connection, but I'm right, aren't I? This is Parnassiinae work.'

Slowly, still wary, she sits back down. 'It looks like it,' she admits. 'Except I'm not dead.'

Her father tried to kill her. She knew – or at least she suspected – but it's different, somehow, having a stranger tell her they recognise his work. She lied to herself for so long, trying to pretend she still believed he never meant to hurt her, but she *knew*.

And Ronan wonders why she ran.

'Yes, non-lethal hits are rare for Parnassiinae,' Daragh agrees. 'But it wouldn't be the first time they've used a slow-acting poison to make a point. There was an ambassador—' He breaks off. 'The details don't matter. But the reports suggested the poison was encased in a coating that broke down slowly over time, releasing the toxin into the bloodstream only after some weeks had elapsed. By the time the target became sick, the agent was long gone, and it was virtually impossible to prove it was Esperan work. If something similar is happening here, it could be that the casing has only just begun to break down.'

So this is only the prelude to something much worse. 'Meaning these are just the first symptoms.'

'Meaning it's possible we can remove the capsule before any more poison is released into your bloodstream,' says Daragh. 'We can't counteract it effectively without an antidote, but it might give you a fighting chance.'

It takes a second to realise he's giving her good news. 'You can remove it?'

'Me personally? I'm not sure. It would depend where exactly—'

'Can you get it out?' she asks urgently.

He hesitates. 'Let me do an ultrasound to locate it,' he says at last. 'I'm not sure what it's made of, so an X-ray might not pick it up. But a slow-acting poison like this would have to have been inserted, not ingested. Do you have any bruises or scars that might help me find it?'

Isabel has more than enough scars, and none of them are likely to tell Daragh anything useful. But there's a small patch of mottled bruising above her hip, and when she mentions this, he nods.

'Okay. We'll start there. Take your T-shirt off and pop up on the bed for me. Don't worry,' he says, seeing her stricken expression. 'I've seen it all before.'

She doubts that, but she does as he asks, and sits shivering on the bed.

He takes one look at her and sucks in his breath. She waits for the interrogation, but all he says is, 'Have you had these scars checked over to make sure they've healed properly?'

It's not what she expected. 'You're not going to ask how I got them?'

'Do you want me to?' Isabel shakes her head. 'I thought not. Have they been treated?'

'Mostly.' She runs her hand along her lower abdomen, across the thick, knotted line that bisects it, marred by the small wounds of rough stitches. 'This one didn't heal like it was meant to.'

'That's a big scar,' says the doctor. 'When did that happen?'

'About a year and a half ago.'

'Ah.' Daragh frowns. 'Is that why you no longer menstruate?' When Isabel nods, he looks closer. 'They made a real mess of that.'

'It was okay ... before,' she says. 'I was healing. And then it – then my parents didn't give me enough time to rest, so the stitches tore. They insisted on treating it themselves, and now it's like this.'

'I see,' he says. 'I noticed you're taking hormone replacement therapy, so your ovaries—'

'Yeah, they're, uh, not there any more.'

'How much isn't there?'

'Let's just say I definitely won't be having children.'

That doesn't bother her: she can't imagine a future for herself that involves children, and doesn't care to. But she does care that she was stabbed, that she nearly died – *would* have died, if Michael hadn't been there. All because her parents sent her on a job she wasn't ready for, signed off by Toni fucking Rolleston and her moss-green eyes.

'It's a drastic approach, to remove your reproductive system at that age,' says Daragh, a hard edge to his tone. 'They didn't try to save it?'

'My parents told the doctors not to bother.'

'I see.'

'Nobody asked me what I thought.'

'I see,' he says again. Now the hard edge seems more like anger, though she's fairly sure it's not directed at her. 'And

102

this burn on your chest, that's Comma's handiwork as well, I suppose?'

Isabel doesn't have to ask how he guessed. The burn's in the shape of a butterfly, Comma's logo traced in the damaged contours of her skin. 'Sort of,' she admits.

Daragh mutters something that sounds a lot like, '*those bastards*', although he's all professionalism when he asks, 'Forgive me, Bella, I know I said I wouldn't ask, but are you willing to tell me what happened?'

The trouble with staying silent for so long is that when you're eventually asked to speak, the words have buried themselves so deep they can't be found. 'I don't . . .'

'Anything you say is in the strictest confidence,' he promises. His critical medical eye is gone: it's sympathy on his face as he looks at her now. 'I want to help you.'

And for some reason she believes him, or maybe she's just sick of the secrets, of always swallowing her truth. But still the words are strangled, barely more than a whisper, as she says, 'I was eleven years old. My mother wanted to teach me a lesson. My father was the one who held me still.'

He closes his eyes for a moment, swears quietly, then opens them, a new resolve in his expression. 'Okay,' he says. 'Okay, Bella. I'm going to put some gel on your stomach now and then I'll dim the lights to help me see the screen. Is that okay? Tell me if you need me to stop.' She nods. 'Then let's see what we can do to help you.'

11

HELPO (HELP)

Daragh's brow creases as he fiddles with the display, trying to make the grainy image of Isabel's abdomen clearer. Finally, he sits back. 'What I don't understand,' he says, 'is why Comma would do this.'

I didn't know, Ronan said, like what happened in the lab wasn't Comma's responsibility. *Your father is missing.* And her own words: *You think he's defected?* Ian Ryans has proved he's working to his own agenda, and maybe poisoning her is a part of that. She can't see what he stands to gain from her death, but perhaps she's outlived her usefulness to him.

'I'm not sure that Comma did,' she replies.

Daragh frowns at this remark, and she realises she probably shouldn't be dropping hints that Comma have lost the loyalty of their deadliest poisoner. Before he can ask what she means, she says, 'Where is it?'

'Here.' Daragh points to a raised bump in the middle of the bruised area.

A tiny mark. She thought the enemy was out there in the city – her parents, the guilds, the police – but it was here all along. In her stomach, her intestines, the space where her womb used to be. *I'm dying.* She doesn't have the energy to be afraid any more. She wants it to be over.

'Can you get it out?'

'I think so.' He passes her a roll of tissues to wipe the gel from her stomach. 'But I can't fix the damage it's already done, not without knowing what it is or how to make an antidote. And for that you need a poisoner, not a doctor.'

'I'm not going to the guild.' She doesn't have the words to make him understand, not in English, not in a way that makes sense to him. She tries anyway. 'I don't know if they knew about this. But it doesn't matter, because even if they didn't know, they *did* this, you understand? They didn't stop it.'

'Yes,' he says. 'I understand. They failed you.'

Failed. She wants to ask Daragh if he knows about Cocoon. Maybe she's not the first patient he's seen with scars they're too young for. Maybe there have been others who got out, and—

None of them really got out.

'So will you remove it?'

He hesitates. 'Our facilities aren't designed for this type of operation. I'm only considering it because delaying will do more harm than good.'

Isabel gestures to her scars. 'I've had worse.'

Daragh grimaces. 'Yes, I can see that.' He sighs. 'Okay. Follow me.'

The corridor is dark, lit only by the pale glow of emergency lighting. 'Everyone's gone home?' she guesses.

He props open the door of a tiny operating room. 'The clinic's not usually open this late. It's just us.'

She's alone in this building with a man who's about to cut her open. Maybe if she were less tired, she'd be afraid. *I'm dying anyway. Nothing to lose any more.* It's liberating, somehow, knowing there's nothing left to fear.

Daragh invites her to sit on the operating table while he fetches his equipment. 'Local anaesthetic will be safest, considering the stress your body's under, but if you want a general—'

'No.' The last thing she wants is to be knocked out. She might trust Daragh more than any other doctor she's seen in the last five years, but that's saying very little. 'Local's fine.'

'All right. Let me know if you're in pain.'

He keeps up a running commentary as he works, ensuring she's never taken by surprise. Several times he pauses to remind her that she can tell him to stop if she needs to. Even that small illusion of control over the situation feels strange and new.

She can't look at what he's doing, so she focuses her attention on the far wall of the room. It's been painted with a huge spreading tree, the leaves gold and green and silver, with names written on them.

'Who are they?' she asks. 'The names?'

Daragh follows her gaze. 'People the clinic has helped,' he says. 'They donate money to keep it running, and we add their names to the tree. Or their friends donate in their name.'

So many names. If she lives, will hers join them? Will they write *Bella Nicholls*, or will it be *Isabel Ryans*?

That depends, she thinks, on who it is they're saving.

Daragh grunts in concentration and withdraws his tweezers, a tiny pellet held between them. It's not much bigger than a grain of rice. 'So small and yet such a nasty piece of work,' he says, dropping it onto a tray. 'Absurd, isn't it?'

Isabel nods. She doesn't know what she was expecting, but this tiny *splinter* wasn't it. She knows size isn't everything – a grain of polonium eight times smaller would be fatal – but still it feels wrong to be afraid of something so minuscule.

Daragh stitches up the incision and covers it with a fresh dressing, then drops the pellet into a sample bottle and seals that inside a small box. 'Can't be too careful,' he says, seeing her watching him. 'I have no idea what's in that thing, but we'll play it safe.'

'What now?'

'Now I'll stuff you full of vitamin supplements in the hope of keeping you alive long enough to create an antidote, and you take that poison to the guild and set their poisoners to figuring out what it is.'

'I can't.'

'Then take it to a freelancer. I'm a doctor, Bella. I can treat your symptoms, but I can't reverse-engineer the nastiest poison I've encountered in ten years of this job.'

'But—' Freelancers can't be trusted. They're as cruel as the guilds, and their loyalty can be bought by anyone who offers the right price. Isabel can't pay enough to be sure they won't double-cross her. But she's dying, so what choice does she have? 'Fine. Any suggestions?'

'I'll give you the contact details of someone I've worked with before.' Daragh seems relieved that she's agreed. He rummages around for paper and a pen. 'Her name's Grace Whittock and—'

'Grace Whittock, the librarian?'

Daragh stops halfway through writing the number on the back of an appointment card. 'Shit,' he says. 'You're at the Fraser, aren't you?'

'She's a poisoner?'

'She mainly specialises in non-lethals, and she's good with antidotes. This might be too complex for her, but I trust her, at least.'

Grace Whittock, freelance poisoner. Isabel reassesses all her interactions with the librarian in light of this new information. Is that why Grace felt familiar – a danger so well known it almost seemed like safety? Her anger's offset by relief at not having to deal with a total stranger. If Daragh trusts Grace . . .

The doctor is waiting for her response. She pushes aside her fear and tries to be practical, because if she allows herself to get emotional about this, she'll have to face the fact that she's dying.

'Can I have a copy of my test results?' she asks. 'It'll give

Grace more to work with and might help her figure out what's in the poison.'

'Good idea,' says Daragh. 'But first, let me give you a couple of vitamin shots and an immunosuppressant to see if we can stabilise your system. It feels like sticking a plaster on a missing limb, but it might help. Next week we'll do another blood test to see whether things are going in the right direction.'

Afterwards, as she puts the printouts in her bag and listens to Daragh's instructions about the aftercare for her new wound, Isabel asks, 'Why are you doing all this for free?'

He shrugs. 'Because no one else is going to help you, are they?'

And she can't say he's wrong about that.

On Friday, Isabel's running late after her paper round, so it's not until break that she takes her printouts and all her courage to the library. In her head, she rehearses what she's going to say to Grace.

'Hey, Bella.' Emma's lounging behind the library desk with her feet on the table. 'Grace is off sick today, so I'm in charge. Need any help?'

'What?' It comes out as a whisper.

'I know, right? Can't believe she left me in a position of authority. *Big* mistake.'

'She's not here?'

Emma swings her feet off the desk and looks more closely at Isabel. 'Are you okay?'

She means to say, *I'm fine*, but what comes out is, 'I'm dying.' Then the tears follow, the ones she swore to herself she wouldn't cry.

'Oh, shit.' Emma slides out from behind the desk. 'Here. Grace left her office unlocked. Let's go in there.'

Inside, Isabel tries to stop sobbing, palms pressed against her eyes. She's been choking back these tears since she left the clinic last night, and the only thing helping her hold it together was the thought that Grace could help. But now . . .

'Here,' says Emma, putting a glass of water and a box of tissues next to her.

'I'm sorry,' she stammers. 'I'm sorry, I . . .'

'Don't apologise. Cry as much as you need to.' Isabel expects Emma to leave and go back to surveying her library kingdom, but the other girl sits down on the desk as though she'd happily stay there all day.

Isabel runs out of tears eventually, and it leaves her feeling wrung out and humiliated. She wipes her face and takes a sip of water. When Emma opens her mouth to speak, Isabel cuts her off. 'I don't want to talk about it.'

'I was going to ask if you wanted a hug.'

'A hug?'

'Yeah, you know, a sign of affection that makes you feel better when you're crying uncontrollably in the library instead of hanging around the canteen, or whatever normal kids do at break.'

'Right.' Isabel musters a small smile. 'Well, normal is overrated.'

'True, but hugs aren't.' Emma eyes her. 'So?'

'A hug sounds nice,' admits Isabel. Hugs have always felt dangerous, the perfect opportunity for a knife between the ribs, but she's able to forget that for a moment as Emma's arms encircle her. She's dying anyway. There are worse ways to go.

'I take it Daragh didn't give you good news,' says Emma, drawing back.

'Not exactly, no.'

Emma pulls her feet up onto the desk so that she can sit cross-legged. 'I know you said you didn't want to talk about it, but it might help.'

Talking about it is too much like admitting it's real. 'I don't know how,' Isabel says truthfully.

'Are you really dying?'

Because of course Emma jumps straight in at the deep end. Isabel shrugs, as though it doesn't matter that she won't see her eighteenth birthday. 'It tends to be a side effect of getting poisoned.'

'You've been *poisoned*?'

Maybe she shouldn't have said that. It's becoming harder and harder to keep track of what she's supposed to care about. The walls she's built are cracking, the secrets spilling out, and she doesn't have the will to hold them back.

'It's bad,' she tells Emma, looking down at her hands. They're so pale she could be dead already. 'We don't know what it is, but it's bad. And I . . . I don't know who I can ask for help.'

There's a pause, and she waits for the inevitable questions, but all Emma says is, 'That's shit.'

'Yep.'

'Daragh will figure it out, though, won't he? You haven't given up yet?'

It's not 'giving up' to be realistic about her chances. 'Not yet,' she says, because it's what Emma needs from her.

Emma twists her fingers uncertainly. 'You know, when Jean . . .' she begins. 'I mean, I know a little about what it's like to find out you're dying, and . . . you don't have to deal with this alone. You could come home with me tonight if you want company.'

Isabel swallows. 'Why?'

Emma pushes her glasses further up her nose. 'Why not? You're my friend.'

'I am?' *You don't even know my real name.*

'Sure.' She doesn't hesitate. Whatever criteria Emma has for friendship, she's decided Isabel meets them – even though almost everything she knows about her is a lie. *Except the fact that I'm dying*, thinks Isabel morbidly. 'Bella, I know what it's like to be on your own, afraid of anyone who's nice to you, afraid that everything good is temporary.'

'You do?' How can Emma know? There's no shadow of sadness on her face, no clues to the life she might have led.

Emma's smile is sad. 'I do. I was so sure that everything was going to be taken away that I convinced myself it wasn't real in the first place.'

The only thing that's ever been real for Isabel is being on her own. She's never had anyone she trusted to watch her back, never dared assume someone would catch her when she falls.

'Did you mean it, about coming home with you?' she asks, blinking back more tears. If she starts crying again, there'll be nothing left of her. 'I don't think I want to be alone.'

She feels sick at the thought of finding Ronan Atwood in her kitchen; she doesn't have the strength to tell Comma to fuck off again when all she wants to say is *save me save me save me don't let me die of this don't let this kill me*. If he offered her a deal today, she can't promise herself she wouldn't take it.

'Of course I meant it,' says Emma. 'I'll meet you at the gate at the end of the day.'

Isabel nods. The end of the day. She can make it to the end of the day.

12

HISTORIO (HISTORY)

Emma's house is in south-east Lutton, close to the
Weaverthorpe boundary. Most of the houses in the terrace
are typical of the area: red brick below, light-coloured pebble-
dash above, with gutters and woodwork painted bright colours
to match the front doors. The last house, however, stands out.
Colour trails down from the window frames and streams
across the walls like a fine, rainbow cobweb, the pigments
coagulating in corners in the shapes of small animals
and mischievous faces that peer out under sills or above
gratings. From the little Isabel's seen of Emma's artwork,
it's comparatively restrained, but the house is a riot of colour
compared to its neighbours.

'Juvenilia,' Emma says, grinning. 'It's the first house I ever painted. Me, Leo and Jean did it, right after her diagnosis. Still can't believe Mum let us.'

Isabel pictures Leo and Jean looking a little like Emma – the same flyaway hair, the same dimple when they beam, the hands that are never still while they talk. 'How old were you?'

'Thirteen,' says Emma. 'Jean ...' She hesitates. 'It was already terminal when they found it. I think that's why Mum let us paint the house – she wanted us to have that memory, all three of us together. Also,' she adds, her tone deliberately light again, 'she suspected I'd paint *something*, and wanted it to be something she knew about.'

She unlatches the gate and leads Isabel through a small garden planted with vegetables and flowers. 'Mum?' she calls out, unlocking the door. 'Bella's here.'

Isabel's hand stills halfway through unzipping her jacket as a woman comes out of the living room. The two of them stare at each other: Isabel, frozen, her badly cut fringe falling into her eyes; the woman, equally still, with her moss-green eyes and a nose that's been broken a few too many times.

'Bella,' repeats Toni Rolleston, as though tasting the word. Her eyes dart to her daughter and back to Isabel, and she manages a tight smile. 'It's nice to meet you.'

She can't be Emma's mother. They look nothing alike, and anyway Emma is – and Toni is – and this isn't possible ...

Isabel's tensed to run, muscles taut and ready. *This isn't happening.* But Emma's there, expression open and cheerful, and Emma's never there in her flashbacks. Which means this is real. And Emma's smile is real too, so either she's in on it, or she has no idea that she's led Isabel straight into a trap.

Toni's still standing there, pretending nothing's wrong, like she's not a nightmare incarnate in this brightly painted home.

'It's nice to meet you too,' Isabel says, voice rough. It's the hardest lie she's told so far. 'I'm sorry, Emma didn't tell me your name—'

'Toni.' So she's using her real name. Of course it's only Isabel who has to hide. She's surprised there's no painted butterfly among the other artwork on the house, declaring allegiance for all the world to see.

There's a long pause, neither of them sure how to pretend they've never met when the brands of their past acquaintance still burn on Isabel's skin. Emma, oblivious to the awkwardness, says, 'I'll put the kettle on. Tea, Bella?'

'Please,' she says, without taking her eyes off Toni. 'That would be nice.'

The moment Emma's safely in the kitchen, Toni says, 'Some warning would have been nice, little Moth.'

'Don't call me that.' Toni, of all people, should know why she hates that nickname; should remember why Isabel was a restless child, flitting from dark room to dark room in search of somewhere to hide from her bad dreams and the monsters that haunted her waking world. The butterfly of night. They always saw her as Comma before they saw her as human. Saw her as a knife more than as a child. 'Does Emma . . . does she know what you are?'

'Funny, I was about to ask you the same question.'

116

The way Toni says it, it's like she expects Isabel to be grateful that she hasn't immediately destroyed her cover. But she can't be grateful when it's *Toni fucking Rolleston*, who signed off on the assignment that nearly killed her. And she's *here*. She's Emma's mother.

How the *fuck* can she be Emma's mother.

'Are you guys going to stand in the hallway forever?' Emma calls from the kitchen.

'We're coming!' Toni looks at Isabel: 'She doesn't know anything.' The plea's implicit: *don't tell her. Don't ruin this.*

Toni doesn't deserve this lie, but Isabel can't tell Emma the truth about her mother without outing herself. Mutually assured destruction. She forces a smile, baring her teeth. 'I won't tell if you don't,' she says, and follows the embodiment of her nightmares into the kitchen.

Emma brings the tea´ over to the table, her forehead wrinkling in concern. 'Are you okay, Bella? You look like you've seen a ghost.'

A ghost would be preferable. 'It's been a long day,' she says, leaning against the counter instead of taking a seat. Absently, she picks up a framed photo and looks at it: a family shot. Emma must be about ten. There's a teenage boy, dark-skinned and beaming, and a girl maybe a year or so younger than him; with her pale, freckled skin and fair hair, she looks the most like Toni, but the resemblance is superficial at best.

Leo and Jean, presumably.

'You don't look alike,' she says neutrally. It's an understatement, and it doesn't come close to what she wants

117

to say to Toni: *I didn't know you had children.* Except it's more like: *How? How could you be part of Cocoon while they were waiting for you at home? How could you tuck them in at night knowing what was happening to me?*

Emma says, 'We're fostered.'

Right. That explains why Isabel never detected a hint of Toni in her. 'All of you?'

Toni nods. 'Why don't you sit down, Bella? You look tired.'

'I'm dying,' snaps Isabel. 'Of course I look tired.' She sees the shock on Emma's face and moderates her tone. 'I'm sorry. It's been—'

'A long day,' Toni finishes. She's managed to make her expression sympathetic, pasting on the 'concerned mother' mask as though she thinks Isabel can't see the truth. 'Emma told me you weren't very well.'

What else did Emma tell her? Not enough for her to work out who 'Bella' was, at least: her surprise at seeing Isabel was genuine. The fact that her pseudonym hasn't yet reached the entire guild should be a comfort, but somehow it's not.

She takes a seat at the kitchen table, the furthest from Toni, and wraps her fingers around the mug Emma pushes towards her. Why did she come? *I don't think I want to be alone.* Pathetic. All Toni can offer her is a noose to tie around her own neck.

Isabel looks at Emma and says the only thing she can think to say: 'I didn't know you were adopted.'

'Fostered,' Emma corrects, an edge to her voice. 'My parents left Espera when I was seven.'

118

People don't just *leave* Espera. You need a visa, permission from the guilds and, most of all, you need somewhere to go. Smugglers can help you circumvent the first two issues, but it's harder once you're out – if you get that far.

'They abandoned you?'

Emma shrugs, staring at the table. 'Maybe they thought a child would give them away,' she says. Her voice is the flat monotone of suppressed feelings. 'I don't know how they got out. I don't even know if they *did*. Sometimes I imagine them living happily in some other city, other times I imagine them shot by the border patrol before they made it past the wall. Makes no difference to me. I was fostered half a dozen times; ended up in an orphanage in Hunmanby. Then Mum took me in.' She glances up at Toni and smiles. 'She was the only one willing to make the effort to turn a feral creature like me into a person again.'

'You weren't that bad,' her mother protests.

Emma raises an eyebrow at Isabel. 'I was a "problem child",' she says, making the inverted commas with her fingers. 'I had "behavioural issues".'

'Well, those do tend to be the labels institutions use when they've decided not to bother any more,' says Toni. Isabel doesn't miss the quick glance the woman shoots in her direction. Whatever issues Emma had must have seemed trivial after dealing with Isabel and Cocoon.

'And now you can't get rid of me.' Emma grins. 'Luckily, I'm an absolute delight.'

Seeing the fond look Toni gives her daughter feels like

barbed wire against Isabel's skin. How can the woman who helped train her be allowed *this*? This normality, this love, this child who isn't irredeemably fucked up?

'And the others?' she asks, swallowing her bitterness.

'I had Leo and Jean since they were babies,' says Toni. 'I'd never planned to add a third, but when I met Emma . . . I changed my mind.'

Emma raises her hands as though to say, *It's true, I'm irresistible,* and then gets to her feet. 'I need the loo. Back in a minute.'

The kitchen door swings shut behind her, and Isabel and Toni are alone. Silence falls, a stand-off without weapons, but it's Isabel who strikes first. 'Fuck you, Toni.'

'Isabel, I'm . . .'

'You're what?' she says. 'Sorry?'

'If I'd known it was you that Emma had befriended, I'd have done this differently. Planned it better.'

'If *I'd* known,' says Isabel, 'I wouldn't have come.' Her next words are forced out through gritted teeth. 'You can't tell my parents I'm here.'

'If they care, they already know. I'm retired, Isabel. I've got nothing to gain from selling you out. Besides, last I heard, Ian and Judith were MIA.'

Retired. It seems funny that you can retire from ruining people's lives. 'So now you live here, in your sweet little house, with your sweet little fake children, and you pretend to be a civilian?'

'I *am* a civilian, and they *are* my children.'

'Fostered,' counters Isabel. 'Not even adopted.'

'Adoption would have given them Comma affiliation, whether they wanted it or not, and I didn't want them anywhere near the guild.' Toni sips her tea. 'I was trying to keep them safe.'

Isabel spits her response. 'I didn't think protecting children was a priority of yours.'

She waits for Toni to shout, or threaten her, but she only sighs and braces her forehead against her fingers. She looks old and tired and sad. 'It doesn't matter what I say, because you won't believe me, but I was against Cocoon from the start.'

'Right. So against it that you volunteered to help out.'

'They should never have been training minors. I told them that. They wouldn't back down, so I proposed safeguards: a minimum age, the consent of the children and the opportunity to leave if they chose. Comma didn't listen. They didn't want me meddling, but I thought if I were part of it, I could stop things from getting too bad.'

'Are you trying to justify it to yourself, or to me?' says Isabel coldly. 'Because a sob story doesn't change shit.'

'I made so many mistakes.' Toni closes her eyes. 'You were so young. I couldn't have done anything, but I should have tried. I should have done something.'

Isabel swirls her tea around her mug. 'So when you fostered Emma, was that you trying to prove to yourself that you weren't a complete fuck-up?'

'I was trying to save her,' says Toni. 'Not many loving parents are keen to give their children to the guild for training,

121

it turns out, and with Cocoon being top secret they could hardly recruit openly. So they took kids nobody cared about, which meant kids from orphanages. They sent me to Hunmanby, and there she was: ten years old, severe abandonment issues, prone to panic attacks and bursts of rage. And, crucially, no attachments. No family to care whether she lived or died. She was exactly what Cocoon was looking for.' Toni looks up, eyes moist with tears she doesn't deserve to cry. 'Actually,' she says, 'she reminded me a little of you.'

Isabel has nothing to say to that. She doesn't want to think about her younger self reflected in Emma's pain. But Toni's still talking.

'I was too much of a coward to save you, Isabel, so I saved her instead. I fostered her before Comma got their hands on her file, and I convinced myself I'd done something noble when they took a couple of older kids instead.'

'But you didn't leave.' Because this is where Toni's saintly tale falls apart. 'You stayed,' Isabel points out, 'right to the end. You're the reason I nearly died.'

'I know.' Toni swallows. 'I thought I was helping, but that was when I realised I couldn't make Cocoon anything other than completely evil.'

Her confession requires something from Isabel: understanding, forgiveness, absolution. But how can she let go of the fact that Toni saw what Comma were doing and didn't save her?

'Did they know?' she asks. 'Leo and Jean?'

'Leo found out when he was sixteen. He didn't take it well,

and I still don't think he's forgiven me. Jean never knew, and by the time Emma was old enough to understand, I'd retired. I've promised Leo I'll tell her eventually, but I haven't been brave enough yet.' Toni downs the rest of her tea and wipes her mouth, placing the mug firmly on the table in front of her. 'I made a lot of mistakes, Isabel. My children were my chance to do better, and time after time I've come so close to screwing that up too.' She reaches out and takes Isabel's hand. 'For what it's worth, I'm *deeply* sorry for how completely I failed you.'

Isabel jerks her hand free. There's a rock in her throat, heavy and immovable no matter how hard she swallows. All she can think about is Toni saying, *She reminded me a little of you.* And yet Emma is this: colour and sunshine and mischief and an outstretched hand and that broad, dimpling grin, hope in human form. And Isabel is this: broken glass and barbed wire and a knife clutched in bloody fingers, nothing but a weapon or a wraith. She has never, until now, thought there was anything else she could have become.

Her left hand curls easily into a fist, damaged and defensive. She stares down at it and tries not to think about a world where it's whole, where she's whole, where somebody saved her and she didn't have to drag herself out of hell alone.

'I'm glad,' she says with difficulty, 'that you saved Emma, at least.' Then she stands and walks to the kitchen door.

'Isabel—' Toni begins.

'You were right about one thing. You *are* a coward.'

Toni has the wisdom not to argue. She doesn't stop Isabel as she flings open the door, but she comes to a halt anyway. There on the other side is Emma, eyes wide and lower lip trembling. Her expression is terrified, furious, disbelieving, as she stares from Isabel to her mother.

She heard. How long was she standing there? How much does she know? Isabel opens her mouth to speak, but no words will glue together the shattered lies strewn between them now.

'Mum?' Emma's voice cracks. 'Mum, is it . . . ?'

Is it true? The words die on her lips, her voice failing her, and Isabel's frozen to the spot, unable to fix yet another life she's destroyed.

'Emma, I'm sorry . . .' Toni begins, but that's confirmation enough. Emma's choked sob is just about audible as she turns and runs up the stairs. A door slams.

Isabel wants to go after her. She can't undo what's said, but she can . . . she can explain, can't she? Say *something* useful when Emma's entire world is crumbling? At the very least, she could apologise for being the reason her friend found out this way, because she didn't know. She wouldn't have come if she'd known.

'Don't,' says Toni, before she's taken a step towards the stairs. Isabel looks back at her. Her expression is bleak. 'She won't want to see you, Isabel. I think you should go.'

'But—'

'This is my mess to clean up.'

But she was meant to be my friend. But this was meant to be safe, and new, and normal. But, but, but—

'Good luck with that,' says Isabel, and she lets herself out of their house.

124

13

REKUNIĜO (REUNION)

Isabel's shitty evening gets worse when she reaches the tram stop and finds they're running emergency maintenance on the line, forcing her to take a bus home. It crawls through the Espera dusk, bookended by the lights of other vehicles making the same interminable journey, the roads packed and slow. Halfway home, she starts to cry, tears rolling down her cheeks faster than she can wipe them away. She staggers down the aisle, ignoring the curious looks of other passengers. The weight of her school bag throws her off-balance, and she has to clutch the rail beside the driver's window.

'Can you let me off?'

'Not till the next stop,' he answers, without even looking at her.

She slaps the window. 'Open the fucking doors before I hit the emergency button and do it myself.'

He swears at her, but opens the doors. Isabel flips him off as she disembarks into the chilly evening. She's not sure where that attitude came from. Maybe it's a side effect of dying.

The cold air dries her tears, but she can't stop sobbing. The anger and betrayal are choking her: Emma's friendship was meant to be new, and good, and instead it's exactly as shit as everything before. Seeing Toni Rolleston has made her afraid again, like no time has passed and she's still a terrified twelve-year-old.

Her first kill. She was *twelve*. Isabel swears and kicks the metal barrier separating her from the traffic, again and again until a sharp pain suggests she's broken a toe. A few cars slow as they pass her, drivers probably wondering if she's drunk. When somebody calls out, 'You okay?' she swears at them too.

Hoarse from screaming, she stumbles the last half-mile back to her flat and drags herself up the stairs, ready to collapse into bed and stay there until everything stops being so fucking awful.

And then she stops dead.

Her front door's ajar, which means there's somebody in her flat. Not Ronan; he'd never leave the door open. So: somebody else. Isabel's unarmed, reluctant to test the Fraser's anti-violence policy by taking a knife to school, but she readies herself to fight, tension coiling in her body. She pads towards the door and nudges it open, wincing when the hinges squeak, and slips inside.

There's a young man sitting on the settee, a dirty rucksack by his feet. His head is propped on his hand, his eyes bruised with fatigue. When he hears her come in, he scrambles to his feet.

'Isabel,' he says. 'Finally. I was beginning to think I'd got the wrong flat and I didn't know how much longer I could wait before they found—'

'Michael,' says Isabel. 'What the fuck are you doing here?'

She's conscious that she's a mess, her face blotchy with tears. Her toe throbs, begging for attention, but her focus is on the young man in front of her. Michael Griffiths.

When Isabel was nine, she became the youngest member of the newly founded Cocoon, Comma's highly secret and controversial minors' training programme. It was completely illegal but that, like the fundamental inhumanity of turning children into murderers before they'd had a chance to be anything else, didn't stop the guild. At first, for Isabel, it was an after-school club – a chance to hone the skills she'd learned from her parents almost as soon as she could walk, a place where she got stronger and faster and cleverer and forgot what it meant to be a child. Over time, it became something more, consuming her life: it made lies of her friendships and filled her school record with absences. But at least she wasn't the only one. At least she wasn't alone any more.

She was twelve when they recruited Michael, then fifteen and a recently orphaned ward of the guild. They might never have had much to do with each other, except that, eighteen months ago, they were both sent on a job neither of them was ready for. Michael was responsible for fumbling the shot that got Isabel stabbed, but he also saved her life by keeping pressure on the wound until the extraction team arrived. His quick thinking is why the Ryans' family took him in after Cocoon was shut down. Her parents' protégé.

And when Ian and Judith disappeared, so, they'd all thought, did he.

The sight of him brings a wave of memories. Michael's hands on her bleeding stomach, his desperate face: 'Is she going to live?' Michael teaching her card games at the kitchen table – then teaching her to cheat. Michael bandaging her hand even while saying, 'No, you must have got it wrong. Ian wouldn't . . .' when she was finally coming to terms with the idea that Ian *would*.

And then: Michael standing between her and the back door as she clutched the holdall containing everything she dared take when she ran. 'Where are you going?' The fear, the certainty that he'd raise the alarm and give her away, and her lie: 'For a walk. I'll be back soon.' The way he stepped aside as though he believed her, when he couldn't have done.

He didn't help her. But he didn't stop her either.

And now he's here, in her flat.

'I've got to talk to you,' he says. 'Your parents—'

'How long do we have?' There's a bag by the front door, always packed. Even allowing for her toe, she could be gone from here in two minutes flat. Fat lot of good that does her when she has nowhere else to run.

'What?'

128

'How long till they get here?'

'No, they're not ... they're not coming. I left, Isabel, like you did. I needed to warn you, I—'

She cuts him off. 'Stay here.' They're not coming. She doesn't have to run. But she can't have this conversation right now, not like this, so she ducks into the bathroom, the only place she can hide from him.

She won't think about what Toni Rolleston said. She won't think about the look on Emma's face. She splashes her face with water, clips back her overlong fringe and regards herself in the mirror. She looks like she's dying, but at least it's no longer obvious that she's been sobbing by the side of the road. Good enough to fool Michael? Maybe not. He knows her better than anyone – well enough to see straight through her.

It'll have to do. Retrieving the first aid kit from under the sink, she squares her shoulders and goes to face Michael and the memory of her parents.

He's moved from the settee to the kitchen table, his back to her. He's lost weight, his wristwatch sliding halfway up his forearm, clothes loose on his bony frame. His hair's clipped short, but she can still make out the white streak behind his ear where a small scar robs it of pigment. The auburn looks redder when it's short like this. He turns as she approaches, and she sees that his nose is crooked in profile. *Broken again*, she thinks, and this time she wasn't there to wrench it straight for him before it healed. It must be recent.

They punished him? Stupid question. Of course they did.

Isabel takes a seat, propping her injured foot on one of the remaining chairs and peeling off her sock. 'You shouldn't be here,' she says. 'You have two minutes to tell me why you came.'

'What happens in two minutes?' he asks with a slight smile.

Isabel doesn't smile back. 'I decide whether I'm going to kill you.'

His smile fades. She can tell he's weighing his words with care and she half expects him to blurt out a speech, but all he says is, 'Your parents have defected.'

Is that meant to be news? 'To Hummingbird?' she asks mildly, examining the mangled mess of her toenail and reaching into the first aid kit for an antiseptic wipe. The toe is swollen and angled strangely; definitely broken.

'No, they . . .' Michael chews his thumbnail for a moment. 'They've set up their own guild. It was your father's idea.'

Their own guild. Whatever she was expecting, it wasn't that. 'I see,' she says, mind racing. There's no way this won't end in blood when the other guilds find out.

'Ian backed out of a Comma deal and undercut them.' Michael sounds a little desperate now, like he thinks she can't tell how serious this is. 'He made the sale himself and kept the money to fund his own organisation with contacts from outside. And he . . . he poisoned you and drugged you so you'd forget.'

What does her father want with his own guild? Power? Money? She'd have thought he had enough of both already. 'I see,' she says again, keeping her voice neutral.

'Is that it?'

Isabel finishes cleaning the blood from her toe and looks up. 'What do you want me to say?'

'Something more than "I see", considering I just told you that your dad poisoned you.'

She looks down at the toe. It's almost as much of a mess as the rest of her life. 'And that's meant to surprise me?'

'You *knew*?'

Not for sure. 'Now I do,' she says, reaching for the microporous tape to bind her broken toe to its neighbour. 'I knew I was sick. I knew he was missing. Didn't know he'd been fucking with my memory, but it explains a lot. Do you have anything to tell me that's actually news?'

'Ian's the only person who can cure you.'

Isabel pauses, tape in hand. 'Is that what he told you?'

'It's the truth. Comma won't be able to find him. They cleared out his lab, took all his notes, but there's no way they can figure out his poison before it kills you. Without your parents, you'll never get the antidote.'

'Hmm.' She finishes bandaging her toe and snips the end of the tape, putting the roll back on the table. 'I think that was more than two minutes. Which one of them came up with this plan? My mother, right? You always did worship her.'

'No, she didn't ... I didn't ... I'm here to warn you.'

'Trouble is,' says Isabel, 'I don't believe you. Because running away from my father to help me would be brave and self-sacrificing, and while you're many things, Michael, a martyr isn't one of them. So why are you *really* here?'

He's staring at her as though he thinks she was serious when she threatened to kill him, but maybe he's grossed out by her foot. It's certainly not looking its best.

'They've defected,' he says again, and she's about to interrupt when he adds in a small voice, 'and they didn't take me with them.'

Ah.

'So that's it, then?' she says. 'They abandoned you, and you came running to me. When you said you left, I thought maybe you'd grown a backbone.'

'I could have gone to Comma,' he says, like he's defending himself. He has a kicked puppy look about him. 'But I thought you should know. About them.'

Isabel wiggles her toes experimentally. A flash of pain shoots through the broken one, but at least she doesn't seem to have cut off the circulation. 'I'm surprised they didn't take you,' she says honestly. 'It's not like them to turn down a willing minion.'

'After you left, your mother ...' He hesitates, and she notices again his broken nose. 'She said it was my fault for not stopping you, that they'd only kept me that long because of you.'

'Must have been hard for you,' she says, dimly aware that she's being a dick but unable to stop herself, 'after all that time you spent projecting your mummy issues onto her.'

The insult's too true to be a joke, and Michael doesn't bother trying to argue with it. His mother's death was sudden: she was out of the city on what should have been a straightforward contract hit, except the client double-crossed Comma and it

132

was *her* body that was dragged out of the river and sent back to Espera like a warning. Shell-shocked and in mourning, Michael ended up in Cocoon because there was nowhere else for him to go, and that was a vulnerability Judith Ryans knew too well how to exploit.

'I never saw her like that before,' he says. 'Isabel, I'm sorry. I should have listened to you.'

'Yeah,' says Isabel. 'You should have done. But it's too late now, isn't it?'

'But I—' He breaks off. 'I let you leave. I didn't tell them—'

Isabel cuts him off. 'You *let* me leave?' she echoes. 'Wow, thanks, you're a real hero. Finally, after years of abuse, I escaped, and you didn't have me dragged right back to where I started. Well done! Here's your bloody medal.'

'There's no need to be a bitch about it.'

'It's my trauma. You don't get to tell me how to deal with it.'

'Right, because obviously I had such a great adolescence,' says Michael. 'I can't tell if the highlight was Mum's murder, being recruited into Cocoon without being asked what I thought, or listening to the guild debate whether to murder me or just kick me out onto the streets after that job went wrong, but clearly—'

'*Clearly* neither of us had a great time,' interrupts Isabel. 'But you're not exactly the saviour you seem to think you are.'

'I tried to be your friend,' he shoots back. 'You're the one who kept pushing me away. I never asked for your parents to take me in, but I didn't have a lot of options. Fuck me for taking what I could get and sticking it out as long as I could, I guess.'

'Yeah,' she agrees. 'Fuck you.'

They lapse into silence, neither willing to break the stand-off.

Michael sitting at the kitchen table, teaching her card games – a small kindness in that isolated eighteen months between her injury and the day she left her parents' house. Bandaging her hand. Returning from errands in the outside world that Isabel wasn't allowed to see, bringing back books and games that she kept hidden in a shoebox under her bed and had to leave behind when she ran.

It wasn't friendship. It couldn't be. But it was something.

'My parents would never have let us be friends,' says Isabel finally. 'You know that, don't you?'

'Who cares what your parents wanted?'

'They'd have used it against us. Another way to manipulate us.'

Don't get attached to someone who can't defend themselves, her mother would say, over and over. And Michael couldn't, could he? If they wanted to hurt him to punish her, he couldn't have stopped them. Better to make them think she didn't care.

Better still to make sure she genuinely didn't.

Isabel turns away. It wasn't as bad for him. They didn't treat him the way they treated her, but she still left him behind. She hadn't realised how much it was weighing on her until now.

Michael sags, slumping back in his chair. 'So that's it?' he says. 'That's why you refused to be friends with me?'

Isabel shrugs. 'If we were friends, they wouldn't have let you stay. Anything good always got taken away.'

There's a long pause as he processes this. At last he shakes his head and swears. 'I'm sorry,' he says.

'Yeah,' says Isabel. 'So am I.' Because they might not have been friends, but Michael's a fellow survivor of Ian and Judith Ryans, the only person in this city who understands what her life was like before she ran.

And it fucking sucked for both of them.

She could tell him to leave. She could point out that Comma will welcome him with open arms if he'll help them find Ian and Judith. But she's got precious few allies, and she owes him her life. So she says, 'Tea?' like it's a peace offering, and because Michael knows her, he recognises it for what it is and accepts both the drink and the olive branch.

Isabel makes tea. As she brings their mugs over, he retrieves a battered pack of cheap playing cards from his bag and places them wordlessly on the table between them.

She looks at them and huffs a laugh. 'All right,' she says. 'One game. For old time's sake.'

14

ĈIFRO (CODE)

Over their game of cards, Isabel tells Michael about the Fraser, about Emma – the outlines of the new life she's building. She can't shake the feeling that she's trying to prove something to him. She tells him about Toni, too, and watches his expression harden at the name. So he remembers her. Of course he does: that job nearly got both of them killed.

In return, he tells her about the hostel he's found in Grindalythe, seven to a room, next to the manufacturing plant. He tells her the other men know him as Matthew, that he spent the last of his cash on his fake ID so he's picked up a factory job, and that he hasn't slept properly in days because one of his roommates snores. All of this is disclosed with a wry, self-deprecating smile, as though it doesn't bother him, but Isabel can see the strain in his face and wishes, for one uncharacteristically philanthropic moment, that her tiny flat were big enough to offer him a place to stay. But he doesn't ask, and she doesn't offer.

'Do you have a plan?' he asks, gathering up their cards after beating her for the third time in a row and shuffling the pack again. 'For dealing with the poison?'

Isabel watches him shuffle for a moment and says, 'There's a freelancer. She might be able to help me with an antidote, but I haven't asked her yet. Beyond that, I don't know.'

'You can afford that?'

She has no idea how much Grace charges. 'I have a paper round,' she says, as if Ashvin pays her enough to commission a poisoner. 'I'll figure it out.'

'And is it safe to go to a freelancer?'

Safe. The word fills Isabel with a pang of loss, an aching nostalgia for something she never had. 'It's my only option,' she says, taking the pile of cards he slides towards her. 'I have to try, right?'

'Of course, but . . .' Michael shrugs. 'I meant it about your father being the only one who knows how to deal with this poison. Maybe you could, I don't know, negotiate with him.'

'My father doesn't *negotiate.*'

'Are you sure? Because if he wanted you dead, I don't think we'd be having this conversation. The fact that he's got a vested interest in your survival gives you leverage.'

'Sure, he doesn't want me dead,' says Isabel, the camaraderie of the card game dissipating into her old fear. 'Just dying and

137

desperate enough to beg him. That's what this is about, isn't it? He wants to control me, the way he always has.' Did he know she was going to leave, or was it just that he could see his daughter getting older, harder to manipulate? Surely if he'd had an inkling of her plans, he would have stopped her.

'He's underestimating you,' says Michael earnestly. 'You ran away once; you can do it again.'

As if that's all there is to it. 'It took me fifteen months of planning,' she says. 'Months of stealing money, little by little, hiding my tracks every step of the way. Do you have any idea how difficult it is to co-ordinate a new life when you have no contact with the outside world? And if you think he won't make it harder a second time, *you're* underestimating *him*.'

'So you're resting your chances of survival on the idea that some second-rate freelancer can find an antidote to a Parnassiinae poison?' He shakes his head. 'We don't even have his notes. I went back to his lab and Comma had gutted the place. Hard drives, notebooks, everything – they took it all.'

Isabel frowns. 'What?'

'I said Comma cleared out his lab,' Michael repeats. 'They took half the lab techs for questioning; the others have gone underground. I guess he took them with him.'

'You went back there?'

'I thought I might find something I could sell.'

The idea of going back to her father's lab is bad enough; the thought of stealing something – even something he'd left behind – has her gut clenching in fear, waiting for the inevitable punishment. Sure, she siphoned money from her parents' bank account for months before she ran away, but that's different.

'Comma took his notes . . .' she says slowly. 'You think he'd have written anything about the poison?'

Now it's Michael's turn to frown. 'Probably? I mean, I assume he took anything useful with him, though he would have had duplicates. But they'll be deep in the bowels of Comma by now. We'd never find them, unless you plan to ask them for help.'

'I don't need to,' she says, getting to her feet. 'Because they asked me.'

Michael watches, perplexed, as Isabel crosses the room to her wardrobe and unearths the thick file of printouts that Ronan left with her. She drops it in the middle of the table, and their cards scatter in flurries.

'What's this?' he asks.

'Ian's notes. Apparently his codes are causing Comma all sorts of trouble. Ronan Atwood thought I might be able to advise.'

'*Ronan Atwood* gave those to you?' He takes a handful of pages from the top of the pile and looks them over. 'I mean, I can see why they're not making much headway, but . . . you made a bargain with Ronan Atwood?'

'Of course I didn't,' says Isabel. 'What do you take me for?'

'Somebody trying to survive,' says Michael pragmatically, putting the papers back on the stack. 'But this shit's indecipherable. I'm pretty sure it's a write-only code.'

'I don't think so.' She wondered that at first – of course she did. But these are her father's own records, material he might want to come back to, and that means he'll have ensured he can decode it again. And if *he* can break it, then so can Isabel. Eventually.

It's been a while since she last tackled something like this, but she's fairly sure she remembers the principles. It'll be her memories of her father she has to work harder to get back.

Speaking of memories ... 'When you said he drugged me to forget,' she says, trying to sound unbothered, 'forget what?' She knew there were gaps in her recollections, but she'd half figured that was her brain's way of protecting her, not another piece of violence inflicted upon her. 'That he poisoned me, or was there more?'

Michael shrugs. 'Maybe it was habit.'

'"Habit"? You mean he did it before?'

His hesitation tells her everything. 'I thought you knew,' he says.

Isabel feels ill. 'Evidently not, if I was being drugged to forget it.' *Habit.* 'How long?'

'I don't know. Not long after I met you, I guess, but it's hard to be sure.'

Five years, then.

If even Michael could tell she was missing time, why hadn't *she* known? Why hadn't she noticed? She has plenty of bad memories of the lab, so what is it that her father took from her – more of the same? Or something worse?

'Why?'

'I don't know.'

'Why not?' she demands, suddenly pissed off. 'You come

here pretending you have all the answers, but you're guessing, aren't you? You don't know any more than I do.'

He quails under the force of her glare. 'I know he poisoned you,' he says, in a hoarse voice, 'because he made me hold you down.'

Of course he fucking did. As if this couldn't get any worse. 'He what?'

'He said it was only temporary, that it wouldn't hurt you and you wouldn't remember. That's how I knew—'

'Wouldn't *hurt* me?'

'Your mother objected. They'd been arguing, and she stormed out – that's why Ian used me instead. I think he'd have kept me out of it otherwise. He certainly didn't tell me what was going on.'

His words echo her nightmares: hands around her wrists, pinning her down; hot breath on her face; a sharp pain in her side that went on and on and on. Whatever memory suppressant he used, it hasn't entirely robbed her of the truth.

Isabel slumps back in her chair, letting her anger diffuse. 'Fuck,' she says, with feeling.

'There was nothing I could have done.' Michael sounds almost timid. 'I wanted to find you sooner, to warn you, but it's taken this long to track you down.'

She doesn't blame him. She knows how impossible it is to refuse her father's orders. But while Michael's a welcome ally – she's been desperate for somebody she can be honest with – she wishes he'd brought actionable intel with him. Something she can use to save herself.

Instead, all she's got is a pile of encrypted files she can't read and the name of a freelance poisoner.

And herself. The one thing she's always had.

'Okay,' she says. 'So it's up to me.'

'Isabel . . .'

'You're right,' she says. 'I got out once. So I'm not waiting around for somebody else to save me – and *no fucking way* am I begging my father. Which means it's up to me.'

Michael looks at her stubborn jaw, the steel in her gaze. 'Not on your own,' he says, folding his arms and sitting back in his chair like he's settling in. 'I'm not leaving until we fix this.'

She's grateful for the solidarity, but she also remembers that Michael was hopeless at codebreaking. And, if she's honest, she's not sure she wants an audience while she does this. Not when she doesn't know what she might find in those papers.

She tells him as much, expecting him to argue and bracing herself to make a fight of it, but all he says is, 'All right. You've got a phone?' He holds out his hand for it, adding his number to her contacts and handing it back. 'If it gets too much, if you need someone, or if you want to play blackjack at three in the morning, call me.' He pulls on his battered trainers, grabs his rucksack and heads for the door. Then he turns back. 'Oh, and seriously, get new locks. These took me about three seconds to pick.'

'Thanks,' she says, before adding with a hint of a smile, 'Say hi to your roommates from me.'

'I absolutely will not,' he says, and grins like they're friends.

And then he's gone, and Isabel's alone in her flat with the fact that she's dying.

It seeps back gradually, now that there's nothing to distract her from it – the pain, the fear . . . the rage. It takes her a while to recognise the latter, but that's what it is. *Fury.* Because she deserves better than this. She deserves a *life*, and instead her body's falling apart from the inside, just when she was finally learning to live on her own terms.

Is Michael right? Is it possible she could negotiate with her father? Does she want to live badly enough to put herself back in his power? If she survives, Ian Ryans would never let her walk away. He'd rather see her dead than free.

It's late; she should eat something, get some rest. But she has no appetite, and she can't ignore the sense of possibility and dread that seeps from the pile of documents on the kitchen table. Knowing her luck, they're nothing but a record of all the worst moments of her life. But maybe, if the universe is kind, these notes can save her . . .

She takes the top sheet from the stack and sits staring at it for a long moment.

Ian Ryans' codes aren't that complicated. Not on an encryption level. If anything, they're less secure than the codes Comma uses for internal comms, which are designed to be used once only and are nearly unbreakable as long as that rule is kept. Her father prefers codes based on memorised phrases, which means decoding one can often provide the key to another. That weakness is exactly why they were phased out under guild policy, but Ian has never given a shit about their policy.

Now, of course, Isabel's beginning to see why he might not have wanted Comma reading his files.

Insecure code or not, his notes are a nightmare to decrypt, largely because they're all written in a minimum of three languages and two alphabets. He'll use Esperanto transliterated into Cyrillic characters, or render Russian into the Latin alphabet, and jumble both up with German, English, French ... It makes identifying the key phrases virtually impossible, and even if you manage that, the resulting text is incomprehensible without strong language skills, which few Esperans have. It used to drive Isabel to tears when he 'forgot' to decode the recipes he gave her to work from, guaranteeing hours of slow, frustrating work before she could embark on a task.

No doubt that was the idea. But the result is that Isabel has a knowledge of his coding style that she doubts anyone else in the guild can match, a solid basis in every language he spoke, and a dogged determination that would make Comma's most dedicated codebreakers look like shirkers.

Thanks, Dad, thinks Isabel grimly, and tears a sheet of squared paper from her maths book to start drawing up the charts that will help her break this.

The night is surrendering to the early hours before she identifies one of his code phrases, but once she has that, the first few pages unravel easily. She decodes fragments from each page, searching for anything that will tell her whether these are the notes she needs before she bothers to solve the rest. But none of them offers her formulae and explanations. Instead:

At home in the lab ... quite the little scientist ... perhaps combat isn't her strength ... no memory of the experiment ... doesn't suspect anything.

This report is about her.

Isabel tastes bile and swallows hard. Whoever printed the files – Comma, presumably – included the dates and filenames in plain text in the top margin, but she doesn't have to try to match the dates to know this is one of the occasions she doesn't recall. Ian must have drugged her over and over again. Maybe it made it easier for him if she didn't remember her pain. She wouldn't know to be afraid of the lab, or what he might do to her there.

Her heart breaks for her younger self – a girl who didn't know, who couldn't have saved herself even if she did. Someone should have got her out. Someone should have seen it, and got her out.

The next page is more of the same:

She was very weak by the time we gave her the antidote; the dose may have been too high. I always forget she's small for her age.

Twelve.

She used to like working in the lab. It was a chance to escape the training room, learn something new. She doesn't remember when it became as painful as the rest of her training, or when she became aware that he was testing on her, but these notes suggest it's earlier than she ever knew.

145

How long did she spend doubting herself? Her mother encouraged it, told her stories that clung to her memories and warped them until she hardly knew what was real. Part of her brain still says her parents never wanted to hurt her, that the punishments were because she needed to learn, that she was responsible for her own pain.

These files tell her it was real. Concrete, objective evidence that they hurt her. Maybe somewhere in this pile there's a record of the day her father pressed her hand in acid. Will there be a description of the way she screamed, or just a cursory note?

She'd still been recovering from her stomach wound and the subsequent surgery. She wasn't fit enough for physical training, so she spent her time in the lab, but the medication gave her hand tremors, and the acid spilled, and her father—

And she realised she could spend her entire life doing exactly what he wanted, and it would never keep her safe.

She wonders if he knows that that's the day she started planning her escape.

On the next page, his code phrase has changed. She starts again with the laborious process of searching for patterns, for clues, for anything recognisable as a word that might be the string that, once pulled, will unravel the rest. It's dawn by the time it resolves into words – a list this time, straightforward enough, if that's an appropriate term for an account of the various substances with which he poisoned her and how she reacted. Some he tested on himself and some he tested on both of them, comparing how their age and physical make-up affected the symptoms.

Some of them she remembers. Others are holes the shape of a memory, slowly filled in by his words. She's buried them deep, but bones come to light eventually.

Isabel keeps reading, until this code phrase, too, has no further secrets to offer. The words and formulae amalgamate in her head, and she grabs a pen and a scrap of paper, scribbling whatever she remembers. Some of it's gibberish, and some of it resembles the formulae in her father's notes. Her handwriting becomes erratic, the letters tangled and overlapping, but she can't stop, can't slow down, can't let these memories slip away, even though her heart's pounding hard enough to crack a rib, because what if one of them is the answer? She can save herself, can get this out, can fix the bloody destruction her father has wrought in her body. She just has to remember – has to make it make sense – has to break through the fog clouding her mind and remember remember remember remember . . .

She pushes the papers away and breathes. Five things she can see: nib on the pen, lines on the page, grain of the table, ink on her finger, ripped corner of her maths book. No. She squeezes her eyes tightly closed and then opens them again, trying to shake her tunnelling vision. Five things: her school bag, the empty chair opposite, the clock on the oven, yesterday's washing-up, the morning light coming through the window. Better. Five things she can hear: her ragged breath, the dripping tap, the humming fridge, the bell of a passing tram, footsteps in the flat upstairs.

She's in her flat. Just her flat. Alone. As safe as she'll ever be. Calmer now, she goes back through the pages she's decoded, looking for dates and detail. It's clear that none of these mentions the poison in her body, only other, older cruelties, long since sold to world governments or used by the guild. It's not that she expected it to be that easy, but she still feels a moment of shattering defeat when she sees how many pages of code remain unbroken. The answer could be in any or none of them.

Maybe this time, her father has actually managed to kill her.

15

VERECO (TRUTH)

The weekend passes in a mess of naps and codes and pain, time blurring until it's as incomprehensible as the jumble of letters Isabel's slowly untangling. The thought of Toni Rolleston and the awful look on Emma's face is replaced by single-minded focus on the problem at hand, but it gets her nowhere: none of the pages she's able to make sense of tells her anything that might save her.

So on Monday, Isabel races through her paper round and goes in search of Grace Whittock before school starts. She doesn't want to: asking a freelancer for help is risky at the best of times, and asking a freelancer *who works in her school* is a clear sign of her desperation. But the pain's getting worse every day, and she needs all the help she can get.

She's almost at the library when the door opens, and she finds herself face to face with Emma.

The other girl won't meet her eyes, and seems content to let the encounter pass without remark. Isabel grabs her arm, forcing her to stop. 'Emma—'

Emma wrenches her arm free. 'I don't want to talk to you.'

'I wanted to check you were okay.' Pathetic. Truth be told, she's been so preoccupied that she hadn't even thought about what she'd say if she ran into Emma.

'Why would you care?' asks Emma. 'You've been lying to me since we met.'

And Isabel really can't argue with that. 'How much ...'

'How much did I hear? Enough to know that you're Comma.' Emma's tone is low but vicious. Isabel glances around; there's nobody nearby, but that doesn't mean a school corridor is a safe place for this conversation. 'I made Mum fill in the gaps afterwards.'

'I left, Emma,' says Isabel. 'I'm not ... I don't ...'

'Doesn't change the fact that you've killed people, though, does it?' Emma pushes past her. 'So unless you want the whole school to know you're a murderer, I'd think twice about talking to me again, *Bella*.'

And she's gone. Isabel stares after her bleakly, the threat meaningless compared to the heaviness that settled on her chest when she saw the disgust on Emma's face.

When she finally makes it inside the library, Grace is at her desk, repairing a battered paperback. Isabel glances around to check they're alone, then says, 'I need your help.'

'Sure, what is it?'

'I need an antidote.'

Grace puts down the glue. 'Ah,' she says. 'Who told you?'

'Daragh Vernant.'

The door opens and a student wanders past, nodding at Grace before heading towards the shelves. 'Let's go into my office,' says the librarian, and leads the way.

Inside, with the door firmly closed, Isabel hesitates. How much should she say? How much *can* she say? But there's no time to worry about whether she can trust Grace – to be helped, she has to be known, no matter the risk.

'We haven't identified the poison, but we know it's bad.' She finds herself speaking quickly, before she loses her nerve. 'It was inserted intramuscularly, coated with something that delayed its effects. Daragh's removed it, but without the antidote the damage will continue. I don't have the formula, but I do have the pellet itself and printouts of my blood test results, if that helps.'

Isabel waits. Grace blinks a few times. 'Bella,' she says. 'This is . . .'

'If it's too complex, I understand.'

'Complexity isn't the issue here.' The librarian takes off her glasses and cleans them on her jumper. 'I'm sorry, I'm just . . . You've been poisoned? Are you sure?'

Her surprise is understandable, but they don't have time for this. 'I wouldn't be here if I wasn't.'

'I . . . right, of course.' Grace puts her glasses back on. 'Do you know who by?'

She's probably only expecting a guild name, but, instead, Isabel throws her a test: 'Daragh thinks it's Parnassiinae work. Does that mean anything to you?'

It's clear from Grace's wide eyes that it does. 'Every poisoner worth a damn knows the Parnassiinae lab,' she says. 'Their poisons are ...'

'Legendary?'

'I was going to say *horrifying*. Why would Comma be coming after you with this?'

The fact Grace is clued up on the big players suggests that she isn't completely useless as a freelancer, so Isabel gives her another nugget of information. 'I don't think it's Comma. I think it's personal.' Then she adds, 'Parnassiinae is my father's lab.'

The librarian takes a moment to absorb this. 'Your name's not Bella Nicholls, is it?' she asks, after a pause.

It's a relief to let go of the lies. 'No. I'm Isabel Ryans.'

She nods. 'It's nice to meet you, Isabel. You said you had test results?'

Isabel passes them over. 'Daragh's included his analysis at the end, and I've added the compounds I've managed to identify. This,' she continues, pointing to a highlighted section, 'looks like traces of a memory inhibitor. I have it on reliable authority that my father drugged me, and this is as close as I've got to identifying what he might have used.'

Grace looks from Isabel to the paper and back again. 'You're probably right,' she says faintly. She's clearly finding it hard to reconcile her idea of Isabel with the girl standing in front of her, but she flips back and forth through the rest of the pages, occasionally pulling a face. At last she says, 'This is the work of a sadist.'

'You'd be right there.'

'I'll be honest, I don't know how much I can do for you. The memory inhibitor I can counteract, but depending how long it's been in your system, the antidote may not have much effect. As for the rest . . . a poison this complex is way beyond me. I'm not sure it even technically qualifies as a poison – it's not so much doing damage as tricking your body into damaging itself.'

'So you can't fix it?'

'There isn't a freelancer in this city who could counteract this kind of biological weapon.' Grace drops the test results onto the desk. 'I want to help you, but Parnassiinae work . . . it's in a league of its own. If you really think this isn't a Comma hit, you're best off throwing yourself at the mercy of the guild. Nobody else has the skills and knowledge to undo this kind of violence to your system.'

'What about somebody they trained?'

'Well, perhaps. But where we might find . . .' Grace looks up slowly and meets Isabel's eyes. 'Oh. But you—'

'I spent years working in my father's lab. He wanted me to follow in his footsteps.' How much of it she can remember is a different matter; she's still trying to get to grips with what he stole from her. 'And I have a solid theoretical background too.'

'I heard rumours that Comma were training kids,' says Grace cautiously. 'I didn't believe they were true.'

Isabel shrugs. 'They've stopped now.' It's funny how her near-death experience scared them into shutting the programme down, when they'd known all along that it was putting children at risk. 'Look, if I could do this alone, I would never have asked you, but I can't. With your skills and my knowledge, maybe there's a chance.'

'Bella,' begins Grace, then corrects herself: 'Isabel. I don't want to give you false hope. This is *way* above my pay grade. I don't know if I can do anything for you.'

'But you'll try?'

The librarian regards her for a moment, then sighs. 'I'll try. That's as much as I can promise.'

'Thank you. That's all I'm asking for.'

Grace looks at the pages again, at Daragh and Isabel's handwriting in the margins. 'You worked in your father's lab,' she says thoughtfully. 'What did that entail?'

'Well, a lot of the time he was experimenting on me,' says Isabel. She momentarily regrets her blithe tone when she sees the horror on the librarian's face. Right, because that's fucked up and *not* something she's supposed to throw around casually. She remembers Mortimer calling her 'obviously traumatised' and wonders whether it's always been obvious to everyone except herself – whether she should have pieced together sooner that what was happening to her wasn't right. 'I mean . . .'

'Did you ever help *make* the poisons?' asks Grace, interrupting her before she has to figure out how to mitigate the awfulness of this revelation.

Isabel pauses before answering. 'Yeah, sometimes. Older inventions, simpler things. Nothing recent that I remember, but that doesn't necessarily mean anything.'

'Right.' Grace taps her pen against the formula in the margin. 'This memory suppressant ... it's already broken down a lot, but the fact that there are still traces of it in your system means counteracting it might recover some memories. Do you think that would include anything about this poison?'

'What, like I'll magically remember the formula? I doubt it.' More likely all it'll give her is the memory of her father poisoning her in the first place, if that. It's been a month since she left – the damage is probably already done.

'I agree – it's a long shot,' the librarian admits. 'But it's our best chance. Isabel, I specialise in non-lethals – stuff people use to spike their co-workers' food so they spend two days in the bathroom, that kind of thing. It's not classy, but the way I see it, diarrhoea's a more fitting revenge than the death the guilds would deal. It saves a few lives every year, and it pays the bills, so it's what I do. Not poison like this.'

Her meaning's clear: however much she wants to help, all she can offer is a stay of execution. If Isabel wants to live, she needs to go to the guild.

She can't. She won't. Maybe Grace is right, and the formula's hiding in her own brain. Maybe Michael's telling the truth, and only her father knows it. Either way, there has to be a solution that doesn't involve going to Ronan Atwood and paying whatever price he asks.

'One thing at a time,' Isabel says, a little unsteadily. 'We tackle the memory suppressant first. The rest comes later.'

Grace nods. 'Okay. I'll try to have it for you tomorrow.'

It's the illusion of control, at least, the tempting placebo effect of feeling like she's taking action. She leaves the printouts with Grace and heads to class, trying to push it all from her mind, which is easier said than done when she's fatigued and in pain.

It doesn't help that she has Woodwork today. Ever since she overheard Mortimer's argument with Grace, she's been bracing herself for confrontation, but he was mysteriously absent from last Wednesday's class. She doubts he'll be off again, and she's tempted to hide in the nurse's office until the end of the period.

She doesn't. Sure enough, Mortimer's back, although she's spared his safety exam because he wants the whole class to watch today's demo. Isabel lurks at the back and manages to avoid eye contact until the last five minutes of the lesson, when he asks her to fetch some printouts from Reprographics for him.

It's on the other side of the building and the lesson will be over by the time she gets back, but she doesn't have a good reason to refuse. Distrust prickles in her belly, but she leaves her bag under the workbench and sets off.

Sure enough, when she returns, the classroom's empty. Even Mortimer seems to have disappeared. She stacks the pile of worksheets on his desk and goes to collect her bag, turning her back on the empty room as she crouches to retrieve it.

A hand touches her elbow. She whips round, fingers closing on the wrist and *twisting*, prompting a grunt of pain. Too late she recognises the green plaid shirt that Mortimer was wearing earlier. She lets him go and backs away, but the workbench is behind her and she can't go any further, and he's blocking her path to the door.

Hesitantly, Isabel looks up.

Mortimer is massaging his wrist, expression pained. He raises his eyebrow. 'Well, I guess that answers one question,' he says. 'Ekde kiam ili trejnis vin?'

How long have they been training you?

Isabel freezes. Esperanto. Guild tongue. But how can *Mortimer* be guild? Does Comma have spies at the Fraser now, keeping an eye on her? Or is he Hummingbird, perhaps, undercover here to spot talented students they might want to recruit?

Talented at . . . Woodwork, though? Something doesn't add up.

'I don't understand,' she says carefully in English, sidling along the workbench in the hope of extricating herself from her corner. 'I'm sorry, I don't speak Esperanto.'

'Ĉu ne?' *Don't you?* He's still wincing and rubbing his wrist, but there's no malice in his expression. Still, there's a knowingness that worries her. In English, he adds, 'Most people wouldn't have reacted like that.'

'I'm . . .' There's no good excuse for how she behaved. 'I'm sorry. I didn't meant to hurt you.'

'I think you did,' he says wryly. 'At least, you meant to hurt someone. Whether it was me is another matter. And, for what

157

it's worth, I'm sorry for startling you. I thought . . .' He shrugs. 'It doesn't matter what I thought. I guess I got my answer.'

'So you were testing me,' says Isabel warily. 'Trying to see how I'd react.'

'Yeah, funnily enough, nearly breaking my wrist wasn't actually one of the options I'd considered. In hindsight, that was short-sighted.' He forces a smile that does absolutely nothing to reassure her. 'So I'm guessing it's Comma, right? Unless you were lying about living in Fordon.'

He waits.

Reluctantly, she drops the pretence of ignorance. 'You first,' she says. 'Hummingbird?'

Mortimer shakes his head. 'Fuck, no, I'm not guild. They don't have a lot of use for carpenters, and I've less use for them.'

'But you speak Esperanto.'

'I thought it might come in handy. *Know thine enemy*, as they say.' He runs his hands through his hair. 'I figured your family were top six and I got the impression you were running from something – probably Comma's attempts to recruit you. I didn't realise you were trained. Guess I underestimated you.'

By 'top six', Isabel knows he means the six departments that form Comma's central core, as opposed to adjacents, who form the seventh and largest category. For a civilian and a carpenter, Mortimer seems far too clued up about the inner workings of the guild.

'You and everyone else,' says Isabel, edging a little further along the bench. At the far end, there's a chisel. Maybe if she can

158

grab that, she can ... what? Stab him in the neck? Murdering people has so far not proven the best way to deal with problems.

'So how far did you get?' he asks. At her blank look, he clarifies: 'With training. That's why you ran away, isn't it?'

It hits her then that he doesn't know about Cocoon. He knows too much, but that particular secret is safe. He thinks she's a recent recruit, drafted in from the fast track at whichever spon she attended – enough information to screw her over, but not enough to do the same to the guild.

'Far enough to know it wasn't what I wanted,' she says evasively, and glances towards the door. She doesn't really want to hurt Mortimer, but if he tries to stop her ... 'Are you going to hand me back to them?'

'To Comma?' He seems surprised that she'd even ask. 'Why would I do that?'

Isabel shrugs. 'People do a lot of things for a lot of reasons. They'd probably pay you. At the very least they'd owe you a favour.'

'I don't need guild favours,' says Mortimer, tone hard.

'Then why are you testing me?' she asks. 'Why are you so bothered that I switched schools? I was at Linnaeus, by the way,' she adds. 'Since I know you've been poking around. Congrats – you caught me.'

Understanding dawns on his face. 'You heard me talking to Grace.'

'She was right when she said it isn't your business.'

Mortimer steps back as if he's only just realised that he's got her cornered. 'I was worried about you.'

Obviously traumatised. 'I'm fine,' she tells him. 'I got out.'

Even Mortimer looks unconvinced by that, and he doesn't know she's dying. 'Bella, I—'

'I'm fine,' she says again, more firmly. 'Except that you've made me late for Maths. I have to go or Miss Carey will have my head.'

He lets her go.

Only when she's outside the classroom, catching her breath with the closed door behind her, does Isabel realise that, despite her fear, she never truly believed he wouldn't.

16

KULPO (GUILT)

The following afternoon, after another restless, painful night and a dismal school day that seems to last several years, Isabel heads to the library. Acid fear scratches her throat at the thought of what getting rid of the memory suppressant might reveal. Nothing she's decoded in her father's notes so far has been anything she wanted to know about her past, but she can't back out now.

Grace is sitting at her desk, her head in her hands.

'Is now a bad time?' asks Isabel.

The librarian looks up blearily. 'What? Oh. No. Come in.' With the door safely closed, Grace adds, 'You didn't tell me that Emma's mother is Comma.'

'I didn't think it was relevant,' says Isabel honestly. 'How did you find out?'

'Emma told me, while having a breakdown in my office at lunchtime. She didn't out you, by the way – she's angry, but she kept your name out of it. If that means anything.' It does, more than Isabel will admit. 'Is there anything else you didn't think was relevant that I should know before we go further with this?'

The words slip out. 'I killed Ian Crampton.'

She's expecting shock, or at least surprise, but Grace only nods. 'I figured as much.' Then she spins her chair towards the mini-fridge in the corner and says, 'So, this antidote. Are you ready?'

'I ... yes, but ...'

'If you're having second thoughts, I don't blame you. You don't have to do this.'

'It's not that.' What's the etiquette for things like this? It feels rude, however she phrases it. 'It's ... how much will it cost? I don't have a lot of money.'

The librarian drums her fingers on the arms of her chair. 'I hadn't thought about that,' she admits. 'How about we put it on your tab and figure it out later?'

'Look, if you're doing this out of pity ...'

'It's not pity, Isabel,' says Grace, sounding faintly exasperated. 'I said, we'll figure it out later. Right now, you're seventeen, with no income, and you're dying. Seems to me that tackling the "dying" part is our first priority. The money can wait.'

Isabel would be relieved, if she had the strength to feel anything except tired and in pain. 'One more thing,' she says. 'Mortimer Sark.'

'What about him?'

'I heard you talking, before. I heard what he said about me. He might have figured out that I'm guild.'

'Ah.' The librarian looks rueful. 'At the time, I thought his paranoia had got the better of him. I've been rapidly reconsidering that position. So when you say, "might have figured out" . . . ?'

'He doesn't know I've been poisoned, or that I was trained as a child, but he knows enough to get me kicked out of the Fraser. Even the fact that I lied on my school record would do that.' And starting over was hard enough the first time, when she had the money and resources to create her new identity. She's not sure she can do it again. Which means if Mortimer screws her over, she either has to say goodbye to education entirely, or go back to Comma and Linnaeus. She might as well have taken Ronan's deal.

'Want me to poison him?' asks Grace.

Isabel looks up, shocked. 'No!' she says instantly. 'No, of course not. Would you really – wait.' The librarian's mouth is twitching. 'That was a joke.'

'Mostly,' Grace agrees. 'Despite his many flaws, I consider Mortimer a friend, and I'd rather not poison him. But if you'd asked, I'd have considered it. Something nasty, but non-lethal.'

And there Isabel was, thinking Grace wouldn't be the one to protect her. 'I appreciate the offer,' she says, with genuine feeling, 'but please don't poison Mortimer.'

'Message received. Does he know about Ian Crampton?'

'Nothing concrete, and he can't prove anything, but . . . I can't get kicked out, Grace.' It seems odd to be worrying about her educational future when she's at risk of not having any future at all, but if she doesn't at least *pretend* she'll live through this, she won't be able to keep going. 'Do you think he'll turn me in?'

Grace considers this. 'No,' she says finally. 'Mortimer's a busybody, and too observant for his own good, but he wouldn't do anything he thought might hurt you. And since he thinks you're running from the guild, he's not going to make any sudden moves unless he's sure it's the right thing to do. You don't need to be afraid of him.'

Isabel nods. Grace's reassurances don't mean Mortimer wouldn't accidentally land her in hot water, but it's a relief to be able to downgrade her assessment of the threat he poses.

'Okay,' she says. 'So, this antidote . . .'

'It will take a couple of hours to kick in,' says Grace, retrieving the syringe from the mini-fridge. 'And it's probably not going to be a whole lot of fun. You'd best go straight home afterwards.'

That probably means vomiting. Isabel's becoming far too familiar with the rim of her toilet bowl at this point.

'You're sure you got it right?' she asks, eyeing the clear fluid.

'I'm good at my job. *Both* of my jobs. Are *you* sure you want to go through with this?'

There's still time to back out. Until that needle breaks her skin, she can walk away and keep the shallow peace that comes from forgetting.

'I'm sure,' says Isabel.

It doesn't hurt. Hardly even registers, compared to

everything else her body's going through. Grace sticks a small plaster over the tiny drop of blood that wells up, and offers Isabel some water. Then she says, 'I could speak to Emma for you, if you want. Maybe she'd listen to me.'

'And say what?' asks Isabel.

Grace Whittock opens her mouth, and then closes it again.

'I'm seventeen and I've killed four people, Grace.' It's the first time she's ever put it in such bald terms. 'I'm not exactly prime friend material.' There's no way to fix this, to make it palatable or convince Emma that Isabel's a good person deep down. They both know it's not true, and Isabel's sick of lies.

'She might listen to me,' says the librarian again, unconvincingly.

Isabel swings her rucksack onto her back. 'You've done enough,' she says. 'The rest of this is on me.'

'Stulta putino.' Her father's voice. 'Faru ĝin denove.'

'I can't.' Shaking hands. A holdall hidden in her wardrobe, half packed. A secret phone under the mattress. A moment of defiance–despair–destruction: 'I can't.'

'I told you to do it again. Where are your notes?'

'Here, but—'

'Kia malbela fekero. What is this? Are you even trying?'

'I can't do it.'

His voice is too quiet, a heavy cloud weighing down the sky before the lightning strikes. 'Why not?'

'It's too complicated. I've never done anything like this before. Please, I'm so tired. It's been hours. I just—'

165

'You'll stop when it's done.' He looms over her. She doesn't dare back away, her knuckles white on the edge of the workbench. 'This isn't too hard for you, noktopapilio.'

'It is. Please.'

His sigh is full of disappointment. 'Will you tell your mother that, then?'

Fingers so tight on the workbench they ache. 'No, please, I tried. You've got to tell her I tried. I'm doing my best.'

'I've got to?' A mistake. She's made a mistake. She braces herself, muscles like cheese wire, taut and deadly. 'Is this your best, Issy? Because it seems to me like you're not trying.'

'I am! Please, I've been here for hours and I can't—' A sharp pain in her cheek. She stumbles back from the slap, tasting blood.

And then his hands are there, soft, wiping away the blood, cradling her face. 'Issy, Issy, Issy,' he says. 'I know you don't want to make me unhappy. Perhaps I pushed you too hard – is that it? It's been a while, hasn't it? Maybe we should refresh your memory of what these ingredients do. I'm not surprised you forgot.'

Pulling free of him will only make it worse. Her eyes fill with tears she's not allowed to cry. 'No, I remember, I remember! Please don't—'

'Well, then, if you remember . . .' He lets go of her face. 'I'm a busy man, Issy. I have business to attend to. When I get back, I want this done. Understand?' She nods. 'There we are, little Moth. I knew you had it in you.'

He has his keys in his hand as he walks to the door. He's

166

going to lock her in, leave her here to starve until she can make sense of this vicious formula, this nightmare poison he's dreamed up. It can't be done, she knows that – it's a madman's weapon, inhuman and impossible – but he swears it can be made, that she can make it.

She has no choice. She hears his key turn in the lock and allows herself a sob, a breath, a truncated breakdown, and then she reaches for the sheet with the formula written on it, his handwriting black and spidery against the white page. She—

—wakes up.

Isabel stares at the ceiling above her bed, her breathing shallow and painful. She remembers. She *remembers*. It wasn't her father who made this poison.

She did this. She made this awful cruelty, and now it's unmaking her.

For the first time in her life, she's sorry to have woken from a nightmare. A few more moments and she'd have had the formula and a chance of a cure, but now she's no better off than before, and she has to live with the knowledge that it was her hands which transformed this torture from hypothesis to death sentence.

It's some forsaken hour of the morning without a glimmer of light from outside, but she's too keyed up to go back to sleep. She sets the kettle boiling for a cup of mint tea to settle her stomach, her gaze drifting towards the files still waiting to be decoded. Is the answer in there? Would she know it if she saw it? Or is this memory good for nothing but taunting her?

167

She takes out her phone instead. The clock reads 04:23, and she has three unread messages. The first two are from Nick.

> Hope you're okay, haven't seen you around much.

Then, later:

> If you're still up for trying that club, I've got the details from Rob. Let me know. No pressure.

She hasn't even told him she's sick. She wouldn't know where to start.

The other message, to her surprise, is from Emma.

> Why are you talking to Grace? Don't lie to me.

It was sent several hours ago, so Emma's probably asleep. That gives her time to figure out a reply. There are a dozen innocent reasons Isabel might be talking to the librarian, but she knows what Emma's really asking: *Is Grace guild too?* And Isabel's not about to insult Emma by pretending she can't read between the lines.

But Grace's secrets aren't hers to spill, which means she has to think carefully about what to say. She's about to put the phone back in the pocket of her school bag when it buzzes with an incoming call.

Michael.

'I could have been sleeping,' she says, answering it.

'You could have been,' he agrees. 'But I figured if you were, you wouldn't answer.' His voice is low and hoarse, like he's hardly awake himself. 'I'm glad you picked up.'

'Has something happened?'

'Nightmare,' he says. 'I'm sorry, I shouldn't have bothered you.'

'It's okay.' It makes her feel better to know she's not the only one having a shitty night. 'I had one too.'

He chuckles softly. 'What a pair we make. So well adjusted.'

'Cocoon's greatest assets,' she agrees, swapping the phone to her other ear. She can hear traffic and a distant car alarm in the background. 'Where are you?'

'Sitting on the fire escape of the hostel,' he says. 'Didn't want to wake the roommates. Though, frankly, Gregory is snoring like a rowing machine, so he would deserve it.'

'A rowing machine?' says Isabel, startled into amusement.

'Yeah, you know, a dragging sound in, and then *whoosh* – he lets it all go. I've never known a man with such congested nostrils.'

'Poor Gregory.'

'Poor *Gregory*?' echoes Michael. 'Poor me, more like. I am *so* close to smothering him in his sleep.'

'I wouldn't advise it,' says Isabel. 'It turns out that murdering people is generally frowned upon.'

'No, really?' he says. 'You astonish me. So, do you want to go first, or shall I?'

'What do you mean?'

'Nightmares. I'll tell you mine if you tell me yours.'

Did you know I made the poison? she wants to ask, but he'd have told her if he knew, wouldn't he? 'The usual,' she says, picking up a pen and spinning it between her fingers. 'My father. The lab.'

'Right.'

'What about you?'

He exhales static, crackling down the line. 'Also the usual. The job. You bleeding to death in front of me. Except this time your parents don't take me in, and Comma just has me murdered.'

'Oh.' He referenced that before, the way they'd debated his fate. She didn't know execution had been on the cards, but the guild has never liked loose ends. No wonder he came to her and not Comma. 'So when you're not calling me in the middle of the night, how do you usually deal with nightmares?'

He laughs. 'Drink until I fall asleep again,' he says. 'I wouldn't recommend it. I've heard good things about therapy.'

'Yeah?'

'Maybe we should try it.'

'Maybe.' She glances at the clock. 'I should go. Might still manage a power nap before my paper round.'

'All right, I won't keep you.' There's a pause, and she thinks he's hung up, until he adds, 'Thanks for picking up. I needed that.'

Isabel smiles, though he can't see her. 'Goodnight, Michael,' she says. 'Don't murder Gregory.'

'I'll do my best,' he assures her, and hangs up.

It never would have occurred to her to call him. But she needed it too, this small moment of connection – a reminder that there are other people in the world who know what happened to her, and that it was real, no matter how untrustworthy her memories are.

She can't trust much these days, not even the inside of her own head, but at least she's not alone with the doubts and the nightmares. It's a small consolation, but it's all she's got.

17

BATALHALTO (TRUCE)

'Good!' says Ashvin. 'You're early. I was hoping you would be. Alfie called me at five this morning to say that he's ill. Five! What am I meant to do with that? Here – you can take these too, can't you? It's only a short route. The details are in the bag.'

Isabel takes the bag automatically. It's a lot lighter than her own. 'But—' she begins.

Ashvin cuts her off. 'You're reliable. I've heard no complaints. I trust you with this.'

She's about to tell him that she hardly has the energy for her usual route, let alone a detour, but then she glances at the contents of the bag. It's not the *Echo* – that much she could have guessed. But she wasn't expecting the dense grey typescript and heavily recycled paper of the *Weekly Bulletin of the Free Press*.

She looks at Ashvin. She didn't think he was the type. He sees the question in her face and says, 'News is news. Business is business. You'll take it?'

I trust you, he said, and clearly that's true, because it's not only his neck on the line – it's everyone's whose address is on the list as a subscriber. Reading the *Bulletin* isn't enough to make them a target by itself, but it's enough to make the guilds start keeping tabs, looking for evidence of abolitionist activity, and if they find it . . .

And Ashvin's handed her that information like it's no big deal.

'I'll take it,' she says, looping the bag's handles over her shoulder. 'No problem.'

She's tempted, once she's out of Ashvin's sight, to read the paper herself. She's never been this close to a Free Press publication before, and she's curious to know how much of it is ideology and how much is intel, passing round information that ordinary civilians shouldn't have. But if she stops now, she'll be late for school, and proving to Ashvin that he was right to trust her might pay off in the long run.

It's a drab morning, the autumnal air too chilly for a jumper but slightly too warm to justify a coat. Clouds hang indecisively over the crowded rooftops of Lutton, threatening rain, and the dismal grey light washes the colour out of the paintwork. Isabel falls into her usual rhythm: fold the paper, post it through the letterbox, be extra quick at the house with the big dog, pet the grey cat that sits on the postbox at the end of the street. She's a little slower than usual and has to stop to rest a few times, but at least her early start makes up for that.

Alfie's route overlaps with the last few streets of hers, so when she's down to a handful of copies of the *Echo*, she takes out his list, triple-checking every address before she posts the papers through the doors. Screwing up with the *Echo* means a disgruntled customer and a confused non-subscriber. Screwing up with the *Bulletin* . . . she doesn't want to think about it. At least none of them seem to be early risers. Their houses are still dark, so there's little risk of running into anyone.

Until the last house. She's halfway up the front path when the hall light clicks on. Her instinct is to shove the paper through the door and run, but she's barely reached the porch when the door opens.

Give them the paper and leave. Don't make eye contact. Don't let them see your face. She fumbles in the bag for the newspaper, holding it out blindly. 'Here.'

'Bella?' says an incredulous voice, and she slowly raises her gaze. Mortimer is standing in the doorway, looking from her to the copy of the *Bulletin* she's handed him.

Shit.

They regard each other for several moments. It makes sense now: his Esperanto, his knowledge of the guild, the way he called them his 'enemy'. Isabel had thought that was a joke, but she should have realised that Mortimer's an abolitionist. No wonder he was so interested in somebody he believed had

174

run away from Comma. He was testing her because he thought she might be sympathetic to his cause.

And now she holds his life in her hands. Never mind that he can get her expelled – she could get him on a Comma hit list with one word to the right person. She can see from his expression that he knows it and is waiting to see what she'll do.

The old Isabel would have done it, she realises, the one who never imagined leaving her parents' house. She wouldn't have hesitated. And now, when she's trying so hard to persuade herself that she got out and isn't going back? Where do her loyalties really lie?

Before she's come to a decision, Mortimer says, 'Please tell me Alfie is not lying in an alleyway with his throat cut.'

Of course he knows the delivery boy's name. 'He's ill,' says Isabel. 'I do the *Echo*. Ashvin asked me to fill in.'

'Well, that's a relief.' He gives her a tight smile. 'I was wondering why he was late.'

She inclines her head towards the paper. 'You should take that inside before someone sees it.'

'Someone else, you mean,' he says, tucking it under his arm. 'There's not much point hiding if you're going to turn me in.'

It's a challenge and a question, and Isabel doesn't have an answer. She could trade this information. Offer him to Ronan like a human sacrifice, buy herself some time, or intel, or anything that might help her survive. But . . .

I was worried about you, Mortimer had said.

And she's not Comma's any more.

'Good thing I'm not going to, then,' she says, tucking the

empty bag into her *Echo* satchel. 'Not unless you give me a reason to.'

He raises his eyebrow at that. 'Blackmail, Bella?' he says mildly. 'That's a dangerous game.'

She shrugs. 'I've played worse.'

'Yes,' says Mortimer thoughtfully, 'I can believe that.' He salutes her with the newssheet. 'Well, then, see you at school.'

It's not an alliance – more of a stalemate. But for the first time in too long, Isabel feels she might be in control of the situation, a tiny shred of power reclaimed. And after weeks of feeling helpless, that's a heady rush she can't resist.

She drops off the last few copies of the *Echo* and trudges to the tram stop. Perching on the metal bench, she replies to Emma's text while she still has the courage.

I was talking to Grace because she's helping me.

'You look terrible,' says Nick. She hadn't even noticed him. 'Are you okay?'

'Not really,' says Isabel, trying to remember what day it is, what the point of this is, why she's here. 'Rain check on that club idea? I think I overcommitted myself this term.'

He seems relieved that she's offered an excuse instead of pretending the conversation never happened. 'Paper round taking it out of you, is it?'

'Something like that.' Maybe it's Wednesday. Is it Wednesday? She feels like she hasn't had a Wednesday in a while.

Her phone buzzes just as the tram arrives. She retrieves it

one-handed, using the other to scan her travel pass, trying not to lose both in the crush. It's a message from Emma.

> Is she guild?

> No.

Isabel wants to tell Emma the whole truth, but Grace's secrets aren't hers to tell. For now, the simple negative will have to do.

They're almost at the Fraser when her phone buzzes again.

> Are you lying to me?

> No.

> Are you really dying?

> Yes.

> My father poisoned me.

She doesn't get a response to that one until halfway through first period.

> Did you kill Ian Crampton?

This time she hesitates before answering.

> Yes.

Then she asks a question of her own:

> Do you hate me?

The wait for Emma's reply is unbearable. Isabel finds herself checking her phone every few seconds, as though she might have missed the vibration.

Finally, as the bell shrills overhead, the message comes through:

No.

What a sweet, precious gift of a word.

It gets her through the rest of the morning, and, at lunchtime, Emma falls into step beside her as she leaves her locker. 'Hey.'

'Hey,' says Isabel, surprised. 'Does this mean you're talking to me again?'

'Don't get used to it. The second shit gets weird, I'm out of here.' Emma gives her a little sideways smile that isn't quite her old grin but is close enough to lighten Isabel's heart. 'I'm still pissed that you lied to me, for the record. But I talked to Leo, and he pointed out that you were just trying to stay alive, and if I'm going to be mad at anyone, it should be Mum, who kept this shit from me for *years*.'

'I'm sorry for being the reason you found out,' says Isabel. 'I really didn't know.'

'I know,' says Emma. 'And at least I know now. Leo said she promised to tell me eventually, but ...' She grimaces. 'I'm mad at him as well, if I'm honest, but rage is relative, so I'm staying at his for the moment. I don't think I can face Mum for a while.'

Isabel nods. If she were Emma and had suddenly found out her loving foster mother had lied to her for most of a decade, she'd probably want some space to process that too. 'So you don't hate me?'

'I don't hate you.' It's not a warm day, but by silent agreement they gravitate towards a bench on the muddy playing field instead of the warmth of the canteen. Emma perches on the back of it, feet on the seat, while Isabel positions herself warily on the arm. 'I mean, don't get me wrong, it fucks me up to know that you've killed people. But the more I think about Cocoon, the more I realise it wasn't your fault. You were a literal child. *That*'s fucked. And I'd be a dick to hate you for that. So here we are.'

Isabel swallows. Emma makes it all sound so simple, and while she's not sure it's as clear-cut as that, she's just grateful to have her friend back. 'Thanks,' she says, not knowing what else to say.

'But in return, will you be honest with me? No more lies. I've had enough of people hiding things from me.'

'I'll try,' says Isabel doubtfully. 'Some things are … difficult to talk about.'

'Start with Grace,' says Emma. 'You said she wasn't guild, but if that's true, how come she's helping you?'

'No more lies' suddenly feels a lot harder than it did five seconds ago, if she wants to keep Grace's secret. After a moment's internal argument, Isabel gives in. 'She's a freelance poisoner,' she says, 'and she's good at antidotes, so she's helping me treat my symptoms.'

Emma's face is blank, wiped of all expression. 'Well, fuck,' she says. 'I had tea at her *house*.'

It's not quite the reaction Isabel expected. 'That's it?'

'Oh, I'm deeply pissed off that yet another authority figure is lying to me, for sure. But I already hit maximum rage capacity, and there's nothing left in the tank, so, yeah, for now, that's it. I'll yell at her later, when I've worked up the mental energy.'

'Right.'

'Frankly, I don't have the bandwidth to process this. So my mum's a murderer! So you're the product of Comma's super-secret child training programme! So the librarian's a poisoner! My brain's checked out, Bel. I've given up.'

Bel. The nickname catches her out, distracting her from her anxiety about discussing this in a public place.

'You called me Bel,' she comments.

'Did I? I guess I did.' Emma shrugs. 'If you hate it, I won't do it again.'

Isabel shakes her head so fast she's momentarily dizzy. 'No, I . . . I don't hate it.'

'Cool.' Emma takes out her lunch and unwraps a sandwich. Isabel tries to muster the appetite to do the same, but her nausea wins out. 'So,' says her friend, through a mouthful of food, 'Grace is helping you, you said. But what about Daragh?'

'He wants to run more tests.' As if that'll help. 'I'm heading over there after school.'

Emma frowns. 'I didn't think Daragh worked Wednesdays.'

'Yeah, either he likes me, or I'm a new and exciting kind of dying that he wants to study. Either way, he seems determined to fit me into his schedule.'

'Let's hope it's the former. What've you got this afternoon?'

'Double Woodwork.' The prospect of nearly two hours with Mortimer isn't appealing. 'I'm considering skiving so I can nap before my appointment, though.'

'I'll help you,' says Emma immediately, and looks offended by Isabel's surprise. 'What, you thought Grace was lying when she called me a delinquent? If you want a way out of class in the middle of the day, I'm your girl. She thinks I'm a reformed character, but it's more like being a library prefect gives me immunity. Somehow, nobody ever suspects I'm up to no good.'

'You can do that? Get me out of lessons, I mean?'

The other girl looks at her with pity. 'What did they teach you in assassin school?' she asks. 'Clearly nothing useful.'

'We weren't exactly encouraged to bunk off.'

'More's the pity. You look like shit; you definitely need to get out of here.' Emma grins, shoving her lunch back in her bag. 'Have you found the old gate yet?'

She thought she'd located all the exits, but she was more focused on the buildings than the grounds. 'There's another gate?'

Emma hops down from the bench. 'Yep. I'll show you.'

Isabel hesitates, glancing around to make sure nobody's observing their escape. It seems funny to worry about breaking a rule like this, after everything she's done, but this school is a bridge she doesn't want to burn. 'Are you sure you're okay skipping class for my sake?'

'I have a free period. It'll be an hour before anyone realises I'm gone.' She holds out her hand. 'Come on.'

181

Isabel takes it, and lets Emma lead her across the field.

The old gate is half hidden by a copse of trees in the corner of the field. It's held shut with a rusted padlock and overgrown with brambles and the remains of a neglected box hedge. But to the left of the gate, the chain-link fence that runs around the field hangs limply from its concrete posts. It's easy enough to clamber over, although the ground's slippery with mud. Emma steadies Isabel when her weakened legs threaten to give way, and then they're out.

'The school doesn't know about this?' says Isabel.

Emma snorts. 'Of course they know. But they leave it like that so the teachers can sneak out for a smoke.' She hasn't let go of Isabel's hand, and it seems wrong, somehow, to pull free. Isabel tells herself she needs the support when she's so unsteady on her feet, but she's not sure that's the whole truth. 'So where now?' says Emma. 'You wanted a nap, right?'

She does – she wants a night's sleep or a week's or a year's, a temporary death until she stops feeling so bone-tired – but Emma doesn't hate her and the relief flooding through her has set her humming.

'That artwork you showed me,' she says. 'Have you done any more?'

Emma's smile is blinding, a supernova. 'Fuck yeah I have. Want me to show you?'

Isabel nods. She could probably find it alone, wandering the streets until she spotted Emma's distinctive style, but she doesn't want to. It's easier to see Espera's beauty when Emma's beside her, and if she's not going to have many more of these moments – *don't think about it like that you're not going to die you're not going to die* – she wants to make the most of it.

They catch a tram into central Espera, and Emma takes Isabel on a walking tour of her world, a city made entirely of brightly painted alleyways and hidden squares emblazoned with art. Some of the paintings are hers and some aren't; she lets Isabel guess which, and beams when she's right. Some are wistful and delicate, pastoral scenes out of place among crowded city tenements; others are angry, hopeful, defiant. Here and there, the walls have been scoured clean with pressure washers, and all that remains is a trace of colour and a sense of threat.

'There was an abolitionist mural here,' says Emma, running her hands over one of these blank spaces. 'A painting of the city with the gates open and people streaming out. It went up overnight.' She touches the rough bricks as though she can still feel the image there. 'They got rid of it almost as quickly. Sometimes it takes months for them to notice, but I don't think this one was even up a week. It must have been reported.'

The blank wall is like a wound, shocking and painful. 'You could paint something new,' suggests Isabel, although she can't imagine what might fill it; she doesn't know how to create pictures in her head the way Emma does.

'Maybe I will,' says Emma. 'If someone else doesn't get there first.'

They carry on their tour, but Isabel's flagging, leaning heavily against the wall whenever they stop. There are no benches in these backstreets, and puddles are still pooling on the concrete. 'Anywhere to sit around here?' she asks, humiliated to need it.

'Shit, sorry, you should've said something,' says Emma. 'There's the cemetery, I guess. It's just around the corner, and they have benches. Can you make it that far?'

She'll have to. Isabel grits her teeth and dredges up the strength to follow Emma through the wrought-iron gates and along the carefully marked paths, until they reach a bench surrounded by fallen autumn leaves, a few brave orange souls still clinging to the branches over their heads.

She sinks gratefully onto it, and her gaze falls on the gravestone ahead of them. *Jean Aran.* She glances sideways at Emma. 'Is that—'

'My sister.' Emma has a curious lack of expression on her face, like she's not sure what she's feeling so has opted out of expressing anything until she figures it out. 'Sorry if it's weird to bring you here. Autopilot, I guess. I come here a lot when I've been painting. I like to tell her about my work.'

'It's not weird,' says Isabel, although she wouldn't know. 'It sounds like you loved her a lot.'

Emma lets out her breath in a long rush. 'Yeah,' she says. 'I did.'

Isabel would be happy to sit there in silence, drinking in the time together until her appointment with Daragh. The cemetery's peaceful, and strangely full of life in a way that few parts of Espera are. Even in autumn, with the leaves falling and most of the flowers gone for the year, it's rich with plants and busy with insects.

But after a while, Emma starts to speak, so quietly it's not clear whether she's talking to Isabel or herself or Jean.

'When Mum first took me in,' she says, 'I was so angry, because I was so scared. Scared that I was going to get left behind again, passed around like a package nobody wanted, until eventually I'd be forgotten in a corner somewhere. And I didn't know how to be scared without falling apart, so I let it make me vicious, and nobody wanted to come near me. I kept thinking Toni would take me back to the orphanage, or that none of it was real and I'd wake up and find I'd never left. But at night it was harder to be angry, and that's when I used to panic. I'd hide under the blankets so that nobody would hear, but one night Jean heard, and she came to sit with me. Helped me ground myself. And then the next night, and the next, and the next. She held me until it was over.'

Isabel looks at the grave. It's a simple marker, but somebody has kept the plot clear of weeds, and she thinks in the summer it must be covered in flowers.

'When she was gone,' Emma continues, 'I didn't know what to do. I'd got so used to having her there, I'd forgotten how to be alone.' She scuffs the ground with her toe. 'You know what sucks? How when someone dies they just … stay dead. Like, once they're dead, that's it, that's for ever. And you keep thinking if you wait long enough, it might change, and you can see them again. But it never does. Everything keeps going and changing, and you want to know what they'd have said or thought, but you can't, because all that's left is the picture of them that lives in your head and they'll never surprise you again.'

She doesn't say it like it needs an answer, but Isabel presses her shoulder against Emma's and says, 'I know one thing she'd have thought.'

'Yeah?'

'That grief could have made you cruel, but it didn't. It made you kind.'

She thinks she understands, now, why Emma wouldn't leave her to have her panic attack in the toilets by herself. Why she cares that Isabel's sick, even though she shouldn't. Her debt's not to Isabel – it's to a sister who will never come to collect it. But she'll pay it however she can.

Emma leans her head on Isabel's shoulder. 'Your standard for kindness is low,' she points out, but she stays there like she finds it comforting, and they sit like that until it's almost time for Isabel's appointment.

And then Emma takes her hand and helps her up, and they walk to the clinic together.

18

ĈANO (TRIGGER)

Thursday is a fog of lost words and scattered thoughts, language skittering away when Isabel tries to think. She attempts to push away her fear, but it's impossible to ignore the poison eating away at her mind, destroying every train of thought. When she gets home from school, she doesn't even bother to look at her father's files; breaking codes seems impossible when she can hardly remember her own name.

You're wasting time, Isabel, whispers a little voice in her head. *Comma could save you. Your father could save you.*

But she will not put herself back in their power.

Friday brings a sharper mind and a sharper pain: a deep ache that gnaws at her stomach, her throat sore and lips swollen as her body self-destructs from the inside out. Ashvin takes one look at her and sends her back to bed, and while it means sacrificing her pay for the day, she can't bring herself to argue. She's so tired she just stumbles away and half crawls back to her flat. She ends up sleeping through her alarm, trading school for drifting in and out of a grey wakefulness on the settee.

She's made it as far as the kitchen table and is staring helplessly at an indecipherable page of Ian's code when Daragh calls her. All he can offer is a strong dose of bad news. In a gentle, apologetic voice he explains her results: she's getting worse. The source of the poison might be gone, but the blood test is showing more traces, not fewer. It means the immunosuppressant isn't working and the poison's spreading, recruiting her antibodies to do its dirty work, making her own body into a weapon.

How very like her father that is.

'I'm sorry,' Daragh says, 'but this is bad.' And what she hears is, *You're losing.*

Dimly, she hears him explaining her options, pressing her once again to consider accepting help from the guild, using words like 'prognosis' and then, the less responsive she seems to his suggestions, 'palliative care' and 'pain management'. But she will not die like this. Nor will she go to her father and beg him to save her, which seems to be the only rope anyone can throw her as she drowns day by day in the encroaching blackness of the poison. Never mind that he's missing, that she might not be able to find him even if she tried – she will not try. She refuses to give him the satisfaction of seeing her come crawling back.

And she won't go begging at Ronan's door, either.

When Daragh's exhausted himself listing new ways she could surrender, Isabel says, 'Do you have Grace Whittock's number?'

'Yes, but—'

'And she has a lab, presumably?'

'Bella, whatever you're planning . . .'

'I'm *planning* to fix this,' she says. 'Are you going to give me the number or not?'

He gives her the number.

Which is why, on Saturday, Isabel's hesitating at the bottom of the steps up to a detached house in north Lutton, and Michael's saying, 'Are you sure this is a good idea?'

She asked Michael to come because she needed the company and she didn't think this was something Emma should get involved in, but now she's second-guessing her decision. Maybe it would be easier without witnesses to see how she's swaying on her feet, her vision blurred and breaths painful. Three times on the journey here he asked if she was okay. Three times she lied to him and said that she was. Even Isabel doesn't believe that's true any more.

'Do you have a better one?' she asks.

'Yes, and it hasn't changed since the last time you asked.' *Go to your father. He wants you alive: you can negotiate with him.* Nobody in this city knows Isabel as well as Michael does, and he still doesn't understand her at all.

'I can do this,' she says, though the coloured lights of the road's solar panels are strobing in her fogged vision and she wants nothing more than to close her eyes. 'But I – I might need a bit of help getting up the steps.'

Michael swears under his breath, but he gives her his arm and she makes it to the front door, pressing the doorbell once, twice, three times as Grace instructed her.

The librarian looks different outside school. Her warm jumper and collared shirt have been replaced by a tight-fitting, long-sleeved T-shirt and dark jeans, and for the first time, Isabel realises that Grace is fit, muscles toned from more than lifting books. Even her short hair looks less fluffy and more deliberate.

'Come in before you collapse,' she says, helping Isabel stagger over the threshold. 'And you must be Michael. Isabel told me you were coming to help out.'

Michael gives an awkward smile. 'She might've overstated my competence.'

'Don't worry,' says Isabel. 'I made it clear that I'm the brain and you're the brawn.' She certainly doesn't have any brawn of her own, not at the moment; she's leaning on the hall table just to stay upright, careful not to knock any of the accumulated junk and post onto the floor. She wants to take a minute or ten to recover from the walk from the tram stop, but if she waits, she'll lose her nerve. She looks at Grace. 'Everything ready?'

'Near enough. Did you bring the sample?'

'Sample' is such an innocent word for the pellet that Daragh removed, but Isabel nods. The plan is to break the compound down into its constituent parts and analyse those to determine the main ingredients of the poison. Once they've done that, they'll know whether it's possible to make an antidote.

Well, that's half the plan.

Grace leads them both along the hallway, past the stairs, to a locked door that requires a thumbprint and retinal scan before it swings open to reveal a small but well-equipped laboratory. At the sight of it, Isabel feels her stomach clench. She has to steel herself to cross the threshold, memories threatening to overwhelm her.

That's the point, though. She's made good progress with her father's files, but several stubborn pages are resisting her attempts to decode them. One of them carries the most recent date of anything Ronan gave her: the twentieth of August. Barely seven weeks ago. The date nags at her, but whenever she tries to remember what might have happened that day, all she feels is an abstract sense of dread.

If there's a record of the poison anywhere in those notes, she's convinced it's on this page. A day she can't remember, less than two weeks before she ran ... it has to be. But she's thrown every trick she knows at the code and got nowhere, her father's logic impenetrable. Her best hope of decoding it is to remember how it was written in the first place, to draw together the tantalising shreds of her nightmares until the fragments of memory coalesce into a whole.

Given time, maybe her memories would return naturally and she'd be able to save herself, but time is the one thing she doesn't have. Yesterday, Daragh told her that her kidneys are failing; it won't be long until the poison triggers a vicious cascade and the rest of her organs follow suit. She needs her memories back *now*, and Grace's lab is the closest she can get to her nightmares without going back to her father. Maybe being here will trigger a flashback that will help her fill in the blanks.

It might not work. But it's the best idea she's got.

Isabel sinks onto a stool with relief, pulling on a pair of gloves and accepting the goggles Grace passes her. 'Michael, do you have the sample?'

'Here.' He takes the box holding the poisonous pellet and places it on the bench beside her. 'Anything you need me to do?'

Isabel eyes the machine next to her, impressed despite herself. When she asked Grace whether her lab was equipped for high-performance liquid chromatography, she was afraid the answer would be 'no', or that Grace's kit would be an elderly and inefficient machine the size of a small cupboard. Instead, it's a modern, self-contained unit – not top of the line like the one in her father's lab, but no shabby piece of equipment, either. That'll make this easier.

'Not yet,' she says. She needs to do as much of this herself as she can, if she wants to break down the barriers in her mind that are hiding her memories from her. It's too much to hope that muscle memory will kick in (if she could ever trust her body, she can't now), but working by proxy will put her too far away from the action to remember anything. 'Do you have a magnifying glass?' she asks Grace.

The librarian nods, retrieving one from a drawer. Carefully, Isabel removes the capsule from its vial and positions it in an empty glass dish in front of her.

It's the first time she's had a good look at it, and, until now, she hadn't fully understood what it meant to have received a sub-lethal dose. The coating's still intact, but degraded enough to become permeable and allow the slow release of its deadly payload. If she'd left it even a day longer before removing it, she'd be dead. As it is, she's probably only here because of Daragh's interventions.

And it's so *small*.

She puts down the magnifying glass and gives the others a shaky smile. 'All right. Let's do this.'

The first step is to extract the poison into the solvent, making a solution that can pass through the machine. It's unavoidable, but Isabel still hesitates with the capsule clasped in tweezers just inches above the solvent. She only has this tiny pellet to work with: if something goes wrong, they have no back-ups, no further samples to analyse.

Still, she's used to having no second chances. She lets it fall.

Such a small action. But it brings back a childhood spent in a lab, learning to mix chemicals until they turned bright colours or spat flames. Her father, teaching her to test their acidity with little strips of coloured paper. Praising her when she got it right. Writing increasingly complicated tasks on the board at the front and watching her struggle to complete them, refusing to let her leave until they were done.

Her father, testing her own creations on her, watching impassively as she writhed in pain. Her father, demanding she mix her own antidote, even as she vomited blood into the sink.

Memories, Isabel tells herself. Just memories. But her

hand's shaking as she draws the solution up into the syringe, and she fumbles the filter three times before she has to give up and let Grace fix it in place and inject the solution into a vial.

'You're okay,' Grace says quietly, as she slots the vial into place. 'It's okay. Tell me what you need me to do and I'll do it.'

Isabel bites her lip, frustrated with her own powerlessness. She wants – she *needs* – to do this. But the scar on her left palm is testament to the last time she ignored her unsteady hands in a lab, and if she ruins this by being stubborn, they're worse off than before.

'I'm fine,' she says. 'Just got to wait for the results now, right?'

'Right,' says Grace, and gives her one last wary look before moving to help Michael prepare the next stage of the process. Once they've separated the ingredients of the compound, they'll run them through a mass spectrometer, and if they're lucky, that'll get them the chemical formulae they need to identify them.

Isabel's watching the results from the first stage come through on the monitor. Each peak on the graph is a different component in the mixture, and it's kind of beautiful to look at, in a fucked up way. The complexity alone makes it a masterpiece – a dozen ingredients working in harmony to destroy a body from the inside. Her father may be a monster, but he's also a genius, and she can't let herself forget that.

Grace leaves Michael and comes over. She lets out a low whistle when she sees the screen. 'This is a bastard of a poison,' she says, which is an understatement. 'You really can't remember anything?'

The graph tugs at Isabel's mind with the same nagging familiarity as the date on her father's notes, but it's an itch she can't scratch, memories that refuse to surface. 'Nothing useful,' she says. 'I guess we're doing this the slow way.'

But slow is better than giving up. Slow is still hope. Isabel waits for the monitor to tell her it's ready, and then she removes the tray of test tubes from the fraction collector. The compound has become a dozen individual ingredients, each of which holds its own secrets and needs to be analysed, no matter how many steps that involves.

She's exhausted at the thought of it, but as she takes the first test tube from the tray, Isabel feels a tiny thrill of anticipation too, buried deep beneath the brain fog of illness and fatigue. It's not that she's missed her father's lab, but she feels almost as though she's been operating at half capacity, pretending to know less than she does. Being ordinary. Playing a part. Here, away from prying eyes and her civilian cover story, she doesn't have to be anything other than who she is.

Quite the little scientist.

The test tube slips between her fingers and shatters against the workbench. Isabel flinches away as the liquid puddles around the broken glass, spreading across the surface like it's searching for her. *Shit.*

'Are you okay?' Grace says.

Of course she's not okay. She smashed the test tube, lost the ingredient – that's one they'll never analyse, one they

195

can't figure out and can't cure. Now there'll be something missing, no matter how well they analyse the rest. She fucked it up, because she's a failure who shouldn't be in a lab, because she always messes everything up and her father was right when he—

'Isabel,' says Grace sharply, snapping her out of it. 'Some of it splashed on your gloves. You should change them.'

Right. Contamination. That's the last thing they want when they're trying to figure out what's in this thing. She swallows, moving away from the bench and peeling off the soiled gloves, while Grace cleans the mess. She imagines she can feel the poison seeping into her skin and eating away at her, though she knows the drop that landed on her was too dilute to do any damage.

As she turns on the tap to wash her hands, Grace passes the next of the test tubes to Michael – no more accidents – and looks back at the results from the chromatography. 'That's weird,' says the poisoner, highlighting a section and looking closer at it. 'What is that – some kind of protein?'

'A protein?' echoes Michael. 'What do you mean?'

Isabel scrubs her hands at the sink, as though she might rub away the skin and her scars. *The poison's gone.* It doesn't feel gone. She doesn't feel safe.

'I'd have to break it down before I can analyse it further,' says Grace. 'But at a guess, it's some kind of spider venom.'

Fucking *spiders.*

The sound of the running tap is like white noise, static, impossibly loud and meaningless at the same. She's forgotten how to turn it off. She's forgotten how to move, paralysed by the fear trickling through her, turning her blood into acid that burns and sears like hate. *Some kind of spider venom.* Of course it is. Of *course* it is. She should have known from the moment she discovered it was her father's work. And now . . .

Isabel stares at the pale hands in front of her, trembling as though they might shake themselves to pieces and leave small bones littered across the grey counter. Only the burn scar on the left tells her they're hers. She's untethered, sliced loose by the memories, and then sensation returns in the form of panic clawing at the inside of her throat, and she becomes embodied again. Incarnate and terrified.

'Issy?' Her father steps towards her and she retreats from his raised hand, but she's backed up against the counter. She fumbles for a weapon, but there's nothing within reach, no scalpel or syringe she could use to fight back, and—

'Bella,' says a voice. A woman's voice. Grace Whittock, because it's Grace's lab, it's Grace's house. She squeezes her eyes shut and opens them again, and it's not her father in front of her, it's Michael, his hands now loose at his sides. He wasn't . . . he wasn't going . . . he never meant . . .

She takes a long, shuddering breath, and begins to sob.

19

HEREDO (INHERITANCE)

Isabel curls up on the settee in Grace's living room, a mug of tea warming her hands and a blanket around her shoulders. She's chilled to the bone, hollowed out from crying and unable to stop shaking.

'Should've seen this coming,' she says, with a shaky smile. 'Went into this *trying* to trigger a flashback. It was never going to be much fun.' Though maybe 'flashback' is the wrong word for half a dozen memories piled on top of each other in an inchoate mess of panic. 'I thought . . .' She looks at Michael, perched awkwardly in an armchair. 'I thought you were my father. I . . . lost myself.' No, that's the wrong phrase. It's more that the lab stripped away all the artifice, leaving behind the core: Isabel Ryans, her father's daughter.

She will never stop being afraid, and she will never be anything other than his.

'It's okay,' says Michael, though it clearly isn't. Outside the lab, he's unthreatening, nothing like her father, and it's hard to see how she could ever have confused them.

'In your place, I don't think I'd have had the courage to set foot in a lab again,' says Grace. 'The fact that you dared tells me you're brave.'

Not brave. Just an echo of her father, running the same tracks over and over again, tracks that lead to the same dead end.

'It doesn't matter,' she says, staring dully into her mug. 'It's hopeless.'

'It's not hopeless,' says Grace. 'The missing ingredient is a setback, but the rest—'

'And the spider venom?' Isabel interrupts. 'Even if we knew what species, you know how hard it is to get antivenom without a guild licence, and smugglers are slow. And that's only *one* ingredient. Fuck knows how hard the rest of them are to counteract.'

Maybe if she had the formula, she'd know how much of a chance she has, how central a role the spider venom's playing. But all she remembered was fear, and that won't help her decode the notes she's sure will give her the answer.

'Well ...' Grace begins, but gives up, unable to think of anything comforting to say. She knows Isabel's right. 'What now?' she asks instead.

'Honestly?' says Isabel. 'I have no idea.' And she's so fucking *tired*. So ready to close her eyes and never open them again. Why does it have to be up to her to fix this? Why does she always have to save herself?

'Then we find your father,' says Michael, yet again. 'He'll know how to fix it. He might even have antidotes left over from testing.'

'No.' It sounds like a sob. 'You know we can't. Once he has me back, he'll never let me go again. How can you not see that?'

'You never needed him to *let* you go before.'

'We don't even know where he is!' She slumps down on the settee, the outburst robbing her of her remaining strength. 'How are we supposed to negotiate with a ghost?'

'We can find him,' says Michael stubbornly. 'No one can hide a whole guild for long.'

'Comma haven't found it.'

'Comma don't have us.'

Grace looks at the two of them – Isabel huddled and hunched under the blanket, Michael declarative, gesticulating wildly – and says, 'Michael, can you give us a moment?'

'Don't tell me what to do,' he begins. 'I don't even—'

'Fuck's sake, Michael,' Isabel interrupts. Even to her own ears, her voice sounds pathetically thin and weak. 'Give us a minute, would you?'

He scowls, but leaves the room. The door slams behind him.

'You didn't tell me your father was missing,' says Grace carefully, when he's gone. 'And what Michael said, about hiding a guild—'

'He's defected. That's what I meant when I said this wasn't Comma's doing. Parnassiinae's gone rogue.'

The librarian sucks in her breath. 'I can't imagine Comma's very pleased about that.'

Isabel shakes her head. 'They're not.'

'So if this wasn't done on Comma orders, do you think they'd be open to negotiation?'

She pictures Ronan's face, the implacable violence of his bargains. 'They've already tried. I turned them down.' She doesn't mention that by decoding so many of her father's papers, she's a considerable way towards fulfilling the conditions of Ronan's second deal. She doesn't want his help and everything that comes with it – and the longer she can keep these vicious formulae out of guild hands, the better. 'Look, Grace, I don't know if I can do this any more. Any of this. I'm so tired.'

'I know.' Grace puts her mug down and sits next to Isabel. 'Nobody would blame you for giving up.'

'You're saying I should?' asks Isabel unsteadily.

'No.' Grace takes Isabel's hand and squeezes it, running her thumb along the backs of Isabel's fingers. 'I think you have so much more to offer than what you've been given the chance to do so far.'

'Do I, though?' She has to force herself not to pull free of Grace's grip. 'In that lab, I . . .'

'You realised how much you've inherited from your father, and that scared you.'

Isabel turns to look at her. 'How did you know?' she whispers.

There's a moment of silence, and then Grace says, 'My mother was Hummingbird.' It tells Isabel everything she needs to know. Then she adds, 'You won't always be afraid, Isabel.'

I don't remember how to be anything else. 'I made this poison,' she says. It's the first time she's said it aloud, and her voice shakes. 'Me. Not him. I'm the reason this is happening – I'm exactly as bad as he is.'

'You are *not* exactly as bad as he is, Isabel Ryans,' Grace tells her. 'You were a child, and he shaped and abused and manipulated you until you became the person you are today. And that girl still has enough humanity left in her to know she wants to be something more. The person your father tried to create is only part of who you are and only a fraction of what you're capable of becoming.'

Isabel pulls her hand free, hugging her knees close to her chest inside the blanket. She does want to be something more, but the fight's taking more from her than she's got to give. 'At least if I died, it would mean not going back to my father,' she says.

Grace looks hard at her. 'Do you really believe that?' she says. 'That dying is better than going back to him?'

There has to be another way. These can't be her only two options. But right now, with the threat of begging Ian for help hanging over her, she's struggling to remember why she wants to live. 'Can you blame me?' she says. 'After what he did?'

'I'm not blaming you for anything,' says Grace. 'I just needed to know. And if that's truly how you feel, then I'll respect your decision.'

'I want . . .' begins Isabel, but she has no idea how to finish that sentence. *I don't want to die.* It feels more and more like a lie. Survival takes energy. Survival requires her to want it. Isabel doesn't know how to want anything any more, except for this to be over.

Total organ failure. That part, at least, should be quick.

Grace says, 'I can keep analysing the samples. See what else I can identify, make antidotes. If that would help.'

Partial cures, partial treatments, enough to take the edge off the blade that's killing her, but not enough to remove it. Is that enough? No. But it's something. 'You'd do that?'

'I can try.'

Isabel leans her head back against the settee. It's so heavy; it feels like her neck will snap with the weight of it. 'Then let's do that,' she says, and closes her eyes. 'I'm sorry. I'm so tired.'

Grace tucks the blanket more closely around her. 'Then sleep,' she says. 'I'll talk to Michael, and I'm going to phone Emma.'

Isabel opens her eyes with some difficulty. 'Why?'

'She makes you feel better.'

The truth has always seemed like a complicated thing to Isabel, but Grace's words are so simple. 'Oh,' she says, and closes her eyes again. Maybe when she wakes up, Emma will be there and everything will be okay.

Michael's gone before Emma arrives, muttering some excuse about needing groceries. Isabel doesn't push it. She can tell he's prickly around Grace, uneasy about trusting a freelancer with their secrets and frustrated by his own helplessness. She can't blame him for either.

Emma holds her hand while Grace gives her a cocktail of incomplete antidotes based on the few ingredients they've identified so far. It's a fragmentary salvation that's not enough to offset the cumulative symptoms of the fact that she's dying, but two hours later when Grace drives her home, she's able to stagger up the stairs, so maybe something in there worked.

She sleeps through Sunday, but on Monday, despite all logic suggesting she should stay in bed, she ignores Ashvin's protests and the drizzling rain to limp through her paper round and drag herself to school.

Double Physics passes in a meaningless blur, equations shattering against the wall of her pain. At break, she can't manage the stairs to the library; can hardly make it to her locker, and stands there staring into its depths like it might help her remember that she wants to live.

'Bella,' says a voice. Emma's voice. She turns to see her friend, soaked to the skin. The drizzle must have given way to the downpour that was threatening. 'Can we talk?'

Isabel glances up and down the corridor. 'Here?'

Emma shakes her head. Her expression's shell-shocked, her eyes bloodshot and sore, as though she's been crying. Whatever brought her here, it's something awful. 'Somewhere private,' she says, voice cracking. 'Please?'

There's a classroom across the hall that's rarely used and always unlocked; Isabel's taken illicit free-period naps in there once or twice. Inside, it's dim with grey light, rain lashing against the windows. She closes the door and waits for Emma to speak, but her friend seems unable to find the words.

As gently as she can, Isabel asks, 'What happened, Emma?'

And Emma says, 'Grace Whittock's dead.'

20

MALGAJNO (LOSS)

The world goes quiet. Numb. A little emptier than before.

Isabel leans on a desk, looking out of the window at the sodden courtyard. The rain thunders on the concrete, grey on grey like the static in her head. Water blurs the outlines of the world, smudges real and unreal until everything is stripped of meaning. *Grace Whittock's dead.*

She stares at the rain until her words come back and then says, 'What?'

'Grace is dead.' Emma's boots are coated in mud, her clothes drenched. She tries to wipe her glasses on her T-shirt, but it's too wet to make a difference. Isabel watches her with blank incomprehension, unable to fathom the steps necessary to offer help.

'She can't be.'

'I saw her body, Bel.' Emma's voice is hoarse. She pushes her sodden hair out of her face. 'It's definitely her. She was . . . she was shot. Right through her heart.'

'But . . .' Isabel swallows her worthless objections. It doesn't matter that it's not fair. 'How did you find out?'

Emma stares out at the rain too. The lights of classrooms in the building opposite aren't enough to brighten the overcast day, the heavy charcoal clouds drawing night over the late-morning sky.

'I was meant to be helping her transport the second year reading scheme materials. I messaged her asking if she needed help getting them to the car or if I should just meet her here, but she never answered. Grace *always* answers my messages,' she adds fiercely. 'Always. So I went over this morning and when I got there . . .' She swallows. 'Her body was on the front steps. I think they rang the doorbell and killed her when she answered.'

If Isabel was a good person, a normal person, she'd ask Emma how she is. Hug her. Hold her as she trembles, braced against a desk like it's the only thing keeping her upright. But all Isabel can say is: 'Who?' *Please not Comma, please not Comma, please not Comma.* As if it makes a difference.

'There was . . . they had . . .' Emma takes out her phone and opens her camera roll, averting her eyes as she passes it to Isabel. 'I didn't want to take a picture, but somebody had to, somebody had to tell someone, and . . .'

Isabel's seen a lot, but none of it's prepared her for the sight of

Grace's lifeless body with a spider carved into it. It's grotesque, the spider's bulbous body a bloody mess on her cheek, its legs extending across her face. The bell shrills overhead and they both ignore it, the cacophony of the crowded corridors meaningless background noise to the horror of Grace's death.

A third guild, claiming the mark of a spider. Isabel looks at the image for as long as she can, then powers off the screen. 'Shit,' she says. 'My parents.'

A third guild means a power struggle. It means Comma and Hummingbird moving to eliminate the threat, regardless of the collateral damage. Michael told her it was happening, but it didn't feel real until now. And if she had any doubt that this was her father's idea, the spider dispels it.

Emma takes back the phone. Her hand is shaking. 'You know,' she says, her wavering voice undermining the light tone she's aiming for, 'the more I learn about your parents, the more I understand why you are the way you are.'

A killer. Her father's monster. Just as bad as they are. 'Well, they do say that about apples and trees.'

'That's not what I meant.' But Emma doesn't clarify. She sinks down onto the floor, leaning against the wall, and hugs her knees to her chest as though trying to hold herself together.

Isabel hesitates, then sits down next to her. The words come finally, years too late. 'Are you okay?'

Emma scrapes at the mud on her left boot with the toe of her right. 'No,' she says. 'No, I'm not.'

No, she's not. Isabel feels the crushing weight of her own inadequacy and guilt. Grace was helping her and now she's dead, and she can't fix that. She wants to sit here on the floor until it stops being her fault.

'I'm sorry,' she says.

'You didn't do this.'

'Somebody must have told them she was helping me. This is because of me.'

'It isn't.' Emma's voice is small but firm. 'It's because they're bastards. This is on *them*, not you. And I hate them.' She repeats this, louder. 'I hate them!'

Her voice echoes in the empty classroom. Soon someone will come and find them not in lessons, and Isabel will have to tell them that Grace Whittock is dead. Which isn't fair, because Grace Whittock shouldn't be dead, and those shouldn't be words she has to say.

Isabel says, 'We should go somewhere else. Somewhere ... safe.'

Emma turns to look at her, and Isabel knows what she's seeing. She saw it herself in the mirror this morning: her too-pale face, lips sore and swollen, eyes bruised with exhaustion. She couldn't be bothered to try to disguise it with make-up. She can hardly eat now, her throat closing up when she swallows as though every food is an enemy, but her body's too close to shutting down to remember how to feel hunger.

Nowhere is safe from this.

'Okay,' says Emma. 'Where?'

Her flat isn't safe; Ronan found it, Michael found it, her parents could find it. Emma's house means Toni. And school is this: Grace Whittock is dead.

'Mortimer,' she says.

'Mortimer?' repeats Emma. 'The Woodwork teacher?'

Isabel nods. She doesn't know what made her say it, but she doesn't have a better idea. It's not that she trusts Mortimer, but at least she knows for sure he isn't guild. He'll know what to do – who to tell about things like this, what forms to fill in so that someone can fix it. And someone can fix it, can't they? They can fix the fact that Emma's been crying, that she walked through a storm to get here, that she used to have Grace and now she doesn't.

Mortimer will know. He knows all the rules.

'Won't he be teaching?'

He's *meant* to be teaching Isabel, she realises; she should finally be taking his safety exam, provided he hasn't forgotten all about it. The idea that his classroom could be dangerous to her feels absurd. 'We'll go next period,' she says. 'He uses fourth for marking. I've seen him.' It's a long time to wait, but she doesn't have the energy to move, would be content to stay here curled up against the wall forever.

Emma seems to feel the same way, because she doesn't argue. After a few minutes of silence, she starts crying again, covering her face with shaking hands. 'I'm sorry,' she says. 'I'm sorry, I shouldn't, I ...'

'It's okay.' It's not. Emma's crying, and she can't make it better. 'Would you like a hug?'

'A hug?'

'Yeah, you know, a sign of affection that makes you feel better when you're crying uncontrollably in an

210

empty classroom instead of actually going to lessons like normal kids do.'

Emma's smile is small and watery. 'Might need to reconsider the idea that normality is overrated,' she says. 'But, yes, I would like a hug.'

Isabel hugs her with all the awkwardness of insufficient practice. Emma is still dripping wet, and her hair soaks Isabel's T-shirt in seconds. She doesn't care. Her friend squeezes her so tightly that she can't catch her breath, and she keeps holding her, feeling her shudder as she cries, the sobs shaking her to pieces. Emma's meant to be the strong one, but this has undone her, which means Isabel can't cry, can't let herself collapse, has to hold herself together so that at least one of them is whole.

'Who else am I going to lose?' says Emma, and Isabel has no answer.

All she says is, 'We'll make them pay, Emma. We'll make them pay for everything they've done to us.'

When the next bell rings, they wait until the sea of students has passed. Emma's almost as unsteady on her feet as Isabel as she pulls herself upright, face drawn and pale, and Isabel doesn't dare lean on her for support as they make their way to Mortimer's classroom. It's a relief to stumble through the door and find him sitting at his desk with a pile of marking.

'Bella, you weren't—' He catches sight of Emma, soaked and sobbing, and finishes, '—in class. I'm guessing you had a good reason. Here.' He grabs chairs for them both, catching Isabel's arm as she wavers, and retrieves the orange biscuit tin from his desk to place it in front of them, lid open. Only then does he say, 'What's happened?'

'La bibliotekisto mortis,' says Isabel. *The librarian is dead.* English feels slippery and meaningless, grief robbing her of words, and it's a relief to know Mortimer will understand when she slips into her native language. 'Emma found the body.'

He swears. 'Who would . . . why would they kill Grace?' he asks, following her lead and switching to Esperanto.

'Because she was helping me,' says Isabel. She feels the weight of all her guilt settle heavier on her heart. 'Because she was my best chance of surviving without them.'

Mortimer frowns. 'What do you mean?'

Too late, she remembers he doesn't know. 'I'm dying,' she says bleakly. 'My father poisoned me. And Grace is, I mean, she *was* a freelance poisoner, specialising in antidotes. She was trying to help me counteract it.'

He looks like he's been hit around the head with a brick. She feels momentary regret for throwing so much at him at once, but it's not like life has exactly passed it to her in manageable bites with time to adjust in between. It's all one accelerating pile of fuckery, and she lacks the energy to break it down for him.

'Fuck,' says Mortimer, with feeling.

'Yeah,' Isabel agrees, because that just about sums it up.

'What are you saying?' asks Emma, looking between the two of them. Her gaze settles on Mortimer: 'You speak Esperanto? Are you guild?'

'She's telling me what happened,' he explains gently. 'And, no, I'm not guild. But you're Emma Westray, aren't you?'

With considerable suspicion, she nods.

Mortimer pushes the biscuit tin towards her. 'I know your brother, Leo. We have ... mutual friends.'

From the shifty look on Mortimer's face, Isabel's fairly sure he's talking about the Free Press, which means his subscription to the *Bulletin* represents more than a casual interest. She wonders if Toni knows her son's an abolitionist. Probably. No wonder he was so pissed at her.

Emma takes a biscuit. 'You know Leo?' she asks, still uncertain, but beginning to soften.

'He talks about you a lot. I hoped we'd get the chance to meet in person.' Mortimer smiles at her, then glances over at Isabel and switches back into Esperanto. 'So. You're sick, and Grace is dead. Which guild are we dealing with here?'

She swallows. 'Neither. A third guild.'

'A third guild,' he repeats.

'My parents. It's a long story.'

'I'm getting that impression.' He appraises her. 'Are you going to tell me any of it?'

She has to. For him to help, she has to – and he has to help, because she's got nobody else to turn to now. She looks Mortimer straight in the eyes and says, 'Have you heard of Cocoon?'

The word hangs heavy and poisonous in the air between them. Mortimer glances at Emma. 'Does she ...' he begins.

'She knows. I don't have secrets from Emma.'

He hesitates a moment longer, then says in English, 'I heard a rumour. The *Bulletin* was rife with it a couple of years ago, but I thought they were trying to stir up trouble. I didn't think it was actually real. So you're saying Comma are training minors?'

'Were,' corrects Isabel. 'Not any more.'

'And you were part of it. That's what you were running from.' She nods, and he looks thoughtful. 'And Ian Crampton?'

She could lie, but frankly, she's too tired. 'I killed him.'

He suspected, she knows that, but still the silence yawns ominously long before he says, 'Would I be right in thinking you're not on the best terms with Comma right now?'

'That would be ... accurate enough. Are you going to turn me in?'

He seems surprised by the question. 'What, to Comma? It seems like they already know.'

Isabel shrugs. 'Or to the school, or the Free Press. I don't know.'

Mortimer shakes his head. 'You came here running from the guild and asked me for my help. As far as I'm concerned, the enemy of my enemy is my friend. Your secrets are safe with me.'

Isabel has a lot more enemies than she has friends. 'My real name's Isabel,' she offers, a tentative gesture of trust. 'Isabel Ryans.'

'Isabel Ryans,' he repeats. 'And you said ... you said your father poisoned you?'

214

'Parnassiinae,' she says, testing him, and when his eyes widen in recognition she adds, 'You were right. Top six.'

Mortimer runs his hands through his hair. 'I hadn't counted on it being *that* bad,' he admits. 'And Grace was helping you? And—'

'And now she's dead,' says Emma. She's drawing patterns in the fine sawdust on the workbench. No, not patterns. A spider.

'I don't know what to do,' says Isabel honestly. 'I don't know who else knows that my parents have defected to form their own guild. I don't know what will happen when the Met finds Grace's body: whether they'll treat it as guild or homicide. I didn't know who else to tell, so . . .'

'So you told me.' Mortimer looks exhausted. 'But I don't know how to help you.'

I don't know how to help you. The words sink into her chest like lead. Of course he doesn't. She shouldn't have told him in the first place. All she's done is surrender her secrets – Cocoon, her parents, Ian Crampton.

'I thought – you're an abolitionist, aren't you?' she says desperately. 'Maybe you know something we don't, somebody who can help?'

'There's a difference between reading a newspaper and being a revolutionary, Isabel,' he says gently. 'I'm afraid I know a lot less than you think.'

'Then what's the fucking *point*?'

In his position, she'd already have gone to the Free Press. She doesn't understand why he's passing up this opportunity to screw Comma over. It probably wouldn't break them, but it would weaken them if the city knew they'd trained children, if *Hummingbird* knew they'd trained children . . .

And why not? If the edifice of Comma cracks and falls, wouldn't she be safe?

No. They'd kill her first. She wouldn't live to see it brought down.

You're not going to live anyway, says that little voice in her head. Strange how she almost forgot that. Strange the freedom that comes with remembering: Isabel Ryans is dying, and that makes her invulnerable. Nothing left to lose and nothing left to live for. And it's liberating, a morbid relief, until—

Emma says, 'So what do we do now?'

Emma.

Isabel doesn't deserve her, this friendship offered so freely despite the violence that binds their families together. She doesn't deserve any of this – her new life, her hopes and dreams – and maybe that's why it seemed a fair trade and an appropriate sacrifice, to deny herself survival if it would deny her father what he wants. Yet at the sound of Emma's voice, something inside her roars defiantly into life.

Without Grace, there's no way she's going to figure out this antidote. Not on her own, not without a price. But it turns out Isabel does still have something to live for, and that something is this: Emma's smile, her art, the possibility of friendship, the unfamiliar taste of laughter. Everything she never had, and doesn't want to lose.

'What we do now,' she says, 'is fight back.'

And she takes out her phone and dials Michael's number.

He answers on the third ring. 'Isabel? Are you okay?'

No. She's falling to pieces and only her rage and her hope is holding her together. *I want to live. I'm not done yet. They will not rob me of this.* She says, 'I'm going to need your help.'

His reply is immediate. 'Anything. What do you need?'

'I need,' she says, 'to find my father.'

21

PLANOJ (PLANS)

Her flat's quiet, the silence broken only by the hum of the fridge and the distant noise of traffic. Isabel still hesitates in the doorway, listening for telltale signs of danger, before she finally lets herself drop her guard and her school bag.

Michael's working a late shift to cover for a colleague, but he said he'd be over tomorrow. Emma left school at lunchtime and headed to her brother's place – the safest place for her, probably, because Isabel's parents know Toni, but they don't know Leo, so they've got no reason to go after him. Isabel misses her already.

She's exhausted from dragging herself through the school day, but she has work to do if she's going to locate her father. She's two-thirds of the way through decoding his papers. Until now, she's been focusing on the lab reports, looking for clues that might lead her to the poison, but it's time to study the pages she's overlooked.

As she curls up on the settee with the files, Isabel can't help but wonder why her father would have done this – any of this. Poisoning her is one thing – cruelty from Ian is never unexpected, even if his exact intentions are obscure to her. But why start his own guild, when Comma's always given him whatever he wanted? Grace wasn't exaggerating when she said his poisons were legendary; his reputation for concoctions that are as subtle and inescapable as they are deadly keeps Comma well supplied with clients, and they've never had reason to refuse him anything.

Except . . .

Cocoon.

Isabel doesn't know who made the final decision to shut the programme down. She woke up from surgery and they told her it was over, like that meant anything at all in that moment. She was too sedated to feel much, but she remembers her father's rage, how he fought to make them change their minds. The fact that she'd nearly died didn't seem to give him a moment's pause.

And just like that it's obvious what he's doing in this spider guild of his. He's training children, just as he trained Isabel – the one thing Comma won't permit him. Maybe he hasn't got that far yet, but it must be his ultimate plan.

So that's the *why*, but what about the *how*? He'd need allies, but he's good at talking people into doing what he wants, and

219

he has any number of contacts outside the city, smugglers and suppliers and buyers alike. Is it too much to hope he might have recorded any of those deals in these files? Probably. She can't be sure Ronan gave her everything, and she suspects he didn't. For all she knows, she's missing something crucial.

And she's so *tired*, weighed down by pain and grief. She's been in problem-solving mode, refusing to let herself process Grace's death, because she has no idea what she should be feeling, how upset she's allowed to be. She hardly knew Grace, and her grief pales into insignificance beside Emma's mourning. But the librarian was helping her, and more than that, she was kind. It's wrong that somebody so kind could have died like this.

But if she thinks about that, she has to let herself feel it, the whole bloody mess of emotions, and she doesn't *do* grief. She understands death, not mourning: knows the moment the spark of life leaves somebody's eyes, but not how to process the fact that somebody's gone who shouldn't be.

Gone, and not coming back.

It's too much, all of it: her father, the pain, the spider carved into Grace's cheek. She's running out of strength to keep fighting, exhaustion filling her bones with lead and her mind with noise. Blackness creeps in at the edges of her vision, and she pinches the soft skin of her wrist. But she's so numb it hardly registers, and the pain can't pull her back from the brink of unconsciousness.

When she wakes, the sky's turned inky black outside the window, the only light a dim glow cast by a streetlight in the alleyway below. The clock on the oven reads 23:13, and for a few moments she lies frozen on the settee, trying to remember how she got there. The last thing she remembers is *her mother's voice* – no, she was here – *a gun in her hand* – she was sitting on the settee, she was here – *a man with his back to her* – was she here? – *a gun in her hand and a dead man with his back to her and her mother's voice: good girl good girl it's okay you're my good girl* . . .

She was here. It's a nightmare, a memory: she's not a child any more, and she's not *theirs*, either.

She's seventeen, she's safe, and she got *out*.

One day maybe that will feel true.

The morning light is pitiless and grey, rain battering the window. Isabel grudgingly concedes that she's not well enough for her paper round and sends Ashvin an apologetic text. It's not the loss of pay that bothers her – she has bigger problems than a scant handful of shillings – but the fact she's letting him down. And the fact that it's another symptom of her civilian life slipping between her fingers.

With every piece of normality she loses, she feels more and more like she never left Comma behind.

School, too, is more than she can manage. She makes herself a mug of tea and settles in with the remaining files, no longer looking only for formulae and lab reports, but names, addresses – anything that might get her closer to finding her father.

The early hours have given way to morning by the time

she has any luck. At first, it just seems like a string of figures, but it quickly becomes apparent that these are her father's accounts – and considering the code they're in, she suspects he kept these transactions hidden from the guild. She's never thought too much about how the guilds make their deals, though she knows they have buyers in governments all over the world, either directly or via third-party arms dealers. It makes sense that they'd have private buyers, but the dates on this page suggest Ian's been cutting deals behind Comma's back for at least three years.

Was he always planning to leave? Or was he just trying to make some extra money on the side? Every time she thinks she understands his motivations, he proves her wrong. It should be a relief that his mind's workings are so different from her own, but it isn't.

Her phone buzzes and she drags herself away from the files to answer it. 'Hello?'

'Are you going to school today?' asks Emma.

Isabel glances at the clock. It's halfway through second period and she's picked up her phone, so she thinks her answer is obvious, but she responds anyway. 'No. Are you?'

'No.' Emma sighs. 'I can't. Grace was . . . she made school bearable for me.'

Isabel has no idea what to say to that. 'I'm sorry,' she tries, inadequately.

'I couldn't sleep. Every time I tried, I just . . . Her body, Bel, it was so awful, you can't imagine. Or . . .' She forces a laugh. 'I guess you can.'

Isabel's seen plenty of dead bodies, but none that she cared about. 'Not really,' she says honestly. 'Are you okay?'

'No,' says Emma. 'No, I'm really not. Leo's at work, and I'm alone, and it's all I can think about. I didn't know who else to call. The others, the school – do they even know she's dead?' Her voice cracks on the word. 'Shit.'

Isabel doesn't have a lot of experience with friends, or comfort, or how to help somebody whose world is falling apart. But she knows she doesn't want to be alone either.

'Come over,' she says instinctively. 'I'll text you my address.'

'Really?' Emma sounds so hopeful.

'I mean, you might just have to sit and watch me break codes and read boring files, but—'

'Anything's better than this,' Emma says fervently. 'If I start crying again I don't think I'll ever stop.'

'Then, yeah. Come over.' Isabel squints at the page in front of her, comparing it to her transposition chart for the financial documents. It looks like the code's hardly changed between the two. 'The company's terrible, but . . .'

'I'll be there as soon as I can,' Emma promises. 'I'll bring lunch, okay?'

'Mm-hmm,' says Isabel, swapping the phone to her other ear so that she can grab a pen and test her theory. 'See you soon.'

Same code phrase, except for one word. Can it be that simple? It only takes a moment to adjust the chart and then the code's unravelling, the words taking shape as she exchanges letters and numbers.

74 Gauntlet Drive. New webs, bigger flies.

Dimly, she becomes aware that Emma's hung up. She texts over her address before she forgets, then sits staring at the one on the paper.

Gauntlet Drive. She doesn't know it, but she only really knows her way around Fordon and Lutton, so that's not surprising. Her shattered tablet takes a long time to load a map of Espera, provoking a hiss of annoyance, but finally it struggles into action.

Central Espera. Not far from the Sunshine Project.

Is this where she'll find her father? It seems impossible that he could be hiding in plain sight, and the district's poor, ill suited to guild activities. But maybe that's a point in its favour – it's the last place Comma and Hummingbird would think to look for him. She looks at the file's date: late July. Recent enough to be worth pursuing, surely?

She considers texting Michael, but he said he'd be over by eleven, and it's safer not to share a discovery like this over an unsecured line when either or both of their phones could be tapped. While she waits, she untangles the rest of the page, but it's all either inconsequential or incomprehensible, nothing as clear as the address at the top. *Gauntlet Drive.*

Almost an hour later, Emma arrives. 'So this is where you live,' she says, hanging her damp coat on a hook near the door and easing off her trainers. 'You know, it's not as grotty as I imagined. You said it was a studio, so I figured the bed would literally be in the kitchen. But there's actual furniture in between.'

'Truly, it's palatial,' Isabel agrees. 'Tea?'

'Yes, please.' While Isabel's putting the kettle on, Emma wanders over to the table, picking up the papers scattered there. 'You can read this?' she says. 'It looks like a typewriter threw up.'

'It's encoded.' Isabel points to her transposition charts, painstakingly drawn on squared paper in increasingly shaky handwriting. 'But, yes, I can read it. Eventually, and very slowly, and only if my father isn't being too much of a bastard with his codes.'

Emma, wide-eyed, looks through the charts. 'Are you a genius?' she asks, apparently sincerely.

'No,' says Isabel. 'Far from it. I just have … extremely specific skills.' She finishes making the tea and brings the mugs over one at a time, trying to keep her hands steady. 'Here. Make yourself comfortable. I—'

Before she can explain about the address she's found, Michael arrives. He lets himself in without ceremony, pocketing his lockpicks as he closes the door behind him. 'Sorry I'm late,' he says cheerfully, peeling off his sodden hoodie. 'The weather's miserable out there.' His expression sobers when he sees Emma. 'Oh. I didn't realise we'd have company.'

Emma's look of alarm reminds Isabel that the two of them have never actually met. 'This is Michael,' she says hastily. 'He's the one I called yesterday. He's going to help. Michael, this is Emma.'

Michael eyes Emma. 'Toni Rolleston's kid,' he says, half a question. She nods uneasily. 'Huh.'

Emma looks back at Isabel, still uncertain. 'Another butterfly?'

Isabel winces. She knows the civilians have their own nicknames for guild members, and 'butterfly' is one of the milder ones, but there's still something casually dehumanising about it. 'Something like that.'

'We grew up together,' adds Michael. He holds up a drenched plastic bag. 'I brought food. I assumed you wouldn't feel up to making anything, Isabel.'

This is a reasonable assumption: Isabel's appetite has been diminishing along with her strength, and she doesn't remember the last time she ate a full meal. Which might explain why her brain's full of dust and screaming. 'Thanks.'

'If I'd known you'd be here . . .' he begins, looking at Emma.

'I brought my own,' she says, with a tight smile. 'And for the record, I wasn't expecting *you*, either.'

'Well, devastated as I am not to be the topic of conversation at all times, I'm sure you'll get over the surprise.' He takes a plastic box from the bag and holds it up for Isabel's inspection. 'Pasta bake. It's early for lunch, but depending on when you last ate . . .'

'I could probably eat now,' Isabel agrees. 'Plates are in the cupboard to your left.'

He puts the container in the microwave and turns to face her. 'Made any progress with those files?'

In response, she pushes the page across the table. 'I decoded this this morning. Gauntlet Drive – do you know it?'

He shakes his head, but Emma says, 'I know it. I've painted there a few times.'

'It's dated July,' says Isabel. 'It's the closest I've got to pinning down a location. Even if they've moved on—'

'There might still be clues,' finishes Michael. He points to the next sentence: *New webs, bigger flies.* 'And this?'

'Not sure,' she admits. 'Maybe some kind of catchphrase. Whatever they've named their guild, I think the logo is a spider.'

She only gave him the absolute basics about Grace's death, wary of the unencrypted line, and he hasn't seen the photo. But he doesn't question her reasoning. 'Fitting,' he says, 'for your father.' Before she can respond, the microwave beeps, and Michael busies himself serving up a steaming plate of pasta. 'Here, eat. You need your strength.'

He's always been a good cook, though she's never known whether he learned out of interest or necessity – her mother always gave him the chores nobody else wanted. She breathes in the smell of food and tries not to let her nausea show on her face.

'Thanks, Michael,' she says, picking up the fork. But one mouthful and her throat is shredding itself, her lips numb and swelling, and she can't breathe—

'Fuck,' he says, as she gasps for breath, and she hears Emma demanding, 'Did you just fucking poison her?' all furious and defensive.

Michael's rummaging desperately in his bag. 'No, I didn't pois— Get out of the way,' he snaps. 'She's having an allergic reaction.'

Anaphylaxis. Isabel never used to have any allergies. She drags in another painful breath and feels Michael slam

227

something into her thigh – his EpiPen, she realises, as her heart pounds against her ribcage.

'Shit,' says Emma. 'What does she need?'

'To go to a bloody hospital, but that's not exactly an option, is it?' Michael sounds scared, voice high; he's popping pills out of a blister pack, crushing them into powder that he tips into a glass of water. 'Here, Isabel, can you drink this?'

She swallows a little, chokes, swallows again. It seems to take a year to drain half the glass, the sense that she's suffocating only slowly receding.

'Was that your EpiPen?' she manages, as her throat clears. 'You shouldn't—'

'I'll get another one,' he interrupts. 'Are you okay?'

Not really. He's right – she needs a hospital. But if that were possible, she wouldn't be this sick in the first place.

'What did you give me?' she says, eyeing the empty pill packets.

'A shit-ton of antihistamine. It'll help, but it's not enough.' He glances at Emma. 'Sorry for yelling. I panicked.'

Emma waves away the apology, looking as rattled as if she were the one whose immune system just tried to kill her. 'What did you react to?' she asks Isabel.

'No idea,' she says honestly. The way the poison's fucking over her system, it could be anything on her plate, and she doesn't fancy trying to narrow it down.

'But you need to eat.' There's genuine concern in Michael's face, an unfamiliar expression. 'Are there any foods you know are safe?'

'I had some crisps yesterday, and I didn't die.'

'That's a start. You've got potatoes?' She nods, gesturing vaguely towards the cupboard. 'Then I'll make you some mash. Don't die before it's ready.'

As he retrieves the potatoes, peeling them with brisk, efficient movements, Emma says, 'We should call Daragh.'

'No,' says Isabel. If Daragh knows she's having random histamine crises, or whatever the fuck just happened, he'll insist she goes to the guild because it's too late for anything else. 'We have to find my father.'

'Isabel, you could have *died*!'

She gives Emma a tired look. 'Yeah,' she says. 'That's kind of why we're doing this.' It's hard for Emma, who doesn't have Isabel and Michael's history of life-threatening experiences. But Isabel's out of energy to be comforting. It's as much as she can do to retrieve her tablet and call up the map again. 'Number 74 just looks like a house,' she observes.

'Wait, you're planning on *going* there?' says Emma.

'No, I didn't think I'd bother following up on the only lead I've got,' says Isabel. 'Of course I'm planning to go there.'

'You're not strong enough,' she begins, at the same time as Michael says, 'I'll go.'

They both turn to look at him, standing by the stove. 'What?' he says. 'I'm as invested in this as you are, and I'm not dying. I can go there later and see what I can find.'

'And if he's there?' says Isabel. 'He'll scarper on seeing you and there'll be no chance to learn anything.'

'And if he *is* there, you want to face him?' Michael counters. 'You sure about that?'

She falls silent. She doesn't want Michael riding into battle on her behalf. He might be a fellow survivor, but she can't relinquish control over her only chance of making progress. The thought of seeing her father makes her throat close up all over again, though, and no EpiPen can help with that.

'We'll all go,' says Emma. 'Tomorrow. Michael can go ahead to scout for immediate danger, and me and Isabel will follow when it's safe.'

You're supposed to be keeping out of this, Isabel wants to say, but she's fairly sure Emma would win that argument, and her friend obviously has no qualms about skipping school. She's more surprised that Michael doesn't try to argue either. Instead he says, 'Are you sure we can afford to wait until tomorrow?'

They both look at Isabel and she hears the unspoken question: *how long do you have?*

'No choice,' she says. 'Right now I couldn't walk to the door.' The allergic reaction has robbed her of what little strength she had left.

Michael sighs, draining the potatoes and mashing them. 'All right,' he says finally, bringing over the plate. 'Get yourself on the outside of that. If it doesn't kill you, I'll agree to this insane plan to trudge halfway across the city to a mystery location that could hold all sorts of horrible dangers.'

Isabel gives him a wan smile. 'We'll meet you at the tram stop on the main road,' she says. 'I'll be the one who looks like they're dying.'

22

DISFALO (COLLAPSE)

Emma calls for Isabel at nine in the morning, despite her insistence that she could get the tram into town by herself. 'You *could*,' Emma said, 'but that doesn't mean you should. This way, if you collapse, I'm there.'

Isabel isn't going to collapse. She's laced herself into her strongest boots, and their solidity holds her firm. She has two knives concealed about her person, their familiar weight a comfort, and the indecipherable page of code, the one dated the twentieth of August, crinkles in her back pocket. It's a strange good luck charm, but she's curiously unwilling to let it out of her sight.

The rain has stopped, but the air's still cold enough to make her shiver. It feels like she's always cold these days.

They've missed most of the school traffic, and the tram is nearly empty.

'So,' Emma says, slipping into the seat next to Isabel. She looks tired, shadowed by sleeplessness, but her tone is bright. 'Michael. What's the deal? Friend, ally, weird co-worker you can't get rid of?'

'He saved my life,' says Isabel.

'Yeah, I saw, but—'

'Not then. Before.' She stops herself adding, *when your mum nearly got us both killed.* 'He's my friend.'

Emma wrinkles her nose, apparently unconvinced. 'Did you really grow up together?'

'Sort of. He lived with my family for a while.'

'Huh.' She glances out of the window. They're passing into Weaverthorpe, the grey sky lightening to white. 'Well, if you trust him, then you trust him. He kind of gives me the creeps, though.'

Isabel suspects that's because it's harder for Emma to forget that Michael is Comma. *She*'s pathetic and dying and in need of help; Michael's not. That makes him seem dangerous. But it would be rude to imply that Emma's afraid, so she keeps this thought to herself.

As they approach the city centre, Emma asks, 'If we get off a stop early, do you think you can walk the last bit? I want to show you something.'

'Sure.'

'Positive? You don't have to say yes. I took pictures, I can—'

'I'm sure I can walk an extra five minutes, Emma. If it turns out I can't, we'll text Michael to come meet us.'

232

Emma still looks unsure, but she doesn't argue. When they reach their stop, she helps Isabel navigate the step down onto the pavement.

'What do you want to show me?' Isabel asks, still leaning on her for support. But Emma only shakes her head and starts to walk. Isabel allows herself to be led through the alleyways of familiar art until they reach the pressure-washed wall where the abolitionist painting was scoured away.

It isn't blank now.

Isabel blinks, looks again. Her own face stares at her, surrounded by a maelstrom of colour – at least, she thinks it's her face. The figure has a purple mohawk, an eyebrow piercing, and a safety pin through their left ear. They're dressed in a leather jacket and ripped jeans, with a T-shirt that loudly proclaims this to be A MATTER OF ART AND DEATH. But they have Isabel's strong, straight eyebrows and defined cheekbones, the same lopsided quirk to the lips that passes for her smile. In one hand, they hold a large, dark moth. In the other, a can of spray paint labelled DISOBEDIENCE.

It's Isabel and it isn't. It's a bold Isabel, a mirror-image Isabel, an Isabel rebuilt from the skeleton up.

She doesn't have to ask whether it's Emma's work: she recognises the style, the use of gold and silver for the highlights. 'When did you do this?'

'Last night, mostly.' Emma twists a strand of hair around her fingers. 'Couldn't sit still any longer, you know?' She's watching Isabel carefully for a reaction. 'Do you hate it?'

'*Hate* it?' repeats Isabel incredulously. The person in this painting isn't dying. They're more than a killer, holding a future in their hands. 'No, I don't hate it.' She traces the painted face with reverent fingertips, pausing on the piercings. 'You turned me into a punk.'

It was meant as an observation, but comes out sounding accusatory. Emma just grins. 'I know,' she says. 'It's great, right?'

The girl on the wall stands with feet planted, eyes up, demanding to be noticed. The real Isabel commands nothing, not even her own body. But something about the painting tugs at her, hooks itself deep into her gut so that she can't look away. She's caught by the defiance in that safety pin through the earlobe: *the only person who will damage this body is me*. Transfixed by the power in those clothes, that aerosol can: DISOBEDIENCE.

She's never felt less punk rock than she does now, exhausted and in pain and searching for someone she doesn't want to find. But for a second, she allows herself to imagine a world where this portrait tells the truth.

'Pretty great,' she agrees. 'Not entirely convinced by the hair, though.'

'No? Damn, I thought it suited you.' Emma runs a critical eye over the picture and Isabel. 'Maybe an undercut? And ... blue. Blue would look good on you.'

It would match the beds of her fingernails. Isabel shoves her cold hands into her pockets and tries to ignore the spreading numbness. 'Maybe when I'm not dying, you can do my hair for me.' Her parents trained her to be invisible. They'd hate to see her like this, staring out at the city through colour and rage.

Her gaze rests on the moth in her alter ego's hand, slightly too large to be held. *Little Moth.* This painting, at least, imagines a world where she has a choice.

'I wasn't sure,' says Emma hesitantly, 'what you'd think.'

Isabel looks at her. 'It's amazing,' she says. 'It makes me feel ...' *Alive. Like I belong. Real.* She lets the sentence fade away and hopes the ellipsis says what she can't.

Emma smiles. 'Part of the art, part of the city,' she says. 'Now let's go and find Michael.'

Easier said than done. Halfway to their meeting place, Isabel stops to lean against a wall, her legs threatening to give way beneath her. Her chest's tight, her breaths coming shallow and painful.

'Okay?' Emma asks hesitantly.

The world goes black for a moment, but she snaps back to consciousness so fast she doesn't have time to fall. She forces herself to smile. 'Just need a break. I'll be fine in a minute.'

And she is. She tells herself repeatedly: she's fine. She straightens up, relying on Emma for balance, and takes several steps without collapsing, so that means she's fine. She can breathe enough. Nothing to worry about.

It takes an eternity to reach the tram stop where Michael's waiting. He rushes to take Isabel's other arm, though she tells him she can manage (she can't).

'It's just around the corner,' he says. 'There's no visible danger, but it's hard to be sure.'

It doesn't look like much. The last house in a crowded terrace, apparently deserted, with windows dusty and neglected above rotting sills. It looks like it's been empty since long before July, but even through the fog of death clouding Isabel's eyes, she can see the subtle signs of security enhancements – scanners and traps to protect the building against all but the most determined intruder.

'Okay then,' she says. 'Lead the way.'

The retinal scanner next to the door is cracked, and the fingerprint reader beside the keyhole is blank and lifeless. When Michael nudges it, the door gives beneath his touch, swinging open to reveal an empty hallway.

Too empty. As they step tentatively inside, they see that the dividing wall with the next house has been knocked through to create a large, open-plan downstairs. It's been stripped of carpets and furniture, and there's nothing left except chips in the door frame where equipment was hastily removed.

'Well, whatever used to be here,' says Emma, 'is definitely not here now.'

Michael lets go of Isabel and she hears him running up the stairs, slamming open doors on the upper floor. The sound echoes in empty rooms. If there was ever anything in this house to prove Ian Ryans was here, it's been systematically removed.

Except for one thing. Isabel takes a step back, tugging Emma with her, trying to get the room in perspective. It looked random at first, lines of dirt on the floor where furniture has been dragged away, but it isn't.

'Look.' It's a whisper, and her hand is unsteady as she points, but Emma looks, walking across the room to be sure and then back to Isabel. 'You see it?'

Emma nods. She sees it. They're standing in the middle of an enormous spider's web, spray-painted onto the stripped floorboards.

New webs, bigger flies.

'This is a trap,' says Emma, voice tight with fear.

Because of course it's a fucking trap.

If Isabel wasn't dying, she'd have noticed it sooner: the silence. How empty the street is, how the house seems to be holding its breath. It's not the silence of neglect. It's the quiet of an ambush the moment before it's sprung.

She's reaching for a knife when she hears the click of a gun and a shadow falls over the doorway: a figure in black, masked and anonymous. She shoves Emma to the ground as a bullet clips her shoulder, sending her spinning. It hits the far wall and a shower of plaster cascades to the floor. Before he can fire again, she throws the knife. Her hand shakes and it only hits him in the leg, but it's enough to make him lower his gun. It buys them a few seconds, but there's another man approaching from the kitchen and all Isabel can think about is getting Emma out.

Her friend's wide-eyed and frozen where she fell. Isabel grabs her arm, but she's not strong enough to pull her to her feet. The two of them scramble backwards instead, away from the advancing figures – except there's no way out behind them, and backed up against the wall with nowhere to run, Isabel feels hopeless dread overwhelm her. She fumbles for her other knife, but she's shaking too much to grip it, let down by her failing body.

The nearest intruder raises his gun. *Emma's not meant to die here*, thinks Isabel, as if she has a choice in the matter, and throws herself in front of her friend's body. And—

The gunman hesitates.

It's only a second, but it's enough. Michael comes crashing down the stairs, grabbing the first guy, wrenching the gun from his hand. It skitters across the floor and Isabel snatches it up, aims blindly, fires – a *bang,* shatteringly loud – and the second agent's down, a bullet in the thigh. But now the first has yanked her knife from his leg and is going for Michael's throat. Michael blocks him, but not completely; the blade catches his shoulder and he lets out a grunt of pain before Isabel's second bullet catches his assailant in the stomach.

Emma makes a whimpering noise.

Isabel drops the gun, exhausted by the effort. Michael is swearing, pressing his palm to his injured shoulder. 'Are you hurt?' he asks. 'You're bleeding, did they get you?'

She hadn't even noticed the blood. She touches her injured arm and feels only a haze of pain, the sound of gunshots still ricocheting inside her head. 'They weren't trying to kill me,' she says faintly. 'He was aiming for Emma.'

Michael doesn't question this assessment. 'Then your parents sent them, and there are probably more of them.'

Emma says, 'Are they dead?'

He follows her gaze to the fallen figures. 'Not yet. But they won't be following us. Let's go before someone else does.'

Isabel's parents sent them. To recapture her, presumably, and kill anyone who might constitute a loose end. Which means they knew she would be here. She should probably care about that, wonder if her father knows she has his files. But the empty room's still a dead end – he isn't here, the antidote isn't here, the answers aren't here. Even as she forces herself to her feet, she feels a curious emptiness. Anger and fear both seem miles out of reach. All she feels is . . . lost.

She doesn't remember falling, just remembers hitting the ground, the impact of her kneecaps against the floor, her palms slamming into the boards. Her vision goes black at the edges, but she forces herself to stay conscious. She's okay. So she fell. She'll get back up again.

Emma yells Michael's name, but she can't see them, either of them, her eyesight blurred and useless. She hears an awful rattling gasp and wants to ask if they hear it too, until she realises it's her own breathing, shallow and panicky. It takes a few more breaths for the pain to register like fire in her chest.

Her heart, staccato and emphatic, desperately pounding as though if it beats hard enough it can get the poison out. Her gut, full of knives and burning. Every inch of her, pain.

Total organ failure.

And they have no leads left to follow.

'We've got to get her to Sunny's,' Emma is saying. 'Your shoulder – can you lift her?'

Before Michael can answer, they hear it: the crunch of footsteps on gravel, coming from the garden. Someone's here. 'Gonna have to,' he says, heaving Isabel into his arms. A hiss of pain escapes between his teeth. 'Get the gun. You know how to shoot?'

'Of course I don't know how to shoot!' Emma's voice is high and panicky.

Michael swears again. 'Then let's get the fuck out of here before you have to.'

Isabel's head sags against Michael's chest as he starts moving. She hears another gunshot – way too close for comfort – but he doesn't slow, and she can hear Emma's breath coming ragged beside them, so whoever fired, it didn't hit either of them.

'I'm not leaving you, okay?' Emma's saying, over and over. 'It's going to be okay, Isabel. You're going to be okay, I promise.'

It's not far to the Sunshine Project, but by the time they get there, blood's seeping through Michael's shirt and there's a pained gasp to his breath. Through flickering vision, Isabel sees Emma at the desk, demanding to know which room Daragh's in; hears her say, 'She's *dying*, Leo!' and then they're moving again, down the corridor towards the consulting rooms.

The sound of raised voices reaches them from the other side of the closed door. 'What do you mean, she's dying and you let her walk away?'

Ronan Atwood. Isabel would recognise his voice anywhere.

'What else should I have done, Ronan?' Daragh responds. 'Held her against her will? Forced her to undergo *more* non-consensual surgery? She made a choice.'

'She's seventeen; she doesn't know what she wants. You were supposed to call me. That was the deal.'

That was the deal. It hits her like a bullet in the gut. He knows Ronan, has a deal with Comma, has always known who she is. Daragh Vernant – safe, civilian, separate – made a deal with Comma.

She should have known she'd never be free of them.

'Comma's done enough damage already,' says Daragh.

'Oh, for fuck's sake, let's not make this about your hatred of the guild. Three more weeks and you can—'

'This isn't about me, Ronan!' He's yelling now. 'Just because nobody else cares about her choices—'

Emma shoves open the door, cutting off whatever else he'd have said. Daragh leaps up. 'I told Leo I was— Oh.' He's seen Isabel, Michael's bloody shirt, the whole mess. Even Ronan, perched on the edge of the desk, looks taken aback, a curse springing to his lips.

'Help her,' begs Emma. 'She's dying. Help her.'

Isabel has no options left. No more possibilities, no more straws to grasp at. There's only this: she's dying, and she hasn't found her father, and Ronan Atwood is here.

Isabel tries to say: *I'll give you my father's files if you fix me.*

Isabel tries to say: *Stabilise me long enough and I'll save myself.*

Isabel tries to say: *You owe me a life, after everything the guild has done.*

Isabel says: 'I'll do . . . whatever.'

It's a quiet surrender. It's easier than she thought it would be, letting go of herself and everything she fought to keep.

241

23

SAVO (SALVATION)

Isabel wakes in a room with grey walls so pale they're practically white, oxygen tickling her nose and what feels like a dozen tubes in her arms. She tries to push herself upright but fails, sinking exhausted onto the pillows.

'You're awake!' says a voice from the doorway. She turns her head. Daragh's green scrubs are a speck of colour against the monochrome, his smile kind. 'How do you feel?'

How does she feel? Fucking awful. She doesn't remember how she got here. She remembers Emma's painting, the colours, the empty house. She remembers the sound of gunshots, the blood; remembers falling, and then . . .

She made the deal.

She told Ronan Atwood she'd do whatever he wanted.

Isabel closes her eyes, turning her face away so Daragh can't see her expression. She gave up. All this time, all this fighting, and she walked right back into their arms and told them to take what they liked.

So much for her new life.

'That good, huh?' says Daragh, and she remembers that he lied to her. He let her believe she was safe, when he was Comma all along. *You were supposed to call me*, said Ronan, because they'd discussed her, because Daragh knew who she was from the moment she walked into his office. What an idiot she was to trust him, just because he was kind.

'Where am I?' she asks, without opening her eyes.

'Chadwick Green. It's a Comma hospital in Weaverthorpe.'

'Are Emma and Michael okay?'

'Michael's fine. His shoulder needed a couple of stitches, but it'll heal.'

'And Emma?' At his silence, her panic returns, her mind conjuring images of her friend lying lifeless and spider-carved like Grace, limbs askew. She tries again to sit upright. 'Where is she? She promised she'd be here, why isn't she here, is she okay?'

'She's safe,' says Daragh. 'She's at home.'

Why doesn't that sound like the whole truth? 'She said she wouldn't leave me.'

'She's a civilian,' he says apologetically. 'For security reasons—'

'She's Toni Rolleston's kid!' *She's safe. She's alive. They're just being bastards.* She's never been so relieved to encounter guild bureaucracy.

'I know,' he says. 'I'll see what I can do.'

But if Comma says Emma's not allowed in, Daragh can't overrule it. Isabel knows how this works. She made the deal – her life's the guild's now, her fate in their hands, and their word is final.

Maybe she should have died, rather than live as an indentured assassin to these people. But she doesn't want to die. She's tired and hollowed out, but she doesn't want to die. She wants more colourful days, Emma's art and Emma's smile, before she lets monochrome rooms like this one rob her of life.

It's too late to change her mind now. *I'll do … whatever.* She has no doubt that Ronan will take every drop of blood offered in those words. He's too clever not to realise what she's given him.

Struggling to prop herself up on her elbows, she sees what she missed from her previous vantage point: the single black butterfly in the corner of the white bedspread. And there, another, next to the door handle. Another by the window. Staking a claim on the room so there's no doubt who owns it.

Who owns *her*.

'Ronan's not subtle, is he?' She catches Daragh hiding a smile, but clarifies anyway: 'The décor. It's a bit much.'

He shrugs. 'Comma hospital, Comma décor.'

'And Comma doctor.' He's silent, so she pushes harder. 'I heard the way you spoke to Ronan. You let me believe you weren't guild, but you know him.' Never mind that he was

244

sticking up for her, that he sounded *furious* about what the guild had allowed to happen to her – he still lied, and the betrayal feels raw and bloody.

Daragh sighs, taking off his glasses and cleaning each lens with care. 'Yes, I know Ronan,' he says. 'He's my cousin.'

She wasn't expecting that. Maybe because knowing Ronan has a family is dangerously close to thinking of him as a person, rather than the humanoid representative of Comma. Maybe because Daragh's warm brown skin is worlds apart from Ronan's paper-white colouring. If she squints, she can see the shadow of a resemblance in the shape of their noses, but not enough to change the fact that Ronan's face is eminently punchable, and Daragh's is not.

'Your cousin?' she repeats incredulously.

'Our mothers are sisters.'

'I know how cousins work,' Isabel snaps, still pissed off. 'So, what, he told you to keep an eye on me?'

'He gave me the name you were using and told me to keep it on file at the clinic, to fit you in if you came to us. He thought you might run out of your meds.'

That explains how easily she got an appointment, though her pride smarts at the idea that Ronan didn't think her capable of navigating the black market. 'Planting a doctor at Sunny's to treat one runaway seems like a waste of resources.'

'No, I ...' Daragh seems wrong-footed by this. 'I already worked there. I've worked there for years.'

'But you're guild.'

Daragh shrugs. 'Yes,' he says simply. She wants to demand

245

an explanation – why would a Comma doctor work in a non-profit civilian clinic? – but her fatigue's weighing on her, her eyelids already drooping. He says, 'Get some sleep. Your body needs rest.'

'I'm still dying, aren't I?' she asks him, as he tucks the blankets in around her. His hands are gentle; it's the butterfly on her bedspread that feels like a lie, not his kindness. It doesn't make sense that he's here. Comma is Ronan, her parents, bargains and violence and cruelty, but somehow, impossibly, Comma is also Daragh.

'Yes,' he says, quiet and honest. 'You're still dying. We gave you several blood transfusions to stabilise your condition, but we don't have an antidote, and we don't know how to undo what the poison's done to your immune system. Yet.'

Isabel closes her eyes. Of course they can't save her. She always knew they wouldn't be able to. At least dying will get her out of the deal she made.

To every cloud a silver lining.

She drifts in and out of consciousness, waking periodically to find different nurses in her room or different tubes in her arms. When Daragh's there, he explains the different treatments – the blood transfusions, the dialysis – and what her latest round of test results said, though most of it means little to her. When he's not, she pretends to be unbothered by the violation of her body by needles and tubes, ignoring the crushing anxiety of being trapped in bed. It's easier when she's barely lucid and can let herself drift, floating loose towards the inevitable gravity of total implosion, only sometimes remembering that she's supposed to be staying alive.

But inevitably those patches of clarity give way to the strange iridescence of her dreams – dreams that might be hallucinations or memories or both, all of them full of blood. Sometimes they have a soundtrack. She thinks she recognises the sound of herself screaming.

She wakes, clammy and sweating, from one of these nightmares to find Daragh at her bedside.

'It's all right,' he says. He doesn't touch her, but his hand is there and she grabs at it just to feel like she's real. His grip is steady and strong. 'It was a nightmare. You're safe.'

She's clinging desperately to the hand of a Comma doctor and he's the only person in this building who gives a shit what happens to her. She's not safe. Nothing about this is safe.

'I want to see Emma,' she tells him, for what must be the hundredth time.

'Ronan said—' he begins, also for the hundredth time.

'Fuck Ronan. I want to see her.'

'I'm sorry.' Almost hopefully, he adds, 'Maybe I can arrange for you to speak to her on the phone?'

It's a pathetic consolation prize: she wants Emma *here*, wants her colours diffusing across this desaturated room and chasing away the impersonal monochrome of Comma. But Isabel snatches at it anyway. 'Yes. I want to talk to her. Please.'

'Okay. I'll look into it.' She feels his warm fingers on her wrist, taking her pulse. Too erratic. Slow and fastfastfast and then a pause, so long it's like the beats have stopped, before it

247

thunders back into life. She feels her heart stutter in her chest and reluctantly begin again, pushing poisoned blood around her ungrateful body. 'You know, the nightmare . . . it's good, if it's a memory,' he says. 'It means the treatments are working.'

It doesn't feel like they're working. Maybe her mind's a little less foggy, her thoughts a tiny bit sharper, but she knows her chances are slipping away. 'They still haven't cracked the antidote, have they?' she says. 'Even if they figure it out, the poison's already rewritten my system to hurt itself.'

Daragh looks away. 'There are . . . challenges, it's true,' he begins. Then he sighs, dropping the pretence. 'You should already be dead, Isabel.'

She likes him a lot better when he's honest with her. 'You don't think I'll make it, do you?' She sees it in his face, every time he looks at her test results. In the way he looks at her when he thinks she's asleep.

'The traces of neurotoxins we've been able to identify should have been enough to kill you, and they've been combined with a dozen other things. I'm not sure how you're still breathing.'

A ghost of a smile. 'Spite,' she tells him.

And years of spider bites and needle pricks and tainted food and crying on the bathroom floor waiting for the sickness to pass. Isabel's resistance is incomplete and hard won.

Daragh adjusts her pillow, helping her move her head to a more comfortable position. 'Well,' he says, 'try to hold on to that spite a little longer, and you might make it through this.'

A tiny capsule.

Lying there under the microscope, pitifully small for the hours of work and tears it represents. She has to concentrate to stay upright, eyes and hands steady as her father inspects her work.

'This isn't what I asked for,' he says, frowning.

Mouth dry. Nails against her palm. 'I ... modified the approach slightly. Aerosol administration would have posed a risk to the agent, since there's no effective pre-exposure antidote. A solid capsule protects the handler, eliminates the possibility of collateral damage, and makes it harder to detect.'

'Did I ask you to plan the hit?'

'No, but—'

'No,' he interrupts, 'I did not.' But he's still peering through the microscope. 'Tell me about the coating.'

'It's designed to break down gradually inside the body. The symptoms will slowly worsen, but by the time the target realises it's poison, they'll have had a lethal dose. They'd never figure out the antidote in time.'

'How long?' he says.

'It depends on the body mass of the target, but a month, maybe. With intramuscular delivery.'

He nods, still examining the pellet. 'A pneumatic delivery of some kind, presumably,' he says. She nods. A modified pen and a clumsy collision, or that old trick of an umbrella tip to the calf, and the mark walks away with a tiny injury and a bad mood, never suspecting that they've been poisoned. 'It's small enough that it could work. But a month's a long time. The aerosol would have been faster.'

'Fast enough to get the agent caught,' she says, and then bites her lip, because that sounds a little too close to criticism to be safe. 'That is – this is better for remaining undetected. No collateral, no witnesses ... the target would struggle to pin down when it happened, and meanwhile the agent's a thousand miles away and still running. They'd know it was us, but they could never prove it.'

'And invisibility is power.' Her father looks up from the microscope. 'Well, little Moth, let's see what that clever mind of yours has done. Show me the changes you made to the formula.'

She tries not to let her hands shake as she hands him her notes, knowing he'll punish her if she shows fear. She did it. She made his impossible weapon, better than he ever could. He has no reason to hurt her.

Not that that's ever stopped him.

He examines the notes carefully, following each calculation with his finger. When he reaches the end, he places the pages down on the bench and looks at her, and he smiles.

'Incredible,' he says.

He's not angry. He's ... proud.

He looks at her work and he knows: she is capable of his ingenuity, his creativity, his vicious sadism and total disregard for the suffering of others. There is nobody else within Comma who could do what she has done, and there is nobody who could have made her into this except him.

The deadliest weapon Ian Ryans ever created was his daughter.

Isabel is awake.

Her hospital room is lit only by the sickly green of the emergency exit sign and the glare of the hallway light slicing under the door. She stares at the ceiling, looking for patterns in the dancing green refractions, and tries to remember how to breathe. It's hard to tell these days whether it's fear or the neurotoxin in her blood robbing her of air.

She drags in a breath, lets it go, reaches for another. Five things she can hear: a siren outside, footsteps, the distant rattle of a trolley on another floor, the quiet hum of machines, her lungs failing. Five things she can see: the ceiling, the corner of the door, a narrow strip of light, the glint of green on the IV stands, her own death approaching.

'Daragh?' She doesn't have the strength to yell, and it strikes her how awful it would be to die like this, when she finally knows how to save herself. Then she remembers her call button and presses it repeatedly until the doctor comes running.

'What is it?' he asks.

'There was a paper. In my jeans pocket when I came. Where is it?'

Daragh takes something from the table, presses it into her hand. 'Is this it?'

She unfolds it with shaking hands. *There.* Not her father's code at all. No wonder she couldn't break it, expecting to find his mind at work behind this.

Because it was always her own.

Daragh finds her a pen, a clipboard to lean on. Shaking with the effort, she pulls free the knot of her own encryption, lets the code unspool into meaning. Her report. Her formula.

By the time she reaches the end, her handwriting's barely legible. She takes a moment to gather her strength, then draws a line beneath it and begins to write. Each word is a heartbeat, stuttering and unsure. Her body protests, lungs screaming. *Just one more day*, she begs it, *just give me a day – half a day – an hour.*

The pen drops from her fingers onto the bed.

It's enough.

It's all she has.

'La antidoto,' she says, as Daragh takes the clipboard from her. 'Jen ĝi.' *That's it.*

They'd never figure out the antidote in time. But the poison wasn't designed to be used against its creator.

Daragh's already reaching for his phone. She's fading out of consciousness, dimly aware of the urgency in his voice as he tries to organise her salvation, his terse commands. All her own urgency seeps away. She's done her part. Daragh has the formula, and that means they can save her, doesn't it? It means there's still a chance she'll wake up from this.

She's done enough.

She's fought enough.

She has nothing left to give.

Isabel closes her eyes and surrenders to the blackness.

Her heart

       fastfastfast slow

            slow

                s l o w

   stops.

24

Rezigno (Surrender)

There is no relief in waking, only noise.

The scream of machines. Shouts and shocks and shattering, the Morse code of her heartbeat ricocheting amidst cracked ribs. And pain – there's pain too, devouring her bones as scorched flesh melts away under the white heat of agony. It would be a mercy to be allowed to scream, but her lungs are folding in on themselves and her vocal cords snap like violin strings, like whiplash, like abandonment.

She never thought dying would hurt like this.

She would have fought harder, if she knew it would hurt like this.

25

RELEVIĜO (RESURRECTION)

'Welcome back.'

Death feels like a hospital blanket under her fingers and a cool pillow against her face. Isabel opens her eyes. Daragh is sitting by her bedside, dark shadows under his eyes and stubble on his cheeks. She opens her mouth to speak and is surprised to find that she can.

'I'm alive?' she says, disbelief plain despite the hoarse rasp of her dry throat.

'Just about.' His smile is weary. 'It was touch and go. Your heart stopped twice.'

'And people said I didn't have one.'

The doctor laughs harder than the weak joke merits. Relief,

she realises. He thought she'd die – and, more surprisingly, he'd have cared if she did.

'You're in intensive care,' he tells her. 'Still in Chadwick Green, in Weaverthorpe. We took you off life support this morning, once we knew your heart wasn't going to stop again, but we'll keep you here until your condition is more stable.'

'What day is it?'

'Saturday. It's the twentieth of October.'

People at school will be wondering where she went. She hopes Ashvin found someone to replace her, that he doesn't begrudge her disappearance, although she suspects she wouldn't get her job back if she asked for it.

Except she won't be going back. Not after making a deal with Comma.

She closes her eyes, suddenly tired again. 'Is it gone?' she says. 'The poison? Did you make the antidote?'

'Yes.' He squeezes her cold hand in his, and she senses pride in his fervent affirmative. 'Yes, it's gone. You gave us the key.' He saved her. Kind, lying, guild-allied Daragh Vernant saved her. 'You're safe.'

Then why do I feel like I'm rotting from the inside?

Being alive is exhausting. Her body remembers being dead, tries to claw itself back into the grave of that momentary oblivion, but the machines around her drag her out again and again.

'What now?' she asks.

'Now you sleep, and heal. It'll take time to fix the damage that was done to you.'

Was done. A passive turn of phrase for such an active brutality, a violence that can never be fixed. When the poison's gone and her body is healed, there will still be this: she made this poison, and her father used it against her.

And if not against her, he'd have used it against someone else, or sold it to someone who would. She knew that and she made it anyway, and she has the audacity to rage that it's *not fair*, that she *doesn't deserve this.*

She should have known after that first flash of memory. Or in Grace's lab. Or when she killed Ian Crampton without even having to try. But it took until now for the truth to sink in: it's entirely fair, and Isabel Ryans only has herself to blame.

Daragh would have her sleep, rest, live, because Daragh sees her as a girl that the guild failed to save, and he wants to help her.

It was always herself she needed saving from.

Her body remembers being dead, so sleep comes easily.

Recovery is a slow bitch of a process, almost as agonising as falling apart.

Isabel wakes every morning in pain. Sometimes the memories hit so suddenly that she lies paralysed until the gentle tickle of the oxygen in her nose soothes her into breathing by herself again. Days pass before she can stand, though time means nothing inside this sterile cage. She walks to the window, supported by an IV stand and Daragh's arm, and it feels like running a marathon.

She has to train Daragh out of apologising every time she

clutches her aching ribs. As if she'd begrudge him breaking them when he was fighting to restart her heart. As if she'd resent being alive.

But sometimes . . .

Sometimes it feels less like recuperation and more like being in Cocoon, except with a heart monitor and oxygen tank by her side. The way they coax her into moving again, curling her fingers around objects until she has the strength to pick them up, encouraging her to stand, walk, move as much as she can within the limitations of her barely functional body. The way they test her memory and brain function, but instead of asking her about history or setting her maths problems, they want to know which arteries cause the swiftest death if cut, which poisons are hardest to detect, how to break bones with minimal force.

She answers their questions anyway, and she's always correct. She knows a thousand ways to kill people. She can't trust her own memories, but she knows this.

'Your cognitive abilities improve every day,' says Daragh, lowering his flashcards. 'This is all information stored in your long-term memory, so it's a good sign that you can access it. It suggests that repeated exposure to memory suppressants hasn't done extensive damage.'

'That sounds like something you should be happier about,' she observes.

He sighs. 'Of course I'm pleased. It's a good sign. But I wish . . .'

'That Comma weren't training me?' They're kidding

258

themselves if they thought she wouldn't notice. 'I made the deal. I knew this was coming.'

'You were dying,' says Daragh. 'You weren't of sound mind and body and it certainly wasn't a free choice. I've tried to tell Ronan that, but—'

'Sure it was a free choice,' she says. 'A shitty choice, between dying and killing, but it's still a choice and I still made it.' She looks at him. 'Aren't you guild? Shouldn't you want this?'

'I work for Comma,' he says, as if that's clarification, but guild is guild. 'I . . .' He shrugs. 'I don't think *you* want this.'

It doesn't matter what she wants. She's proven again and again what she's good at. Nobody made her kill Ian Crampton, but she did it, because that's who she is. Take away the fear and the poison and all that's left is Isabel Ryans, the Moth, a killer to the core. Fighting it hasn't done her any good, so she may as well embrace it – isn't it better to walk freely into this with her chin up than for Ronan to force her?

A few memories dribble back from those confused moments at Sunny's. 'Ronan said you hate the guild,' she says. 'Is that true?'

Daragh weighs his words carefully, and finally says, '"Hate" is a strong word to use for the institution that's allowed me to get where I am today. But I've never been comfortable being part of this.'

'Then why are you?'

She must see a dozen nurses each day, but Daragh is the one constant, always there when she wakes with his quiet voice and gentle hands. She doesn't understand him, and she wants to.

He shrugs. 'I wanted to be a doctor.'

'You could have done that without the guild, couldn't you?' There are civilian doctors, she knows. Guild ones are better trained, but the option is still there.

'Not when you're from an industrial,' says Daragh, and gives a little half-smile at her surprise. 'Yeah. Ronan may be my cousin, but we're not a guild family. We grew up in Ganton, where most people go from school to the factories to the grave. Ronan was the one who saw that the guild could give us more. He knew I wanted to be a doctor, so he convinced me to apply for Comma sponsorship. I could study medicine, and all it would cost would be ten years working for them, as long as I passed basic training.' He shrugs. 'It was – is – a good deal. Of course I took it. It was my only chance to be a doctor, and most of the people I treat aren't killers, just adjacents and their families. I've delivered *babies*.'

'You sound like you're trying to convince yourself,' says Isabel.

Daragh huffs a small laugh. 'Believe me, I've spent enough years trying to square it with my conscience. I almost convinced myself I could be part of Comma without being complicit in what the guild does. Until Christopher.'

He lapses into silence. 'Christopher?' she prompts.

'My partner,' he says, almost unwillingly. 'We were going to get married, when we weren't so young and broke and distracted. He was an artist.' He pauses. 'He painted Sunny's.'

Isabel notes the past tense and guesses where the story's going. 'He's dead?'

Daragh nods. 'Hummingbird. It was ... pointless. That's

260

what always got me. He got in a bar fight with this rich guy – and I mean *rich*. He was a civilian – a lawyer – but he had guild protection and the ear of every smuggler in Espera. And worse than that, he knew Chris's name. He kept telling me nobody would call a hit on a drunk civilian mouthing off in a pub, but he was wrong. They found him three days later. I was at work when they told me.'

Isabel shifts on the bed, rearranging her pillows, then leans back. 'Cue moral crisis, I'm guessing.'

'Something like that,' he says. 'I never knew which of my patients were killers, you know. I had that redacted from their files, because I was trying to pretend it away. I'd stitch a dozen wounds and convince myself I was doing something good, but for all I knew, they'd turn around and kill someone as soon as they walked out of the hospital – someone like Christopher, who meant everything to me. Realising that, three years into a ten-year contract with no get-out clause . . . it was unbearable. I used to wander the city after work, trying to figure out what to do, and everywhere I looked were reminders of him. His art, plastered across the walls. He must have tagged half the city. I followed it across Espera until I wound up at Sunny's, and when I asked them about it, they told me he'd painted it over the course of months and refused to take a penny for his work. The inside, too – he painted the tree of gratitude, the one you saw. I don't know why he never told me.'

Isabel places these jigsaw pieces carefully into the Daragh-shaped puzzle inside her head. 'So that's why you work there,' she says. 'Guilt.'

'Yeah, perhaps you could call it that.' He puts the flashcards down and walks over to the window, looking out, his back to Isabel.

'How much longer?' she asks him.

'What?'

'Your ten years. How much longer?'

He hesitates. 'Five days,' he says finally.

Five days. Five days, and he leaves her. Five days, and he hands her care over to some faceless Comma practitioner, leaving her at their mercy. Five days, and he'll be out, living the life he should always have been living: helping civilians and children and the innocent. And she'll still be here.

She won't let herself panic about that. She's not allowed to panic about that.

Daragh turns to look at her. 'Isabel,' he says, in a tone that suggests her fear's written plainly on her face, 'I'm not leaving you.'

Fragile hope. 'What?'

'I'm not passing your care over to anyone else. Frankly, I don't trust them.'

'But your contract . . .'

'For years I told myself that being part of Comma meant I could make it better. This is my chance to be the part of the guild that's better – the part that doesn't fail you.' He's so earnest that she can't meet his eyes, staring at her hands instead. 'Because they did, Isabel. From the day I met you at Sunny's, all I saw was how completely and utterly the guild screwed up. You were a child, and the people who should

262

have nurtured you chose to neglect and abuse and misuse you instead. I've seen your scars, and none of that should ever have happened. And I can't fix it, or stop Ronan using you however he wants to use you, but I won't abandon you either.' He turns back to the window. 'Not if I ever want to pretend I'm a better person than my cousin.'

She swallows. 'You don't have ... you could ...' He shouldn't stay for her, when he has the chance to walk away. She wouldn't, if she were him; she can't imagine throwing away her freedom for somebody else. But she can't bring herself to tell him that she doesn't need him to stay.

'I'll be here until you're better,' he says. 'Not only until you're not dying. Until you're safe.' She has never been safe. 'Every step of the way, Isabel. And then, maybe, I'll leave, but not before.'

Safe.

She never thought she'd find it here, in the hands of a Comma doctor.

26

KORINKLINO (AFFECTION)

'You missed my birthday,' says Emma, approximately three seconds after picking up the phone.

'What?'

'My birthday. It was last Monday. You were too busy being "mostly unconscious".' Isabel can imagine her making air quotes with her fingers. 'I'm eighteen now.'

'I'm sorry,' says Isabel, caught out. 'I didn't know.'

Emma laughs. 'It's okay. I know you'd have come if you weren't literally dying at the time. And if they'd let me into the hospital, I'd have brought the party to you.'

'You had a party?'

'Not really. I went for a meal with Leo and Mum, hung out with some school people. Pretty quiet.' Isabel's relieved to hear that Emma and Toni are talking again. Toni doesn't deserve it, but Emma does, and she'd hated the thought that she wrecked their relationship for good. 'Leo and I are competing to find the worst possible romance novel, but after the three he gave me as a present, I don't think I have a chance. I have *so* many questions about every step of the process that went into publishing a story about star-crossed lovers from different guilds. I mean, what kind of meet-cute happens over a dead body?'

'And the guilds allow this?' says Isabel. 'It's not Free Press or something?'

'Fully legal,' her friend assures her. 'Whack, right? They're actually not terrible, once you get past the premise . . .'

'I'll take your word for it.'

Emma must have her on speaker, because Isabel can hear the gentle chime of a spoon against the edge of a mug and a clink as she puts it down. 'And you? How are the near-death experiences going?'

'Apparently I actually died.' She didn't think she wanted to talk about it, but now that she's hearing Emma's voice, she finds that she does. 'Daragh says my heart stopped twice.'

'Huh,' says Emma. 'But he saved you, didn't he?'

'No, this is a phone call from the afterlife.'

'Oh, damn. Resurrected Isabel comes with sarcasm. That's an impressive doctor you've got there.'

She feels herself smiling. 'He is.'

'Good,' says Emma emphatically. 'Otherwise I was going to fight him on your behalf. I mean, hello, it's *Daragh Vernant*, people like him for a reason – though I'm reconsidering his awesomeness now we know he's been Comma this whole time, because that's fucked up. I would *not* have guessed that.'

'It's okay,' says Isabel. 'He probably won't be Comma for long, so you can go back to thinking he's awesome.'

'Oh? How come?'

'His contract's about to end, and I don't get the impression he'll be renewing.' She bites her lip. 'And you? Are you okay? After what happened at Gauntlet Drive ...'

There's a long silence. 'I think it'll be a while before I can forget watching you shoot someone in front of me,' Emma says. 'I thought I'd have nightmares, but so far it's been more of a daytime haunting.'

No nightmares is the best she could have hoped for. 'I wish you hadn't had to see that.'

'It's weird. I knew you were trained, but somehow seeing it is different. You made it look ... easy.'

'I missed,' Isabel points out.

'You didn't kill them,' Emma corrects. 'That's not the same thing. You saved my life.'

Isabel swallows. She'd half thought Emma would want nothing to do with her, after seeing what she was capable of. 'Do you know what happened to them? Afterwards?'

There's a clatter of plates in the background. 'After you collapsed, Ronan sent a team over there. Mum says one of them got away – the one you didn't shoot – but the other two are in custody. I don't think they've said anything useful yet, but that's not our problem, at least.' Emma pauses, then adds,

'I don't think I've ever been that scared in my life. You were dying, and they were shooting at us, and—'

'Yeah,' agrees Isabel, guilt weighing heavily on her. 'I'm sorry. I should never have involved you in this.' She feels responsible, not only for Emma's fear, but also for Michael's injury, the damage it must have done when he carried her. Daragh keeps assuring her that he's healing well, but it doesn't ease her worries.

'I'm the one who insisted on coming,' says Emma. 'It wasn't your fault.'

But Isabel knows those men were there for her. She knew it the moment the gunman hesitated. Her father doesn't want her dead, he wants her *his*, whatever it takes, and this whole city's full of traps. If Emma had been caught in the crossfire, she'd never have forgiven herself.

'Are you coming back to the Fraser?' asks her friend.

'Have you?' says Isabel, deflecting. The question of her future is one she'd rather not discuss with Emma. 'Gone back, I mean?'

'No,' Emma admits. 'I went once, spent three periods jumping at loud noises, and then hid in Mortimer's classroom for the rest of the day. He's been calling round to Leo's with my homework ever since. I can see why you like him.'

'I never said I liked him,' says Isabel. 'We're just . . .'

'Blackmailing each other. I know. He told me. You have a *weird* approach to friendship.'

'He told you?'

'Well, not exactly, but I figured it out. I don't think he'd ever

267

have told anyone about you, you know. It seems at odds with the way he thinks he's under some moral imperative to offer people biscuits at every possible opportunity.'

'Did you . . .' Isabel pauses, trying to figure out how to word her question. 'What did you tell him?'

'The truth, mostly. I didn't tell him about Gauntlet Drive. But I told him you collapsed and were in hospital. He asked if it was a Comma hospital, and I said yes. He asked what they'd demanded in return, and I . . . didn't know the answer to that.'

Isabel doesn't know either. She's had no visits from Ronan Atwood, no ultimatums, but she's constantly braced for them.

'So?' prompts Emma. 'What *have* they asked for in return?'

She sighs. She should've known she couldn't avoid this conversation. 'Nothing yet,' she says, which is true, even if it doesn't feel like it. 'But there'll be something. I don't think I'm coming back to the Fraser, whatever happens. You should probably tell Nick Larrington that I changed schools.'

'He asked after you,' says Emma. 'The day I went in, I was collecting some of my stuff from Grace's office, and he was working in the library. He said he'd texted you, but you hadn't replied.'

'I don't have my phone.' She doesn't know what happened to it when they brought her here. Come to think of it, she has no idea what's happened to any of her stuff – whether it's still at her flat, or in a skip somewhere if her landlord's noticed that she hasn't paid her rent. 'Tell Nick it's not personal, will you? I appreciated his attempts to be friends with me, however misdirected.'

'Misdirected?' echoes Emma incredulously. 'What's that supposed to mean?'

'I'm not exactly worth befriending.' It's not self-pity – it's an objective truth that she needs more from Emma than Emma needs from her. She's a parasite, leeching off the goodwill of others with nothing to offer in return.

'Well, that's ridiculous,' says Emma. 'Are you saying I fucked up when I decided to befriend you?'

'Maybe.' She swaps the chunky hospital phone to her other ear. 'If you hadn't, Grace would still be alive, you wouldn't have found out that your mum's Comma, and—'

'Okay, well, first of all, my mum continuing to lie to me isn't a *positive*, and as for Grace . . .'

'She's dead because of me. You can't deny that.'

'She's dead because somebody killed her. That's not your fault. It fucking *sucks*, but it's not your fault.'

'But you hate the guilds,' says Isabel. It feels important, somehow, to remind Emma who she is. Just because Isabel's losing herself, doesn't mean her friend has to. 'You saw me shoot someone, for fuck's sake. Why haven't you walked away from me already?'

'You don't get to tell me how I feel,' says Emma. 'And anyway, you're not the guilds.'

But she is. Comma is written into her skin, her blood, her bones. When she dies and they cut her open, they'll find that butterfly mark of ownership carved into her heart. 'I'm a killer, Emma.'

'You're a seventeen-year-old girl whose father poisoned her.'

269

'Both of those things can be true.' She takes a deep breath. 'I ... I made the poison. I created it. I'm the reason it was that bad.' It's no easier to admit it to Emma than it was to tell Grace. 'This is my fault.'

'Oh, for the love of Espera ...' begins Emma, biting back expletives. 'Isabel, this isn't your fault, and the fact that you made the poison doesn't mean you deserved to die. Are you honestly trying to tell me you think you deserved all that pain? That because you're not some perfect, innocent child, every bad thing that's ever happened to you is in some way justified?'

Isabel is silent. When Emma puts it like that, it sounds ... absurd. But she does, doesn't she? Deserve it? She was willing to let that poison be used on others, so it's justice of a sort that it ended up being her. A cruel justice, but justice nonetheless.

'I can tell from your silence that you're being an idiot,' says Emma. 'So whatever you're thinking right now, stop it.'

'I've killed four people,' says Isabel. 'More, if you count those who died because of the work I did with my father in the lab.'

'You mean all the times he tested poison on you?' Emma's good at this, throwing Isabel's own words back in her face. 'This isn't some kind of cosmic retribution. Next you'll tell me you deserved what your parents did to you.'

Emma doesn't get it. She'll never get it. The Isabel she knows is an idealised Isabel, a victimised Isabel. Not Cocoon's greatest success story, who took to killing like a duck to water. 'I know they were wrong,' she says, but she hesitated too long.

'Bel,' says Emma seriously. 'I know they fucked you up, but tell me this: if you saw another child going through what you went through, would you say they probably deserved it and walk away without trying to help?'

'That's different.'

'Is it? How is that different?'

Other children aren't Isabel. 'I don't want to have this conversation, Emma.'

'Okay,' says Emma. And for a second Isabel thinks that'll be the end of it, until her friend says, 'But I'm curious. I know your dad's a poisoner, but what about your mum? What does she do?'

She doesn't want to talk about her mother either, but she's not willing to sacrifice her connection to Emma by hanging up, so she says, 'She's a contract killer. Field agent. Swallowtail, if that means anything to you.'

'Not really,' admits Emma, which is understandable; there's no reason she should've paid attention to Comma pseudonyms. 'What part do you think she played in all this? The poison, the new guild ...'

Isabel has been trying not to think about that, which is her usual state of being when it comes to Judith. 'Michael said she was against the poisoning, that my parents had argued about it. But wherever they are, they're together, so clearly it wasn't a deal-breaker.'

'She was opposed to it?' Emma sounds surprised. 'But surely that's a good thing.'

She sees the number on her heart monitor ticking upwards

271

and tries to relax her suddenly taut muscles. 'Not when it's my mother,' she says. She knows Emma will want answers, but fear's closing her throat and stealing her words. She manages: 'She's the reason I have a butterfly burned into my chest. She probably opposed the poison because she thought it was letting me off easy. That's all you need to know.'

Emma swears. 'She *what*?'

'Leave it, Emma.'

The questions stir up memories she's been fighting to keep buried since she left her parents' house. Her father's a sadist with no regard for her suffering. But her mother . . . her mother's worse. Her mother is the bruises under her clothes where they won't show, the lies that twist her memories into something unreal until she doubts her own sanity, the constant shame, the gun in her hand that took the last shreds of her innocence. Her mother is the promise that nobody would listen to anything she told them and the fear that kept her from testing it.

She knows she doesn't deserve what they did to her. But knowing isn't the same as believing, when all her life she's been told the opposite, her mother's voice warping truth into lie and reality into delusion. Her father's drugs aren't the only reason she struggles to trust her recollection of events.

In the background, on Emma's end of the line, she hears a door slam and the rattle of keys. 'Emma?' calls a voice. 'I think I've got a new top contender. It's about—'

'I'm on the phone, Leo.' Footsteps. 'Oh, wow, that's . . .'

'Yeah. Is it Isabel you're talking to? Maybe she'd get a kick out of it.'

'Somehow I doubt that.' A door closes, and then Emma's walking back towards the phone. 'Sorry. Leo's friends work in a library and they were having a sale. He's brought an even more horrifying contender to the Worst Romance Novels of Espera table.'

Isabel would happily discuss bad romance novels in excruciating depth for hours if it gets her out of talking about her mother. 'Do tell.'

For a moment she thinks Emma won't let her change the subject, but her friend must realise that persisting will only result in Isabel having a panic attack, because she says, 'Well, it's about an agent who falls in love with her target, so we're off to a strong start there.'

'Yikes.'

'It's love at first sight, of course.'

'Of course,' agrees Isabel. 'She'd be pretty bad at her job if she had time to get close.'

'"The assassin reached for her blade,"' reads Emma, in a dramatic voice, '"but pity stayed her hand. She hadn't felt this way in years, but when she saw how his dark hair framed his face on the pillow, she couldn't help but—"'

'I will hang up on you.'

'Oh, but there's a juicy bit on the next page, listen—'

'Hanging up right now.'

Emma's laughter rattles the tinny speaker of the hospital phone. 'I'll spare you the vicarious smut-reading if you promise to stop with the self-loathing.'

It's not self-loathing. It's honesty. 'I'll try. No guarantees.'

'Then call me tomorrow, so I can yell at you about it again.'

A tiny smile tugs the stiff muscles of her face. 'Okay.'

'I'll be waiting.'

Isabel imagines Emma waiting for her phone to ring. It fills her with a sense of wonder that somebody would want to hear her voice, would pick her as the recipient of their jokes about bad novels.

'Tell Mortimer,' she begins impulsively, and then hesitates. 'Tell him ... I'm grateful he was worried about me.' It's not enough. He's a loose end, and she can't help feeling like she's reneged on whatever agreement they had. *The enemy of my enemy* ... but she's not, is she? Not any more. 'And that I owe him a pack of biscuits.'

'I'll tell him,' says Emma. 'He'll be glad to hear from you.'

A month ago, she wouldn't have believed that. But it's starting to feel like it might be true, that people out there give a shit what happens to her.

After Emma's hung up, the thought of her mother lingers like a bad taste. But Isabel clings to those brief moments of laughter, those jokes – this friendship she never thought she'd have. And for a little while, it keeps the fear at bay, a shield between her and the past she'll never truly leave behind.

27

ELEKTOJ (CHOICES)

Daragh has finally declared Isabel well enough for visitors –
guild-approved ones, anyway, which pretty much just means
Michael, since there's no one else in the guild she wants to see.
But she's missed him, and when she asks him if he'll come, he
agrees so quickly that she suspects he missed her too.

So it's a surprise when Ronan Atwood turns up in her
doorway instead, his grey suit a dark smudge against the
whiteness of the room. He takes in the sight of her with
flinty eyes.

'You look like you're feeling better,' he says.

Isabel has been pacing the length of her room, seeking
any reprieve from the boredom of convalescence. There's
little to be found; the small window looks out over a dull

Weaverthorpe terrace of narrow houses, confirming her suspicion that whenever Daragh stares intently out of it during their conversations, it's less to do with the scintillating view and more because he doesn't want to look her in the eye.

'Better enough to be bored out of my mind,' she says. 'Why are you here?'

'I thought we might discuss the terms of your arrangement with Comma.'

She's been anticipating this moment since she woke up in the hospital, but Isabel still feels her stomach clench. 'You want me to work for you.'

'You said you'd do anything.' Ronan takes a seat on the room's only chair, which has the curious effect of ensuring he has to look up at her. It doesn't make her feel any more in control. 'Obviously, this is premature. You're still in recovery. But I thought we should talk about it, so that we both know where we stand.'

'There's nothing to talk about.'

'There's plenty, but let's start with your father's files. We retrieved them from your flat, and I have to say your codebreaking skills surpassed my expectations.'

Isabel resumes her pacing. 'I didn't do it for you.'

'No,' he agrees. His pale hands are folded in his lap, corpse-white against the dark cloth of his trousers. 'But if you *had* taken my offer, none of this would have been necessary. You do realise that, don't you?'

Of course she realises that. Ronan offered her medical care and she turned him down to keep clinging to the illusion of her independence, only to find herself utterly in his power. She doesn't need him rubbing her fuck-ups in her face.

'What do you want from me?'

'I want you to work in the lab.'

Isabel's blood runs cold, and she freezes mid-step. It takes a moment to remember how to move so that she can turn to look at him. 'What?'

'You're the only person currently in the guild who was trained by your father, and you've proven your capabilities. The modifications you made to that poison—'

'Nearly killed me.'

'—were inspired. With your father gone, we need somebody with his skills, to do for us what he did.'

It never occurred to her that in saving herself, she'd given them the formula. That Comma now has the poison – *her* poison – to use as they see fit.

'No,' she says. 'Not what he did. I can't . . . I *won't* be like my father.'

She won't take over Parnassiinae and spend her life thinking up crueller ways to kill people. The fact that she's capable of it is exactly why the idea terrifies her.

'Okay,' says Ronan, realising his mistake. 'Not what he did. But you could be useful—'

She cuts him off. 'I want you to destroy it.'

His forehead creases in a perplexed frown. 'What?'

'The formula. The poison, if you've tried to make it. I want it destroyed.'

'Isabel . . .'

277

'It's not my father's work, it's mine, and I never agreed to give it to the guild. You have no right to it.' Destroying it won't save lives. Comma has other poisons, all as deadly, and changing the means doesn't change the end. But the idea of them using her work . . .

'It would be considerably against our interests to destroy such a valuable weapon,' begins Ronan.

'I don't care. You don't need this poison. My father already undercut you, so it's not going to net you much on the international market, and there are other poisons that are faster and easier. The only reason you'd use this one is if you want your target to die terrified and in unimaginable pain. And I'm telling you to destroy it.'

I will not become my father. As long as this poison exists, that door remains open and that version of Isabel survives.

He's silent for a long time. She pictures the gears in his head working as he tries to compute this unanticipated hurdle, because whatever he was expecting of Isabel, it wasn't this.

'Destroy it,' she says again. 'Everything I gave you – the notes, the pellet. And when you find my father . . .' The words stick in her throat. She assumes they're still looking for him, but she doesn't dare ask what their plans are. Whether they're going to kill him. Whether he'll suffer for what he's done.

'You want us to destroy his copy too,' Ronan finishes, when it becomes clear she isn't going to complete her sentence.

'I wouldn't have decrypted his files,' she says. 'Not if I'd had a choice. I can't take it back now, but I wouldn't have done it.'

Ronan's eyes are lazy pools of brackish water as they rake over her, utterly merciless. 'You're very demanding, for somebody who already owes us her life.'

'You want me,' Isabel points out. 'You're the one who wouldn't let me leave. You could have left me alone and then I wouldn't owe you anything.' The fact that she'd be dead is neither here nor there.

'You're right,' he acknowledges. 'We do want you. But let's say, for argument's sake, that you have the power to dictate terms here. Say we agree to destroy the formula. What could you offer us that would make that worth our while? What will you give us in return?'

She has nothing to offer. Nothing that will be enough, nothing that will get her out of this. 'What do you *want*?'

Ronan shrugs. 'It seems a waste, to send a brain like yours out into the field. But if you're not interested in the lab . . .'

If Isabel had been thinking straight, she'd have known this was his plan. He wants her back in the field – wants her to kill again, take contracts, become everything that Emma hates. No doubt he only offered her the lab so that this seemed like a concession instead of a life sentence. It's not that she doubts she can do it, because she knows exactly how good she is at killing. She could be everything Ronan wants her to be.

But becoming that means losing everything: her hope of another life, her conscience, the only friend she's ever had. Because if she agrees to this, there aren't enough lies in the world to stop Emma from seeing her for who she really is.

'I'm not strong enough yet,' she objects. 'I haven't even left this room.'

'There's a training gym downstairs.' He gives her a tight, insincere smile. 'I'm sure by the time I find a job to suit your talents, you'll be almost back to your old self.'

So that's it. She can either kill with a knife in her hand or she can let them use her poison to rip people apart from the inside. And what kind of a choice is that? She's as much a murderer in the lab as she is in the field.

'And you'll destroy it?' she says. 'If I agree to ... whatever, you'll destroy it?'

'Of course,' he says. Then he adds, 'You are, after all, a significantly more valuable weapon than one poison.'

I'm not a weapon, she wants to say, but she is. She always has been.

'Okay,' she says. It was meant to sound defiant, like she's got what she wants out of this conversation, but it comes out as a whisper. Lost and broken. *I'll do anything. Just don't turn me into my father.*

Ronan gives her his reptilian smile. 'Then we're agreed,' he says silkily. 'I'll be in touch.'

As soon as he's gone, she walks back over to the bed and sits down, legs weak.

'Isabel?' says Daragh from the doorway. 'I saw Ronan in the corridor. Are you okay?' She nods, but her breath catches in her throat and her shoulders hitch, making a liar of her. Daragh crosses the room, sitting down beside her. 'You're okay. I'm here. What did he say to you?'

Isabel shrugs. 'Came to follow up on the deal.' There has to be a better word for a bargain struck on the brink of death. 'Wanted to discuss my *future*.'

Daragh sighs. 'Of course he did.' He brushes Isabel's fringe out of her eyes. 'But he can't overrule me if I say you're still recovering, you know. So if you need me to spend the next six months getting in Ronan's way, I will.'

She forces a smile. 'Thanks, Daragh,' she says, though she can't see the point in delaying the inevitable. Then she adds, 'Are you *sure* you're Ronan's cousin?'

He frowns, confused. 'Yes.'

'And you grew up together?'

'Yes.'

'Then how come he's a dick and you're not?'

He laughs, his expression clearing. 'Would you believe me if I said he's not as bad when he's not at work?'

'No,' says Isabel honestly. 'Because the idea of Ronan outside of Comma just made my brain implode a little. So, what, he has *hobbies*? A personality? Don't tell me – he lives in a flat, instead of being stored in a filing cabinet somewhere in his office?'

'He has a house,' Daragh confirms. 'And a cat.'

'A *cat*?'

'She's very cute.'

'You're fucking with me.' She waits for him to agree, but his expression is innocent and guileless. 'You *are* fucking with me, right? You can't actually mean that Ronan Atwood has a cat?'

281

'Her name is Rory.'

Isabel stares at him. '*What?*'

The doctor takes his phone from his pocket and opens the gallery, flicking through until he finds what he's looking for. He hands it to Isabel.

It's ... definitely a cat. A small, black cat, with an oddly cheerful expression. And to remove any doubt as to whose cat it is, there's Ronan in the background, holding a mug and laughing.

'That was taken last month,' says Daragh.

He's wearing *jeans*.

Isabel's brain physically hurts trying to reconcile the picture on the screen with the Ronan she knows. 'But he's a *bastard*,' she says. 'He's ... I don't understand.'

Daragh shrugs. 'He's ambitious. He knows what he wants, and he'll do whatever he has to do to get it. Some people would consider that admirable.'

'Do you?'

'That depends on what it entails.' He puts his phone away. 'I'm sorry for letting him ambush you. Michael should be here soon. Is there anything you need before I go?'

Isabel shakes her head. 'I'm okay,' she lies. He gives her shoulder a last squeeze and leaves her be.

Michael arrives a few minutes later. 'Well, you look about four thousand times less awful than last time I saw you,' he says. 'I feel like I'm witnessing some kind of resurrection.'

'Dead girl walking, that's me.' She gives him a lopsided smile. 'And you? How's the shoulder?'

'I mean, the bodybuilding career's on hold, but other than that ...' She's missed his sarcasm, Isabel realises, a speck of familiarity to break up the monotony of hospital life. 'I was lucky. The knife missed everything vital. Daragh's been lecturing me about not pulling my stitches by overworking it, but other than that, I'm good.'

'And ... mentally?' He told her he still had nightmares about their last job together, the last time she nearly died. It can't have been easy watching her collapse again.

He grimaces. 'I'd be better if I knew where your parents are hiding ... and what they're planning. I feel like I'm constantly waiting for the next trap.'

What they're planning – that's the tricky part. The poison didn't kill her. The gunman hesitated. Her father wants something, and she doesn't know what it is, and that scares her. Whatever the ambush at Gauntlet Drive was meant to achieve, she's not sure it's over yet.

'Emma said Comma took prisoners,' she says. 'Have they talked?'

'Not yet. The guy you shot in the stomach isn't doing too well.' She should probably feel guilty about that, but she doesn't. He threatened Emma, and she'd have done worse than shoot him if she hadn't been dying at the time. 'The other guy either knows nothing, or your mother's done an excellent job training him to resist interrogation.'

Anyone allied with her parents deserves what they get, but there's no world where Comma interrogation is anything but a living nightmare. Maybe the gut shot was the kinder option.

283

'Will you tell me if you hear anything?' she says. 'Nobody seems inclined to tell me much.'

'Of course,' says Michael. Then he adds, 'Though I doubt they'll tell me either. Ronan offered me a job in logistics.'

Isabel winces. Michael might not want to be a field agent, but a low-level adjacent role like that is both an insult and a threat. Comma aren't going to let him walk away, knowing what he knows – they want him where they can see him. But they don't value him. 'Could be worse,' she says.

'True,' he admits. 'They could have accused me of conspiring with your father and had me executed.'

She gets the impression Michael spends a lot of his time anticipating the moment Comma finally decides he isn't useful enough to keep alive. It's a fear they both share, but Isabel, at least, has the peculiar comfort of knowing that, right now, they won't let her die.

'They won't . . .' she begins, searching for words of comfort.

'Don't, Isabel. I'm fine.' He pulls his battered deck of cards from his pocket and holds it up. 'Daragh said you were bored. Want a game?'

It's a transparent effort at changing the subject, but Isabel agrees gratefully, taking the cards he deals her.

'So,' he says, as they start to play. 'What's the plan?'

'The plan?' she echoes.

'To find your father.'

He says it like it should have been obvious, but it's clear they're operating on two different levels. 'But we figured out the antidote.'

'Yeah, and?' Michael frowns at her. 'He's still a threat, Isabel.'

Isabel fidgets with one of her cards, running her nail along the edge. 'I don't think he wants me dead,' she says. 'You said it yourself. If he did, we wouldn't be having this conversation. And at Gauntlet Drive—'

'That doesn't mean he can't still hurt you.'

'It means he wants me back.' She plays her card, though she has a shitty hand and Michael's already winning. 'So chasing after him would be doing exactly what he wants me to do. I'm safer staying out of his way.'

'Safer?' echoes Michael. 'In Comma?'

She cringes at the judgement in his voice. 'Look, it's complicated . . .'

'I thought this – all of this – was what you were trying to leave behind. Weren't you supposed to be getting *out*?'

'Exactly,' she says. 'Out means not going back to my father. Out means not putting myself back in his power!'

'So you'll put yourself back in Comma's instead, is that it?' She's surprised by the vehemence in his voice. 'What deal did you make, Isabel? What did you promise Ronan?'

Isabel stares down at her cards. 'That I'd go back in the field,' she says. The moment she says it aloud it starts feeling real. 'That I'd . . . that I'd kill for Comma again.'

She looks up just in time to see the disgust on Michael's face. 'How could you do that? Your civilian life—'

'Was already over. It was over the moment I got sick.'

'You didn't have to go back in the field!'

'It was that or the lab – what would you have had me do? I can't go back there. Not after everything.' Michael doesn't understand, he wasn't there, he doesn't know what it's like to see your nightmares in the mirror every day. 'He'd have turned me into my father.'

'So you're so determined not to turn into Ian that you'll become Judith instead.'

Isabel flinches like she's been punched. She isn't her mother. She won't be her mother. 'That's not ... I'm not ... It would take a lot more than a few contracts to make me like her.'

'Would it?' he says, discarding his cards on the bed. 'Because it looks to me like you're more willing to kill than to stand up to your father, so I'm not seeing a lot of difference there.'

'That's not fair!'

'Then tell me which part of this *is*!' Michael spits. 'I thought we were on the same page. I thought you wanted to make your father pay for everything he did to us, to Grace Whittock, to—'

'Of course I want to make him pay!' She wants him to bleed for all the pain he ever caused her. She wants him beaten and bloody and burning from the inside. But whenever she thinks about coming face to face with him, all she wants to do is run. 'But I can't, okay?'

'That deal you've struck with Ronan, it's never going to protect you,' says Michael, gathering the cards and shoving them back into the pack with sharp, aggressive movements. 'You know that, don't you? Ronan doesn't care about us, or anything we went through. He's never going to make Ian suffer for what he did. The only way you'll ever get vengeance is if you hunt your father down yourself.'

'And then what – kill him?'

'You want to, don't you?'

Isabel tries to imagine killing her father, but can't, just like she can't let herself feel the rage that Michael wants from her. He wants her on his side, all passion and violence, demanding redress for what they went through. Fellow survivors, armed to the teeth and coming for revenge.

But if she takes down the wall between her and her emotions, they'll drown her.

'I'm not you, Michael,' she says.

'No, you're a coward,' he replies. 'When did you stop running, Isabel? When did you decide Comma was a safe place to rest?'

When she realised she had nowhere else to go.

Bella Nicholls is dead. That future, that freedom, was lost the moment she begged Comma for her life. And while Ronan can't put a knife in her hands and force her to kill for him, he doesn't have to, because he knows if he keeps her here long enough, makes her feel trapped enough, eventually she'd kill just to see the sky again.

'Michael—'

'Forget it.' He stands, swinging his rucksack onto his back. 'Call me if you get bored of being Ronan's pet murderer and decide to take control of your own life again.'

'Don't,' begins Isabel, horrified to hear her voice crack. 'Please don't go. Don't leave me on my own again.'

'Don't leave *you*?' he echoes. 'You've got a whole guild around you! What about me, Isabel? What about those of us that Comma doesn't want? I thought we were in this together.'

'We are.' But it doesn't feel like it. Not when Michael's been offered a job in logistics – a shitty job, an adjacent job, but a kind of freedom that Isabel will never, ever be offered as long as Ronan considers her a useful weapon. 'I'm just trying to survive, Michael.'

He doesn't soften, but he hesitates. 'Aren't we all,' he says. And then, 'Call me when you change your mind. I'll be waiting.'

Which is almost a promise. Almost friendship. Isabel will take whatever she can get. 'I will,' she tells him, and means it. Even if she can't see herself changing her mind about this.

28

KONSENTO (ACCEPTANCE)

Isabel spends the next two weeks in the training gym, slowly relearning the feeling of power over her own body and trying to outrun her bad dreams. Daragh keeps warning her not to push herself too hard, but if she sits still, she has to think, and she can't bear being alone with the inside of her head right now.

When did you stop running? She didn't. It was always her parents she was running from.

The day Ronan comes to see her, she's only just finished her warm-up. She steps off the treadmill when she sees him in the doorway, and takes the slim, cardboard wallet he hands her. 'A job for you,' he says pleasantly.

When she looks at the profile inside, she thinks there's been a mistake. 'Sixteen,' she says aloud. 'He's ... sixteen?'

'Intel suggests he'll be at a club called Dancejo on Saturday. That gives you a few more days to train.'

The mark's sixteen. 'Since when did Comma kill minors?'

Ronan's lips are a thin, displeased line. 'Since your father defected with a very expensive poison and you refused to give us use of the formula.'

'Don't you fucking *dare*—'

'It's good money,' he says, cutting her off. 'We aren't currently in a position to overlook that. Will you be ready on Saturday, or do you need more time to prepare?'

She stares at the file. She can't get past the boy's age. Sixteen. She knows better than anyone exactly how much of a shit Comma gives about the rules and the gentlemen's agreements that limit their current activities, and still something about that number feels jarring. Unspeakable.

'What did he do?' she asks. As if there's a good reason for a teenager to have to die.

'That's none of your concern.'

'But there's a reason, right? If it's good money, that means it's a commission, which means somebody wants him dead. Who would call a hit on a sixteen-year-old?'

'That,' Ronan repeats, 'is none of your concern. Suffice to say they have enough money to be worth our attention. Will you be ready?'

It's a test, clearly, to see whether she'll cross this line. Whoever the client is, they're rich as fuck and morally bankrupt, and maybe that's all that matters to the guild, but she doubts there are many takers for the job. Even Comma agents have qualms when it comes to killing children.

But if Isabel refuses, whatever comes next will be worse. He's got her in a corner, back against the wall without a way out. Exactly where he always wanted her.

I'll do anything. Ronan's pet murderer. Her life in their hands. Isabel closes the file. 'Yes,' she says. 'I'll be ready.'

Her training feels different after he's left. Every knife in the target brings to mind the photograph in the file; the thud of her heartbeat whispers, *sixteen, sixteen, sixteen.* It doesn't matter, she wants to say. It doesn't make a difference if he's sixteen or twenty-six or sixty: a death's a death and a job's a job.

But it feels like it matters.

When she's done, she takes a moment, sitting on the bench with her towel around her shoulders, eyes closed. She hears the sound of familiar footsteps, and then somebody sits down beside her.

'You don't have to do this,' says Daragh.

Isabel opens her eyes. 'Don't I?' she says, taking the ice pack he offers her and pressing it against her still-healing ribs, wincing at the cold.

'I know you believe going back into the field is inevitable. But I told you I'd get in Ronan's way and I meant it. You don't have to agree to this, not now.'

She never told Daragh about the deal she made the last time Ronan paid her a visit. About the debt she owes him, about the promise she made herself, about everything she's trying not to become. She doesn't want him to forgive her for her choices.

'It would have happened eventually,' she says. 'May as well maintain some control over the timing.' As if she had any of that.

In a voice as gentle as the one he used when she was dying, he says, 'This is a knife you're using on yourself, Isabel. You're pre-empting the pain of someone else doing it to you.'

Ronan's already twisting it in her back. 'Or maybe I'm accepting that I'm good at killing people. Don't psychoanalyse me, Daragh – neither of us will like what you find.'

He sighs. 'I'm not psychoanalysing you, but I am trying to help. Whatever he said to you, you still have options. If you like, we can work them out together.'

She tries to imagine telling Ronan she wants to join the medical division and asking him to send her to med school, or taking a job in intel, where she can hide behind the scenes and lie to herself about the blood on her hands. Daragh may be able to kid himself that he can excuse his part in the guild's atrocities, but Isabel's never been good at that kind of deception.

'This,' she says, tapping the file, 'is my best option.'

Daragh picks it up. 'It doesn't have to be,' he begins, flicking the wallet open, and then he freezes.

So he didn't know.

He came here looking for her because Ronan told him she'd taken a job, but evidently he left out the details. She should've seen that coming: there's no way Daragh would have been this calm if he knew what the contract entailed.

'This is a child,' he says, and looks at her, as though checking she knows that.

Isabel gives him a tight smile. 'We have that in common.'

'Isabel, you can't—'

'A death's a death,' she says. 'A job's a job. I already told Ronan I'd do it.'

'*Why?*'

She could tell him, of course, about the poison, her formula, the rock and the hard place she's trapped between. He'd be sympathetic. It would fit with his image of her: the victim forced into monstrosity, his opportunity to redeem himself. He needs her to be broken and traumatised because that way he can fix her and pretend it makes up for a decade as a cog in the blood-soaked machinery of Comma.

But deep down she's exactly as awful as every other villain he's treated, and she doesn't know how else to show him that, except by letting him believe this is her choice.

'Why not?' she says. She expects him to tell her it's immoral, that the guild shouldn't be targeting children, that she should have tried harder to negotiate her freedom.

But he just looks at the file for a very long time, and then closes it. 'Are you going to tell Emma?'

The question knocks her bluster out of her. 'I . . .'

'The details, of course, will stay within the guild. But the fact that you're killing again would be a big thing to keep from her.'

His tone is very careful and even, as if he's not sure how she'll react.

'I'll tell her,' she says, though she doesn't know how.

'And that doesn't worry you? How she'll respond?'

So that's his *why not*. Because if she does this, she's throwing away the one good thing in her life. Joke's on him, though: she's been waiting for it to be taken from her since the first time Emma smiled at her.

'It doesn't make a difference,' she says. 'This was always going to end with her hating me.'

'Why?'

'Because I ...' Because she's guild. Because she's fundamentally unlikeable. Because she doesn't know how to be a good person, let alone a good friend. 'Because why wouldn't she?'

Daragh stands. 'You're allowed to be loved, Isabel,' he says. 'You know that, don't you?'

Does she?

Is she?

By whom, by him? So that he can offset his guilt about being part of the guild? Or by Emma, who doesn't see her for who she really is, who still thinks she has the capacity to be more than someone who'd kill a child rather than live with her father's ghost behind her eyes?

There's a long pause while Daragh waits for her to answer and she waits for him to leave.

In the end, he breaks first, placing the file on the bench beside her and turning to go. At the door, he stops. 'I wanted you to know that,' he says quietly. 'That's all.'

And when the door to the gym has closed behind him, Isabel covers her face and begins to sob.

'So,' says Emma, sounding disapproving. 'What has you so busy that you only found time to call me *twice* this week? I'm hurt and appalled by this neglect, Bel.'

She should tell her. Isabel's been trying to work up the courage all week, knowing there's only so long she can drag this out – the sooner she rips the plaster off, the sooner she can get on with healing. But she can't bring herself to do it. *A few more days*, she keeps thinking, *a few more days with Emma not hating me. Just give me that, just give me this small lie.*

'I'm sorry,' she says, still too much of a coward to spit it out. 'All the physio, you know, it's . . . a lot.'

'Physio,' repeats Emma. Her tone suggests she knows there's more to it than recovery, but she's too kind to force Isabel to lie by asking her if she's training again.

The implied curiosity's almost worse – it makes it harder to judge how much she's guessed. Isabel says, 'I'm getting stronger, but it'll be a while before I feel like my old self.'

'When do you think they'll let you out of hospital?'

'I'm not sure.' That much is true. She can't leave this place until Daragh's certain it's safe. That means figuring out what she can eat without one food or another triggering anaphylaxis, for one thing, thanks to the number the poison did on her histamine response. Then there's the issue of money. At the last count, she had roughly a crown to her name; her commission for the job Ronan's given her will change that, but first she has to go through with it.

Emma sighs. 'I miss you. I wish they'd let me visit. Mortimer must be getting sick of me.'

'Is he still bringing you your homework?'

'Yeah. Though I think he really comes to see Leo. He asked after you again today.'

There has to be a neutral way to ask Emma if anything Mortimer's said indicates he might take what he knows about Cocoon to the Free Press, but Isabel hasn't found it. She says, 'Do you trust him?'

'Yes,' says Emma immediately, knowing what she's really asking. 'And Leo does too, and he's a good judge of character. Mortimer wouldn't expose you, Bel.'

Because that's the risk. To accuse Comma of training children, he'd need proof. Proof that Isabel and her scars and her father's files could adequately provide.

'You can't know that,' she says.

'Yes, I can. He knows how badly the guild fucked you up, and there's no way he'd put you through the trauma of a media storm. Especially since Cocoon's no longer active, so it's not like he'd be protecting anyone.'

'But it would hurt Comma.'

'Maybe, but I don't think he's the rabid abolitionist you think he is. He wants you safe more than he wants to undermine the guilds.' Emma laughs slightly. 'You know, he joked about sending you a block of wood so you can learn to whittle, but apparently you never passed his safety exam.'

This surprises a huff of laughter out of Isabel. 'Yet people seem determined to give me knives anyway.'

The joke lands badly, into an awkward pause. Then Emma says, 'Isabel, have you ... has Ronan ...'

'Had a miraculous change of heart and decided to let me off the hook for what I owe the guild? No.' She swallows. 'I made a deal, Emma. I know you were hoping there'd be a way around it, but there isn't.'

'You were dying.'

'It doesn't matter.'

'But you have options. Daragh—'

'It doesn't make any difference. Whether I'm a contract killer or a medical worker, as long as I'm part of Comma, people will die because of me. At least when I'm holding the knife I'm being honest with myself.'

'I still think you could fight this if you wanted to.' When Isabel doesn't immediately respond, Emma says, 'Is that what it is? You don't want to?'

'I don't know what I want, Emma,' she says, and it feels like the first honest thing she's said in weeks. She wanted a normal life, but she failed at that. She wanted to live, and here she is, alive, lost, her future formless and unknowable. 'I'm good at this. It's . . . normal to me, in a way that nothing else is. I know it's wrong, but I don't see anyone else getting punished for the shit they do.'

'You can do more with your life than kill people, Bel.'

'Can I, though?' All her attempts to be something more have failed, brought her right back where she started. 'I feel like you've created an idealised version of me, one that's a victim who can't be blamed. But I killed Ian Crampton because he was there and because I could, and now he's dead. And that's on me. That's who I am.'

There's a moment of silence, and then Emma says, 'You know what I think? I think you killed Ian because you were afraid, and you don't know how else to deal with a threat.'

'And the rest?'

'I think you've been afraid all your life.'

She can't argue with that. Her fear and her rage and the blood on her hands are all part of the same picture, a smudged portrait of a girl.

Emma says, 'You've spent your life starved of choices, starved of love, and you think that the person you are now is all you'll ever be. But it's only a shadow of what you're capable of becoming. And I think,' she adds more firmly, 'that right now you think I'm an idealist who refuses to see that you're nothing more than what your parents made you. But you're wrong.'

Isabel's protests die in her throat. 'I . . .'

'You think all that's inside you is darkness, Isabel, but I see light there. It's small and it's starved, but it's there. And I wish you could see it too.'

'A candle can't do much against a black hole.'

'So light another candle.'

Isabel swallows. She wishes she believed in Emma's fantasy. She wishes there was an Isabel who could be soft and gentle, could be full of friendship and kindness, if only given the chance. But that Isabel never existed, and what's left are these broken shards, cutting anyone who tries to put her back together.

'I'll do what Ronan asks of me,' she says. 'I made a deal. I'll keep my word. And you have to decide if you can live with the knowledge of what I'm capable of.' *Leave now. Make it easier on both of us.* 'This is me, Emma. Not some imaginary person you've created in your head – this. I've only ever been this.'

'I know who you are,' says Emma. 'You're a girl who made shit choices because all you were given were shit options, and now you're fucked up and you're trying to push me away because you don't know how to deal with anyone giving a shit about you. But this is a defence mechanism, and it's not going to work.'

Silence.

'Fine,' says Isabel. 'Stick around. But don't be surprised when you don't like what you see.'

'Fuck you, Isabel,' says Emma.

But she doesn't hang up, and neither does Isabel.

29

INFANO (CHILD)

The music is so loud that Isabel can't hear herself think.

She knew, theoretically, that clubs were like this, but it's her first time experiencing it in person. The bass pounds in her ears like a pulse as she pushes through the crowd of teenagers trying to dance, most of them still in the awkward pubescent stage where they aren't fully aware of their limbs.

She's already spotted the mark, talking to friends on the other side of the room. Even by the standards of this crowd, he's young, a childish rounding to his features that he'll never have the chance to grow out of.

She's too on-edge to act now, so she works her way through the room to the bar. It's underage night at this popular Weaverthorpe club, and it seems like every under-eighteen in the west of the city is here. The venue isn't serving alcohol, which saves her having to excuse her sobriety, although it means everyone else is equally alert and sober. A few boys glance at her as she leans against the bar; a few girls, too. She meets one girl's eye, raising her eyebrow, and the teen flushes and looks away. It feels a little like power, but it's not a game Isabel's ever been interested in playing.

Instead she sips her drink, surveying the room and trying to calm her nerves. She can see the mark's friends trying to persuade him to dance, but he's resisting. Distracted, she thinks; he'll be easy enough to lure away. When her glass is empty, she shakes off her anxiety and gets up, moving as smoothly as she can across the packed room.

Someone blocks her path. 'Bella?'

It takes a moment to place him, and then— 'Nick?'

Shit. Too late, she remembers him inviting her to this club, weeks ago, in another life. She should have known there'd be people here from the Fraser, but it's just her luck that it's one of the few who'd recognise her on sight.

'It *is* you!' he says. 'Wow, you look . . . different.'

She can't tell if he's referring to her clothes or her overgrown hair or the ravages left by her near-death experience that still linger in the shadows of her face, but it doesn't matter. She tries to keep her voice light as she says, 'I didn't know you'd be here.'

Clearly she doesn't succeed, because Nick looks taken aback as he says, 'Yeah, well, there's no need to sound so disappointed. There are a bunch of us here. Want to join, or are you with . . . friends?'

'I'm with . . .' She gestures in the approximate direction of the mark. He hasn't moved from his corner, but if Nick doesn't get out of her way, she'll miss her opportunity. 'People.'

'So I can see.' He steps out of her path. 'Well, wouldn't want to keep you from your "people".'

'I'm sorry.'

Nick shrugs. 'For what? The disappearing, or the fact that you're not even going to tell me where you've been?'

'Both,' she says, though 'sorry' is the wrong word to express this curious tangle of obligation she feels. She knows she *should* be sorry, that she's wronged Nick, somehow, in the way that she disappeared and because she isn't here to fix things, only to make them worse. She's not sure that she *is*, but feelings – her own, or other people's – remain an inaccessible mystery, as difficult to identify as they are to express. 'Sorry' will do. It's all she can offer him, but she knows it's not enough.

He's still watching her as she pushes through the crowd, and it's a distraction she doesn't need. Isabel tries to shake it off. The job's her highest priority; nothing else matters.

She finally reaches the mark and, half shouting over the music, asks him to dance. She's rewarded with a grudging acceptance, and his friends jeer good-naturedly as he joins them on the floor. For a while, she finds herself pressed against him by the movement of bodies around them, hardly needing to move to look like she's dancing.

The mark's interest in her only grows the longer they're squeezed awkwardly together. 'Want to get some air?' he says, gesturing towards the door that opens onto the alley by the club.

He's practically doing Isabel's job for her. She lets him lead her outside, his smile a teenager's attempt at suave confidence or a wolfish grin.

'I haven't seen you here before,' he says.

'I haven't been here before,' she replies, trying to sound more like a teenager new to the joys of underage clubbing than a contract killer on a job. 'It's not what I expected.'

'Oh yeah?' He moves closer, and she's struck by a sudden terror that he's going to try to kiss her.

And then he puts his hand on her thigh and the whole charade falls apart.

Isabel's skirt is short, her top skin-tight – there are limited hiding places for concealed weaponry, and she's strapped her knife to her thigh. His fingers brush against the holster's thick strap and his eyes widen, as though he knows exactly what it is and why she's here.

They're close enough that, if she wanted to, she could kiss him. Instead, she whispers almost directly into his mouth, 'Don't move.'

He freezes, a catch in his breath that she feels against her lips. 'You came here for me, didn't you?'

She lowers her right hand to the catch on her thigh sheath, her leg still pressed against his. 'Yes,' she says. 'I did.'

'I didn't tell anyone.' He's panicking without moving, smart enough to keep still. 'He made me swear – I didn't – I've kept quiet.'

'I'm just doing my job,' she says, sliding the knife free. 'I don't make the decisions.'

'Please.'

But she's not here to listen to him beg. The knife slips easily between his ribs, and he falls towards her, his lips moist against her neck. She holds him there, feeling his breath slow and falter, until his heart stops throbbing in the bony chest pressed against her, and then she lets the body slump against the wall. Death diminishes him, makes a child of him; it strips away the pretence of maturity, and all that's left is the corpse of a teenager and a void inside Isabel where the guilt should be.

She thought maybe it would feel different, but a death's a death, and he died the same as anyone.

The door to the club slams open. 'Bella?' Nick's voice. *Shit.* 'I thought I saw you come this way. I wanted to . . .' He's seen her. 'Bella?'

Slowly, Isabel turns. 'You should've stayed inside, Nick.'

He sees the knife, the blood, the body, and his breathing becomes more laboured. 'Shit, is he . . . is he dead? Did you . . . ?' He staggers backwards. 'You killed him. He's just a kid and you killed him. He must be like sixteen.'

'Nick,' she begins.

'You're guild, aren't you?' He's backed up against the door now. It's a fire exit that only opens from the inside, and she can hear him cursing under his breath as he tries to wrench it open. Eventually he gives up, pressing his back against it as though he can disappear through the wood. 'Is that why you left school? Emma said you were sick.'

'I was.' Why did it have to be Nick? Why did he have to

follow her, when he could have stayed inside where he'd have been safe?

'But that boy ...' He looks over her shoulder at the mark. 'You killed him. I thought ... I thought the guilds didn't kill minors.'

'You thought wrong.'

'Bella ...'

A stranger in his position would already be dead. *No mercy, no hesitation, no witnesses*: the three rules of surviving in the field. But it's Nick. Soft-hearted Nick Larrington, who cries over the deaths of strangers. Who was kind to her even when she didn't deserve it.

Who has seen her face, and knows what she's done.

'Please,' he's saying, 'I won't tell anyone what I saw. I had no idea that you—'

'I'll make it quick,' she says, because that, at least, is a mercy she's permitted. 'You won't even feel it.'

'You can't kill me. *You* can't kill *me*. I thought we were friends.' He's shaking. He looks like he wants to run. '*Fuck*. You wouldn't, you wouldn't kill me, you can't.'

'Nick ...'

'Don't.' He's gauging exits and escape routes, as if he's not the one who failed PE because of his asthma. 'Don't come any closer, Bella, I swear I—'

'You'll do what, Nick?' she says, stepping forward. 'You'll scream? You think they'll come for you? You think they can move faster than I can?'

He's sobbing now. 'Please don't do this, Bella.' He uses her name like he's trying to recall her to herself, but he's trying to bring back a ghost. There's no point appealing to Bella Nicholls for mercy when it's Isabel Ryans holding the knife.

'I have to.'

'You don't,' he says. 'Whatever your guild said to you, whatever they promised, this isn't your only choice. *Bella.* Please!'

Isabel moves quickly, pinning him against the locked door, knife jammed under his chin. 'You know nothing about my choices.'

'I know that killing me doesn't have to be one of them. I swear I'll keep my mouth shut. No one will know what I saw, I promise.'

'Promises mean nothing to Comma,' she says. 'You'll slip up eventually. Next week, next month, next year. You'll open your mouth and they'll take you out anyway. It's easier this way.'

'Is that what happened to Emma?'

If he'd punched her, she'd have flinched less. 'What?'

He takes advantage of her distraction to twist free of her grip, slipping out from under her arm faster than she'd thought he could move. 'Is that why Emma hasn't been at school?' he says. 'Did you kill her too? And the librarian, she died – was that because of you as well? Are they dead because of you? Or are—'

He stumbles, looks down, and seems dimly surprised to see her knife in his chest and blood spreading rapidly across his shirt.

306

'You . . .' he begins.

'I'm sorry.' Still not the right word. Still the only one she's got.

Nick stares at her, crumpling to his knees. 'Bella,' he begins, but whatever he was going to say is lost as he dies.

She retrieves her knife, wiping it clean on his shirt; her own top's sticky with the mark's blood. With one bloody finger, she draws the guild symbol on the mark's forehead: a comma for a body and three curved lines forming the outline of wings, the warped silhouette of a butterfly. After a moment's hesitation, she draws the same symbol on Nick's cheek.

And now she has to go.

If not for the blood, she'd wait until a group left the club and try to blend in, but after the mess she's made, she needs to leave as discreetly as possible before the boys' friends come looking for them. She sticks to the shadows, avoiding main roads, and by some miracle gets back to the hospital without being stopped, despite the blood on her outfit.

The lobby's empty. She leaves signing off on the hit until the morning and heads to her room, stripping off her bloodstained clothes and throwing away the ones she knows she'll never wear again. She takes a shower, washing away the traces of the mark's dying kiss against her throat. The job's done, but the encounter with Nick has unsettled her.

Is that what happened to Emma? She's not going to be able to hide this. Emma will join the dots, realise Isabel's killing again, and everything that hasn't already been taken from her will come crumbling down.

And the worst part is how easy it feels. *When did you stop running, Isabel?* She wonders what Michael would have made of her there in the alleyway, the mark pressing against her, greedy for something she wasn't offering. She wonders what he'll think when he learns she killed two teenagers in the space of minutes. If he'll be repulsed by her, or if he knows how it feels not to have to pretend you care just to be able to live with yourself.

It should be harder than this, to live with herself.

She pulls on her pyjamas and crawls into bed, trying not to think about the evening's work. She killed Nick. The mark – *Oliver, he was a person and his name was Oliver* – was a job, but Nick Larrington tried to be her friend. He cared about her. And when Emma knows about *that* …

He's just a kid, Nick said, and she imagines tomorrow's headlines, screaming that Comma killed a minor. Just a child, just a child, just a child.

But as her dreams drag her away from wakefulness, all Isabel can think is, *So was I.*

30

HOMŜTELO (KIDNAPPING)

'You were dreaming,' says Daragh, when Isabel opens her eyes. Her cheeks are wet with tears, and she wonders if she cried out. 'Was it about last night?'

Isabel struggles into an upright position, only half awake, and sees him standing by the window with his back to her. 'Not exactly.'

'Are you sure?' That's the tone of voice she calls his 'therapist voice'. 'Do you want to tell me about it?'

'Not really.' Telling Daragh about it means thinking about it, and thinking about it is dangerously close to letting herself feel any of the emotions that haunt her at night, when the walls she builds so carefully by day come crumbling down in her dreams. There's only one way Isabel knows how to survive, and it isn't by getting in touch with her feelings.

'It was your first voluntary assignment,' he says. 'And you killed a child. Each of those on its own would be—'

'Let me revise my answer,' she interrupts, since he doesn't seem to be getting the message. 'I definitely don't want to talk about it. Please stop attempting therapy on me when I've only just woken up.'

'It's almost noon, and you need to get up. Ronan wants to talk to you.'

Abruptly, the weight of what she did last night hits Isabel. 'Oh, shit.'

'Oh, and you made the front page.' Daragh tosses a newspaper onto the bed. She pushes it away without looking at it. 'They're speculating about you, you know. Well, about Comma's newest. No calling card means no pseudonym to claim the kill.'

She doesn't want to put her name on this, to give the city a target for its condemnation. Only *La Revuo* publishes pseudonyms alongside obits, but somehow word spreads beyond the pages of the guild newspaper and across the rest of Espera. *Three Swallowtail kills this month*, people say, if they're the kind to keep track of that. Or: *Nothing from Skipper in a while. Do you think they've retired?* Those kinds of comments are made with relief, or fear: an older agent off the circuit, no longer a threat, means a new one coming to take their place and their name.

Isabel doesn't need a recycled nickname. She has her own: *Moth*. A name for a butterfly that strikes at night.

She pushes aside the duvet and climbs out of bed. 'I don't get why they care so much,' she says, hunting for clothes.

'The mark was young,' says Daragh. 'It makes a difference.'

She could do without his disapproval on top of everything else. 'How long until Ronan gets here?'

'Half an hour, tops. You should probably figure out what you're going to say to him.'

But when it comes to it, she has no excuses.

'So,' says Ronan. 'You fucked it up.'

'The mark's dead, isn't he?'

'You killed a witness.'

'I didn't think you'd want him alive.'

'There shouldn't have *been* a witness in the first place. Let alone another teenager.' He pauses, as if she didn't already know how disappointed he is. 'I understand you knew Nicholas Larrington in some way.'

'He went to my school.' *He was my friend.* No. She can't think about that. Nick stopped being her friend the moment he saw her with the mark. 'He recognised me in the club and again in the alleyway. It was a clear identification and I was compromised, so I eliminated the threat the only way I could.'

'Which would be admirable, in a case less controversial than this one.'

'Controversial?'

'The mark was a minor, Isabel. And the motive was ...

311

personal. Some weren't sure we should have taken the job in the first place.'

She doesn't see how that's her problem. 'And yet you did.'

'And *you* killed two teenagers and marked them in blood.' He raises his eyebrow. 'That's a little melodramatic, don't you think?'

What she wants to say is: *I didn't have a pen.* What she says is: 'I wouldn't have killed Nick if I thought there was another way. He saw me. I couldn't let him walk away.'

'That wasn't your decision to make.'

So many rules about murder. She doesn't see the point – either you're a killer or you're not, and she's way past the point where the details matter. 'I didn't exactly have time for a consultation.'

She waits for the inevitable punishment, using all of her willpower to sit firm in her chair and not let him see that she's afraid. Finally, Ronan says, 'Don't let it happen again.'

She stares at him. 'That's it?'

'You're right. He had to die. But that's not up to you. You're not judge and jury, Isabel Ryans – you're the executioner, nothing more.'

So who *does* make those decisions – Ronan? Who decides which commissions they'll take, which motives are good enough, what price is high enough? She's never given it much thought. It's easier to follow orders than consider who makes them.

'Got it,' she says. 'Don't kill anyone without making somebody else do paperwork about it first.'

Ronan's mouth twitches in a barely suppressed smile, and she feels a tiny thrill of victory. He holds out a metal business card case. 'Here. This is for you.'

Isabel opens it gingerly. When it doesn't explode or release a cloud of toxin, she takes out one of the cards inside. It's made of good-quality cream cardstock, a simple black border a few millimetres from the edge. In the centre, in crisp, red ink, is Comma's symbol: a comma for a body and three curved lines in the shape of wings.

'You got calling cards printed? Already?'

He shrugs. 'I saw no reason to delay.'

She turns the card over. There, in the middle, in small sans-serif letters:

noktopapilio | moth

'I know that's what they used to call you,' he says. 'The butterfly of night.'

'Did they tell you why?' She runs her thumb along the edge of the card, feeling the bite of it against her skin.

'It doesn't matter why,' he says, so either he knows and doesn't like it, or he's got less access to Cocoon records than she thought but won't admit it. 'The city needs a name. To know there's a new player in the game.'

She puts the card back in the case and slips it into her pocket. It's not like there's another name she'd have chosen, if they'd asked, but the nickname still makes her uneasy. And they didn't ask.

'It suits you,' says Ronan, watching her.

'Being a dick suits you,' she retorts.

A fleeting glimpse of a smile. 'Must be why I do it,' he says. 'While I'm here, let me give you this.' He hands her a phone, a sleek, black handset that makes her old phone look like the cheap crap it was. 'The encryption means you don't need to code your messages, but I'd be careful what you say, and to whom.'

For the first time since she arrived in hospital, Isabel has a line to the outside world. And all it cost her was two people's lives. 'Thanks,' she says uncertainly.

'You're welcome,' says Ronan. 'You earned it.'

Knowing it was paid for in blood makes her never want to touch the phone again, but she puts it in her pocket anyway. 'This doesn't make me like you,' she tells him. 'Daragh might think you're not so bad, but I'm beginning to think he'd see the goodness in a machine gun.'

'It's always been one of his endearing qualities. Fortunately, I don't need you to like me. Only kill for me.'

'I'll kill for you. I won't die for you.'

'That sounds fair.' Ronan holds out his hand. It's papery and dry, but his grip is firm. 'Welcome to Comma, Isabel Ryans.'

So this is it. The end of the road she set herself on when she ran away from home. Did she really think it would take her anywhere else?

Ronan makes for the door, then pauses. 'If Nick Larrington was a pupil at your school, I assume your friend Emma also knew him.'

314

Isabel's mouth goes dry. 'A little.'

'Somebody will need to tell her that he's dead.'

Did you kill her too? Are they dead because of you? Isabel's ruined everything. Destroyed any hope of this friendship surviving. And she has no idea how to fix this.

'She'll see it in the papers,' says Isabel. 'But I'll ... I'll tell her, when she calls.'

'Do that. And Isabel?' She looks up. 'Don't let the headlines go to your head.'

When he's gone, she picks up the newspaper Daragh gave her and skims the article. She tells herself she's trying to get a better sense of which facts are in the public domain, but really it's a punishment. Somehow it sounds worse, splashed across the front page of the local news, and she has no right to look away when she's the one who did it.

> Oliver Roe, 16, is survived by his parents and four younger siblings ...

If Emma sees this paper, how long before she realises it was Isabel? If she wasn't a coward, she'd have confessed already, but she skipped their last couple of calls rather than lie to Emma's face. Now she finds herself weaving together excuses in case her friend doesn't already know. She could say Ronan forced her into it, but what difference does that make, when she was still the one holding the knife?

Her anxiety bites at her as she dials Emma's number at their usual time. She runs through her excuses as she listens to the phone ring, scripting a hypothetical conversation and trying to anticipate her friend's questions. She hates herself for every lie and she hates herself more for the truth. Her thoughts are beginning to spiral by the time the line clicks and goes dead.

Emma didn't pick up.

Emma didn't pick up. She imagines her friend watching her phone, waiting for it to stop ringing, because she doesn't want to talk to a murderer and a liar.

She tries again. The phone's ringing gives way to the abrasive hum of a disconnected call, but she's frozen; it takes too long for her to remember how to hang up. She calls Emma's home phone instead, in case she's misplaced her mobile, but there's nothing.

If Emma wanted to, she'd have picked up the phone. Emma *always* picks up.

Which means Emma knows, and she hates Isabel for it.

Of course she does. Murder was bad enough, especially for Comma, especially of her own volition. But Nick was someone they knew, an innocent bystander. How could Isabel ever expect Emma to forgive this?

She stays sitting by the phone, unable to move. She hardly notices when an alarm shrills elsewhere in the hospital and every security officer runs to deal with it. Why does she care if there's an intruder? None of it means anything, because Emma hates her.

The door slams open, startling her out of her fog, and a vaguely familiar young man storms in. Security guards follow moments later, grabbing his arms, ready to drag him away as he says, 'They've taken Emma,' in an urgent, desperate panic. 'Isabel, Emma's gone, they've taken her—'

At the sound of his voice, she recognises him: Leo. 'Stop!' she tells the guards. 'Let go of him. It's okay, he's not a threat.'

They stop trying to drag him from the room, but they don't let go of him. 'He doesn't have security clearance to be here, Miss Ryans,' says one of them.

'Call Toni Rolleston. Tell her Leo's here. *Go.*' Isabel's expecting them to argue, but evidently her new status as a fully fledged Comma murderer affords her some authority, because they let him go and step away, one of them already reaching for his phone. She looks back at Leo, his words beginning to sink in. 'What do you mean, "Emma's gone"?' she asks him. 'What is this?'

'I came home and she wasn't there,' he says. 'I thought she was trying to see you, maybe. She didn't say anything to you?'

Isabel shakes her head. 'I haven't heard from her in a couple of days. I ...' *I did something awful and I think she hates me.*

Leo swears. 'I knew it. When I first found the letter, I thought it was a joke. But why would anyone joke about this? Look.' He shoves an envelope into her hands, already ripped open along one edge.

Isabel has to read the letter inside about four times before it registers as a ransom note. There's no signature, except for a bulbous, black spider, almost identical to the one carved into Grace's body.

She looks from the page to Emma's brother and back,

and finally understands what he's telling her. 'Emma's been kidnapped.'

Leo nods, sinking into the chair and covering his face with his hands. 'I came home and she was gone,' he repeats. 'I was supposed to be looking after her, but I failed.'

Emma's been abducted. Emma is *gone*. It's not that she didn't want to answer the phone – she couldn't. She doesn't hate Isabel. She probably hasn't even seen the news, which means there's still a chance Isabel can fix this, but . . . but she's been kidnapped. By the guild who killed Grace.

By my parents, she thinks, and her moment of relief turns to fear.

31

Preparo (Preparation)

Toni Rolleston pushes her way through the agents blocking the doorway. 'Leo, what's going on? You know you shouldn't be here. When they called me, I thought—' She breaks off when she sees their expressions.

Wordlessly, Isabel hands her the note.

Toni only has to read it once before she grasps its meaning. She sends the security agents away, commanding one to fetch Ronan and another to switch off that damn alarm. Leo has fallen silent, curled up miserably in the uncomfortable chair. His gaze, like Isabel's, is still on the ransom note.

'What happened?' Toni asks him. 'I thought she was staying with you.'

He flinches at the implied accusation. 'I was at work,' he says. 'I came back and she was gone. The door wasn't forced, but they got in somehow, because the note was on the table.' He looks up as Ronan and Daragh arrive, then away, as though afraid to be caught looking at Comma agents. 'I fucked up. I was meant to protect her and I fucked up.'

'No,' Toni begins, softening her tone. 'No, you didn't. This isn't your fault.'

'They want our attention,' says Ronan. He takes the note from Toni and glances at it. 'And our money, apparently.'

'It's bait,' says Daragh. 'We know what they really want is Isabel.'

It's always been Isabel they wanted.

'Okay,' says Toni, pacing. 'Well, we're getting Emma out. We can't . . .' Isabel's never seen her unsettled like this, her usual icy confidence frayed to breaking point. 'Ronan, I know the policy on ransoms, and I know she's a civilian, but we can't leave her in there.'

'I know that.' Ronan traces the spider mark on the paper with his finger. 'This could be our chance to gain access to the Ryans' guild, access we wouldn't otherwise have. But we need to be strategic.'

Isabel's mind is full of static. *They've got Emma they've got Emma they've got Emma.* She tries to refocus on Toni and Ronan discussing the ransom, but the words wash over her, incomprehensible. They've got Emma.

'It's my fault,' she says. 'My bastard parents think they can kidnap my best friend to get to me, but—'

'Which makes it their fault, not yours,' interrupts Daragh. 'You can't blame yourself for this.'

She ignores him. 'I won't let them hurt her the way they hurt me. I'm getting her back.'

Ronan says, 'We can't do anything until we know more. I'll call a meeting, get things moving. Leo, is it?' Leo looks up, eyes wide. 'Go home. This isn't the place for a civilian.'

Leo's about to argue, but Toni cuts him off. 'Please go home, Leo,' she says. 'Daragh will show you out.'

He doesn't look happy about it, but he goes. As the door closes, Ronan says, 'And I suppose you're about to say you didn't tell him where the hospital was, or how to get in.'

'I didn't,' says Toni tersely. 'And if you think I'd have needed to, you underestimate my son.'

'*You* underestimate how close he came to getting shot by security,' counters Ronan. 'If you would only register them—'

'Don't start this again, Ronan.' Toni sounds tired, like they've had this argument before. 'I know he shouldn't have come. But he's protective of his sister. He wants her to be safe.'

It would be wrong to say that Ronan softens, but for a moment it seems like he puts his claws away. 'And she will be, Toni. We'll get her out.' Then he looks at Isabel, and he's all business. 'If you want to be involved in the retrieval, you need to train. Perhaps Michael could help you.'

'What are you . . . ?' Isabel begins, but he's already walking away, Toni at his side like an equal.

What are you going to do? What are you willing to sacrifice? Isabel sits frozen for a moment longer in the now empty room, her questions unvoiced and unanswered. Does it matter what they're planning? She'll do anything they ask, if it'll save Emma.

She pulls on her training gear and clips her hair back, texting Michael on her way down to the gym. She doesn't know if he'll come. *They've got Emma* – why should he give a shit? Especially if he's seen the news, knows what she's done and where her deal with Ronan led her. But maybe ... maybe he'll see that leaving an innocent in the hands of her parents is unconscionable, no matter what other disagreements they've had.

She can only hope so.

After a few jittery minutes waiting for a reply that doesn't come, she tosses her phone onto the bench and throws herself into training. Her fear's like a demon inside her, only satisfied by violence. She's so absorbed it takes a while to notice Daragh leaning against the wall, watching her throw knife after knife at the target.

As she's yanking them out of the board, she looks over at him. 'Well?'

'You're getting stronger,' he says. 'But your emotions are getting in the way. You're not thinking logically.'

'You mean I care too much about Emma to wait around for someone else to save her? No shit.'

'I mean you'll make mistakes unless you stop to think before you act.'

He's right, either way: her emotions are the problem. If she hadn't let herself get attached, Emma wouldn't have been taken, and now the kidnapping has thrown her completely off balance. If something happens to Emma, she'll lose the only real friend she's ever had.

She has to prove she's worth that friendship, which means getting Emma out. Not because rescuing her will earn Isabel forgiveness for what she's done – after Nick, her friend will probably never speak to her again. But because she can't leave someone she cares about in the hands of her parents.

'I'd ask you how you're feeling,' says Daragh, 'but I get the sense you'd rather throw knives at the wall than talk about it.'

'Aww, it's almost like you know me.'

'Isabel, I know you care about Emma,' he begins. She responds by taking aim once more. The knife hits the centre of the target with a dull *thunk*. 'And I know how you feel about your parents. It might be helpful to process that.'

'There's nothing to process,' she says, throwing another knife. 'They're bastards. No one got me out. They've got Emma. I've got to get her out. Simple, easy to follow, non-negotiable.'

Daragh watches her throw the rest of her set of knives and then, as she's retrieving them, says, 'You're not the only person invested in Emma's welfare. Toni won't rest until she's safe. You don't have to take sole responsibility for this.'

'I know.'

'Do you?'

The final blade is wedged deeply in the target, and it takes all her strength to yank it free. 'Of course. But I—'

'You want to be involved because you feel like this is

323

your fault. I know. But you're not the only person carrying this burden.'

It *is* her fault. Her parents aren't trying to lure Toni Rolleston into their guild – it's her they're after. That makes it her responsibility to fix it.

Michael arrives then, looking flushed, and saves her from further discussion about her feelings. 'What's going on?' he demands. 'You said they took Emma?'

'I'll leave you to it,' says Daragh. He kicks aside the doorstop as he goes, giving them some privacy.

Michael heads straight for Isabel. 'Are you okay? I came as fast as I could. Who's "they", your parents?'

She nods. 'Ransom note. Spider logo for a signature.'

He swears. 'I heard about your kill last night. Do you think they guessed it was you?'

Isabel stares at him. 'What?'

'I mean, they had no way of knowing you survived the poison until now, right? But if they saw the news and realised it was you ...' He sees her expression and backtracks. 'I'm probably wrong. It all happened so fast, they can't have known ...'

'No.' That would make it unequivocally her fault. She kills Nick, they take Emma – a vicious domino effect of losing the only people who've ever been kind to her. 'They can't have known, they can't have, there's ... there's no reason they'd think it's me, right?'

'Nothing in the papers,' Michael confirms. 'You're the talk of the city, but it's speculation, nothing identifiable. The

324

civilians are terrified, Hummingbird's intimidated and the rest of Comma ...'

'Is wondering when we started killing minors. I know.' All this fuss, and they don't even know about Cocoon.

'So you're going after them, right?'

He doesn't say *finally*, but she hears it. Reluctantly, Isabel nods. 'I don't know how we'll find them, or get the ransom money, but ...' She draws in a shaky breath. 'You were right. This isn't over. And we have to get Emma out.'

Michael nods. 'Then let's train.'

But no matter how hard she pushes her body for the rest of the session, she can't achieve that white-noise brain space that training usually lets her reach. All she can think about is Michael's suggestion that her kill is what drew her parents' attention: the confirmation that she survived. She was safe as long as they believed she was dead. She should have let them go on believing that.

And even if that's not what forced their hand – even if they don't know it's her – with the media screaming about the kill it'll be impossible to hide for ever. If they get Emma back, Isabel's going to have to tell her everything.

When. *When* they get Emma back. Because there's no way she's letting her parents take anything else from her.

32

PROMESO (PROMISE)

An unfamiliar doctor wakes Isabel the next morning with the news that Ronan Atwood wants to see her. She asks them where Daragh is, and gets no answer. Scowling, she heads downstairs to see why she's been summoned.

It's the first time Ronan has asked her to come and see him, instead of coming to her; the first time she's had a choice, though it doesn't feel much like one. She hesitates outside his office door, hearing raised voices inside.

'Our policy is that we don't pay ransoms,' says a man. 'If we cough up the cash for a *civilian*, that'll only encourage—'

'Don't try to explain our policy to me, Kieran,' says Ronan. 'I *wrote* most of it. Rest assured that I know what I'm doing. Your responsibility is to make sure everything's in place.'

'It will be, but, Ro—'

Ronan cuts him off. 'I'll speak to you later. I need to talk to Isabel.'

The door opens and a man storms past, barely glancing at Isabel as he goes. She pauses on the threshold a moment longer, until Ronan looks up to see what's taking her so long.

'Is there news?' she asks. Her voice sounds small and childlike.

He pushes a sheet of paper across the desk towards her and gestures to the empty chair. Isabel comes in and sits, picking up the page. 'Another ransom note,' he says, though that's apparent the moment she begins to read. 'They want you to go.'

'Me?'

'Isabel ...' Ronan sighs. He looks tired. 'We knew this wasn't about the money.' He reaches over and pulls the note back to his side of the table. 'This,' he says, 'was delivered to us by a fifteen-year-old boy. He collapsed immediately afterwards. Daragh's in intensive care with him now, and, with luck, he'll make it, but it was a strong poison and it's hard to be sure.'

'A child,' she says, voice hoarse. She knew – she'd guessed – but she'd said nothing.

'He hasn't regained consciousness long enough for us to find out if there are more of them.'

Isabel swallows. 'What do we do?'

'I'm not sure.' Ronan taps his pen against the desk. The cheap plastic casing rattles with every impact, and the sound is like broken glass against Isabel's mind. Her fear flays her open, leaving her stripped of defences. 'We knew your father wanted you. He planned for his daughter to be with him in his precious new guild, and if you go, I expect he'll try to convince you to throw in your lot with them – though I doubt he expects it to take much argument.'

Because Isabel has always done exactly as he asked, even when it wasn't enough. 'But he poisoned me,' she says. 'He left me for dead.'

'Then maybe he intends to finish the job.' Ronan's pen beats a violent tattoo on the surface of the desk. 'Of course, the best way to get him to lower his guard is to pretend to go along with it. Make him think he's got what he wants.'

Pretend to put herself back in her parents' power. Isabel feels sick. 'You're saying I should do it. That I should hand myself over.'

The pen stills, the silence abrupt as a gunshot. Ronan looks at it like he'd forgotten he was holding it, then places it carefully in the middle of the desk. 'I think,' he says, folding his hands in his lap, 'that it should be your choice.'

'And if I don't?'

'We can send the ransom. Trust he'll keep his word and let Emma go. Or we can attack his headquarters, but he probably has contingencies in place to eliminate her before we get too close.'

'*Do* you trust his word?' asks Isabel doubtfully.

'When he's made it clear the money's not what he's really interested in? No, not particularly.'

328

'So Emma would die.'

He gives a tight nod. 'Most likely.'

'And the children? If there are more of them?'

'We can't get them out without a way in.'

She appreciates his refusal to soften the blow. The truth falls like a rock onto the table in front of them and lies there, out in the open, impossible to brush aside.

The answer's obvious, of course. She has to go. Her father won't give them Emma until he gets what he wants, and what he wants is Isabel. She opens her mouth to say as much, but the words catch in her throat and nothing comes out.

'Isabel, it will be difficult to face your parents again. To put yourself under your father's control, even for a moment, goes against everything you've fought for these last few months.' It's the most gentle Ronan's voice has ever sounded, and for the first time she can believe that he and Daragh grew up together. 'If you go, then I swear to you, we will get you out. Do you understand me? It isn't permanent. You will leave that place.'

Isabel understands his words, but they mean nothing compared to the years Comma spent failing to get her out. If they couldn't do it when she was a child, how can she trust them to do it now?

Emma will die.

Ronan is a snake and a bastard, but he made her a deal, gave her a second chance. Ronan is Comma and everything they stand for and she's not fool enough to think he's in this for anyone but himself, but right now he's on her side.

She tries, again, to speak, but when she thinks about her

parents her words desert her, replaced by a crescendo of panic: *I can't I can't I can't I CAN'T.*

'We will get you out,' says Ronan again. 'You would only have to pretend long enough to save Emma, and then it will be over.' He sits back in his chair, a little crumpled. It doesn't look like he's slept. 'It's your choice, Isabel.'

Choice is the one thing she's never had.

It feels like minutes pass before she's able to speak, and when she does her voice is barely more than a whisper. 'Why? Why give me a choice now?'

He gives her a taut smile. 'Because my cousin has spent the last three days tearing me a new one for, in his words, being a "manipulative bastard" with no respect for your autonomy,' he says. 'And because your father makes me look like a saint, and while I suspect Daragh has a point, even I would hesitate to send you back to him after what he did.'

Isabel believes him about Daragh; she's not sure she believes in his sudden moral qualms about the use and abuse of children. Either way, it changes nothing. She stares at the note on his desk, but the letters swim, meaningless black symbols on a glaring page. 'Do I have to go alone?'

'The letter specifies that no agents should be sent with you.'

'What about someone who isn't an agent?' She presses the pad of her thumb against her scarred palm, rubbing and rubbing at the skin as though she can rub off the scar tissue and leave it blank and baby-smooth again. The sensation hardly registers. 'Someone they won't consider a threat?'

'Who do you have in mind?'

330

'Michael.' Ronan doesn't immediately answer, and Isabel tries to explain. 'They trained him too. So, if anything, it might strengthen the impression that I'm ... coming back, if he's with me, if it's both of us. Like a peace offering.'

Ronan picks up his pen again and taps the end of it against his chin. 'I can't see them objecting to Michael's presence,' he says at last. 'And it sits easier with me not to send you alone.' The implicit question is plain: *Will you go, then?*

Isabel takes a steady breath in, then releases it. Five things she can see: an ink stain on Ronan's middle finger, the light glinting off his cufflinks, the blocky print of the ransom demand, the grey carpet, her own hands twisting and twisting in her lap. Five things she can hear: the buzz of Ronan's plastic pen as he taps it, the distant traffic, the whir of his computer's fan, her unsteady breath, his words – *we will get you out we will get you out we will get you out.*

She will not leave Emma there.

'Okay,' she says. 'If Michael can come with me, I'll go. And then what? You'll attack their headquarters?'

'The ultimate goal is to neutralise their guild, yes. Once Emma is safe and we've got you out, we'll take action.'

'And my parents? What will happen to them?'

His pen stills. 'That remains to be seen. There'll be a trial, I suppose.'

'On what charges?' His silence is enough of an answer. 'For being traitors to the guild, right? Not for the rest.'

'Isabel ...'

'Because prosecuting my parents for what they did to me

means talking about Cocoon, and even in a guild court that would screw you over.' And because betraying their employers is worse than all the times Ian and Judith Ryans almost killed their only daughter, and all the times they made her wish they'd succeeded. Treason trumps child abuse. 'I should warn you,' she says, 'that unless someone is there to stop me, there's a chance I might kill them.'

'I'd prefer it if you didn't,' says Ronan, his tone even. 'I understand, however, that if fighting breaks out, events may transpire that are outside of my control.'

It's almost permission. 'Thank you.'

'But first, you have to cooperate. I know it won't be easy for you. Play the obedient daughter, do whatever you have to do to make them believe it, until we make our move. We need them to think that they've won.'

It won't be easy, and at the same time it'll be the easiest thing in the world, because Isabel Ryans has been playing this role all her life.

'Do you have any other questions?'

A thousand. None. 'When?'

'Tomorrow. We can't move any sooner. We're mobilising a mixed group – our forces and Hummingbird's, and—'

'You're working with Hummingbird?' she interrupts, surprised.

'Your parents' guild is as much a threat to them as to us – the more defectors they're able to recruit, the more compromised guild security will be. And we have a better chance of success with their help.'

She's always known, academically, that the two guilds are rivals rather than enemies, but she's never heard of them working together. 'And you think we can wait until tomorrow?'

'We've got no choice. Your father won't be expecting an instantaneous response.'

Tomorrow. And then one way or another, it'll all be over.

Isabel doesn't remember leaving Ronan's office; her mind is too busy running through everything that could go wrong. The real fear hits once she's in her room and his words – *we will get you out* – begin to fade under the onslaught of her anxiety. They didn't get her out, they never got her out, she saved herself and now she's agreed to walk back into the monsters' lair and put herself in her parents' power all over again. Based on what, the flimsy promises of a man she doesn't trust? *We will get you out.* How can she possibly believe that?

Her hands shake as she picks up the phone and dials the number for the Fraser, a number she called a dozen times in secret as she laid the foundations for her new life and now calls in desperation as she tries to grasp the fading wisps of it. When the receptionist answers, she asks for Mortimer Sark.

There's a pause. And then:

'Hello?'

'Mortimer? It's Isabel.'

Silence. It occurs to her then that maybe he knows about Nick. If he saw the papers, guessed it was her, he'll know she's a monster. She waits for him to hang up in disgust, but all he says is, 'Are you safe?'

It's the last thing she expected. 'I'm . . .' Is she? Not really. It doesn't matter. 'Mortimer, they've got Emma. My parents.'

'I know. Leo told me.'

Right. And the fact he knows Leo means he cares, doesn't it? So she's not asking for herself, she's asking for Emma, and it doesn't matter what she's done because . . .

'I'm going to get her,' she says. 'But I don't know if I trust the guild to get me out of there. I need somebody to know where I've gone. I need a *civilian* to know where I've gone, to know if I don't come out again.' *He wants you safe*, Emma said. Is that true? Has she ever been worthy of his protective instincts?

She waits, counting seconds of silence.

Finally, Mortimer says, 'Okay. Tell me what you need me to do.'

33

MISIO (MISSION)

'Hey, little Moth.'

Isabel looks up as Michael enters the kit room. 'Don't call me that.'

'Why not? It's on your calling card, isn't it?' He takes a stab vest from the rack, tries it on, then discards it and tries another. It didn't take much to convince him to come with her, although he was less enthusiastic about pretending to cooperate. She suspects he was hoping for a straightforward revenge mission, guns blazing the moment they walked through the door. 'Embrace it. Before the year's out, you'll be the monster of kids' bedtime stories.'

Isabel's mild discomfort turns to annoyance. 'That's not funny.'

'I didn't ...' He trails off, hands full of protective gear. 'You're the one who took the contract. I thought it didn't bother you.'

You're the one who kills minors. Isabel turns away, looking at the clock. 'You're late. Ronan's expecting us at eleven.'

'I'm sorry.' Michael's clearly not talking about his poor timekeeping. 'I didn't realise you were sensitive about it. You didn't seem upset.'

'I was a little distracted by Emma being kidnapped almost immediately afterwards.' Isabel laces up her combat boots and stands. 'I'll deal with the rest when she's safe.'

'Will you really, though?'

Isabel leaves the kit room without answering, and doesn't look back to see if Michael catches the swinging door before it hits him in the face. Only the sound of his footsteps tells her he followed her.

'Wait, Isabel, I—'

'Only one thing matters today,' she says, not glancing in his direction, 'and that's getting Emma out. If you do anything to jeopardise that, I'll kill you myself.'

'Message received.' Michael speeds up until he's walking at her side. 'I'm sorry, I misjudged that.'

It felt more like malice than misjudgement, but Michael, like her, has never been good at knowing when to stop. She lets it slide and keeps walking until they reach the office where Ronan is waiting for them, a rucksack on his desk.

'Is that the ransom?' asks Isabel, indicating the bag.

He nods. 'The fabric's reinforced, the zips are locked, and I

336

suggest not giving them the key until you know Emma's safe. It'll give you a bit of extra bargaining power.' Isabel tucks the small, silver key that he hands her into the zip pocket of her jacket. 'You're armed?'

'Two knives and a small pistol.'

'Michael?'

'The same.'

'Good. Remember, you're not there to fight. Do whatever you have to do to convince them you're on their side, until Emma is safe. Leave the rest to us.'

'I'll do my best,' says Isabel.

'We'll have someone there to meet her and get her out of the way before any fighting starts. We'll act as soon as it's safe.' Ronan's been talking to them both, but now he looks at Isabel. 'This won't be easy. Any of it. I need to know you'll keep your head.'

What is he afraid of – that she'll kill her father the way she killed Ian Crampton? 'I won't fuck it up.'

'Good.' Ronan's smile is dangerous, but she isn't his enemy today. She pities those who are. 'Any more questions?'

'The boy,' says Isabel. 'The messenger. Is he . . .'

'Still in intensive care. I sent Daragh home at four this morning to get some sleep, but he's being looked after.' He doesn't ask why she cares, which is a relief, because she's not sure she knows. She certainly can't articulate it. 'If that's everything, the car's outside. Good luck to you both. I know what you're capable of, and I don't think you need it, but I'll offer it regardless.'

Isabel doesn't trust herself to speak. *We will get you out.* Contingency plans haven't eased her mind. She's walking knowingly into a trap baited with the only person she truly cares about, and she has so much more to lose than she realised.

She needs a lot more than luck if she's going to survive this.

The address they've been given is in Flixton, a tiny industrial borough crammed up against the city's northern wall. An anonymous grey car takes them across Espera, through the narrow streets of the city centre into the wider roads of Fordon. Isabel stares mutely out of the window as they pass through her former home borough. It looks exactly as it always did.

'What will you do if this doesn't work?' says Michael, as they near the Flixton boundary.

'It'll work.'

'And if it doesn't? What if Emma's already dead?'

Isabel's hand tightens into a fist. 'She's not.'

'You don't know that.'

'They only sent the second ransom demand yesterday. She's alive. If they'd killed her, they'd have sent the body and hoped we'd come for revenge.'

Michael hums sceptically. 'Just because that's what you'd do ...'

'I know my parents,' Isabel interrupts. 'She's not dead.'

Michael knows them too, so he knows she's right. The rest of the journey passes in bleak silence.

Finally, a sign declares: YOU ARE NOW ENTERING THE

BOROUGH OF FLIXTON. The car stops, as agreed, a few streets from their destination, and Isabel and Michael climb out.

'This could be a trap,' he says, ever the optimist.

'Of course it's a trap,' says Isabel. 'That's the whole fucking point. We need them to believe we've fallen for it.' If it wasn't a trap, they wouldn't have specified that Isabel has to be the one to bring the money. They wouldn't have brought her here instead of making an exchange somewhere on a neutral street. They want her on their territory, under their power.

They've reached the road. Ahead of them is an ordinary-looking terrace of houses, though as Isabel gets closer, she can see it's only a façade; behind the brick frontage, the houses have been knocked through. The central door bears the number written on the directions.

'Stick to the plan,' she tells Michael. 'It'll work.'

'I'm following your lead,' he assures her, which means it's all on her not to fuck this up.

Isabel takes a deep breath and walks up the path to the front door.

It swings open as they approach, and she has to force herself not to hesitate on the steps. She knows they'll be watching her, and she can't let herself show fear. She steels herself – *it's for Emma* – and steps inside, Michael close on her heels.

And there he is.

Her father.

He hasn't changed at all. He's still a lean, sharp-featured man, greying at the temples, who wouldn't look out of place in any corporate office. The moment she sees him, she feels herself diminishing, making herself smaller, less of a target, and she has to consciously square her shoulders and stand up straight. Her mouth is as dry as her palms are sweaty, the hair on her neck prickling with the overwhelming sense of threat. But when she looks around the lobby, there's nobody lurking in the shadows. No sign of Judith.

Nobody there but Ian Ryans, standing at the bottom of a flight of stairs.

He smiles when he sees her, and ice trickles down her spine. 'Mi sciis ke vi venus, Issy. Kaj Michael! Kia agrabla surprizo.' *I knew you'd come, Issy. And Michael! What a pleasant surprise.*

If she lets herself feel anything, she won't be able to bear this. Already her fear threatens to paralyse her, muscles tightening. Isabel squashes her emotions down into the secret place inside her where they lived for the first seventeen years of her life and puts on the mask her father expects to see. She shrugs off the rucksack, placing it on the floor between them like a barrier.

'I brought the money,' she says. Her English is a small, meaningless act of rebellion.

He regards the rucksack. 'Mi povas vidi tion.' *I can see that.*

'And I'm here. Like you wanted. So you can let her go now. You can let Emma go.'

'Always in such a hurry,' says her father, still in Esperanto. He looks disappointed, which should be satisfying, but it isn't. She hates that it isn't. 'I've got so much to show you, Issy. A whole guild of our own. I wanted to give you the grand

340

tour – you'd like that, wouldn't you? Our facilities here are superior to anything you'll find in Comma. Or Hummingbird, for that matter.'

She wonders how many defectors they've recruited from Hummingbird. 'Let Emma go.'

'We'll get to that.' Ian clicks his fingers, summoning a young man from one of the rooms off the lobby. 'Search them, will you, Joseph?'

Isabel doesn't struggle as she's patted down. Joseph is thorough, finding both her knives and the gun. He takes her phone too, which she should have seen coming. *I still have my fists*, she reminds herself, but Michael's face is resentful as his weapons are taken.

'Now the rucksack,' says her father. 'Open it.'

Her instinct is to obey, but she doesn't have to listen to her instincts any more. 'Not until I've seen Emma.'

'How do I know it's money and not a weapon?' he counters. 'Show me, and then you can lock it up again until I've proved to your satisfaction that your friend is unharmed.'

Make him think he's won. Wearing her old subservience like a mask, Isabel unlocks the padlock and pulls it off. She has the sudden, horrible thought that Ronan might have tricked her, sent her in with a bag of newspaper. Would he take that kind of risk, after all he's expended to keep her alive? She has no idea what he's capable of.

She yanks on the zip, exposing the bundles of notes.

Ian's smile is broad. 'That's my girl.'

Isabel closes the bag, fastens the padlock, and returns the

key to her pocket. 'You've seen the money,' she says. 'Now what? Dear old Mum's here somewhere, I'm guessing?'

This is asked casually, as though it's an idle question and not an attempt to get the worst over with before she loses her nerve.

'She's not, I'm afraid,' he replies, just as casual. 'She hoped to be here when you came, but it can't be helped. You can catch up later.'

He clearly doesn't think she'll be leaving any time soon, but she can't worry about that when she's still stuck on Judith's absence. She should be relieved, but instead the knot in her stomach tightens even further. 'Not here? Where is she?'

'Taking care of some business,' says Ian smoothly. 'Which reminds me. Which of you do I have to thank for the fact that two of my agents are currently in Comma custody?'

Isabel exchanges a glance with Michael. Gauntlet Drive was a collaborative effort: she's the one who fired the shots, but he's the reason she had the gun. He's pale, as though he thinks Ian can see his culpability just by looking at him – after all, Judith isn't here to protect him from Ian's wrath. For her part, Isabel doesn't want to think about what her mother might be doing right now. She has a feeling the unconscious agent won't be waking up and giving his testimony any time soon.

'I see,' says Ian, when it becomes clear that neither of them is going to claim or disavow responsibility. 'So it's like that. You didn't need to hurt them, you know. Their orders were only to bring you to me – you weren't in danger.'

She refrains from pointing out that she was dying at the time. 'And Emma?' she says. 'Was she in danger?'

Ian shrugs. 'What do I care about a civilian? I told them to deal with any loose ends.'

Isabel freezes, fear like needles piercing the wall around her emotions. 'If you've hurt her—'

'Relax,' says Ian, as if it's faintly absurd for her even to ask. 'Your friend is fine.'

As if she'd take his word for it. 'I want to see her.'

'All in good time.' He gives her an unconvincing smile. 'But first, Issy, it's been such a long time since I last saw you. How about a hug for your father?'

She recoils. *Cooperate. Do what he asks. Pretend to be—* 'A hug? After you nearly killed me?' It slips out. So much for obedience. 'You forced me to make that poison and then you let it rip me apart from the inside!'

'That was never my intention,' he says, in the tone he always uses to prove she's being irrational. His mournful expression is transparently unconvincing. 'Let me show you around and I'll explain.'

Cooperate until Emma is safe. That's all she has to do. But it feels like a lot, when she's looking her father in the eye, knowing – perhaps for the first time in her life – exactly what he did to her.

It was hard enough to believe Ronan's promises when she was safe in his office, and it's harder now. She reminds herself that she didn't need the guild to save her the first time around. She got out, and she's staying out.

343

'Fine,' she says. 'I'll have the grand tour. But I don't want you to touch me.'

Her father holds up his hands. 'As you wish. I suppose I deserve that.'

He deserves a knife through the heart. 'And when you've shown me your precious guild, I want my friend back.'

Immediately, his sorrowful expression vanishes, and Ian laughs, dismissing her rage like a childish tantrum. 'Of course,' he says, turning to set off up the stairs. 'Come along, then. The sooner we start, the sooner you get what you want.'

It takes all of her willpower to place her foot on the first step and follow him. Her legs are unsteady, but she refrains from touching the banister, as though it might contaminate her with the pervasive aura of *wrongness* that fills this place. She reaches blindly for Michael instead, and he takes her hand with an encouraging smile. *I'm here*, he mouths.

He's here. She isn't alone, and she'll get out.

'You know, Isabel,' her father's saying, 'I never meant for you to suffer. I wish your mother were here – she's got such a way with words, she could explain better than I can.'

'Give it a go,' suggests Isabel caustically. 'I'm fascinated to know why you poisoned me if you didn't intend to hurt me.'

With a mulish expression that suggests he finds the whole topic tiresome, he says, 'It was *supposed* to be temporary. I left to sort things out here, and your mother was meant to bring the two of you to join me a few days later. Comma were bound to search the lab when they realised I hadn't made the sale for them; I had to protect my creation somehow.'

It takes her a second to understand what he's actually saying, and she stops dead, letting go of Michael's hand. 'You used me as a *hiding place*?'

He keeps walking. 'It was the only way.'

So she was right: he wasn't trying to kill her. The confirmation gives her no satisfaction. At least if he were trying to hurt her, it would mean he saw her as a person – someone worthy of his attention, someone who meant something. But this? This is worse than any sadistic punishment. Because he didn't even care. All he cared about was protecting the exclusivity of his poison, and he was willing to sacrifice her health, if not her life, to do that.

Isabel races up the stairs, the better to confront him. 'How can that have been the only way?' she demands. 'You could have hidden it in your own stomach, or destroyed the sample after absconding with the money. But you put it in *me*?'

'If you hadn't run away, you'd never even have known it was there.'

She flinches as though he's slapped her. 'Don't you *dare* say it was my fault.'

'Look.' They've reached the top of the stairs, and finally he turns to face her. 'If your mother had brought you to join us as planned, I would have removed the capsule, no harm done. The casing would have seen to that. "A thousand miles away and still running", I believe those were your words.' Even now he's weaponising the acts he forced her to commit, using them against her. 'And you did run, didn't you? With Comma watching you, we couldn't get close without exposing ourselves.' He shrugs. 'Still, you're alive, aren't you?'

As if that's all that matters – as if her suffering is only a footnote in the grand story of his guild. She thought he hated her, wanted to see her in pain, but he doesn't care at all.

'My heart stopped twice,' she says. Her voice shakes, anger and tears threatening to choke her. 'My immune system is still attacking itself. I've been in hospital for *weeks*, because you decided to use me as a human hiding place, and rob me of the memories that would have let me save myself sooner.'

Ian's expression doesn't change. 'We've all made sacrifices,' he says, and gestures to the first door on the landing. 'Here. The heart of our operation. I've waited a long time to show you this.'

Like his guild is the only thing that matters to him.

Isabel chokes down the lump in her throat and follows him inside.

34

OFERO (SACRIFICE)

The heart of his operation is an office. Larger and more modern than she'd have expected to find inside a row of houses like this, but still, fundamentally, an office. It has a crisp, minimalist feel, with a dozen curved desks and a wide skylight.

The only aspect that meets Isabel's expectations of her father is the wall lined with embedded glass tanks. Ian heads straight for them, drawing Isabel's attention to the one in the middle. 'How much do you remember about these beasties?'

Fucking *spiders*.

She won't let her father see her discomfort. She forces herself to examine the creature he's pointing to. 'Latrodectus katipo,' she says. 'Native to New Zealand. Endangered.

Venomous to humans.' Donor of the venom in the poison that almost killed her.

He gives a genuine smile. 'I knew you wouldn't have forgotten,' he says. 'This is our namesake, you see.' He gestures to the far wall, emblazoned with their arachnid logo in striking black and scarlet.

'Katipo?' she says. 'Is that what you're calling yourselves?'

'You don't like it?'

She shrugs. 'Doesn't roll off the tongue.'

Michael's been letting Isabel take the lead, as though hoping Ian will forget he's there, but now he asks, 'Are you trying to match Comma and Hummingbird, or replace them?'

He asks in Esperanto, which prompts a brief smile from Ian. 'Mostly the former, for now,' he answers. 'The city needs strong leadership, and undermining the guilds could hurt all of us. Rivalry, on the other hand, is profitable. It drives innovation. Of course,' he adds, 'who knows what might happen as we grow?'

'And you're recruiting from both guilds, right?'

'Yes, some of our members have come to us from Hummingbird.' Ian looks sideways at him. 'You're wondering why we didn't ask you to join us.'

Michael flushes. 'No, I—'

'I understand.' Ian's smile is patronising. 'I'm afraid after Isabel's disappearing act, all our plans were thrown into disarray. Certain things slipped through the cracks.'

Certain things like remembering Michael existed. Isabel sees the look on his face as he realises that he, too, is utterly

348

expendable to her parents. His abandonment, like her poisoning, wasn't a punishment: they simply didn't care.

He's about to say something rash and ruin their semi-cooperative act, so Isabel interrupts. 'Can we see Emma now?'

'But the tour's only just begun,' says Ian.

Apparently he's going to drag this out as long as he can. She gestures stiffly to the door. 'Then lead on.'

The corridor he takes them down must go most of the way through the terrace. It's lined with doors, which Ian points to as they pass. 'Training room. We've installed a simulator so that our recruits can practise with humanoid targets, to help reduce hesitation in the field.' The next door: 'Laboratory. I'm continuing my work, although I have a team of apprentices who'll take over in time. Perhaps you could join them, Issy.'

'No.'

Her flat refusal clearly isn't what he expected. 'But you were so good at it.'

'That was before ...' Isabel's doing a terrible job of pretending to cooperate. She tries again. 'There are things I'm better at. Or haven't you been reading the news?'

That brings his smile back. 'So it is you. Our little Moth.'

'One and the same.'

'Well, you always did take after your mother.'

Isabel turns away so that he can't see her face. 'Is that what you want, then? For me to join you?'

'Of course,' he says. 'Katipo is my vision, the culmination of everything I've been working towards. It's incomplete without my daughter by my side.'

She focuses on her breathing. *We will get you out.* 'If you say so.'

Ian doesn't seem to notice her gritted teeth. He leads them to the final door on the corridor, painted a vivid scarlet. 'Now,' he says, 'let me show you what I'm proudest of.'

Isabel knows what she'll see behind that door before he opens it. Her stomach's in her throat, her blood icy. She wants to stop him, snatch his hand away from the door handle, pretend that if he never opens it, she'll never have to know, and she can keep pretending it's enough to know she'll leave this place.

He opens the door, and Isabel knows: it will never be enough.

It will never be enough, because no matter how many times she escapes her father, there will be others who don't. Others like the children in this room, most of them yet to reach their teens. They have watchful eyes shadowed by nightmares, and she sees them assessing her, trying to gauge if she's a threat.

She wonders how long he's been training them. If it started before or after she ran. How deep the rot goes, how tangled the knots he's wrought in their minds.

'This is what Comma and Hummingbird don't understand,' Ian's saying. 'They haven't changed in fifty years. They're clinging to the manners and propriety of the last century, when outside Espera's walls it's a different world, and no matter how much they pretend they're adapting, they're being left behind. That's why they don't see the value in this. Couldn't see the value in *you*, Issy. How many others your age could do what you've done?'

In her attempt to avoid his gaze, she makes unwilling eye contact with one of the children, a bright-eyed redhead who can't be older than ten, if that. The girl stares back like there's no one in the room but the two of them, and Isabel can't tell if it's a challenge or a cry for help. Maybe it's *get us out of here*. Maybe it's *we're the weapons you refused to be*.

It doesn't matter, either way.

'They shouldn't have to,' she says, wrenching her gaze away. 'No one should have to.'

Immediately she cowers, waiting for a blow that never lands. When she dares glance up at her father, he looks disappointed. 'I see Comma have got to you.'

Not Comma, she wants to say. It wasn't Comma who taught her that she's more than this. It was the heavy bag of papers over her shoulder, the weak morning sunlight filtering through the clouds, the way Nick smiled at her on the tram, how Mortimer saw her as someone worth protecting, Daragh's gentle hands, and above all, it was Emma. Emma who didn't have to escape because the guild never ensnared her. Emma who was loved, and believed Isabel should be too.

'Let them go.' Her voice shakes and the words are hardly audible. She tries again. 'Let them go.'

Ian laughs. 'They're not prisoners here, Issy. They're grateful.'

The way she was meant to be.

Isabel closes her eyes, but it doesn't help, because she can still see the redhead's expression branded on the inside of her eyelids. She stumbles out of the room with the scarlet door and hunches over, fighting nausea. Getting out isn't enough. Not if her father is allowed to do it again and again, and keep doing it as long as he's alive. She doesn't know if she can kill him, but if she doesn't they'll never be free, not her and not any of the children in that room.

How many are there? It doesn't matter. One would be too many.

A hand on her back startles her, but it's only Michael, crouching by her side. 'You okay?' he asks, voice gentle.

She feels hysteria like broken glass in her throat. *Okay?* Of course she's not fucking okay. How can he be so calm, after what they saw in that room? Did he know her father was doing this?

Isabel takes five slow, deep breaths, and then she forces herself upright and looks at Ian. 'I've seen enough,' she tells him. 'Now let me see Emma.'

'But you ...' He breaks off, reconsiders. 'Of course. You want to make sure she's safe, naturally. There'll be time for the rest later. It's not as if you're going anywhere.'

We will get you out. 'No,' Isabel agrees tightly. 'It's not.'

Ian leads them back along the corridor. He fetches a key from the office and takes them down the stairs, through a door Isabel didn't notice on the way in, down a second set of stairs and along a sloping corridor, deeper and deeper into the earth.

There's a bored-looking guard outside the cell, reading a battered paperback. She shoves it guiltily under her chair as they approach, but Ian doesn't reprimand her. He inserts his key into the lock in the middle of the solid metal door, and Isabel hears the bolts clank as he turns it.

The door swings open.

Emma's sitting on the narrow bed on the far side of the cell, her expression fearful and bleary. Her hair's a mess, her clothes creased and stained with sweat, but she's alive. She looks up with eyes full of hope, as though Isabel's a candle in a blackout.

'Bel,' she says. 'You came.'

At the sound of her voice, Isabel's protective instinct flares into life. She crosses the room in seconds, taking her friend's cold hands in hers. 'I'm here,' she says. 'I'm here. I'm sorry I wasn't here sooner. It's going to be okay.'

'You came . . .'

'We're taking you home.' She takes the key to the rucksack from her pocket and tosses it to her father. 'Here. You've got your ransom. Now we're leaving.'

'The ransom was for your friend,' says Ian mildly. 'Not you.'

Because that was always the real bargain: Isabel's life for Emma's.

She closes her eyes, and for a moment the only thing that's real is Emma's hand in hers. There are people waiting. Emma will leave this place and they'll be there, ready to take her home and look after her. All Isabel has to do is let go. Let her friend walk away from her.

She opens her eyes. 'Michael,' she says, 'please will you take Emma?' He hesitates, as though he doesn't understand the request. 'Get her out of here. Her mother is waiting for her. *Please*.'

'Isabel, I—' begins Emma.

'Don't.' Her resolve's already cracking; her friend's voice might shatter it. If she can get Emma out, it will be enough, it has to be enough. She'll follow later, when it's all over. 'Michael, please.' She looks at Ian. 'You've got me, you don't need him. Let him take Emma.'

Her father hesitates, then nods. 'Of course.'

It means losing her only ally, but it's worth it if it means Emma is safe. Isabel blinks back tears as Michael steps forward and puts Emma's arm over his shoulder, lifting her with one easy movement.

'No,' says Emma. 'No, I'm not leaving Isabel here. Let go of me, I'm not—'

But she's no match for Michael's strength. Isabel looks away as the sound of struggling footsteps recedes. *She's getting out*, she tells herself. *Emma's getting out. That was the whole point. That's why I came.*

It takes her a moment to realise she's been left alone with Ian.

When she dares look at him, he's watching her. 'I don't understand you,' he says. 'You had every opportunity in life, and instead you ran away. To what? A mediocre, impoverished life and a civ education?'

'At least it was my choice,' says Isabel. Just like this was her choice. To let Emma walk away and leave her in a cell with her father.

'There is nobody else in this city like you,' says Ian. 'And you'd throw that away.'

'I'd do it again.'

354

He watches her for a few more seconds, until she can't bear the weight of his gaze and has to avert her eyes. 'Yes,' he says. 'I believe that.'

And then he steps back, and the door slams shut behind him, sealing Isabel in the cell.

35

ESKAPO (ESCAPE)

It's impossible to know how much time has passed. Isabel lies curled up on the hard bed, trying not to think about how terrified Emma must have been, not knowing if or when anyone would come for her. She doesn't want to think about whether Michael's managed to get her out, in case he hasn't.

She can't stop thinking about that room with the scarlet door.

She suspected that her father was training children, but actually seeing them was another thing entirely. Until then, part of her didn't know how to care, a part that was bitter and hardened and said, *If I survived, why shouldn't they?* And then she locked eyes with that redheaded girl and saw, finally, what Mortimer and Daragh and Emma saw when they looked at her:

a child. Nothing less, nothing more. It didn't matter what she'd done. She deserved better.

But she can't help anyone locked in this cell.

Isabel takes off her jacket and the stab vest underneath, then unhooks her bra, slipping it out from under her T-shirt and tugging at the seams until the underwire punches through. She rips both sides open. The wires are plastic and thicker than she'd like, but it's better than nothing.

No noise from upstairs tells her what's happening: whether Emma's safe, whether the guild has arrived. She can't tell if she's been waiting an hour or a day, but it doesn't matter. She saved herself the first time around. She can do it again.

The underwires make poor lockpicks. She tries not to let desperation get to her as she fumbles with the lock, until at last the final tumbler clicks into place and she twists. An alarm blares in the corridor when she kicks the door open and edges out into the hallway. She'd forgotten about the guard outside – startled out of her novel by the breach, the woman hardly has time to look up before Isabel wrenches her forward, headlong into a wall and unconsciousness.

She searches the guard for weapons, but only finds a small baton. The twist dial on the bottom suggests it's electrified, and Isabel shoves it gratefully into her belt. It's not a knife, but it's better than nothing.

She thought she remembered the route they took to the cell, but the corridor twists and turns so often she begins to doubt herself. She takes any option that leads her *up*, and as she nears the surface, she can hear the distant sound of fighting. So

Comma came, after all. Maybe she should have trusted they'd want Katipo eliminated, if she couldn't manage trusting them to rescue her, but even that felt like a step too far without proof.

There's a set of doors in front of her, locked fast. Either the lock's harder than the one on her cell or her makeshift lockpicks are too mangled to be useful, because it won't budge. Isabel kicks the door. 'Just – fucking – open!'

'Isabel?' At first she thinks she's imagining the voice on the other side of the door. 'Isabel, is that you?'

It's Mortimer. She feels a sob rising in her throat, threatening to choke her, and realises she never actually believed he'd come for her. She called him because she had to do *something*, had to know she'd tried, but the sound of his voice is as unexpected as it is welcome.

'Yeah, it's me,' she says. 'It's Isabel.'

'Stand back. We'll get the door open.'

She does as she's told, still not certain she isn't hallucinating, and the door shudders with the impact of bullets into the hinges and lock. Her teacher pushes it open with the sound of splintering wood, a trembling torch in his hand shedding a feeble beam of light across Isabel. And behind him is Emma.

'What are you doing here?' Isabel demands at the sight of her. 'Michael was supposed to get you out. You were supposed to be *safe*.'

'He did,' says Emma. 'He got me to the medics before the guild mobilised, but then he went back to fight, and they told me Mum was with them, and I—' She breaks off. 'I had to do *something*. I said I wasn't leaving you and I meant it.'

'I couldn't stop her,' says Mortimer, shoving the gun back into his belt. She wonders where he got a gun. Where he learned to shoot. 'Believe me, I tried.'

'Yeah, *tried* to go rushing blindly in without knowing about the other entrance or where to find Isabel.' Emma reaches out a hand. 'Come on.'

Isabel takes it, but she still doesn't understand what's happening. 'But you ...' she begins, looking at Mortimer. 'Why are you here?'

'Because you called me,' he says, as if it's simple. Maybe for him, it is. 'And when Emma told me you were still in here, I thought you might like some help.'

Emma says, 'There's fighting upstairs, but if we're quick, we can make it out the way we came in. All the attention is on the front door; nobody's guarding the other entrance.'

'I can't.'

'Isabel—'

'You should ... you should get out. Both of you. There's something I have to do first.'

'No fucking way,' says Emma. 'We came here for *you*.' Now Isabel sees that she's armed too, a sheathed knife in her belt, half hidden by her jacket. She can't imagine Emma using it. She doesn't want to. 'We're getting out of here, all of us.'

They don't understand. This isn't about her, this is bigger than her. She can't walk away. 'There are *children* upstairs,' she says, voice cracking. 'My father's training children.'

Emma swears, but Mortimer freezes. 'Children,' he says, in a flat voice.

'I can't leave them behind. I don't trust the guild with them.' Ronan won't let them go free, with whatever knowledge Katipo has put inside their heads. He'll see them as a risk, take them into custody – at least until he knows what they're capable of. And she won't let him. She's not leaving those children behind the way she was left behind.

'Obviously not,' says Emma. 'But you're not going up there alone.'

'I wanted you safe,' she says. 'If I know that you're safe, I'll be able to—'

'Take stupid risks and get yourself killed,' her friend finishes. 'I know. Which is why I'm not going anywhere.'

'She's right,' says Mortimer. 'We're not leaving you alone, and we're not leaving them behind. Do you know the way?'

Only if she can get back to the main staircase, and from the sound of it, that's where the fighting is. 'We have to get upstairs. There'll be a back way, a fire escape or something.'

'We passed some stairs on the way in,' says Emma. 'We took the door they brought me in – it's in the next house over, but the corridors join up.'

'Then let's go.'

Isabel goes first, Emma close behind. Mortimer takes the rear, one hand resting on his gun. She can tell he doesn't want to use it, which only adds to her questions about where it came from. They take several wrong turns through the labyrinthine corridors of the converted terrace, some leading to dead ends and stairs that go nowhere, others where the sound of fighting is louder and they have to double back before they end up stumbling into the violence.

Finally, they reach the second floor corridor, and the scarlet door.

Isabel was afraid it would be locked, but when she tries the handle, it gives easily. She peers inside, one hand out to keep Emma and Mortimer behind her. The room is far larger than she'd realised before, the main space branching off into at least three other rooms. It's practically a self-contained complex, and she wonders how long it's been since the children left this suite. There's no sign of them now. The main hall is dimly lit by a few windows of clouded glass, and in the gloom she can make out the clutter of hastily abandoned tasks. Isabel's heart sinks. Combined with the open door, it looks a lot like the children have been taken already.

Or maybe they're doing as they've been told and keeping out of sight.

She takes a few steps forward, Emma and Mortimer close on her heels. 'The other rooms,' she whispers. 'We need to search them.'

Mortimer nods, moving towards the left-hand door. Emma shivers and moves closer to Isabel. 'This place gives me the creeps.'

It gives Isabel the creeps too. It's unsettling how closely it resembles some of the Cocoon facilities, to the point where reality threatens to merge into flashback. Only Emma at her side tells her for sure that this is *now*, not *then*.

It's too quiet, she thinks. The room must be soundproofed,

because she can't hear the fighting at all. Unless it's over already, and they've won. They're going to win, right? The combined forces of Comma and Hummingbird should be enough to defeat a tiny upstart guild who didn't know they were coming.

Unless they did. Just like they knew Isabel survived, or that she would go to Gauntlet Drive, or that Grace was helping her.

Maybe Katipo has been one step ahead all along.

But if that's the case, it ends now. She catches Emma's eye and indicates for her to take the right-hand door, then focuses her attention on the middle door. Like the others, it isn't locked. Inside is a dormitory lined with sturdy bunks, with a desk and small locker for each pair of beds. On the far side of the room are two doors that must lead to toilet facilities. For completeness' sake, Isabel checks them, but the cubicles are empty.

She emerges into the main room just as Mortimer does. 'Anything?' she asks, gesturing towards the room he came from. He shakes his head, and they both look at the right-hand door, from which Emma has yet to emerge.

Isabel loosens the baton in her belt, and they move towards the final room.

It's a laboratory.

The only natural light struggles through a small, high window covered with a grille, but even in the gloom Isabel's breath catches at the sight of the rows of workbenches. They're littered with abandoned experiments, beakers still half full and notes unfiled, like they've interrupted a training exercise. The glass vials glint in the half-light.

And she knows this room. She's walked it a thousand times in her nightmares. It's a perfect copy of her father's lab, which means there'll be a whiteboard on the far wall . . .

There it is, complete with the remnants of a formula scrawled in childish handwriting. But Isabel has eyes only for what's in front of it.

Emma. She's hunched on a plastic chair, and behind her, half concealed by the poor light, is a figure in dark clothes, a gun in their hands, its barrel pressed against the back of her head.

No.

Isabel's feet have taken root in the grey linoleum, like this really is another nightmare. She can't move, can't speak, powerless in the face of Emma's wide, terrified eyes. This wasn't meant to happen. It wasn't meant to end like this.

The figure with the gun might as well be a shadow, until they speak.

'I told Ian you'd come back for the children, given the chance,' he says. 'You're very predictable sometimes.'

She would recognise his voice anywhere.

Not a shadow, not a stranger.

Michael.

36

MALESPERO (DESPAIR)

Understanding comes only slowly, Isabel's brain refusing to join the dots between Michael and his words and the gun to Emma's head. She takes an involuntary step forward, as though it'll make sense if she can see him clearly.

He presses the gun into Emma's scalp hard enough to make her gasp. 'I wouldn't do that if I were you, little Moth. Stay right where you are.'

'Michael,' she says stupidly. 'Why are you ...'

And finally it clicks.

He was never really on her side. He wasn't abandoned – he was her parents' creature all along. *That*'s how they knew she survived, not because of Oliver. That's how they knew she'd be at Gauntlet Drive that day. And that's how they knew where to find—

Grace. A numbness is spreading through her chest.

'You killed Grace,' she says, and sees Emma flinch. 'Didn't you?'

Michael steps around Emma's chair, keeping his gun trained on her. It brings him out of the darkest shadows, and she sees new bruises blossoming down one side of his face. All trace of sympathy in his eyes has been replaced with steely resolve.

'Yes.' He doesn't even have the decency to look ashamed. He killed Grace. Killed her and then had the nerve to pretend it mattered to him, to encourage Isabel's desire for revenge. Weeks of play-acting, twisting the knife a little deeper into her back.

She should have known he didn't have it in him to run, but she'd wanted to believe he was on her side. Maybe because she needed her parents not to have corrupted him – needed to know they could get out, both of them. Fellow survivors.

But it was a lie. All of it. The way he fed her mashed potato when she was dying, their games of cards, all his concern for Emma – lies on lies on lies, from the moment he turned up at her door.

And now he has a gun to her best friend's head.

Isabel stays very still, trying not to provoke him. 'Where are the children?'

Michael jerks his head towards a door in the corner. 'Out of the way.'

In her father's lab, that was the storeroom. No reason to

assume it's any different here. She can't get past Michael to get to them, nor can Mortimer, so she says, 'Okay. Let's talk about this. Please put the gun down.'

His mouth twists. 'Give me one good reason.'

'Because if you fire that in here, the whole place could go up.' Fuck knows what manner of chemicals are in these cupboards and what damage they'd do if a gunshot went astray. The gas supply alone could blow them all into oblivion.

Michael wavers, but doesn't lower the weapon. 'I said a *good* reason.'

Her words have deserted her, right when she needs them most. She swallows. Looks at Emma. Looks back at Michael, and says, 'Because I'm your friend.'

'Grow up, Isabel,' he says. 'People like us don't have friends.'

But if that was true, he wouldn't be standing here with a gun to Emma's head, because Emma wouldn't have come back for her. 'That doesn't have to be the case.'

'Really? You think Nick Larrington would agree?'

In a voice taut with fear, Emma asks, 'What happened to Nick?'

Michael's laugh is hollow. 'Oh,' he says, 'you don't know.' He looks at Isabel as though expecting her to beg him not to say anything, but she doesn't. She won't tell him to lie to them. Not about this, not after everything. So with a vicious kind of triumph in his voice, he says, 'Isabel killed him.' He leans close to Emma as he speaks, and she flinches away. 'Along with a sixteen-year-old boy. But at least they were paying her for that one.'

Isabel feels Mortimer stiffen beside her, sees the pain in Emma's face. 'No,' says her friend. 'No, she wouldn't do—'

'I'm sorry,' says Isabel. It might as well be a confession.

Michael's smile widens. 'Still think she's going to save you?' he says to Emma, tracing her cheekbone with his gun. 'Still believe your life matters to her?'

Isabel can't look at Emma's face crumpling. She meets Michael's gaze instead. 'I always thought we were alike,' she says, and has the tiniest satisfaction of seeing his surprise.

'Alike?'

'My father's using you, and he doesn't give a shit if you get hurt in the process. Just like me.' She eyes the bruises on his face. 'Let me guess. Gauntlet Drive?' He's silent, but his expression tightens just enough that she knows she's right. 'Yeah, I can't imagine he was thrilled you got his agents shot, even before you handed me back to Comma. I assume that part was unintentional.'

'Judith told me to keep you alive,' he spits. 'You wouldn't have made it here. The Sunshine Project was the only option.' He adds, resentfully, 'I didn't know about Daragh.'

'Oh, so you're taking orders from Judith too?' Of course he is. 'Well, I'm glad *somebody* gave a shit whether I survived. But you really did sell out to—'

'It doesn't matter,' he interrupts. 'Don't you get it? None of that matters.'

It does. It matters because Michael's pointing a gun at Emma and she has to believe she can convince him to put it down. 'We deserved better, Michael,' she says. 'Both of

367

us. What Cocoon did to us, what my parents did to us, was fucked up.'

He huffs a wry laugh. 'You think I need you to tell me that?'

'But you'll let my father do it all again?' She gestures to the door in the corner. 'Those kids deserve better too. All of them.'

His finger tightens on the trigger and Emma squeezes her eyes shut, but he doesn't shoot. 'If you're trying to appeal to my better nature, you should know that I don't have one.'

'I know.' *Keep him talking.* It's barely half a plan, but it's all she's got. 'Only a bastard cheats at cards the way you do.'

This time his laugh is real, pulled from him by surprise more than humour. 'I don't need to cheat to win against you, Isabel, but I guess you never could accept when you're beaten.'

'No,' says Isabel. 'I can't.'

Their gazes lock. His grey eyes are as emotive as pebbles as they hold hers, and she hardly dares blink in case he takes it as a victory.

And in those few seconds when his attention is on Isabel, Emma moves. She kicks away the chair, ducks below the barrel of Michael's gun, and thrusts her knife into his thigh, messy and untrained and painful as fuck.

Isabel sees her chance. She yanks the baton from her belt and twists the dial up as high as it can go before slamming it against Michael's side. He screams and drops the gun.

'Go!' she yells at Mortimer; Emma's already stumbling towards the door in the corner, despite her bloodied hands and look of shock. 'Get the children out, get them ...'

The baton fizzes and goes dead, clearly out of power.

Michael snarls, tries to lurch towards the fallen gun, but Isabel kicks it out of reach and slams the baton down on his head. He staggers and goes down, but manages to grab her by the knees, knocking her legs out from under her. Isabel lands hard, barely avoiding the workbench, and before she's caught her breath, he's already moving, crawling towards the gun.

She pushes herself up and dives to stop him, but it's too late. He already has the weapon in his hand and he's pulled himself to his feet. Too far away for her to disarm him. Too close for him to miss.

Michael smiles and raises the gun.

Isabel closes her eyes.

There's no impact. No burning rush of pain. Just the shot, deafening, and a muffled thump, like somebody falling to their knees. She opens her eyes, expecting to see blood spreading from an injury her nerves haven't had a chance to register, but what she sees instead is worse.

Because there's Emma, on her knees, one hand pressed to her side, a dazed expression on her face as she lifts it away and sees the blood, like she doesn't understand what's happening.

Isabel doesn't understand what's happening.

She doesn't understand why Emma looks up, white-faced; why she says, 'Isabel,' and then chokes, doubling over. She can't grasp what's happening or why Emma's fallen or why there's so much blood, because Michael was going to shoot *her*, wasn't he? She should be the one dying.

Dying. No. Emma can't be dying. Not after everything. Not like this.

The useless baton falls from her hand as she stumbles forward, dropping to the floor beside her friend, pressing her hands desperately against the wound as though she can push the blood back inside. Beside her, Mortimer fumbles with his scarf, as if it might make a bandage. His hands are shaking as he proffers it, wordless, helpless.

Isabel knows how he feels. She takes the chequered cotton, loops it around Emma's torso, tries to put pressure on the wound. Blood soaks through it almost at once. 'Emma, you can't.' The words are futile, but they demand to be said. 'Emma, I came for you, I came to save you, you're not allowed to die on me.'

Emma manages a smile. 'Doing my best,' she says, and closes her eyes.

Somebody sobs, the broken gasp of a child who has been holding back their fear for a very long time. It's a moment more before Isabel realises it was her. 'No.' She repeats it like a litany. 'No, no, no, you can't be dead, you can't be . . .'

But you can't be a killer without recognising death, and Isabel has seen too many lives end to delude herself that Emma might open her eyes again. Still she fumbles for her friend's wrist, searching pointlessly for a pulse. Nothing. Only the blood, and death heavy and oppressive in the room, and every day she spent fighting to survive made worthless in an instant.

All she can do is beg. 'Please don't be dead.'

What would she have to pay, for the power to make her friend obey her? It doesn't matter. The cost doesn't matter, because Emma can't be dead, Emma who is sunlight and colour and hope.

Isabel forces another breath into her lungs, but they're ungrateful, hardly let it in. Her body wants to starve itself of oxygen and die here on the floor next to her best friend. Why should she be allowed to live? What good is she? This is *her fault*.

She's been drunk on death before, served it herself, but it has never tasted so bitter.

'Rule one,' says Michael. 'Don't get attached to someone who can't look after themselves.'

She looks back at him and rage sets her alight. She'd burn herself alive if there was a chance the blaze would kill him too. She has to force the words out through gritted teeth. 'I'll kill you.'

'There's the Isabel I remember,' he says, and gives her a condescending smile. 'Judith would be proud.'

Her world has narrowed to Emma's body beside her, the lab a waking nightmare. She lets loose a scream of rage and launches herself towards him, ready to throttle him with her bare hands if she has to, and with a flash of alarm that wipes the smugness from his expression, Michael raises the gun again and fires.

Isabel grabs his arm and the shot goes wide. Hits a cupboard. Sends vials and jars cascading to the floor, powders and liquids mixing indiscriminately in a puddle on the floor. She scrambles backwards, away from the mess, her own alarm a mirror of Michael's as the reaction begins. First smoke, then fire, growing as it spreads through the spillage, reaching towards the next cupboard and its contents ...

'Fuck,' says Michael, and turns to run.

37

POSTRIKOLTO (AFTERMATH)

He's gone.

Around her the lab is burning, every deadly trick of Ian's feeding the ravenous fire and filling the air with toxic smoke. With an explosion that sends Isabel tumbling backwards into the sharp corner of the workbench, another batch of chemicals catches alight, sending flames sheeting up. She stumbles forward through the haze, towards Mortimer and—

Emma.

She feels like she's shattering, the world ripped out from under her, but there's no time. Not unless she wants this room to become her funeral pyre too. And for a second she's tempted to let herself collapse, let herself crumble at Emma's side and wait for the flames to burn them both into ash the colour of grief. But that isn't how this ends.

'The children,' says Mortimer urgently. 'I'll take Emma, you get the children.'

The children. The whole reason they're here. She wishes she could be the one to hold Emma, carry her away from here, but she's not strong enough. She wouldn't be able to lift her in one smooth movement the way Mortimer does, cradling her like a child. So she swallows her sobs and stumbles towards the storeroom, already struggling to see the door through the fire and the smoke. She can taste acrid fumes in the back of her mouth.

For a moment, she thinks it's locked, but then the handle gives and the door opens, revealing the terrified children inside. At the sight of the fire they panic, one boy beginning to cry, and Isabel feels momentarily lost. She doesn't know how to reassure them. She can't be their hero, their bright bold rescuer come to save the day.

But she doesn't have to be, because these kids were being trained by Ian Ryans, and no soft words will ever counteract any of his orders. She turns back. 'Mortimer, go ahead of us!' she yells. 'Take Emma and get out of here. That way they have someone to follow.'

He looks from her to the children. 'Tell me you'll be right behind,' he says, like he's seen the bleak despair in her eyes and knows what it means. 'Tell me you'll follow!'

'I will! Just go!' It's the truth. She has to get out, because Michael got out, and she can't hunt him down if she dies here.

She looks back at the children and hardens her voice until it sounds like her mother's. 'Unless you want to die,' she tells them, 'you need to get the fuck out of here. See that man? You follow him. *Now.*'

They're all wide-eyed with incomprehension and fear, and for a second none of them move, orders warring with survival instinct. Then one of the boys bolts, darting forward towards the flames and freedom, and the spell's broken – one by one they make a break for the door until Isabel's the only one left, coughing in earnest now that the extractor fans can no longer clear the air.

No. Not the only one. There's a child here still, curled in the darkest corner of the room, with her knees pulled to her chest. She seems insensible to what's happening, rocking back and forth as though the place isn't on fire.

The redhead. The one with the bold, fearless gaze.

There isn't time to take her by the hand and tell her she's safe and that Isabel's trying to help. She reaches over and hauls the girl up. She's not strong enough to lift her, but she grabs her hand and holds it tight.

'We have to go,' says Isabel. 'We have to go, okay?'

By now the fire fills the room, small explosions punctuating the roar of the flames. Soon it'll hit the gas supply and there'll be nothing left but a smouldering wreckage, which means they have to move *now.* She looks wildly around, as if she might magically see another exit, but there's nothing.

'Take a breath. Close your eyes.' She's talking to herself as much as to the child. 'Here goes.'

And the two of them plunge through the fire.

The heat crackles over Isabel's skin, sucking away all moisture. The fire's escaping the lab and into the main hall, ravaging the furnishings, the curtains, the polished wooden floor. Clutching tight to the girl's hand, she puts one foot blindly in front of the other. Her breath comes in ragged gasps, a familiar tightness in her chest, but this time it's the smoke poisoning her. One more step. One more step.

The thundering noise of the fire chases them into the corridor. Isabel kicks the door closed behind them to keep the flames contained and takes a moment to breathe, dragging the cleaner air into her lungs until she feels light-headed. Then she's moving again, pulling the girl with her; the child is silent and shell-shocked, stumbling numbly forward as though there's no power left in her to resist.

As they stagger into the stairwell, she closes that door too, listening to the echo of its slam bounce off the concrete walls. In the subsequent quiet, she hears voices further down. Voices – and fighting. She'd forgotten they still had to get through the carnage before they're free of this place.

'We have to keep going,' she rasps. 'You with me?'

The girl gives a tiny, fragile nod.

They keep going.

Mortimer's waiting for them at the bottom, the other children in a loose cluster around him. They look to Isabel for orders, but she's distracted by the body in Mortimer's arms, grotesque and impossible. *Emma's dead.* It doesn't make any more sense now than it did before.

'They're between us and the exit,' says Mortimer. Behind him, the door to the lobby's been propped open, just enough to reveal the battleground on the other side. Across the hall, Isabel can see the front door, an impossible glimmer of daylight. 'It's the only way out. We can't get to the back door without going back towards the fire.'

She nods and holds out her hand. 'Give me your gun.'

'What?'

'Your gun. Give it to me.'

It's like he'd forgotten he had it. He passes it to her, and she checks it over. Five bullets. Not enough to draw their fire for long. 'Isabel, what are you—'

'Get the children out.'

'You can't go out there!'

She has to. 'Do they have snipers?'

Mortimer shrugs helplessly, but one of the children points to the mezzanine level above the hall. 'Two gunmen,' she says. 'They were shooting, before.'

Isabel nods. 'All right.'

She takes a breath, and steps out into the lobby.

Instantly, she's rushed by two men. She elbows one in the stomach, twisting the gun from his hand in time to aim blindly, hears the thud of the other falling. Another rain of gunfire comes from above and she shoots upwards, aiming for the sniper, but it's impossible to know if her shot connects. The gun in her hand clicks: empty. Someone comes at her with a knife and she smashes the empty pistol down on his head, snatching the blade from his grasp before slicing at the wrist of an agent nearby, who immediately drops their gun. She scoops it up off the floor and swaps the knife to her other hand.

There's a moment of breathless silence, broken by the mechanical noise of somebody reloading.

'Now,' she tells Mortimer.

Still holding Emma's body, he makes a break for it across the blood-spattered lobby, the children following. She sees one of the girls twist expertly away from an agent coming at her with a knife, sees another child disable a fighter with a swift kick to the knees.

But she can't see the smallest of them, the redhead. She turns back towards the stairwell and sees her still crouched there, wide-eyed. *Shit.* Even as she darts back to grab her, there's a hail of gunfire, and Isabel moves instinctively in front of the girl, firing blindly in the direction of the most recent shots. She hears the thump of somebody falling from their perch as she discards the empty gun, letting it skitter across the floor.

All that's left is Mortimer's, with its five bullets.

She turns back to the child. She can't tell if it's terror or stubbornness that kept her from following the others. 'We need to get out of here,' she says, though if she's half-deafened by the gunfire, the girl must be too. 'You see that door? When I tell you to run, that's where you aim for.'

The girl only stares mutely. Isabel swears under her breath. It would be easier to leave her here, but she can't, not after everything she did to get them both this far. She looks out at the lobby again, assessing the situation. It's impossible to tell, in the chaos, whose side anybody is on. She needs an ally, someone to draw fire so that the girl can get out. There has to be *someone* here she recognises, somebody who will help . . .

Someone like Toni.

At first, Isabel thinks it's wishful thinking, but she looks again and it's definitely Toni, struggling against a woman whose hands are wrapped around her throat. Emma had said she was here. Did she see Emma's body in Mortimer's arms? Does she think her daughter's still alive?

Isabel raises her gun and fires, catching the other woman in the shoulder and sending her stumbling backwards. Toni gasps for breath and looks around for her saviour. Her expression goes from grateful to concerned when she catches sight of Isabel and the girl.

Maybe Toni didn't protect Isabel, but she's willing to take a chance on her motherly instincts now. Isabel grabs the girl's hand and runs, moving as quickly as she can across the lobby, but there's still someone on the mezzanine with a gun.

'Toni!' she yells, dropping the girl's hand and shoving her forward. 'Cover her. *Cover her.*'

The girl trips, catches herself, glances back once – and then she runs. Toni moves without hesitation, shielding the child with her body. A shot rings out from directly above Isabel's head and she spins, throwing herself into a position where she can shoot back. There's a thud, and the gunfire stops, but when she turns to see if the redhead made it out, what she sees instead is Toni Rolleston on the ground and the child crouched, terrified, in the spreading bloodstain.

'Go!' yells Isabel again, feeling the word rip itself from

378

her throat. She glances up at the mezzanine – no sign of the shooter – and darts forward, grabbing the girl's elbow and pulling her to her feet. 'Go – that door – go!'

The child goes, passing through into the square of pale sunlight on the other side. Isabel crouches by Toni's side and feels for a pulse; any hope she had that Emma's mother was still alive disperses when she sees the bloody mess where her throat should be. Nothing.

'I'm sorry,' she whispers in her smoke-scratched voice, and reaches out to close Toni's eyes.

Into the ringing silence of the corpse-strewn lobby, her father says, 'Issy.'

At first, she can't tell where the voice is coming from, but then she sees him: sitting on the stairs, bloodied and exhausted.

'You should have kept quiet,' she says hoarsely in Esperanto, pushing herself to her feet and raising Mortimer's gun. Two bullets left. 'I might not have known you were there.'

'You won't kill me.'

'Want to bet?' Her hands are shaking. Exhaustion, probably.

Her father pushes himself to his feet, and Isabel backs away before she can stop herself. 'We gave you everything, Issy,' he says. He looks *old*, a fragility she knows is a lie. Has to be a lie. 'It's not easy being a parent, but we did our best. We gave you every opportunity we could.'

'What you gave me was a death sentence!' Isabel's scars throb against her ribcage, her hand burning as she grips the gun. 'And it wasn't enough to fuck me up, was it? You had to take more children, ruin their lives too. You'll never stop.'

'All I wanted was my daughter at my side.'

'Bullshit!' Her voice cracks. 'All you ever wanted was power, and money, and you didn't give a shit who got hurt in the process.'

She expects him to shout, fight, threaten her. Instead, he starts to cry, and there's something graphically indecent about it. She has to look away from the sight of tears glistening on his gaunt cheeks.

'Can't you find it in your heart to have some pity for your father?' he says.

Her heart? The heart that stopped twice because of his poison? Her heart and the burn scar over it, the ragged edges of the butterfly they branded onto her skin? In her rage, she sees his crocodile tears for what they are. 'You should have kept your mouth shut,' she tells him again, and fires a single shot.

It hits him in the kneecap, and he screams, and Isabel walks towards the square of daylight. Her father calls out, triumphant despite his gasps of pain, 'I knew you wouldn't kill me.'

Isabel looks back, smiles, and raises the gun. One bullet. 'Then you don't know me at all, *Dad*,' she says, and squeezes the trigger.

She doesn't stop to watch him fall before she drops the gun on the bloodstained floor and walks out into the bright winter's day.

38

FUNEBRO (MOURNING)

The days are grey. Pale grey walls, grey bedsheets, Ronan's charcoal shirt. Even Daragh's green scrubs seem desaturated and greyed out. The doctor tells her this is grief. Isabel calls it 'failure'.

'You're safe,' he says, the first time she wakes from a nightmare. And the second. And the third. 'You're safe. You got out, you got the children out. It's okay.'

It's not okay.

The fourth time, two nights after the end of the world, she says, 'I thought I was going to rescue her. But she died.'

'I know, Isabel.'

'She was my best friend.'

'I know.' He sits on the bed and holds her like she's a child, curled up against his chest, but even his warmth can't chase away the awfulness. 'It's not your fault. You did what you could, and you survived. Most people wouldn't have made it out of there in one piece.'

Is she in one piece? It doesn't feel like it. 'I killed my father,' she says.

Daragh doesn't let go of her. 'Do you regret it?'

Isabel's laugh is a faint and heartbroken sound. 'No. He was never going to stop. He … the children … I couldn't.'

Maybe Daragh's horrified, or maybe he understands. He waits for her to tell him the rest, to voice her words instead of swallowing them.

'Michael got away. And my mother. I don't know where she was. She wasn't … there.' If she could feel anything at all, she'd be afraid of what that means. Her mother's still out there. Michael's still out there, getting away with killing Emma, and Grace.

She waits for the doctor to say, *The guild will find them.* But he doesn't. He says, 'They won't always have this power over you, Isabel.'

She doesn't believe him. They made her, constructed her, their blood in her veins, their words on her lips. She's their perfect weapon, all their violence incarnate in the shape of a child; how can she ever be anything but theirs?

Her pyjamas are soft against her skin, softer than they have any right to be when the air around her bites with animosity, full of hatred and enemies. And the sheets are like shrouds, her body so numb as to be dead already. *Like Emma.* She doesn't want Daragh to leave. The moment he lets go, she feels like she'll forget she has a heartbeat.

'What happened?' she asks him. 'To Katipo?'

'Katipo's gone,' he promises. 'Literally, for the most part. The fire in the lab reached the gas supply and destroyed half the terrace almost as soon as you got out.'

She remembers the explosion, in that vague, fogged way that she remembers nightmares. She'd thought it was her world shattering, the enormity of grief hitting her all at once. She hadn't realised it was real.

'And the children?'

'They're safe. Mortimer made sure of that. He threatened to tell the Free Press that Comma were complicit in Katipo training children, and expose Cocoon in the process. Ronan had to give in. Most of them are orphans, but he'll make sure they have somewhere to go.'

She lets go of a small weight she didn't realise she was carrying. 'I'm glad.'

'You saved them, Isabel. You got them out of there.'

At least somebody got out. It feels like there's still a part of her that her parents own, left behind in the fire and the violence. Or maybe it's the loss of Emma that leaves this gnawing ache inside her chest, as though her heart's been ripped away.

Isabel leans her head against Daragh's shoulder. 'Tell me about Christopher,' she says, and feels him stiffen in surprise.

'Why?'

'Because you loved him, and he's gone, and you're not.' The

greyness hasn't taken Daragh. He hasn't suffocated under the weight of his grief like stone in his chest. She wants to know how that's possible, how long it took before he started seeing colours again, before Christopher's paintings were anything other than dusty greyscale.

Daragh sighs, and she thinks at first he won't answer, but then he says, 'He was a better healer than I'll ever be.' He's choosing his words carefully. 'He'd paint anything. Take any job that let him make things colourful. Taught art, painted houses, went out tagging late at night and came back with empty cans and a smile made of sunlight. And those paintings, they were like ... medicine. Watching him work felt like the moment a patient's scans come back clear, or the first second holding a healthy baby after a tough delivery. Like all the disparate parts of me were swept up and made whole again.'

Isabel's eyes are drifting closed, but she doesn't want him to stop talking. His voice is her only shield against the nightmares she knows are coming, and there's a softness to the way he speaks when he talks about Christopher that she could listen to for a hundred years.

'How ...' she tries. 'How did you do it, when he was gone?'

'I don't know,' Daragh tells her. 'There's no knack to it. No secret that makes it easier. You just put one foot in front of the other.' He brushes her fringe away from her eyes. 'But one night I was out in the city, wandering, looking for anything to make those steps easier, and I saw someone stop in front of one of his pictures. They had no idea that the man who painted it was dead, and it didn't matter, because it was beautiful and it made them smile.'

Emma's art is luminous, vibrant, a pale imitation of its creator, not enough to make up for the loss of her – but it's something. A reminder that she trailed her hands across this city's walls and left colour behind her, and the world isn't entirely grey.

'It doesn't get better,' says Daragh. 'They don't stop being gone. But it gets easier.'

'I don't want . . . easier.' Isabel's too exhausted even to cry. 'I just want her back.'

'I know.' He does. She can tell that he does. 'I'm sorry. I wish I had words that would help you.' But he's already done more than enough. His are the hands that stitched her back together. His is the voice that dragged her back to life when she fell. 'Go to sleep, Isabel,' he says. 'I'm not going anywhere.'

'You promise?'

'I promise.'

And he keeps that promise, as he has every night; he's there when she wakes from nightmares of Michael's voice mocking her while Emma dies over and over again in front of her, and again when she wakes herself up crying in her sleep, and again when the first light of dawn creeps through a gap in the curtains.

And when she finally wakes properly to the bright light of mid-morning, she sees him dozing in the chair by her bed, the exhausted guardian angel of a girl who does the devil's bidding.

385

Leo is a parrot among crows, his bright clothes visible from the back of the room. He sits alone in the front row of the funeral, the seats next to him respectfully left empty by mourners who feel unworthy of matching the grief of a young man burying his mother and youngest sister only a few years after losing Jean.

Isabel isn't worthy, but she sits next to him anyway. He glances up, and she thinks he'll tell her she shouldn't be here – in the front row, at this funeral at all – but he just says, 'You changed your hair.'

She did. The mermaid blue is as bright as his outfit, undercut by the shaved side that leaves her left ear exposed, healing piercings still a little swollen. It's an aggressive self-deception: she'll never be as bold or as brave as the painting Emma did of her. DISOBEDIENCE. All it ever brought her was this, and she's a moth dressed as a butterfly, but there's still a sense of power in the colours.

'It was Emma's idea,' she says. 'You're not in black.'

He looks down at his clothes as though mildly surprised to see himself. 'No, she'd ... she'd have hated that. None of us wore black to Jean's,' he adds, a reminder that he's already done this too many times.

Isabel says, 'I'm sorry.'

Leo glances around, checking none of the mourners nearby are listening to their conversation. 'It isn't your fault.'

'It is.'

'No.' He puts the service sheet he's holding onto the seat next to him, a calm and deliberate gesture. 'My mother made her choices. She knew the risks and she went anyway. If she couldn't save herself, you couldn't have helped. And as for Emma . . .'

'She was taken because of me.' She feels sick every time she thinks about the way Emma smiled at her, trusting, as though Isabel was her saviour instead of the reason any of this happened. 'Neither of them would have been there.'

'You got her out,' says Leo. 'She went back for you. That was her choice.'

'She shouldn't have,' Isabel says. She thinks perhaps she's finally hit upon the truth of it. 'She shouldn't have come back for me. She shouldn't have befriended me in the first place. I was dying and she chose me and she *shouldn't* have.'

'She thought you were worth the risk.' Leo shrugs. 'If you'd died, she'd have mourned you, and then she'd have lived on. Now that's your job.'

A third figure slides into their row. 'Isabel,' says Mortimer, in a low voice. 'I don't want to alarm you, but Michael's here.'

Only his hand on her arm stops her from leaping to her feet. 'What? Where?'

'Outside. One of the perimeter guards saw him enter the cemetery.'

The officiant is at the lectern now, tapping the microphone to test it. Isabel looks at Leo, then at the other mourners: people she dimly recognises from the school corridors, now weepy and clutching tear-stained eulogies they're waiting to read aloud. Can she stay? Can she really sit here while they talk about what Emma meant to them, knowing Michael's still free?

No, she can't. She stands and edges out of the row, ignoring the whispers that follow her as she hurries to the back of the room and out into the rain. Before she's gone more than a few steps, she's retrieved one of her knives from her forearm sheath, the other from her boot, holding them loose in her hands.

She looks around for the agents Comma sent to watch the perimeter, but she sees Michael first. Hardly more than a flash of hair and cheekbones, light glinting on drizzle-damp skin, but she'd know him anywhere. He's paused by one of the graves on the far side of the cemetery.

Isabel ducks through an overgrown archway, weaving through the rosebushes they've planted to make this less of a necropolis and more of a park. Has he seen her? He lingers a moment more, then turns to leave. He's limping – she hopes the wound Emma gave him still hurts – but moving swiftly, and she has to jog to circle round and cut him off.

'Stop.'

He looks up. First at her face, her bright hair, and then at the knives in her hands. 'Isabel.' The past week has faded the bruising on his face to a sickly yellow. 'I thought you might be here.'

'Why are *you* here?'

He jerks his thumb over his shoulder to the graves behind him. There, close to a familiar bench, are two open graves. New. Waiting. 'Paying my respects,' he says.

'Your *respects*?' Her fury is blood-hot. 'You're the reason Emma's dead.'

'No,' he says. 'You are.'

He betrayed her. He took everything that meant anything to her. And now he won't even acknowledge the blood on his hands. 'And my mother? I suppose you ran straight to her, didn't you?'

'Hummingbird have her,' he says. 'They found our safe house three days ago. They're probably still questioning her, but she'll be dead soon enough.'

It should be a relief. Why isn't it a relief?

Because I won't get to watch her die.

'I killed my father,' she tells him. 'So don't think I won't kill you.'

Michael laughs hollowly. 'As if I would ever have thought that.'

The knives are heavy in her hands. Her boots keep her grounded on the path; through the rips in her jeans she feels the air against her legs. Steady. Waiting. Poised. *No mercy, no hesitation, no witnesses.* She wants to ask Michael if it was difficult, betraying her like that; if he feels any regret at all. Instead she says, 'You shouldn't have come here.'

He shrugs. 'Got nowhere else to go,' he says, and glances over his shoulder at the graves.

He doesn't look back in time to block the knife from plunging unerringly into his heart.

Hot blood spatters over her and he gasps, a desperate futile breath that won't save him. 'That's for Emma,' she tells him. 'And this,' she adds, thrusting the second knife in, 'is for me. You *bastard*.'

He tries to speak, she thinks, to make some final smart-arse remark, but Isabel yanks the blades out and he chokes as his mouth fills with blood. She stands bloodstained and motionless as he falls, watching his body crumple at her feet.

It should have been harder than that. It feels too easy, anticlimactic, but aren't those the steps of this dance? Find the target, take vengeance, stand drenched in blood, feel the reliable catharsis of violence and let it knit you back together – isn't that how it goes?

But there, in the background, there are still two graves: open, new, waiting.

Unsteadily, she walks over to them. She already knows what she'll see on the neat headstone next to them. JEAN ARAN. BELOVED DAUGHTER AND SISTER. But she hadn't noticed the fourth grave in the row, the small butterfly carving at the bottom the only hint that whoever lies beneath it was part of Comma. It's a little neglected, the grass long, but a small vase of fresh flowers is set on the marble beneath the carved name. ANGELA GRIFFITHS.

Paying my respects, said Michael, because he knew it was the last time he'd visit his mother, just as he knew Isabel would be here. He knew exactly what he was doing, now as always, except this time it was his own life he was playing with. *Got nowhere else to go.* Maybe that's an answer in itself to all the questions she didn't ask him.

Isabel kneels beside the damp soil piled next to the empty graves as the drizzle solidifies into rain. She pinches a clod of earth until it crumbles between her fingers, tries to imagine what she'd say if she were inside with the others. If she went up to that lectern, what would she tell them about Emma? Only that whatever awfulness Isabel's capable of, caring about Emma is the one good thing she's ever done. That Emma was the one bright thing in her life when everything went to shit.

And Emma should have been the one who lived. Because Leo and all those people in there, they need her. Not Isabel. All Isabel does is get people killed.

She swallows the sudden lump in her throat. She wanted so badly to live, but at what cost? Michael's death doesn't fix anything, doesn't make up for the things she's done and all the ways she failed. She wonders if Emma would have been grateful to be avenged, or if she'd have seen Isabel covered in blood and turned away, disgusted.

Light another candle. Emma looked into the heart of what made her awful and still saw goodness there. But all that's left is this: a body, a bloody knife, a deep wound in the earth where they're going to bury her friend. She was never the person Emma thought she was. She was never as good as Emma wanted to believe.

Isabel couldn't save her. All she can do is enact vengeance for what was taken from them, and as she kneels in the soil and lets the rain wash Michael's blood from her hands, it doesn't feel like enough. It will never be enough.

'It's meant to get easier,' she tells the empty grave, and a ghost who can't hear her. 'The knowledge that you're not coming back, that's meant to stop stinging. I thought maybe when Michael was gone, I'd feel peace, you'd be at peace, we'd both … that there'd be peace for us then.' But emptiness isn't peace. It's only a hollow, dug deep under her ribcage.

She stays kneeling, inadequate in her grief, unable to move. As the rain patters thinly against her hunched shoulder blades, she becomes aware of other people around her: black-clad and anonymous Comma agents who lift Michael's body and take it away, somewhere the civilians won't have to see it. A charcoal grey figure comes to stand at her side.

Maybe she saved the children. But she lost everything else: Emma, her hope of another life, herself.

She looks up. 'Time to go, Isabel,' says Ronan Atwood, and he holds out his hand towards her.

Isabel takes it.

AUTHOR'S NOTE

The Butterfly Assassin is fiction – it's set in a fictional city, in a world slightly different from our own, everything shifted just a few inches to the left of reality. But it has its roots in real life, in history, and in my own experiences, and it seemed worth offering a brief glimpse of where some of those roots lead.

The city of Espera is in Yorkshire, not too far from York or Scarborough; the names of its boroughs are taken from place names in the area (with apologies to residents . . . !). It's named after the constructed language Esperanto, created by L.L. Zamenhof in 1887. Zamenhof hoped it would bring unity between people of different countries by functioning as an international language, and no doubt he would be horrified by the use the guilds have made of his language of hope. But if your interest has been piqued, there are lots of resources online for learning Esperanto, and many Esperantists are more than happy to chat about the language. The solar roadways in Espera are also a real invention: interlocking solar panels that can be used to create roads, replacing long stretches of tarmac with something more useful and sustainable. In reality, they've yet to reach the level of functionality that Espera's solar roadways have, nor is a city the ideal place for them (long stretches of open highway in deserts are probably a better candidate), but I like to think Espera put some of its technological skills towards innovation of a kinder sort than weapons development.

Speaking of which ... Espera was founded during the First World War, probably around the same time as Porton Down, the site of Britain's chemical weapons research and development establishment. Porton Down was responsible for developing and refining a number of extremely nasty weapons (including mustard gas, anthrax, and the nerve agent VX), and nerve agents like sarin were tested on humans there. Espera's remit is considerably wider than Porton Down's, encompassing explosives, intelligence, and other weaponry, as well as chemical and biological weapons, and it was an Allied project rather than solely a British one. But the existence of Porton Down supports the idea that the British government would have permitted and funded such a project. Nor are all such parallels historical: to this day, the UK hosts the DSEI arms fair every two years, showcasing the latest in murderous technology to arms company representatives and military delegations from around the world, many of whom have been accused of human rights abuses. It's not hard to imagine Comma and Hummingbird sending representatives to London to hawk their wares and find more clients who might utilise their services. The British military also routinely recruits sixteen-year-olds, and is the only country in Europe and NATO to do so; recruitment statistics from June 2021 show that one in five new recruits to the armed forces (and one in four in the army specifically) were under eighteen. In other words, every time I wondered how the guilds could exist without constant uproar and protest from the rest of the world, I looked at reality, and realised it was entirely plausible.

Britain has never had a closed city like Espera, but they exist elsewhere. In the twentieth century, many closed cities were built for nuclear research and weapons development, the majority of them in Russia. While some of these cities are now open, others remain closed to outsiders. Ozersk is one of those that is still closed – citizens may leave temporarily if they obtain a special visa, but if they move away they can never come back. Despite the city's history of nuclear accidents and the radioactive fallout from these, many of its inhabitants don't *want* to leave: the city is the only place they've ever known, and they've been taught that the outside world is an enemy. It's extremely difficult for outsiders to gain access to the city, and Google's knowledge of its layout more or less stops at the checkpoints on the way in. I was deeply intrigued by Ozersk, and reading about it helped inform my portrayal of Espera and its inhabitants. I also took inspiration from Berlin, particularly the Berlin Wall, in terms of the city's construction and layout, and this was one of the inspirations for the colourful street art that characterises Espera.

And finally, *The Butterfly Assassin* takes inspiration from my own life. At seventeen, I developed debilitating chronic pain in my hands and wrists. I had been on the cusp of independence, and suddenly I was cut off from my hobbies, obligations, and everyday tasks – an abrupt and devastating loss of control. When I began the first draft of this book a year later, I didn't set out to write about that frustration, rage, and trauma, but that's what emerged: a story about losing control, and the desperate need to assert autonomy in a body that feels like it's falling apart from the inside. Along with that, it's a story about being failed by those who are supposed to help. Too often, I've had doctors dismiss my pain as irrelevant, psychosomatic, or a product of anxiety; too often, they've ignored symptoms or failed to run tests. And too often, I've been told that I don't look ill enough, I'm not disabled enough, I'm not trans enough, and I've been denied the support and healthcare I need. It's an alienating and isolating experience, and yet it's one I share with so many of my chronically ill friends, who are constantly having to fight to be heard.

In the eight years since that original injury, I've regained the use of my hands to a certain extent, but I will never forget how it felt to be seventeen and in pain that nobody could explain to me, feeling like I was losing my mind. My chronic health problems continue to take choices from me, and many of Isabel's experiences of pain and brain fog draw directly on my own. I like to joke that my biggest weakness is being incredibly easy to poison: a tiny trace of gluten and I'll know exactly how Isabel feels when my gut punishes me for it. On a good day, my body and I exist in an uneasy stalemate; on a bad day, it's an ongoing fight. You can't have full control over your life unless you have control over your body. Isabel has neither, and I know how she feels, because when I was seventeen, neither did I.

The Butterfly Assassin draws on a period of my life I will always fear reliving, but it also draws on aspects of my identity I find empowering. Isabel is asexual and uninterested in romance because I am, and the friendships she forms with those around her – particularly with Emma – are as deep, fulfilling and meaningful as any romance could be. And, ironically for such a violent story, this book is also heavily influenced by my pacifist beliefs and values: it's a way for me to shine a light on the everyday militarism of our society by placing it in a setting that feels fictional, but which actually has too many real-world parallels, some of which I mentioned above.

There is a lot of rage in this book: at the world, at my body, at the experience of being in pain. But there's hope, too – at least, I like to think there is. Hope in friendship, in recovery, in the essential goodness of people and their capacity to change, in art and colour and biscuits and teachers who care and doctors who actually listen. Isabel's a survivor, and her story isn't over yet.

ACKNOWLEDGEMENTS

After working on a book for your entire adult life, you find yourself with dozens of people to thank and an unshakeable terror of forgetting somebody. So it is with *The Butterfly Assassin*, and, as such, I'm offering here a blanket apology to anybody whose name somehow fell off my radar.

First up: Rory Power. If you hadn't selected me as your mentee during Round 6 of Author Mentor Match, this book would not exist. Your help was invaluable, and Isabel's story is about a hundred times better for it. Thank you to Alexa Donne, for founding Author Mentor Match and bringing us together, and to Beth Phelan for #DVPit, which helped me to find my agent, Jessica Hare. Thank you, Jessica, for liking my pitch and then this book! I promise to keep sending you more weird genre-bending books that I wrote 'by accident' while I was meant to be working on something else. Thank you also to Amina Youssef, my editor, for asking all the hard questions so that I had to actually come up with the answers, and not letting me get away with anything. Except my *-ise* word endings. Special thanks for letting me keep those. And to the rest of the S&S team who took this novel from manuscript to the book you're holding now: thank you for all your work in making this happen.

This book has had an alarming number of beta readers over the years, some of whom I'm no longer even in touch with. I'm inordinately grateful to anyone who has ever given me their thoughts and feedback. Among them, Caspian Robson and Eleanor Smith, founding members of the Ronan Atwood Hate Club, who have been reading my work for years and putting up with my ramblings. Your support has meant everything to me. Torin Audoire, whose furious and devastated comments on the first draft sustained me through every draft that followed: you were the perfect first reader. Cathryn Mullen, who read the very first outline and told me I was trying to write two books at once. You were right, so thank you, and thank you also for the science guidance. CG Drews, Emily Miner and Kiara Medina, who cared so much about Isabel and made sure I knew it. Emmet Taylor, who gave advice about knife-throwing that was worryingly detailed. Richard Masheder and Jonathan Mead, who asked questions about world-building and prompted me to actually figure out the details. All of you – and those now forgotten – have been a part of making this book what it is.

As well as these readers, I've gained so much from my writing friends, particularly Write Club. You guys have let me liveblog my editing process, yell about my insecurities and anxieties, and ramble about off-topic nonsense whenever I needed to. Thank you for all the times you've read my opening chapters, peer-pressured me into keeping going, and otherwise kept me on track to make this book real. I can't wait for all of you to get the agents and deals you deserve.

Thank you also to the other 2022 debuts, who reassured me that, yes, whatever chaos I was going through probably *was* normal for publishing (you never can tell). This year is our year, and it's amazing to think about seeing all your (our!) books on shelves.

This book was a few thousand miles out of my comfort zone in terms of knowledge and experience, and I owe a debt of gratitude to everybody who helped with my research. Thank you to Simon Varwell, my consultant Esperantist, for all the translations and advice, and to all those who helped with the science – the STEM channel of the Gradblr Discord (thanks for helping me set things on fire!) and Zoe Wilson (thank you for all the help with chromatography and chemical analysis!). Any remaining errors are completely my fault.

Miscellaneous thank-yous to my supervisors and lecturers at University College Cork, who always asked how the edits were going, and especially Kevin Murray, who forgave me for neglecting my thesis while juggling edits. Thank you also to Laura, my landlady in Cork, for the excitement and encouragement, and all the nerds of the Mortal Engines Discord server who've been putting up with me for many years now. And to the Muddle Ages, my beloved meme goblins and long-suffering medievalist friends: thank you, and I'm sorry, because you've been getting the worst of me since 2018 and yet have somehow stuck around. Your patience, encouragement, and tolerance for being spammed with snippets whenever I'm editing has been invaluable to me.

And finally, thank you to my family. Mum, you'll hate this book – it's sad, it's violent, and there's swearing. One day I'll write one you can read, but this isn't it. But thank you anyway, and the rest of youse, for all your support and for keeping me alive long enough to write it. Appreciate that.

FINN LONGMAN is a queer disabled writer and medievalist, originally from London. With an MA in Early and Medieval Irish and a BA in Anglo-Saxon, Norse and Celtic, they spend most of their time having extremely niche opinions on the internet. They write YA and Adult novels, and have a particular interest in genre-bending fiction that explores identity and tests moral boundaries. *The Butterfly Assassin* is their debut novel, with a sequel to follow in 2023.